DAUGHTERS *of* LIGHT & LONGING

M.L. STONEBURNER

This is a work of fiction. Names, characters, places and incidents either are a production of the author's imagination or used fictitiously. Any resemblance to actual persons, living or dead, events or locales is entirely coincidental.

Daughters of Light and Longing

Fates of Oscana #1

First edition March 2026

Book Cover Design and Interior Design by Aubrey Joy Rosales | www.facebook.com/designjai

Map Design by Lauren Delcoma

ISBNs: 978-1-0676032-0-5 (ebook) 978-1-0676032-1-2 (paperback)

Published by Buxton Bear Publishing

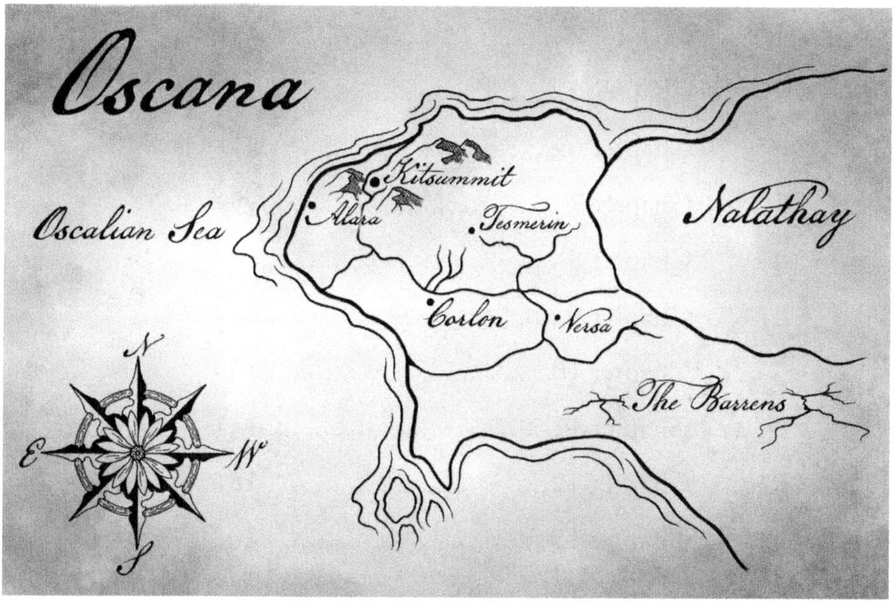
Oscana
Oscalian Sea
Kitsummit
Alara
Tesmerin
Nalathay
Corlon
Versa
The Barrens
N
E
W
S

Contents

CHAPTER 1

Kezra

It never ceased to amaze her how little a human had to bleed before they started to beg. A single drop of blood from the man wallowing in front of her had barely whetted the blade before he'd started snivelling and offering his children in his place. Pathetic. People like him were always so willing to accept an offer from her master, to create an unbreakable bond in exchange for a simple favor, but when it came time to collect, few were willing to pay. Kezra had seen countless men like this before, and knew she'd encounter countless more - men who thought their tears would save them, who thought themselves above the consequences of their choices, cowards so unwilling to face the unknown, they'd sacrifice their children. Kezra despised men like Horace. She almost wished her directions had been different this time, that instead of a single drop decorating the tip of her blade, she could paint it scarlet with his blood. But Kezra couldn't disobey her master, so she'd settled for scaring the man with a small cut to his neck. Although, she hadn't expected him to break so quickly. She didn't even try to hide her disgust when addressing him.

"Your son, Horace? I have to admit I've collected countless payments, and this is a new low." The man's fat jaw quivered as she pressed her blade further into his neck, causing another ruby bead to drip to the ground. Unsurprisingly, Horace descended into further hysterics, perhaps realizing Kezra had no intention of accepting his offer.

"Please! You can't take me away from my family. I'm all they have. My poor wife and son; they'll starve without me!"

"You mean the son you tried to trade for your freedom? He'll be better off without you," Kezra snapped.

"It's the truth." The man continued sniveling. "I only wanted to protect him. At least in Helica, Tylan would care for him. Everyone knows his servants are fed well and treated fairly; at least in Helica, my son wouldn't starve. If you take me, he will."

"Then maybe you should have made a better deal. You're a liar and a coward, Horace, but your tears have no use here. You're coming with me."

"No! Please! You can't!"

As the man continued to descend into histrionics, Kezra pulled out a vial filled with purple smoke. She uncorked it, tipping back the vial and inhaled the smoke while clutching on to Horace. He gagged as the smoke invaded his lungs, choking his cries. Kezra rolled her eyes at the dramatics. Tylan was going to have some fun with this one; she almost felt guilty at the thought. Maybe she should have let him go.

They landed on a solid stone floor: Horace limp and legs akimbo, spread across the floor, Kezra gracefully, staring at the pitiful man. Steps rang out as her master approached, and she dropped to her knees awaiting his arrival. At the sound, Horace unfortunately regained awareness of his surroundings and resumed his fussing in full force. Kezra reached out to clench his jaw between her fingers, squeezing tight as she stared into Horace's red-rimmed eyes.

"Get a hold of yourself," she hissed. "It's time to meet your new master."

The smoke cleared to reveal a tall man with silver hair, tied back at the nape of his neck. He had elegant features: sharp amethyst eyes, a chiseled jawline, silver, arching eyebrows. He might have been considered handsome by most, but Kezra could never see him that way. She had firsthand experience with Tylan's cruelty, and all she could see when she looked at him was the rage perpetually simmering beneath the surface of his refined demeanor and expensive clothes. Today's ensemble consisted of a black tunic and matching breeches embroidered with silver swirls along the side. Kezra wondered which of his bonded was responsible for the hours of careful embroidery. Tylan's eyes alighted on Horace, who had pulled himself up off the floor and was thankfully silent for the time being. Kezra cast her eyes to the floor as she waited for Tylan's acknowledgement. Her neck cramped and the stone floor bit into her knees, but she didn't dare move.

"Well done, bringing me my newest prize, Kezra. This one doesn't look like he came easily." She felt her neck turn cold as Tylan turned his gaze upon her. "You may rise." Kezra obeyed, rolling her neck.

"Thank you, sir. It was nothing." Kezra had found a humble reply was safest; if Tylan thought she was getting too prideful, he made a point to display what true power looked like, and it was never pleasant. Tylan circled the man, stalking his prey.

"Yes, I'm sure. It looks like he put up a fight, nonetheless. But tell me, why is he so…wet?" Horace was indeed a wet, snotty mess from his previous bouts of sobbing, and under Tylan's scrutiny, he started blubbering again. Kezra cringed at the sight.

"This one is in possession of a weak constitution and found himself unable to accept his new circumstances. Fascinating how they're always willing to make a deal, but such cowards when it comes to payment."

"Indeed," Tylan said, voice contemplative. He stood in front of Horace and slapped him once, hard, across the face. The shock of it stopped the wailing momentarily. "There, that's better. Now we can have a conversation." Tylan smiled at the man, displaying his dazzling white teeth. "Let's take a seat."

He snapped his fingers, and chairs appeared. Tylan sat, lounging gracefully, his demeanor so changed it was difficult to recall the sheer violence of the moment before. Horace appeared stunned, but sank down slowly in his seat, seeming dazed.

Kezra shook her head to herself. She had seen this before, and it never ended well for people like Horace.

"Now that we're comfortable, tell me about yourself, Horace. What can you do for me here?" At the mention of his name, the dazed look fled from Horace's eyes and he seemed suddenly more alert.

"Well, as I was telling her," at this point, Horace jerked his head in Kezra's direction and leveled an unhappy glare at her, "I don't have anything to give. Oh no, I wouldn't be of any use to you here. If you could just let me go back to my family, that would be best. I would spread word of you and your mercy far and wide, sir. Anyone who would listen would know of the great Tylan."

Tylan listened, nodding along as Horace spoke. Horace's voice had picked up steam as he'd continued, his words infused with hope at seeing his audience so engaged. Knowing how this would end, Kezra almost felt bad for the man, but then she remembered how Horace had grabbed the little boy by the collar, shoving him Kezra's way as he'd tried to run. She recalled the boy's mother, screaming and crying, offering herself in the child's place, and any remaining sympathy shriveled up and died.

"Pray tell, who is it that says I'm so merciful?" Tylan asked. The man blinked, unsure of how to respond.

"Well, everyone." The man's words came out slowly this time, as if he was reluctant to say them even as they left his lips. "I've heard stories of the gracious Tylan all across Oscana. You're an inspiration to the people. Why, I myself have told anyone who would listen about all the good you've done for my family." Horace gained confidence as he spoke, rattling off compliments in rapid succession while snot dried on his face. Tylan watched in silence, smirking all the while. He held up his hand, silencing Horace.

"It's true, sir, -"

"Horace," the man supplied.

"Horace. It's true I grant favors among the citizens of Oscana - multiplying a grain supply, helping a field of crops grow during a dry season, healing a sick child or two, once someone bonded me to summon back a herd of lost sheep. I do all of this for the poor people of Oscana, but you can't expect me to do it for free. After all, magic always comes with a price; should I bear the cost by myself? Unfortunately, this isn't the type of cost that can be paid with coin, not that any of you have any to pay with regardless, so everyone pays with service. Tell me, Horace, how can you be of service to me?"

"Oh, but My Lord, I'm afraid I have no skills to offer you. Truly, you wouldn't want me wandering about the place mucking things up. My wife always tells me I break everything I touch, and she's a smart lass, she is. But incompetent I might be, my family needs me. Please, sir, let me go back to my family. I'd only make a mess of things here." Horace's voice cracked in desperation as Tylan looked on, appearing to contemplate the man's plea. Kezra knew better. Tylan shook his head.

"I'm afraid I can't do that, Horace. You've already admitted to telling the whole town about me, and I can't have people thinking they won't need to pay for their favors. If I let you go, the next time someone bonds me, they'll think they won't have to pay either, and I can't have that. It's bad for business." Tylan shook his head again, donning an insincere frown. Horace blanched.

"My Lord, please. We can invent a story. I won't tell anyone you let me go if you don't want me to; I swear it. I don't have anything you want. Please let me go!" Horace sniveled. Tylan's smile turned cruel. He drummed his fingers on his chair, turning his gaze to Kezra.

"It would seem someone accepted services without intending to pay for them." Tylan looked at Horace. "Why, that's stealing, isn't it, Kezra?" She gave him a tight nod, words caught in her throat. "Do you know the punishment for stealing Horace?" Tylan held Horace's gaze, his eyes twinkling with malice. Horace shook his head slowly. Any remaining color drained from his face. "Death." Tylan answered.

Horace began blubbering.

"Kezra, please take him outside for my pet to snack on; you know how hungry she gets."

"No, please! Don't do this. I take it back; I can work! I'll do anything you want: clean your rooms, shine your shoes, stitch your clothes, anything! Please."

Horace's pleading fell on deaf ears as Kezra snatched the back of his shirt and started dragging the man, kicking and screaming, toward the door. He thrashed about with desperation, attempting to save his life, but this wasn't the first time Tylan had made this particular request of her, and Kezra was prepared for the fight. She made it to the heavy steel door with Horace in tow, his kicks getting progressively more pitiful as he tired himself out. Kezra wondered if he would try harder if he knew what the door was protecting them from: the pet he was meant to feed.

"Would you mind, My Lord?" Kezra asked, inclining her head in the direction of the door, unable to open it without letting go of the struggling man in her grip. With a wave of Tylan's hand, the door began to creak open, allowing red mist to roll in. The mist swirled around them; Horace's screams increased in volume.

"Please don't! I have a son! Don't let him grow up without a father. Let me live; I beg you."

A roar sounded in the distance, one Kezra was familiar with: Tylan's pet circling the palace in search of fresh meat. Kezra was convinced the beast could smell its victim's fear. An involuntary shudder ran down her spine. The door continued to creep open, and Horace jerked violently away as the space grew, making one last attempt to flee for his life.

"What do you think, Kezra?" Tylan drawled. "Should we save him?" Kezra looked down at the man in her grip with his red-rimmed eyes, his snot-crusted face, the pitiful crack of his voice as he cried, and tried to summon up the empathy a normal person would feel. Instead, she kept seeing his son cry; she saw the still-healing bruises around Horace's wife's throat; she remembered the way the woman gripped her child, pleading with Kezra for the life she had no intention of taking. No, she felt nothing for this man except relief that he would no longer harass his poor family.

"I don't know, my Lord. If he says he's not fit to serve, perhaps we should take him at his word." Tylan raised his eyebrows in surprise. It was out of character for Kezra to accept the death of Tylan's victims so easily, but this time, with the picture of Horace's wife and son flashing through her mind, she knew the world would be better off without him. Tylan nodded, a look akin to pride settling on his features.

"Very well then. It was a pleasure doing business with you, Horace. May you have the afterlife you've earned." At that moment, a black claw the size of Kezra's forearm snaked through the opening in the door. Horace let out an ear-splitting scream at the sight, then promptly fainted, a dead weight in Kezra's arms. "Oh, she's here," Tylan said with undisguised delight. "Throw him out then; she's hungry."

With a huff, Kezra heaved Horace out the door for the beast to consume, then hurried to slam the door shut before it could grab ahold of her as well in its feeding frenzy. There was an awful squelching noise that sounded of tearing flesh, followed by the crunch of snapping bones. It lasted only a moment before the drumbeat of flying wings hit the air, and the beast flew away in search of larger, more satisfying game.

"Shame, I like to hear them scream when they're eaten," Tylan said as he sauntered over. "What did he do to offend you, dear Kezra?" Tylan used a finger to tilt her chin, searching her eyes for something, maybe a reflection of his own cruelty embedded in her heart.

"Who said he offended me?" Kezra asked, holding his gaze. She tried to keep her face expressionless, her tone neutral, giving nothing away.

"It's unlike you to accept an execution so easily. Come on now, he must have done something."

"The coward tried to offer his son in his place," Kezra muttered.

"Is that all?" Tylan let go of her chin and quirked an eyebrow, amused.

"I also have every reason to believe he beat his wife," Kezra added. She looked down at the floor, unwilling to meet Tylan's eye. She knew how he felt about such an emotional reaction.

"Ah, so he offended your moral sensibilities then? I've told you time and time again, Kezra, you've got to let go of those. That bleeding heart of yours will be your downfall."

"Yes, my Lord. I understand."

"I say this because I care for you, Kezra. You can't have a soft heart in this world, or it will eat you alive." Kezra felt his eyes boring into her, but she kept her eyes glued to the floor, shame burning her cheeks. For all twenty years of her life, she'd been tethered to Tylan, and still, she'd never been able to master his indifference. No matter what she said, she wasn't sure she wanted to either. Tylan sighed. "I see it's been a long day for you. Go, get some rest before your next assignment." A slow smile spread across his face. "This one's going to be something special."

Intrigued, Kezra almost opened her mouth to ask about it, as Tylan clearly intended for her to do. But he was right; the fight had been exhausting, and now that Horace was gone, she was battling with a sense of guilt over her complicity in his execution, so with a murmur of thanks, she left and headed for her room. Kezra couldn't stop thinking about the assignment and wondering what it might be, if it would contribute to the growing sense of guilt that was threatening to eat her alive from the inside out. For years, she had been hunting down Tylan's bonded and dragging them to Helica to pay the price. Each time, they pleaded for mercy, and each time, Kezra was unable to grant it, leaving a scar of regret on her heart. When she closed her eyes, she saw their tears, heard the screams of those unlucky enough to meet Horace's fate. She didn't know how long she could keep going until the shame of it crushed her, but Kezra didn't know how to break free. Her bond to Tylan was unbreakable.

Chapter 2
Lennox

"I swear on Altheia, Lennox, if you make us late to service again, the Mother will kill us both."

"The Mother will flay you where you stand for swearing on Altheia," Lennox quipped.

She rubbed her still half-closed eyes with one hand, while blindly reaching around on the floor with the other in search of her robes. The soft light of dawn shone through the window, giving the room a pale golden glow. Lennox tried to pry her eyes open, so they adjusted to the light and spotted her crimson robes shoved in the corner, crumpled and slightly muddy. Lennox inspected the robe's dirt-flecked hem, debating whether it was worse to show up later in wet robes, or on time in slightly dirty ones. She decided speed was more important than cleanliness at this hour, and threw them on, tying the waist with the braided golden cord that worked as a belt, pointedly ignoring the mud-caked fringe. Lennox cringed at the sight, knowing that arriving in dirty robes was as good as asking Altheia to smite her, or at the very least insight the Mother's wrath, but running this late, she didn't see an alternative. It was possible The Mother would overlook her dirty robes, but she certainly wouldn't accept tardiness, and Lennox couldn't get Jasper in trouble yet again by being late for morning prayers.

She braided her hair as quickly as possible, knowing it was far from perfect, then placed the star chain carefully on her head, taking care to ensure it hung directly in the middle of her forehead. Lennox slipped on her crimson slippers, then looked at Jasper, who was pacing around the room. She gave Lennox's outfit a scrutinizing look and let out a sigh.

"The ends of your cord are supposed to be gold, you know, not brown and caked in mud. Don't you have a clean one?" Jasper asked.

"It'll be fine. The Mother won't even notice." Lennox hooked her arm through Jasper's, attempting to lead her out of the room, but Jasper's feet stayed firmly planted.

"The Mother notices everything. Here, take my spare," Jasper said, handing Lennox a gleaming golden cord that shimmered in the sunlight. Lennox took it gratefully to replace her dirty one. Jasper scrunched her nose. "Too bad there's nothing to be done about your robe."

"My robe is fine. It's only the bottom that's dirty. The Mother won't even see it. Now come on, we have to go or we'll be late, and there's no way she'll miss that." Jasper let out another exasperated sigh but hooked her arm through Lennox's.

Together, they rushed from their room up to the temple, heads bowed and hoods drawn. Even after all these years, the view of the temple at dawn still took Lennox's breath away. It sat on a hill in the middle of the country's capital, Tesmerin, where Altheia could preside over the citizens below. Crafted from a pale pink stone and polished to perfection daily by the acolytes, the temple glittered in the soft light of dawn, its colors blending with those of the rising sun. Light gleamed through the open pillars, highlighting the statue of Alethia in the center of the temple. The goddess stood proud, wearing a crown of the sun, moon, and stars carved on top of her head. Lennox often wondered how the temple came to be, as there was no stone like it in all of Oscana, and it was so old scholars often debated what had come first: the city of Tesmerin or Altheia's temple. Lennox liked to think the temple had come first, the city springing up around it under the careful guidance of the benevolent goddess. Although Lennox adored the temple and seeing it in its glory at sunrise, she'd have willingly risked the goddesses' wrath for an extra hour or two of sleep. Surely Altheia didn't love her more for waking before dawn?

Quietly, they slipped into the temple, scurrying to take a seat in one of the back pews since the prayer service had already started. Lennox tried her best to pay attention as The Mother spoke to the acolytes of Altheia's love and wisdom, but the morning prayers were always the same, and her mind wandered beyond the temple to the city below, imagining what it might look like. Acolytes were rarely allowed to leave the shadow of the temple and go to the city below; their duty was to serve the goddess untainted by the ways of the outside world. Once one achieved the level of priestess, The Mother would occasionally give permission to go to the outside city and perform the necessary blessing ceremonies for the children of families who couldn't make their way to the temple. High Priestesses went on to lead temples in the cities around Oscana, but all came from the main temple here in Tesmerin. Lennox often dreamed of leaving to serve in the river city of Corlon, or even to the neighboring country of Nalathay. But for now, Lennox was stuck in Tesmerin under The Mother's watchful gaze.

"May Altheia bless you all with her light," The Mother intoned. Her eyes scanned the back row of pews, landing squarely on Lennox and Jasper.

"And may we honor her with our life," Lennox murmured the standard response, feeling her cheeks heat under The Mother's scrutiny.

With morning prayers ending, Lennox tugged on Jasper's arm, trying to push through the rush of sisters leaving the temple and filtering throughout the compound to study or start their chores. Lennox let out a breath of relief as they neared the door, relieved they'd gotten out of morning prayers unscathed.

"Sister Aphoros, Sister Emerett," The Mother's voice rang out in the emptying temple, laced with authority. Lennox and Jasper stopped and turned to face her. They'd been so close to an escape.

"I'll bet you one full bottle of wine she puts me on temple cleaning duty for a week," Lennox whispered into Jasper's ear.

"I bet she punishes both of us, and it's a full month this time." Jasper tried to sound frustrated, but a slight smile graced her lips all the same. Lennox felt guilty for always getting Jasper into trouble with her, but there was no way in Helica she could survive a month of cleaning duty without her best friend.

They quietly shuffled back to the podium, where The Mother stood, arms crossed, her face stoic. Lennox and Jasper kept their heads down and their hands clasped in front of their bodies. Neither dared to look at The Mother, hoping the sight of their contrition might lessen the punishment. The minutes dragged on in endless silence as The Mother waited for every last sister to filter out before clearing her throat and acknowledging them.

"Do either of you care to explain why you were late to service for the third time this month?"

"It was my fault, Mother," Jasper said quietly, eyes lowered to the floor. "My robes were not suitable for Altheia's temple. Lennox lent me hers so as not to dishonor the goddess."

"Yes," The Mother sniffed. "How kind of Sister Aphoros to lend you her clean set and bear the burden of disgracing the temple by dragging mud on the floors herself. I know you both want to partake in the Bonding ceremony soon and join the ranks of our priestesses, but we cannot have our priestesses showing disrespect to the Goddess and setting a poor example by attending our services late. May you both reflect on your decision to go through with The Blessing while you clean the temple for the next three weeks. One week for each day this month, you have been late. I'll ponder your request to proceed with The Blessing while you finish your punishment."

The Mother turned and walked away without another word, leaving them both to process the punishment in stunned silence. Lennox reached for Jasper's hand only to grab empty space. Jasper had already turned away. The Blessing was a rite of passage to move from acolyte to priestess. Lennox unconsciously touched the gold star dangling on her forehead. Technically, acolytes were eligible for the Blessing two years after they'd earned their gold stars, but everyone needed The Mother's permission to advance, and she did not give it lightly. Usually, sisters waited five years to take the Blessing after earning their stars, and both Jasper and Lennox were well into their fifth. The Mother had given them permission to participate in the upcoming ceremony just a month away, but now Lennox had gone and ruined their chances.

"Jas, I'm so sorry," she said, catching up to her friend.

"It's fine, Lennox," Jasper said with a sigh. "Just please, no more late-night walks for a while, okay? No more dirty robes or sleeping past dawn."

"I swear on Altheia's light, I'll never see the moonlight again. By the time our punishment ends, I won't remember what a star looks like; I'll be in bed before the sun even thinks about setting." Jasper rolled her eyes at the declaration.

"You don't need to be so dramatic, Lex, and you shouldn't swear on the goddess." Jasper peeked suspiciously at the sky, as if expecting a bolt of lightning to fall from it and hit them. "I don't think you could survive without seeing the stars, but just try to keep your robe clean when you gaze at them. Besides, you're unbearable when you don't go out at night, and I can't be expected to deal with you. Just stay clean and get back at a reasonable hour."

"Well, if that's what you insist, Sister Emerett, I'll do my stargazing naked." A mischievous smile settled on Lennox's face, and she waggled her eyebrows suggestively at her friend, who dissolved into a fit of giggles.

"Can you imagine The Mother's face if she caught you naked in the temple garden?" Jasper shook her head. "Altheia save you, Lex. Come on, let's find the little sisters and start cleaning so I can go back to my bed and finish sleeping."

It was sundown before Lennox made it back to her room from a day spent cleaning the temple, her golden hair falling disastrously loose from its braid, robes soaked with dirty water. She threw herself into bed, exhausted - dirty robes be damned. Jasper strode in moments later somehow untouched from her labor scrubbing the temple under the blistering heat of the summer sun. For god's sake, her auburn hair was still braided in a perfect crown around her head, not a hair out of place; her robes were immaculate without a hint of the water splashed across Lennox's. Jasper stood in the doorway, contemplating her friend's disheveled appearance, and sighed loudly.

"Well, at least your robes aren't stained with mud now. Please tell me you gave your spare set to the little sisters for cleaning?"

Lennox tried lifting her head from where she'd collapsed in the middle of the bed to respond and say of course she hadn't. She'd spent the entire day scrubbing the temple until it glistened; when would she have found the time to seek out the little sisters and give them her robes? Instead, she emitted a pitiful moan she hoped accurately conveyed this information, and thumped her head back on the bed. Jasper laughed, and Lennox felt the bed dip next to her as Jasper sat down. She slid two steaming rolls and a block of cheese in front of Lennox's face, a peace offering if Lennox had ever seen one.

"This is all the food I could grab from the cook, but she must have felt some pity for our weary souls because I also made it out of the kitchen with this." Jasper held up a gleaming bottle of ruby wine, jolting Lennox out of bed with excitement. Her body groaned in protest at the movement, wishing only to lay still on the bed and sleep for the next week, but the moment called for celebration. Lennox grabbed her best friend's face in her hands and stared intently into her eyes.

"Jasper Emerett, you are a gods-damned miracle worker and the best friend a girl could have. Statues will be built in your honor for your bravery and service tonight." With that, Lennox swiped the wine and took a swig straight from the bottle. Wine from the temple kitchen was usually spiced in preparation for the mass ceremonies, hiding the taste of alcohol. Nutmeg and cinnamon swirled on her tongue as she took another sip before passing the bottle back to Jasper. Her stomach lurched, and Lennox realized she hadn't eaten all day, so she gobbled down a roll and a bit of cheese, feeling the satisfied fullness of good wine and better company.

"I'd say that's two bottles you owe me now," Jasper said, after taking her own drink of the wine.

"Two?" Lennox asked. "Where in Tesmerin did you come up with that?"

"Well, there's this bottle I already swiped, and you owe me a bottle for the bet you lost." Lennox resisted the urge to point out that neither had won as The Mother punished them for three weeks instead of a month, but she bit back the reply. Guilt swirled in her belly at the potential of her friend being denied the Blessing ceremony. But instead of admitting guilt, Lennox rolled her eyes and threw herself back on the bed for the drama.

"Fine, two bottles of wine it is, but we're still sharing this one. If you drink the whole thing by yourself, you'll be stumbling into morning prayers."

Jasper laughed, handing the bottle back over as she climbed into the adjacent bed, getting ready for another early morning praising Altheia.

"Jas," Lennox said quietly, "we'll get to take part in the next Blessing ceremony, I promise. I'll do everything I can to convince The Mother." Lennox held her breath, waiting for a response. The silence stretched painfully between them before Jasper finally replied.

"I know Lex; I trust you." Doubt laced through Jasper's voice, a dagger to Lennox's heart. She vowed to herself that they would both take the Blessing, no matter what. Lennox couldn't let her down, not again.

The moon called to her. Lennox's eyes fluttered open from a dreamless sleep as she felt the night's presence bearing down on her, beckoning her outside. As it had countless nights before, the starry sky beckoned her to come and play, and she was powerless to resist. Lennox climbed out of bed and snuck out into the moon-lit night. The promise she'd made to Jasper weighed heavily on the back of her mind, so Lennox gathered up her robes, tying the ends into a careful knot, keeping them out of the muddy ground's reach. She made her way to the temple garden, savoring the feeling of its lush grass squishing between her toes. This was her favorite place in the temple, where she came to quiet her mind and still her heart.

The gardens wrapped around the entire perimeter of the temple's land with a tall hedge lining the entire thing, acting as a wall to stop outsiders from getting in without using the main gate. Flowers filled the garden in an assortment of colors: purples, pink, reds, blues and yellow all peeking through the lush greenery and Lennox inhaled their lush, floral scent. But her favorite flower was the small silver bud that bloomed only under the light of a full moon - the lunasha plant. Lunasha plants were a prized possession of the temple. Containing magical properties, they were a highly restricted plant, and only allowed to grow in two places, the temple, or the king's private garden. Whatever magical properties they'd once held had disappeared decades ago, but it didn't stop the temple from growing them, hoping the magic would return with Altheia's blessing. Lennox ran her fingers over the silky petals, letting her imagination wander. If she closed her eyes, she could almost imagine she could feel the magic from the plant humming through her fingertips, settling into her skin.

Of course, she knew this was just her mind playing tricks on her - Lennox had always possessed a vivid imagination. Everyone knew free magic disappeared when the lunasha bloom ceased granting magical properties, meaning no one could wield it themselves any longer, the days of spells and miracles were long over. There were still magical objects, relics left behind from a more glorious age, but those had specific purposes - limits that could not be broken. One such object lived at the temple in possession of The Mother for Blessing ceremonies. Lennox wasn't sure what the object was, or what it did exactly, but she knew once the Blessing was complete, it bound a priestess to the temple. A priestess was unable to leave unless given special permission by The Mother, releasing the bond.

Lennox sighed, contemplating her upcoming ceremony, if it was happening at all. On one hand, she'd trained her entire life to be a priestess, her life and her friends were here. Why wouldn't she want to take the Blessing and become a true priestess? But on the other, Lennox wanted desperately to see the world. She'd never left the temple grounds, not once in her twenty years of life. Like many other young girls, Lennox had been left at the temple as a baby. It was common practice in Oscana for families to give their baby girls to a temple in honor of the goddess they honored most. As goddess of life and light, Altheia had many tributes, but Niveran, goddess of death and darkness was another popular choice as well. The Mother found Lennox as a baby, tucked into a basket neatly placed in front of the entrance gate, no parents in sight.

Lennox tried to imagine her mother, her real one who'd left her in such a precarious position, and attempted to picture her face. She wondered if they had the same golden hair, the same green eyes, or pale skin. In her mind, her mother always had a soft, loving smile. She knew her mother had probably left her here for the same reason as many others - she couldn't afford to feed her, or she was too young, her life too unstable to raise a little girl. At twenty years old, Lennox imagined she was now the same age her mother had been when she'd left Lennox at the temple, but she couldn't know for sure. It made her feel better, though, to imagine her mother as a kind but struggling young woman, one who had possibly meant to come back for her one day but circumstances prevented it. Lennox always tried to tell herself she was lucky she didn't have memories of her mother, unlike Jasper who knew her family. She got to choose how she wanted to picture her mother; she didn't need to know the flawed human being who made the choice to abandon her, but the abandonment hurt all the same. Other families had left a note with their baby, but Lennox's mother had left nothing, just a crying baby in a basket for someone else to find.

With one last glance around the garden, Lennox wandered back to the room she shared with Jasper, trying to shake the melancholy thoughts from her mind. Still, even tucked firmly in bed, the thoughts about what lay beyond the garden weighed on her mind. There was so much out there Lennox had never gotten to see, might never get to see - possibly she could find her family. Once, Lennox had asked Jasper to leave with her, to walk out of the gate and down the hill into the city of Tesmerin, the capital of Oscana. She'd tried to paint an exciting picture: wandering the markets, eating new foods and exploring the hidden alleys of the city, seeing the castle in all its glory before catching a boat at the docks and sailing downriver to another adventure. Lennox tried to say it jokingly, hoping the levity would allow Jasper to play along, but Jasper had been so against the idea Lennox hadn't brought it up again. No matter how much she complained, Jasper loved her life at the temple. She thrived in the routine, adored studying dusty old books looking for higher truths about the gods. Jasper wanted to become a High Priestess; she really thought she'd be able to make a difference in the world honoring Altheia.

So Lennox stayed because she could not imagine abandoning the best friend who had become a sister to her. Instead, Lennox wandered the garden, her own quiet rebellion to the monotony of this life. Sometimes, she wandered closer and closer to the gate, imagining the life she could have if she only pushed it open, took a few steps forward, and just kept walking. But always, Lennox turned around and went back to Jasper. Eventually, Lennox fell into a restless sleep. She dreamt of flinging the gate open and running down the hill to a life filled with magic and adventure, but no matter how she ran, she couldn't escape the shadow of the temple. The vines from the garden grew to an enormous size, wrapping around Lennox's wrists and ankles. The more she struggled to break free, the tighter the plants wrapped around her skin, forever binding her to the temple. She woke in a sweat, not sure if she'd had a dream or a premonition.

CHAPTER 3

Kezra

Tylan promised Kezra an interesting next assignment. That had been a lie. In fact, her time spent watching the golden-haired girl traipse around the temple completing tedious chores was possibly the most boring assignment of Kezra's life. Faintly, she wondered if inflicting this dullness into her life was actually a creative punishment of Tylan's making, but then, Tylan didn't prefer punishments this subtle. A shiver ran down Kezra's spine as she recollected the times she'd displeased her master and he'd unleashed his magic on her. It sent an electric charge through her body, cramping her muscles with unbearable pain so that it was all her mind could concentrate on - pain and pain and pain unending. However, along with the pain came the feeling of power, vast endless power that surged through her blood, and if only she could clear her head from the throbbing pain, she thought maybe she could harness it. Kezra stopped the thoughts before they went any further. She could not harness the magic; she'd tried before with disastrous results. That was not the way to break her bond. No, as dull as watching this girl was, it gave her time to think, and Kezra intended to use it.

As night approached, Kezra rooted herself in a tree within view of the girl's room, settling in for the night. She didn't expect the young acolyte to do anything remotely interesting, so she was surprised when the girl crept out of her room in the middle of the night. Kezra followed safely behind, wondering where she was going. A little thrill pulsed in her chest. Finally, something interesting was happening. The girl tied her robes in a knot, then slunk into the garden where she just sat, absentmindedly stroking the petals of a lunasha plant. Kezra had never seen one before, but she recognized them from their descriptions she'd heard. Watching, Kezra held her breath, waiting for something miraculous to happen - for the bloom to spark to life, for the girl to pluck it and stuff it into her mouth, ingesting the magical properties and activating an ability previously unknown. Instead, the girl continued running her fingers across the petals with a dreamy look in her eyes, doing nothing at all of import.

Kezra let out her breath, shaking her head. She'd been so silly. The lunasha blooms hadn't given magic in decades, thus why people were so desperate for a bond with her master. Eventually, the girl got up and walked back toward her room and then stopped, turning to look around the garden one last time. Kezra froze. She swore the girl's eyes locked onto her, and Kezra had the most bizarre impulse to speak out and let her presence be known. There was a strange humming in her ears, a connection to the girl she hadn't felt before. Then the girl turned and went back to her room without another backward glance. What had come over her tonight? Perhaps the banality of the assignment was driving Kezra slightly mad; she'd need to find something else to do in the meantime if this assignment continued.

With the girl safely back in bed, Kezra settled back into her tree, inventing increasingly ludicrous reasons Tylan would want her to watch the girl. She'd just decided the girl was a long-lost goddess in disguise that Tylan hoped to capture when she felt it- the tugging sensation on the back of her mind. Kezra cleared her head, concentrating on her breathing instead of the constant pull. Purple haze invaded her vision, followed by a stronger, more persistent tug. Her head started to throb with the effort of resisting the summons as she counted the seconds trickling by. She dug her fingers into the tree, wood splintering off in her hands as a battle waged in her head. A last, forceful yank caused her vision to blur with searing pain, and Kezra relented, allowing the purple haze to take her to Tylan. Familiar purple smoke clogged her lungs as it ripped her from the verdant green gardens in the temple of Altheia and thrust her into Helica.

Twenty-eight seconds, Kezra thought as her feet touched the stone floor. It wasn't much of a rebellion, but it was the longest she'd been able to resist a summons to date. Kezra assumed her kneeling position on the stone floor of Tylan's throne room, her head lowered in supplication. Out of the corner of her eye, Kezra could see Tylan standing before her, quietly observing. The back of her neck heated where his eyes bore daggers into her, his anger radiating off him in waves, filling the room. It appeared her small rebellion had not gone unnoticed.

"It seems you took your time answering my summons, Kezra," Tylan's voice was eerily calm. "I can only assume this is because there was something interesting happening you needed to report?"

"I apologize for any delay, My Lord. The girl was on the move; I thought you'd want to know where she was going." Kezra attempted to keep her voice level, hoping this piece of information would be enough to distract him from her defiance. Tylan nodded slowly, and relief rushed over Kezra.

"And did you learn where she was going?"

"The temple gardens. She has taken a special interest in the lunasha plants. She visits the garden nightly and always sits among the lunasha blooms, stroking the petals."

Silence descended upon the room as Tylan chewed on the words. Kezra's neck began to ache from spending so long in her lowered position. Freezing stone bled through her leathers and nipped her knees.

"You may rise, Kezra," Tylan said, just in time to save Kezra from collapsing on the floor. She rose slowly, her joints stiff. Tylan's gaze locked onto her own with unusual intensity. "Did you see anything odd when she touched the lunasha plants?"

"I…no. Nothing." Unused to such attention from Tylan, Kezra's brain stopped working. She combed her thoughts for something to tell him, but all she could think of was that she needed something, anything else to capture his attention. Holding his interest for this long was dangerous.

"Think harder, Kezra. Did you see anything at all?"

She gulped, racking her brain for anything that might appease Tylan, but coming up empty. Kezra debated lying, but quickly tossed aside the idea. Without knowing exactly what he was looking for, making something up was more dangerous than reporting nothing at all. Kezra shook her head.

"No, My Lord. I saw nothing else of note. She seems to be a regular acolyte."

Tylan stared at her a moment longer, searching her face for a lie. Satisfied, he turned from her and began pacing across the room, ignoring Kezra altogether. Her sudden invisibility was dizzying; after an entire life in his service, Tylan's rapid mood changes still left Kezra unmoored. Tylan stomped up to his throne and plopped down, holding his face in his hands as he looked off in the distance. He'd rolled up the sleeves of his tunic, revealing his bare arms, and Kezra's eyes hooked on them. Although she could only see from his elbow to his wrist, she knew his arms were inked completely black from the shoulder down. Unconsciously, she traced the interlocking thin black bands adorning her left wrist - the physical representation of her magical bond to Tylan. Every bond gave both parties a tattoo until the terms of their agreement were met; only then did the tattoo fade away, leaving unmarked skin. Countless bands filled Tylan's arms, turning both of them a solid black. Kezra's heart filled with guilt at the sight. How many souls had she hunted down for him? How many times had a bargain been fulfilled, releasing someone from his service? She knew it happened. People left Helica and went back to Oscana to spread word of Tylan, but she knew there were precious few of them who made it out. She wondered how many souls she'd doomed by dragging them back here. When she'd first started hunting them, she'd tried to count, but over the years there had been too many and she'd lost track.

She ran her fingers over the bands across her wrist again. Hers differed from the others. Usually, a single, solid black line appeared around the arm to represent the bond the moment the deal was solidified. Why did she have two interlocking ones? Her bond was stronger than the rest somehow, allowing Tylan to pull her to him in a way he could not do with his other bonded. That's what made her the perfect servant for him - she could never run away, never escape. The thought landed like a weight in her stomach. Kezra glanced up to see Tylan's eyes focused on her again. She straightened her spine, and put her arms down to her sides, hoping he hadn't been able to sense her train of thought as she'd traced her tattoo.

"You will continue to watch the girl and report back to me if you see anything unusual. Don't approach her or contact her in any way; do I make myself clear?"

"Yes, My Lord." Kezra gulped, eager to put as much distance between herself and Tylan as possible. She'd almost made it out of the room when Tylan called to her again.

"Oh, and Kezra? One more thing." She turned to face him. Tylan's eyes glimmered with malice. "If you ever resist my summons again, there will be consequences."

Kezra nodded without speaking; then fled the room as fast as her feet would take her. Her door banged shut as she pressed her back against the solid wood, letting it provide a false sense of protection from her cruel master. Unbidden, memories flooded her senses - Tylan unleashing his magic through their bond, overloading her senses and burrowing into her skin. The power of it seared her nerves, sent an aching pulse through her mind until her only thoughts were of the pain and immense power. At the exact moment she thought maybe she could endure it, somehow harness the magic coursing through her veins and turn it on her torturer, he ripped it away, leaving Kezra feeling hollowed out and brittle. Tears filled her eyes at the memory, as did shame. As much as Kezra dreaded Tylan unleashing his magic through her bond, she craved it in equal measure. She wanted that power for herself, but that was impossible. It wasn't hers to grasp.

Wiping the tears from her eyes, Kezra stormed out of her room and down the dusty corridor in the direction of her training room - the place Tylan had made her his monster. The echoes of this room carried a different kind of pain; one she knew how to harness. Here, Tylan had worked her until her muscles cramped, made her practice with a sword until her hands blistered, then sparred with her until he'd blackened her body with bruising. Even then, Kezra got up again and again, forced to work her body until the point of collapse to become Tylan's Amethyst Assassin. Such a stupid name, Kezra cringed to think of it. It's what the villagers had named her due to the purple smoke she used to travel. Although she rarely killed anyone, so few people returned that assumptions were made, and the name stuck. Kezra grabbed her sword, closed her eyes and concentrated on breathing, ridding herself of the troubling thoughts. Her body went through the motions of its own accord. She practiced until her muscles shook with exhaustion and there was room in her mind only to think about bed. Back in the small room she called her own, Kezra collapsed on the bed. It wasn't huge or even particularly comfortable, but at least it was better than the tree she'd planned to spend her night in. Exhausted from the day, Kezra fell into a dreamless sleep where the screams of Tylan's victims couldn't reach her.

Waking up in her own room was jarring after days spent outdoors. Helica didn't have sunshine, just a swirling red mist that grew more or less visible depending on the hour. The promise of sunlight was almost enough to make her feel excited about another boring day of watching the priestess. As Kezra went through the motions of readying herself for the day, she found her thoughts drifting back to the question of what was so special about this seemingly ordinary girl.

Kezra replayed her days of watching the girl - she saw her golden blonde hair, her light green eyes, heard her chiming laughter, reminisced on the easy camaraderie between her and the red-haired girl who shared her room. A pang of jealousy lit her chest at the memory. Kezra's only social interactions were with Tylan or with the bonded she hunted down in his service; she wondered what it would feel like to be so close to someone. A small part of her longed to trade places with the nameless blonde priestess. The girl even kind of looked like her, similar eyes, the same lift to their nose - almost a lighter version of Kezra, one untainted by Tylan and the darkness of Helica. Hardening her heart, Kezra shook the thoughts away. The longing wouldn't do her any good, and it didn't matter what Tylan wanted; it was Kezra's duty to fulfill his wish, whatever it was. She ventured back to the training room and grabbed four small daggers, giving her sword a longing stare - it wasn't practical to bring with her on a stealth mission. Kezra went to the cabinet, which held hundreds of vials of Tylan's purple smoke, grabbing one to transport her back to Tesmerin. On impulse, she plucked three extras off the shelf and stuffed them in her pack. Tylan would never notice they were gone, and maybe they would be useful.

For three miserable days, Kezra manned her post, never taking her eyes off the girl with nothing of note occurring. In fact, the more she watched the priestess, the more convinced she became that this was a new, agonizing punishment Tylan invented for her. Day in and day out the routine remained the same: the acolytes woke up at dawn for prayers, followed by chores, breakfast, lessons with the high priestess, time for studying, dinner, more chores, and evening prayers before bed. The acolyte never broke routine once; she'd even stopped her midnight strolls in the garden.

At least she'd finally gleaned a few pieces of information she could pass along: the girl's name, Lennox, that she could always be found in a pair with the red-haired acolyte, Jasper, and that the symbols the acolytes wore on their forehead all marked their rank. Lennox still wore a single gold star, the same as many of the children walking around the temple, which told Kezra that on top of being boring, Lennox was also terrible at becoming a priestess. By the fourth day of watching the same mundane routine, Kezra decided she couldn't take it anymore. Nothing extraordinary was going to happen to this girl, and she planned on telling Tylan as much, so there could be no harm in breaking up the monotony. It felt like a waste to spend her entire time in the country's capital at the temple. Instead, Kezra thought she'd earned a trip to the market.

The walk down the goddess's hill was longer than Kezra initially anticipated, and by the time she spotted Tesmerin's market, she was sweating despite the slight chill in the air. Kezra took a deep breath to steady herself before entering, because even from a distance, she found the chaos of the markets overwhelming. She was used to the quiet, to the isolation of Helica, to the steady undercurrent of desolation and fear. Tesmerin; however, was Helica's complete inverse. The market teemed with life. A handful of vendors had set up shop on the hill leading to the temple, selling prayer beads, replicas of temple relics, and miniature statues of Altheia. The stalls had been spaced evenly apart, allowing Kezra some time to browse, and while the vendors were a little pushy, one glare had been enough for them to leave her in peace. She'd incorrectly expected the heart of the market to be similar.

Instead, the moment Kezra set foot in the market, she found herself being shoved along by the crowd. The deeper into the market she ventured, the more tightly packed the stalls became, and the more aggressive the vendors were with her. They shoved fabrics into her face - silks in bold patterns or fur from exotic animals. They tried to slip jewelry around her wrist and demand payment for things she didn't want, and worst of all , no level of glaring or threats seemed to intimidate anyone. If anything, it just emboldened the vendors further.

"Would you like a pelt of fur, Miss? It comes from the bears of Kitsummit, trapped by the most skilled hunters. It's yours for only eight gold crowns," a vendor called as he pushed the fur into her hands.

"Don't listen to that crook," a short, dark-haired woman interrupted, grabbing her arm. "Here, you want this emerald silk spun from the worms of the barrens. Make a dress to match your eyes and catch the eye of a lord. Much better for you than some stuffy fur and only seven gold crowns."

Kezra shook the woman off, muttering a reply as the vendors called after her. Someone bumped into her right side, throwing her off balance and knocking into the person on her left.

"Hey, watch it!" The stranger yelled.

Her lungs felt tight; sweat beaded her forehead. The smell of sweat and unwashed humans clung to her nostrils. Bright afternoon sunshine blinded her eyes. Kezra picked up her pace, needing to escape the crowd, the noise, the smells. She thought she might throw up or possibly faint. Before she knew it, Kezra was running through the market, pushing people aside in her desperation to get away. People muttered curses at her as she shoved her way through, but she ignored them, moving forward without seeing where she was going.

Finally, Kezra found herself free of the crowd. Suddenly, she could breathe again; her skin didn't feel as tight. In an alley, Kezra leaned her back against a stone wall, taking deep breaths and settling her mind, embarrassed by her body's reaction to the crowd. Men twice her size had tried to kill her, and Kezra hadn't broken a sweat taking them down and dragging them to Tylan. It was ridiculous for the market to cause her so much fear. Feeling centered, Kezra glanced up to take in her surroundings. She was still in the market, but in a much less crowded portion.

Here, the stalls were set up in the shadows. People kept their hoods up, their faces covered as they haggled over their wares. There was a tension Kezra felt familiar with, one she felt every time she picked up one of Tylan's bonded. She wandered around the market, taking in the glittering vials that promised eternal youth, the relics that promised to hold some lingering magical properties. They were likely all fake, a facade for darker things sold by the vendors. Distracted, Kezra bumped into a man selling a bone-white powder from the pocket of his coat. The impact sent the man stumbling; he fumbled with the powder, dropping it on the ground. Spooked, his would-be customer scurried away without a backward glance. Kezra backed away, but the salesman turned on her in an instant, and she spotted the silver gleam of a knife as it flashed toward her. He grabbed her by the throat, shoving her against a wall.

"You cost me a sale, girl. I expect compensation," he whispered in her ear. The man's sour breath was hot on her face. Kezra wrinkled her nose in disgust. Her heart picked up in anticipation of a fight.

"I'll give you one chance to let me go now and walk away unharmed," Kezra said, keeping her voice measured and calm while she spoke. The man threw his head back and laughed.

"Why would I do that when I've got you right where I want you? If you don't have any money, I can think of other ways that you can pay." The man's eyes roved down her body, hungrily taking in her appearance. Her vision turned red. He kept her by the throat with one hand and moved his mouth closer to hers. Kezra spit in his face. "Why you little bitch!" The man yelled, his face turning red with fury. His furious screams turned to howls of pain as Kezra caught wrist and twisted until she heard a snap, freeing the knife. She caught it as it fell, and he released his grip on her throat to cradle the broken bone. Switching positions, Kezra pinned him against the wall, holding the knife to his throat. The man's eyes hardened with anger, but she could taste the fear simmering underneath. She inhaled the scent, savoring it.

"Remember that I gave you the chance to get away," Kezra smiled, slowly pressing the knife into his flesh. Drops of blood fell to the ground, and she prepared herself to make a final swing, cutting his throat when a hand landed firmly on her shoulder, halting her.

"Let him go, child. He isn't worth a murder charge. And there are eyes watching, even here," a soft voice whispered in her ear. The voice belonged to a woman, and the calm in it washed over Kezra, soothing some of her rage, leveling out her pounding heart.

"You're lucky someone came to your rescue. But if you ever try this again, I will find you, and next time, you won't walk away." With those final words, Kezra released her grip on the man who fell to the ground as he tried to stumble away, powders and pills spilling from his pocket as he landed. He gave Kezra one hard glare that seemed to promise pain, but scrambled away without bothering to pick up his belongings. She turned to face the voice's owner as the red slowly faded from her vision.

A small woman, draped in patchwork clothing, faced her. Wild, curly brown hair escaped from the wool attempting to tie it back. The pink and green horizontally striped skirt was a jarring contrast to her orange spotted top, and Kezra found it disorienting to take in the woman's full appearance. She decided to concentrate on the woman's face, which was lined and wrinkled, meaning the woman was either twice Kezra's age or had lived a hard life. But her eyes were striking - deep-set and a shimmering gold that danced with mischief and burned with fire. Despite her small stature, Kezra recognized the eyes of a fellow predator. For her part, the woman held Kezra's stare, unintimidated despite the interaction that she'd just witnessed.

"Are we going to stand here staring at each other all evening until that man gets a guard to come arrest you?" Kezra blushed at the question, realizing she'd been silent for an awkward length of time. She didn't often interact with people she wasn't threatening, and she wasn't sure where to go from here.

The woman shook her head and started walking away. Kezra stayed planted for a moment, unsure if she should follow, but the woman turned back to her and waved her along to follow. After a second of debate, Kezra followed her. What did she have to lose?

They arrived at a shoddy tent that had escaped Kezra's notice earlier. It was clearly homemade, stitched together with mismatched secondhand fabrics, much like the woman's clothing. Worry tickled her senses, but Kezra shook it free. If she felt uncomfortable in the space, she could simply leave. The little woman may have been tough, but she certainly wouldn't be able to outrun Kezra. She opened the flap of the tent, beckoning Kezra inside. Without hesitation, and against her better judgment, Kezra followed.

Inside was surprisingly cozy and larger than anticipated. The woman had made an effort to create a comfortable space. In the center sat a table with two mismatched chairs. Second-hand rugs covered the ground, still vibrant although a little worn. Books in haphazard piles were strewn about the ground. Coupled with the strategically placed candles glowing softly around the tent, the color gave the space a warm, cozy feeling that put Kezra at ease. It was the exact opposite of her cold, impersonal room in Tylan's lair. Her heart lurched at the sight, part of her wishing she had a space like this to call her own. A bedroll peeked out of a covered space in the back of the tent. This woman had let Kezra into her home, and she couldn't help but wonder why.

"It takes strength to let reason override emotion, bravery to release a man you could not trust." The woman said, jarring Kezra from her thoughts. "Tea?" Kezra nodded, and the woman bustled about, pouring brown, steaming liquid into two mugs.

"Some might call it stupidity," Kezra answered, taking the mug. "But I didn't feel like washing blood out of my tunic today. It stains you know." The woman sat down at the table, gesturing for Kezra to do the same. Once seated, the woman leaned across the table, offering her hand.

"You speak so callously of ending a life, but I don't think you're truly so cold-hearted. Give me your hands. Let me do a reading for you." So that was it, the reason the woman had invited her into the tent. It wasn't kindness; it was business. The woman wanted money. Still, Kezra was already there, and she had a warm mug of tea. There wasn't any harm in playing along. She took the woman's outstretched hands, feeling the rough calluses that mirrored her own. Kezra wondered what had caused them. She imagined they were from labors of love, hours spent caring for herself or a family, so different from her own, developed from training, learning to kill with efficiency, to become heartless. The way the woman saw through her cold facade made her uneasy, but she prepared for the reading, anyway. Nothing the woman said would be real; it was all just a show meant to fool the common folk.

"Believe what you'd like," Kezra smirked. "Let's get on with the reading." The woman returned her smirk, nodding. Her fingers closed around Kezra's hands, holding them in a tight grip. For a beat, nothing happened. Then the woman's eyes went pale, almost milky. She wondered if the woman had put in some kind of eye drop before handing over the tea to make it happen.

"An act of mercy from a warrior is no small thing. I see something important in you, but fog and smoke cloud your future. The smoke clings to you, making it hard for me to see you clearly. For your small mercy, I shall try to read your fate." Kezra rolled her eyes, but she had to applaud the dramatics. The performance would be at least worth a few coppers. At least it was more entertaining than sitting in a tree watching the priestess. Kezra decided to encourage her.

"Go on," Kezra said. The woman shut her eyes, concentrating.

Suddenly, the room grew chilly, as if a winter breeze had blown in. The candles flickered. One extinguished. The woman's eyes snapped open, but this time her golden irises were lit with an otherworldly glow. Her grip on Kezra's hands tightened painfully, her nails cutting into skin. When the woman spoke, her voice was cold, deeper than before.

"Two were separated and two will join, dark and light, two sides of the same coin. One a daughter of day, one blessed by night. The fates of the two are tied. Together they will find what they both seek, for if one is without the other, neither will be free." The strange light faded from her eyes, but her grip remained tight. "I don't know what you are, daughter of night, but I fear for you. Worse, I fear you may doom us all." The woman's voice had returned to normal, but it shook on the final words, as though she was afraid.

Kezra wasn't having fun anymore. She wrenched her hands away from the woman's flinging a few coins onto the table. Bolting out of the tent, Kezra ran through the markets, all the way back to the hill. Out of breath, she stopped, replaying the scene in her mind: the woman's cold voice, the chill that bit into her skin, the strange golden glow in the woman's eyes. A shiver ran down Kezra's spine at the memory. As she made her way up the hill, Kezra told herself she was being silly. The woman was a performer, and she put on a well-rehearsed show, nothing more. By the time she made it back to her post, she could almost believe the lie.

CHAPTER 4

Lennox

Two weeks into her punishment, constant exposure to the water and soap needed to scrub the temple had rendered Lennox's hands raw and cracked. Jasper had made a salve for them with plants from the gardens, and they took turns helping apply the salve and wrapped each other's hands in bandages every night as their cracked hands bled. Lennox's heart filled with dread at the thought of another week enduring the same punishment, but she kept her thoughts to herself. She was the reason they were in this mess; she wouldn't make it worse for Jasper by wallowing in self-pity. Lennox bent down to the floor in the fading sunlight, soaking her coarse brush with sud-laden water that dripped onto the floor. Moving in tight circles, she scrubbed away the remnants of the temple's visitors, who left behind dirt and muddy footprints along their way to leave an offering for the goddess.

Keeping the temple clean was a pillar of Altheia's discipline as priestesses, so to keep it spotless a team of at least six acolytes usually worked to clean it on a rotating schedule. However, for their punishment, Jasper and Lennox bore the sole responsibility, and they worked in tandem to keep it clean. They started in the middle, each making their way to opposite ends of the temple, careful not to leave a speck on Altheia's floor. At the beginning of the punishment, they'd tried to talk to each other or pass the time with songs and jokes, but as it progressed, expediency won over. They found it was faster to work in silence. By the time she finished, Lennox could no longer see Jasper. The silence and the glittering pink stone in the setting sun created an eerie feeling of isolation that Lennox struggled to dispel. It always left her feeling trapped, lonely.

Her only reprieve from the tedium was the nights she spent in the garden. Although Lennox hadn't been in the garden for three nights in a row now, too exhausted from a day of rigorous scrubbing to venture out under the moon. She could still feel the night's call, though. In her dreams, Lennox stepped out under the moonlight and wandered through the gardens, brushing the lunasha's silky petals against her skin. Lately, she'd felt another presence there; eyes watching her every move. Although it was just a dream, Lennox liked to think it was a message from Altheia that she was watching over her, ready for Lennox to take her next step and become a full priestess.

"How have you been doing the same chore for two weeks, and yet you haven't gotten any faster at completing it?" Jasper asked, pulling Lennox from her daydream. Lennox let out a little huff.

"I'm going as fast as I can. Not all of us are blessed with your superior cleaning skills."

"Some of us concentrate on getting done instead of daydreaming," Jasper said. She tapped her foot, peering down at Lennox. "Come on, Lex. I practically worked myself to the bone to be done in time for supper. If we don't hurry, there won't be anything left and I'll have to beg the cook for another stale roll."

"You could go without me."

Jasper rolled her eyes, but instead of rushing off toward the dining hall, she grabbed her brush, helping finish Lennox's portion of the temple. The prospect of warm food gave Lennox the motivation to work a little more quickly, and they were done in no time; plus, the second pair of hands certainly didn't hurt.

"I can't believe you got me to do your work for you," Jasper quipped, picking up her bucket and brush.

"I'm just not built for manual labor, Jas." Lennox gave a dramatic sigh to go with the declaration. Jasper shook her head.

"Oh, and I am?"

"You're just so much better at it. It might be best for you to clean the temple next week, and I'll supervise." Jasper ignored her and made her way toward the supply shed to stow away her bucket and brush. Lennox scurried down the hill after her. Outside the temple, the bitter evening air pricked at her raw hands, irritating them. Lennox let out an involuntary wince, regaining Jasper's attention.

"You need to keep your hands wrapped at night, Lex. I'll see if I can gather some herbs for more salve tonight, but it will only work if you actually keep the wrap on so your hands don't keep cracking." In response, Lennox looped her arm over Jasper's shoulder, pulling her close.

"Yes, mother. I'll keep them wrapped." Truly, she didn't deserve a friend like Jasper, one who would gather herbs for them after a long day. Her voice softened. "What would I do without you, Jas?"

"Stay cleaning the temple until midnight with no supper and bleeding hands, if I had to guess."

Lennox withdrew her arm and gave her friend a playful shove, wiping away the unfallen tears welling in her eyes. She really didn't know how she'd have survived without her best-friend who had always been there for her. Both left the temple as children; the two had grown up together, but unlike Lennox, Jasper knew her family. The fifth daughter of a small farming family, they'd left Jasper at the age of two when her family knew they couldn't afford to care for her. However, they'd still visit every couple of years, bringing their offerings to the goddess and checking on the welfare of their daughter. Sometimes Lennox envied it: the way Jasper's mother would hug her, how her sisters would nettle and tease her, the teary-eyed goodbyes when the family left. What must it be like to see your face reflected on someone else's - to know in advance how the years would settle onto your face? Lennox would never know. But every time her family left, Jasper would grow morose. It took Lennox days to pull her out of the darkness clinging to her like a second skin, every time she felt abandoned all over again. For that reason, Lennox thought maybe how she'd been left was better. Perhaps it was more painful to get small glimpses of your family than to never know them at all.

Lennox stumbled as Jasper returned the earlier bump, harder than what she'd received. A smile grew on Lennox's face as she pushed her friend back, harder still. Then she took off running when Jasper stumbled. She stopped several feet ahead and turned back to look at her friend.

"The first one there gets the other's dessert!" Lennox shouted. Jasper threw her head back and laughed. Lennox loved the sound in part for its rarity. So often the serious one, Jasper rarely let go and really laughed. She started chasing after her friend, gaining surprising speed. Taking that as acceptance of the challenge, Lennox took off toward the dining hall. Breathless and smiling, she spotted the dining hall just ahead. Lennox turned her head to look over her shoulder and shout out a victory cry when she ran straight into a solid mass. Lennox bounced back, losing her balance. A panicked yell and a short cry came from the wall she'd run into. There was a loud thump that sounded suspiciously like a body hitting the ground. Lennox hurried to her feet, brushing dirt off her robe as she made her way to the fallen sister. She blurted out apologies, leaning over to help the priestess to her feet. The furious gaze of The Mother greeted her. Jasper caught up, still laughing. All traces of merriment drained from her face at the sight of The Mother sprawled on the ground. The ancient woman stood slowly, refusing help as she gained her feet. Lennox went to sputter out another apology, but Jasper's glare cut her off. Lennox snapped her mouth shut so quickly it hurt her jaw.

"Well, if it isn't just the two young women I came looking for, although Alethia knows, you've both been acting more like girls lately." The Mother paused, taking time to straighten her robes. "I was on my way to inform you both that I've come to a decision about your request to participate in the next Blessing Ceremony." Lennox reached out for her friend's hand, her heart suddenly pounding. She wondered if The Mother could hear it thundering in her chest.

"The two of you are now in your twentieth year. You've grown from girls into women under my tutelage, and while you may sometimes be...difficult, I'm proud of the women you've become." Lennox took a sharp intake of breath, unable to believe her ears. She held it, waiting for The Mother to finish. "You've taken your punishment with grace, never once complaining, and I believe such virtuous behavior deserves a reward. Therefore, I'm granting the two of you permission to participate in the next blessing ceremony. It will take place in ten days under the full moon. As for this little incident, I'm willing to overlook it, provided it does not happen again."

"Yes, Mother." They said in unison.

"Thank you for your generosity," Jasper added.

"Yes, thank you, Mother," Lennox muttered.

"Very well." The Mother nodded. "This is cause for celebration then. Go, make your way to the dining hall for your supper and try not to knock over anyone else along the way." The Mother gave a rare smile with the reprimand before walking away.

Lennox watched as she walked out of sight, maintaining her dignity. The moment she walked over the hill, and hopefully out of earshot, they both started squealing. Jasper pulled Lennox in for a tight hug, beaming.

"Can you believe it, Lex?" she asked, breathless. "We're finally going to be priestesses!" She pulled back, grabbing Lennox's hands in her own, smiling brightly.

"We did it! Now, can we eat, please? Victory made me hungry." Lennox smirked.

"What do you mean, victory? We're walking to the dining hall together, and you knocked over The Mother, which is a cause for disqualification." Jasper tried to be exasperated, but she struggled to fight back a smile.

"Whatever you say. I'm still eating your dessert."

"Fine, eat it. I'm hardly going to be able to eat, anyway. We're going to be priestesses!" With that, Jasper linked her arm in Lennox's, and the two skipped off to the dining hall. Lennox tried to match her friend's elation, but a sinking feeling crept into her stomach. Suddenly, her hunger was gone, replaced by dread.

Lennox sat at one of the dining hall's long tables, pushing her food around on her plate as she looked around the dining hall. In the summer, the dining hall was one of her favorite places with its painted wooden tiles depicting different stories of the goddess. During the summer equinox, the dining hall doors were thrown open so the people of Oscana could participate in a celebration of the goddess with feasting and dancing at the temple. It was the only time The Mother allowed the acolytes to let loose, turning a blind eye to the drinking and dancing so long as it didn't get out of hand. For weeks beforehand, they worked on decorating the hall, preparing for the celebration. Lennox had always loved watching the late summer sun stream in through the open doors as people filtered into the hall. However, the winter was a different story. This late in the year, half the hall was closed down, sitting in darkness as there weren't enough priestesses to occupy the entire space. With dinner almost over, few people lingered in the hall, and the ghostly atmosphere added to Lennox's growing melancholy.

Jasper sat down across from her with a plate full of salted beef and potatoes rich with butter. The scent made Lennox's mouth water, but she found once she brought the food to her lips, she couldn't get it down. She couldn't stop thinking about the blessing ahead, what it would mean. Once she took it, she'd be physically bound to the temple forever, unable to leave without special permission from The Mother. With her mind preoccupied, Lennox was uncharacteristically quiet throughout dinner, and she worried her friend would notice. Luckily, Jasper's exuberance made up for her silence, unable to contain her excitement.

"I can't believe we get to take The Blessing! What do you think it involves? Is there a test? What if there's a test? Lex, we need to study!"

"Jas, we've been studying our whole lives. Whatever The Blessing involves, you're ready."

Jasper bit her lip and nodded slowly.

"I guess you're right; I just want to succeed so badly. We can't fail, Lex." Lennox reached out to grasp her friend's hand, giving it a gentle squeeze.

"It'll be okay, Jas. You're not only going to pass; you'll be the best priestess in all of Oscana." A smile crossed Jasper's face, her worried look melting away. She went back to eating and chatting contentedly, but Lennox couldn't bring herself to participate with the question sitting on her lips.

"Aren't you a little nervous?" Lennox asked tentatively.

"What do you mean? You just told me not to be," Jasper replied, worry creeping back into her tone.

"Not about passing; you'll be perfect. Just…doesn't it bother you that we won't be able to leave the temple?" Lennox couldn't meet her friend's eye as she spoke. She concentrated on moving the potatoes around the plate, swirling the melted butter around.

"Not really. My whole life is here; why would I want to leave? You're not thinking of leaving, are you?"

Lennox's head snapped up at the panicked sound of Jasper's voice.

"Of course not," she said, looking Jasper in the eye. "This is my home; you're my home. I guess I'm just a little sad that I won't get to see everything that's out there."

"We will though; we'll see it all together. The Mother sends priestesses on missions. We'll be missionaries, travelling all over the country to spread Altheia's light. I promise." Jasper's eyes were full of desperation as she spoke; it broke Lennox's heart.

"Of course we will. I'm sorry; I was just being silly." Lennox gave her brightest, most encouraging smile. Jasper let out a sigh of relief and opened her mouth to speak.

Whatever she'd been about to say was cut off by two figures approaching the table - Elana and Rose. The two clung together as closely as Lennox and Jasper; you'd never find one without the other. Elana was short and serious, with wheat-brown hair that constantly fell into her face despite her tight braid and mud-colored eyes. Rose was her opposite, tall and willowy, head always in the clouds. She was ghostly pale, with corn-silk blonde hair and blue eyes so light they verged on white. She looked like a spirit, bound to disappear at any moment, and Elana followed her, keeping her grounded. Both took their roles as priestesses too seriously for Lennox's taste, although it was hard to say if Rose directed her whispering to the goddess or nonsense to a world that existed only in her head. Either way, neither of them were fans of her "antics" as they called them. Lennox didn't know why her dedication mattered at all, as no one had seen the gods in centuries. They were little more than myth now, but it didn't stop the priestesses from acting like Altheia could storm into the room at any moment and smite any who didn't show her proper deference.

"So, I hear you two are finally taking The Blessing," Elana said, nudging Jasper and ignoring Lennox entirely. Elana and Rose were only two years older, but they'd been elevated for four and acted with an air of superiority.

"Yes, The Mother has arranged the ceremony for next week," Jasper replied stiffly. But in her excitement, her voice turned low and conspiratorial, "Is there any advice you can share for the ceremony? Is there a test?"

Elana's eyes narrowed.

"You know that's a sacred ritual, sister. It's simply not discussed."

"Oh, stop, both of you. Sisters don't squabble," Rose said airily. Jasper's cheeks blushed red as she hastily redirected the conversation to ask about lower priestess duties and what to expect after The Blessing. The three of them chatted without noticing Lennox's lack of participation. She moved her attention again to the ceiling, focusing on a tile painted to depict the moon in different phases, a tribute to Altheia's dominion over light. Lennox longed for the real thing, to feel the soft moonlight touch her skin under the night sky, for the fresh air of the gardens. If she closed her eyes, she could almost imagine she was out there.

"Hello, Lennox, are you listening to me?" Elana said, snapping her fingers in Lennox's face.

"I'm sorry, what?" Lennox drew her attention back to the women seated around her.

"I asked if you're ready for The Blessing."

"Of course." Lennox gave her a bland smile, which she hoped conveyed the appropriate amount of excitement. "I've waited my whole life to be bound to the goddess." Elana turned away, satisfied with the banal answer. Lennox thanked the goddess; no one seemed to sense the panic coursing through her.

Weeks passed in a blur. Lennox concentrated on her punishment, growing quiet with nervousness and exhaustion, going through the daily motions with none of her usual levity. Jasper, on the other hand, grew uncharacteristically animated, as though the promise of The Blessing had breathed new life into her. She chattered consistently, painting a vivid picture of how life as a full priestess would differ from that of an acolyte. Her voice filled their bunk, while Lennox gave only nods of agreement, or muttered a placating word when it seemed her friend grew suspicious of the silence. The dull days of scrubbing gave Lennox nothing to concentrate on but her growing sense of anxiety over being tethered to the temple. To brush it away, she focused on a single spot, making it shine to perfection. The Mother nodded approvingly at her work, even going so far as to utter a confirmation of Lennox's readiness to become a priestess, filling her with further dread. The solace to be found was at night, in the gardens. Lennox wandered the path, venturing closer and closer to the path, envisioning a life beyond the path, beyond the temple. She sat in the garden, stroking the silky bloom of the lunasha plants, debating what to do. Before she knew it, it was the day before The Blessing. She envisioned herself taking a vow, magic emerging from The Mother acting like a cord, tethering her to the temple, a tattoo appearing on her arm to display the bond. Lennox felt like she was suffocating. She pushed herself through her day of cleaning as usual, feeling unsettled. Then threw herself into bed without supper, hoping she'd wake feeling differently.

She woke to an almost full moon, bright and heavy in the night sky. It beckoned her to come out and play in the moonlight, to dance through the gardens. As always, Lennox listened. Whether it was the moon's calling or her anxiety, something pulled her into the temple's gardens, barefooted and bleary-eyed. One foot in front of the other, she edged closer to the garden's gate and the path leading into the city. Finally, she reached the tall, black iron gate - the boundary between life as she knew it and the one she dreamed of having. Lennox rested her head on the cool iron, allowing her imagination to run wild with possibilities. Deep in her heart, she knew she couldn't do it, she couldn't take the vow that would tether her to this temple for the rest of her life, but her heart fractured at the idea of leaving the only family she'd ever known. What would Jasper do if she awoke the next morning to find Lennox's bed empty, a bag missing, her gone without a trace? Indecision paralyzed her hand against the gate. She couldn't bring herself to open it, but couldn't find the will to walk back to bed either. With a deep breath, Lennox made up her mind; she reached for the latch to unlock the gate.

"Lennox?" She froze at the sound of the familiar voice, her fingers grazing the latch. With the sound, her courage fled. Guilt wrapped itself around her gut and squeezed until a sob built in the back of her throat. Lennox turned around to see Jasper's blue eyes piercing through the night to gaze back at her. The hurt inside them tore a hole through Lennox's chest.

"What are you doing?" Jasper asked.

"Nothing." Lennox tried to voice a calmness into her voice despite her raging heart. "You know how I love to be in the garden at night. I wanted to clear my head before tomorrow's ceremony."

"But why are you at the gate? You weren't thinking of going into Tesmerin, were you?"

"Technically, we're in Tesmerin." Lennox smirked at her joke, hoping to lighten Jasper's mood. It didn't work. While the temple was technically in the city's heart, it was so far removed from life outside that it practically felt like a different world, and that feeling of isolation had laced into her voice. The joke fell flat. She hesitated before replying again. "Of course I wasn't, Jas. Come on, let's go to bed," Lennox took Jasper's arm, leading her back to bed.

"Don't lie to me, Lennox." Jasper ripped her arm free, whirling around in fury. Lennox glanced around, uneasy. She didn't want the commotion to wake The Mother and get them into more trouble. She wouldn't be able to bear it if her last act before leaving was to land her best friend in more trouble and strip her of the honor of taking the ceremony. Lennox moved further away from the gate, hoping it would appease her friend.

"I'm sorry, Jas. But aren't you the least bit curious about what else is out there? We live in this glorious city, but all we know about it is from books. We're about to throw our lives away without exploring anything else. We could go now, together." Lennox offered her hand. "We could live a real life, Jas. You and I, in it together. Come with me," Lennox's soft voice took on a pleading tone. Her hand hung limply in the air as she awaited her friend's decision, hungering for acceptance and terrified of it in equal measure. In the end, Jasper reeled back, her hand over her heart as if she'd been slapped. Lennox let her hand fall to her side, ashamed.

"If we go now, Lennox, The Mother will never take us back." Jasper's use of her full name made Lennox wince. "After everything we've put her through, she won't offer us this opportunity again if we leave. Besides, I like it here. What the priestesses do is important, even if you can't see it. We are the hope of the people of Oscana. We are who they turn to for the goddess's protection in their darkest times and for her blessing during their greatest triumphs. Eventually, we can apply for missions; we can still see the world. But I have spent my whole life answering this calling. I won't ruin it at the last minute because of your impulse to see the world unencumbered by duty." Jasper sighed, shaking her head. Something in Lennox's chest withered and died; she thought it might be hope. "Besides, even if we did leave, where would we go? We wouldn't even be able to buy a room at an inn. We have nothing without the temple; we'd be beggars on the street. Come to bed, Lennox. Don't throw this away; don't throw me away." The last line broke whatever resolve Lennox had been clinging onto. She only nodded, not trusting herself to speak, and let her friend lead her back to their room. Lennox climbed into bed, guilt and anguish gnawing at her.

"We'll be happy here, Lex. I promise," Jasper whispered before she fell into a sound sleep. But sleep didn't find Lennox that night. Instead, she lay awake all night thinking of how she couldn't bear to stay, but was too cowardly to leave.

One of the few perks The Blessing ceremony offered was the ability to sleep in. Lennox curled herself into a ball under the covers, trying to take full advantage of the late start after a sleepless night. Rays of morning sunlight shone into the room, illuminating everything in a comfortable glow that made her want to believe everything would be alright. She rolled over and glanced at Jasper, who was still sleeping soundly. Her long copper hair glimmered subtly in the sunlight. Unconsciously, Lennox stretched her fingers out to touch the delicate strands in a subtle goodbye. At her touch, Jasper's eyes fluttered open. A slow smile spread across her face.

"Good morning, Lex."

Lennox muttered a good morning back, awaiting a scolding about the night before. The confrontation never came. Instead, they readied themselves for the day in companionable silence. As a peace offering, Lennox braided Jasper's hair for her, delicately placing the star chain on her forehead, knowing it would be the last day she'd wear it. When she was done, Jasper returned the favor. Lennox closed her eyes to savor the moment of intimacy. This is what she had almost given up, what she had almost lost to a moment of impulse. Who else would love her, care for her like this? As Jasper placed the star chain on her head, she lowered herself to whisper in Lennox's ear.

"Thank you for staying." She gave Lennox's arm a reassuring squeeze.

With that, a weight lifted from Lennox's chest. She felt like she could breathe again. Everything was fine. She'd made the right decision, and now she and her friend, whom she loved like a sister, would take this next step together. Arm in arm, they left their room, determined to pass any test The Mother threw their way.

The day passed uneventfully. Other than the privilege of skipping morning prayers in preparation for a late night. They proceeded with their regular chores and lessons, but excitement radiated off Jasper, who beamed even during the most menial chore. Lennox, however, moved through the day as if watching herself from above. She chopped vegetables for dinner in a daze. As she chopped a carrot, she didn't feel its coarse skin in her hands, or the smooth handle of the knife when she picked it up. The spicy smell of the stew she cooked didn't meet her nose, nor did the heat of the fire warm her skin. With every moment the sun passed lower in the sky, she felt further disconnected from her body. Somehow, dinner was cooked and ready to be served without her remembering helping put it together.

Without thought, she bid the cooks goodbye and shuffled to the dining hall with the other acolytes as Jasper appeared at her side with a watchful eye. Through her joy, she'd been keeping an eye on Lennox all day, as though afraid she would flee down the path at any moment unless carefully watched. Jasper didn't need to worry; Lennox had missed her window to run and had slunk into quiet acceptance. Lennox had just grabbed her steaming bowl of stew when a high priestess with a serious face and a severe braid came to collect them.

"Follow me," she said. The priestess turned and set a brisk pace toward the temple without glancing back. Jasper and Lennox exchanged a look before rushing after her.

She led them to the temple. The moonlight illuminated its soft pink pillars, so they appeared to be studded with glimmering silver crystals. Most of the temple was open air so light could shine through, illuminating the pews and The Mother's pedestal in a dreamlike glow. Lennox looked around the temple in awe. For all the time she'd spent in the garden, she'd never seen moonlight grace the temple itself. How foolish she had been to think of abandoning such splendor. They made their way past Altheia's statue, past the rows of pews to the back of the temple where three doors awaited them. The doors were always locked, so Jasper and Lennox had spent years speculating about what could be inside, their guesses growing increasingly outlandish over time. Lennox's latest and favorite theory was that The Mother was hiding a mythical dragon behind the doors, training it to devour misbehaving acolytes. The high priestess strode to the door on the left.

"Jasper Emerett, you will wait in here."

Jasper gave Lennox's arm a final squeeze and strode into the room. The priestess shut the door before Lennox could get a good look inside. She unlocked the door on the right.

"Lennox Aphoros, you will wait in here."

Lennox obeyed, walking in silently, waiting for the high priestess to slam the door and walk away. Instead, she remained in the entryway, watching.

"This is your last opportunity to turn back. You may leave, walk down the hill, and enter the city. You will be supplied with a small bag of coin and civilian clothing to start your new life. Know that if you choose this path, we will not welcome you back as a priestess." Lennox opened her mouth to reply, to accept the money and be on her way, but she stopped herself. She thought of Jasper; memories of their years together played through her mind as she pictured the hurt on her friend's face upon learning Lennox had left without even saying goodbye. She had her answer.

"I will offer my life to the goddess." Without giving a response, the priestess slammed the door in her face. Lennox leapt back, narrowly avoiding it slamming into her nose.

She looked around the room for the first time, taking it in. There wasn't a dragon hiding in the space, which was simultaneously a disappointment and a relief. The room was small, much smaller than she'd imagined. There were fluffy baby-blue cushions on the floor in front of a short wooden table. On the table sat a single lit candle, the sole source of light in the dim room. Next to it was a piece of paper. Lennox sat on a cushion, folding her legs beneath her as she examined the paper in the candle's wavering light. *Take this time to dedicate your heart to the goddess. When your heart is bathed in her light, you may accept her blessing, and we will begin.* The note was unsigned, but she recognized The Mother's curled handwriting. With nothing left to do, Lennox sat in the silence and waited, wondering if her heart would ever truly be open to the goddess.

An eternity passed before the door opened with a click. The Mother stood in the doorway, flanked by the same unfamiliar priestess who had led her to the room.

"Follow me, child." The Mother led her toward the front of the temple. Lennox had expected to meet the moment with a heart beating in anticipation, or with a swirling pit of anxiety in her stomach. Instead, she felt nothing. Whether minutes or hours had passed in that room, it had been long enough to make peace with her decision to stay. They came to a stop under Altheia's statue. Jasper was nowhere in sight. Lennox wondered if she'd already completed her blessing. Would she be waiting for her after to celebrate, or did Lennox get to witness the ceremony first?

Lennox approached the statue with steady steps, holding The Mother's stare as she walked. As she approached, her gaze snagged on the unfamiliar book in The Mother's hands. It was bound in leather, dyed a deep blue. Embossed on the front were the symbols of Altheia in golden gilt - the sun and the moon surrounded by swirling stars. Golden script adorned the binding bearing the book's title. Lennox couldn't make out the words, but she recognized the old language of the gods. It had been briefly introduced in lessons, and she knew she'd learn the full language only after taking The Blessing. It dawned on her that the book must be The Book of Light, the ancient book of Altheia's wisdom. Lennox had read about it before and seen renderings, but the beauty of the book in front of her was stunning. She tore her eyes away from the book to take in the high priestess standing next to The Mother. In her hands was an ornate silver chalice, filled with amber liquid. Lennox steadied her heart and met The Mother's eyes. She was ready to begin. The Mother's grey eyes, though lined with creases and wrinkles from her decades in service, were still sharp and full of bright intelligence. The Mother glanced up at the moon, as if checking to see if it was still full, then nodded to herself.

"Sister Lennox Aphoros, you stand before the goddess under the light of her moon, her sun, and her stars. Tonight, you will pledge your life to her. Should the goddess accept your oath, you will be bound to her for the rest of your days, a vessel to share her light with the world. Do you, Lennox Aphoros, give yourself heart and soul to Altheia? Do you pledge to answer her call, honor her wishes, and reside here, in her home?"

"I do," Lennox said, her voice even. The Mother gave a small, encouraging nod.

"Very well. Then you will drink the elixir of the gods, speak their vows, and seal your promise in your blood." The statement sent a jolt through Lennox's spine, and she looked around before her eyes found the blade resting at the base of Altheia's statue, its hilt wrapped in the same dyed leather as the book with Altheia's symbols embroidered onto it. Yet another holy item from the goddess. The priestess held the cup out to Lennox, amber liquid sloshing as it moved. Hesitantly, Lennox took it, peering at the liquid swirling inside where silver flecks swirled on the wine's surface. The eyes of The Mother bore into her, urging her to make her decision and be done with it. Before she could think further, Lennox threw back the chalice, draining the glass in a single gulp.

Immediately, she could tell something was wrong. As the drink slithered down her throat, the blood heated in her veins. An unbearable pressure built in her muscles, ripping a scream from her lips before everything exploded in blinding white light. There was a startled scream, then a heavy object crashed into her, knocking her to the ground. Desperately, she tried to puzzle out what was happening, why her blood felt hot in her body, where the light had come from, and why her head suddenly throbbed. Then her world went black.

Chapter 5

Kezra - One day before The Blessing

Weeks passed as Kezra watched the acolyte with nothing new to report, and even worse, no new leads on how to break her bond to Tylan. Thoughts of the golden-eyed woman constantly filled her mind, distracting her from her mission. In desperation, Kezra had gone back to the market, searching high and low for the fortune teller, but she'd vanished without a trace. The space where the patchwork tent had once resided now held another vendor; Kezra was beginning to wonder if she'd imagined the whole thing. Not that it mattered. One strange afternoon didn't mean the woman knew anything about old magic or bond breaking. The woman was a talented con-artist who'd made something up for a bit of coin, nothing more. Still, the interaction wasn't helping Kezra's fraying nerves. It had been over a week since Tylan had last summoned her to Helica; he was going to call her back at any time, and Kezra had nothing to report and no sign that this Blessing ceremony was actually going to happen. Tylan might decide the entire thing was a waste of time and keep her in Helica for the foreseeable future. That couldn't happen.

Tylan had never given Kezra so much freedom before; he wasn't likely to give it again.

She pulled out a vial of smoke and twirled it idly in her hand, wishing she could use it to go to Kitsummit. She'd never been in the mountains among the tribe people, but there were whispers about them: whispers that they harbored some remnants of old magic, their leaders guarding the knowledge like a closely held secret. Not a single person from Kitsummit had ever bonded to Tylan. They didn't need his magic there, which gave her hope the rumors held some truth. She sighed, stashing the vial in her tunic, knowing this line of thinking was pointless. As useful as the vials were, they had their limitations. Kezra could only use them to travel to places she could envision; meaning she had to either visit them or at least see an accurate rendering of the place before she could visit. She'd never been to Kitsummit, and as far as she knew, the people who lived there were so reclusive that no renderings existed. Besides, it wasn't just a matter of getting there; she would need people to talk to her if she went, and that would take time she didn't have. Even if she could go, if Tylan summoned her back before she learned anything, but if he found out she'd left her station, the consequences would be brutal. She settled into the tree with reluctance, trying to think of a better plan when she caught the whisperings of a hushed argument.

Kezra moved silently between the trees until she saw the acolyte, Lennox, and a red-haired girl arguing at the edge of the garden. Lennox's hand rested on the iron as though she intended to leave; which was curious. In all the weeks Kezra had spent watching, she'd learned a lot about the routine of the temple, and the faithful servants of Altheia rarely left the temple grounds. Food and supplies were delivered directly to them from the merchants in Tesmerin, virtually eliminating the need to venture into the city. Exactly two priestesses left the temple in the past few weeks, and were dressed for travel and carrying supplies, indicating a journey. Lennox was not. Those priestesses had also been older and hadn't left under nightfall. Lennox walked through the gardens almost every night, but she had never left them. Whatever was happening now, Kezra didn't think it was happening with the elder priestesses' knowledge.

"Don't lie to me, Lennox!" The red-haired girl was straining not to shout, but she looked like she was fighting a losing battle. Lennox tried to pull her down the path toward Tesmerin, but her friend ripped away from her, stumbling back. The scene struck her as a petty argument between friends, and Kezra was quickly losing interest. She forced herself to listen in case there was something useful to report to Tylan. She leaned in closer, trying not to miss a word. The red-haired girl was pleading with Lennox.

"...Besides, even if we did leave, where would we go? We wouldn't even be able to buy a room at an inn. We have nothing without the temple; we'd be beggars on the street. Come to bed, Lennox. Don't throw this away; don't throw me away." On the last words, the woman's voice cracked, and Lennox appeared to give in,following her friend back toward the room. But Kezra was no longer paying much attention. The Blessing. She didn't know what it was, but it sounded significant. It sounded like a reason for her to stay. As she walked away, Lennox gave a desperate glance back over her shoulder and, for a moment, Kezra swore their eyes met, though she couldn't know for sure though, because a heartbeat later, she was enveloped in purple smoke and Lennox was gone.

Smoke stung her eyes as Tylan's throne room came into focus. A sense of agitation filled the room. Tylan was on his onyx dais, pacing back and forth, muttering incoherently. Even though he summoned her, it took him a moment to notice Kezra standing silently behind him.

When he finally spotted her, he whipped around to face her, a madness lurking behind his eyes. Whatever he needed from this priestess was eating at him. Kezra made a mental note to tread lightly.

"What do you have to report?" he asked, skipping his normal power play.

"There's nothing, my lord. She's just a simple girl, training to be a priestess. Perhaps if I had some more time..."

"Time!? You've had nothing but time. You've missed something. What good have you done me wandering around up there? Years of waiting, of watching and planning, raising a defiant, ungrateful child all for nothing." Tylan continued his pacing around the throne room, looking as though he was hunting for something to hurl across the room. Kezra's mind reeled so fast she couldn't concentrate on his movements. Raising a child for nothing. Did he mean her? What did she have to do with some want-to-be priestess?

"There's nothing you've noticed, nothing new to report to me?"

"She appears drawn to the gardens."

"Yes, yes. You told me before. But nothing happens? She just walks as usual?"

"Well, there was one thing. She got into an argument with her friend in the gardens tonight. They mentioned something about a blessing, and not being able to leave the temple." Tylan came to an abrupt halt, the tension in the room starting to disappear.

"The Blessing," he whispered to himself. "Did they mention when it's supposed to take place?"

"Tonight was supposedly their last opportunity to leave the temple, so I believe tomorrow." Tylan nodded, remaining silent. He appeared deep in thought, seeming to forget Kezra was in the room with him. An eternity passed as she waited for him to dismiss her. He finally looked up.

"New plan, Kezra. You'll continue to watch Lennox tomorrow. Make sure she doesn't leave the temple grounds. Watch the ceremony closely. She will be offered a special potion, let her drink from it, but don't let the ceremony continue any further. The Mother will ask her to take a vow - that can not happen."

"How do I stop her from continuing?"

"I don't care, Kezra. Knock her out, set the temple on fire. Figure something out. You're resourceful. But you can not let her take the vow."

"I will not fail you. But after I stop the ceremony, what then? Do I continue to observe?" Tylan was still for another heartbeat, contemplating his next move.

"No. I've waited long enough." He pulled a vial of purple smoke from his tunic and held it out. "The time for watching is done. You will bring her here, to me". Kezra took the vial from him, a quiet agreement to his demand. Tylan whispered under his breath and waved his hand in her direction. The smoke enveloped her, whisking her away to that gods-forsaken tree.

That night, Kezra didn't sleep. Instead, she crept through the shadows of the garden to the dorm room where Lennox slept. Kezra climbed the building, trying to stay silent so as not to wake anyone. Perched on the top of the roof, there was nothing to do but wait and remain alert in case Lennox changed her mind about running away. Thankfully, there were no further escape attempts during the night. In fact, it was well past dawn when Lennox emerged from her room, a change to her usual routine. Kezra's eyes were heavy with exhaustion as she watched Lennox head to the temple for her chores. She debated taking a few quick moments to rest. It seemed unlikely this blessing would happen during the middle of the day, but Kezra couldn't know for sure and if she messed up, if she failed to deliver the priestess to her master…a shiver ran down her spine as an image of a long claw emerging from the mist burst into her mind. Failure wouldn't result in punishment this time; it would mean death. Kezra shook the sleep from her eyes and looked for another vantage point.

The day passed uneventfully. In fact, other than sleeping a little later, there was nothing unordinary about Lennox's day. When she began walking to the dining hall with the other priestesses, Kezra felt the first pangs of worry start to settle within her. The acolytes usually ended their days early, so they were rested for prayers at dawn. Surely there should have been some preparation for the ceremony by now. Maybe if Kezra brought Lennox back before she'd drunk the potion, Tylan wouldn't notice. Worry evolved into full-on panic, sending her heart hammering in her chest as indecision ate at her. She forced herself to wait a little longer before snatching Lennox and returning to Tylan; the ceremony be damned. Restraint was quickly rewarded as a priestess, with a braid so tight it pulled at her face, walked up and grabbed Lennox and her friend, leading them toward the temple. Kezra followed behind them, grateful the sun had already set, as she melted into the shadows. A cool breeze licked her skin, bringing with it goosebumps prickling up her arm. The woman with the braid led the girls up the temple steps, past Altheia's statue, and she separated them into two rooms. Kezra climbed the statue to get a better view. The wind kicked up again, making her shudder. It was going to be a long, cold night.

Worshipping Altheia, Kezra concluded, involved a staggering amount of waiting. Finally, an old woman shuffled up the steps. The same priestess from earlier was by her side. The old woman was a tiny, frail-looking thing, nearly half the height of her accomplice, with a face covered in deep, ancient wrinkles. A strong wind could have snapped her in half. A feral smile spread on Kezra's face; there would be no resistance when she pounced on Lennox. The woman held a leather-bound book in her hands. The writing on the cover wasn't legible from Kezra's viewpoint, but even from afar, she could tell it was sacred to them. They handled it with delicate reverence, careful not to break the binding or tear a page. The younger priestess carried a chalice filled with amber liquid in one hand and a knife in the other. Together, they stopped under the statue of Altheia, where a small book rest had been set up. The old woman set down the book carefully, flicking through the pages before finding the right one.

"It's time," the old woman said. Her voice was stronger, more commanding than Kezra had imagined. She quickly adjusted her impression of the old woman. "Get Jasper first." The priestess set down the chalice and knife next to the book and strode to the room the red-haired girl occupied. Jasper she was called. Jasper emerged, trailing behind the priestess before making her way to the statue. She stopped in front of the old woman, looking anxious. Kezra thanked whatever goddess was listening that they had selected Jasper first. Now she would get to see the ceremony and better plan how to stop it. The old woman's voice boomed out in the quiet of the empty temple. Her voice took on a hypnotic cadence as she asked Jasper to pledge her life to the goddess Altheia and make the temple her home. Jasper seemed to grow in confidence as the ceremony continued, swiftly pledging her life to a goddess she'd never seen. Then the priestess grabbed the chalice and the knife. Kezra tensed in anticipation. She watched as Jasper brought the silver chalice to her lips and gulped down the liquid inside. Instantly, a faint silver glow radiated from her skin. The sight of it was a shock; magic wasn't supposed to exist anymore. Kezra waited for a reaction that never came. The old woman simply read from her book as her assistant grabbed the knife and handed it over to Jasper. Jasper sliced her palm, red blood welling in her hand.

"Voveo vitam meam tibi, Altheia. Spondeo ut seviam tibi, ac dumum tuam ut mem recipiam," she chanted, echoing the old woman. She turned over her hand and squeezed the blood onto the temple floor. The marble drank it in, the blood vanishing. The light radiating off her skin expanded, then contracted into her hand with a flash. On the back of her hand, there was now a black design. Kezra squinted, trying to make out the shape. It might have resembled a star, but her attention was drawn to Jasper's forearm, where a thin, black band had formed. Kezra froze, staring at the identical band inked onto her skin, the physical mark of her bond to Tylan. Whatever liquid was in that cup contained magic and the ancient book; it held a spell to activate it. That was why they couldn't leave the temple after the ceremony; it created a magic bond. If that book had a spell to create a bond, then maybe it contained the spell to break one. This mission hadn't been useless after all; the answers she'd been seeking were right in front of her the entire time.

Jasper's hand was bound in cloth, and they led her away. Kezra didn't watch to see where she went. The break gave her a moment to sort through the thoughts flying through her head. Was that how Tylan controlled people? Did he have a book of his own? Did he have a potion like this one? She needed to take that book when she grabbed Lennox, which led her to the next problem. The ceremony progressed quickly. There was a very brief window of opportunity for her to both complete the mission and grab the book. The timing would be tight, and she had to get it right.

Kezra's freedom depended on it. When she brought Lennox to Tylan, his attention would be on his latest acquisition, which would provide an opportunity for her to study the book and make an escape. Kezra could finally be free of him. She bounced on her toes in excitement, fighting the urge to make the grab now and get it all over with. With a deep, steadying breath, Kezra fought back the impulse and attempted to clear her mind to focus on the task at hand. The priestess was back with Lennox, leading her to the same spot Jasper stood during her Blessing. It couldn't have been a better position if she'd planned it in advance, Kezra thought with a smile. She took out a purple vial of smoke, taking care not to draw any attention to herself. Then, she prepared to run.

Lennox took her time walking to where the old woman waited for her under the statue. She seemed to be studying the way the moonlight illuminated the temple, a bright, glittering star in the darkness. The girl reminded Kezra of a wild animal approaching a stranger: cautious, ready to flee at any moment. Kezra could see the emotions ripple across her face, from a look of deep longing to one of resignation. For one fleeting moment, Kezra regretted what she was about to do. She would rip this girl away from her friend, from the only world she'd ever known, to drop her into the isolation and despair of Helica. A shudder ran down her spine as she tried to imagine what Tylan had planned for the priestess. Though if the choice was between this girl and Kezra's freedom, she would sacrifice the priestess every time. Kezra wouldn't, no, couldn't waste this chance. All too soon, the ceremony began.

Too fast, the priestess handed Lennox the chalice. She hesitated for just a moment before letting out a sigh and drinking deeply. As soon as the liquid touched the girl's lips, it was evident something was wrong. What had been a faint light surrounding Jasper now pulsed from Lennox in blinding waves. The ferocity of the light was enough to temporarily stun her, but the old woman appeared unfazed, as if she couldn't see the silver beacon in front of her. Kezra shook her head, coming out of a daze. Then, in one fluid motion, she leapt down from the statue and used her teeth to rip the cork from the vial of smoke. Landing hard on her feet, she ran as fast as she could into Lennox, hooking her around the waist with one hand while using the other to tip back the smoke. As soon as she felt the sweet smoke begin to burn her lungs, she tossed the vial and darted her hand out blindly, snatching around for the book. Screams erupted from the old woman and her companion, but the temple had already started to fade from view. In the chaos, Kezra kept hunting for the book, and at the last moment, before they disappeared, her hand connected with smooth leather binding. Plucking it from the old woman's grasp, they disappeared.

Faintly, the sound of someone screaming registered as Kezra tried to tuck the book into her tunic. The screaming turned to a hacking cough as the smoke invaded Lennox's lungs. They slammed into Tylan's throne room in a heap. Certainly not her most graceful entrance. Scrambling up off the floor, Kezra attempted to drag Lennox onto her feet, but she was dead weight, rooted to the ground. The smoke cleared from her vision to reveal Tylan standing over them. A savage smile lit his face.

"Well done, Kezra. Why don't you introduce me to our new guest?" Lennox looked around with a dazed look. Slowly, she began to take in her surroundings, and terror replaced her confusion.

"I'd like you to meet Lennox." Kezra said. Tylan looked pleased as he moved toward her.

"An acolyte of Altheia, yes? Although maybe you're a priestess now. How does that work if you don't finish your Blessing?"

"What is this place? Where am I? Jasper! Where is she? Jasper!"

"Make it stop!" Tylan snarled, his amusement evaporating, replaced by rage. Lennox started hysterically screaming and intermittently calling for Jasper again, oblivious to the growing threat of violence. The whole thing was giving Kezra a headache. She needed the screaming to stop before Tylan's anger erupted, and she didn't want to see Lennox get hurt. Plus, the guilt about ruining her life was already starting to set in. There was only one option. Kezra marched up to Lennox and slapped her squarely across the face, bringing the screaming to an abrupt stop. Lennox put a hand to her cheek, where a red mark had already started blooming. Kezra refrained from wincing in sympathy. That was going to leave a nasty bruise. Lennox stood there, frozen. Without a second thought, Kezra used the opportunity to grasp Lennox by the shoulders and whisper a warning into her ear.

"You need to calm down. Take a breath and listen to what Tylan says. If you want to get out of here alive, you need to play along. No resistance." She pulled away from Lennox and stood straight, hands behind her back, awaiting Tylan's dismissal.

"Very good, Kezra. You'd done well fetching me such a prize." He glided toward Lennox and looked her over, appraising her like a prize. He ran his fingers through her soft, golden hair. Then he circled around in front of her. Using a finger, he reached out and lifted her chin so she was looking up into his eyes.

"We're going to have fun together. What do you think of your new home? How does it compare to the splendor of your temple?" Lennox just stared back at him, wide-eyed and speechless. "Well? Are you broken? Speak!" Trembling, she clamped her mouth shut, lifting her chin in a small show of defiance. Kezra would have respected the display if the priestess's defiance didn't have the potential to result in their death.

"If I may, My Lord, perhaps our new guest needs a moment to settle in before she's ready. I'm sure her new home is grander than she's used to. She's too awestruck to speak."

"When I want to hear you speak, Kezra, I will give you permission to do so. The opinion of a foolish little girl has no value to me." Tylan held Lennox's chin for a moment longer before stepping away, releasing her. "Perhaps you're right. She needs some time to adjust to her new life." Tylan snapped his fingers, and a servant, one of Tylan's bonded, appeared. "Take our new resident to the room we've prepared. Welcome, Lennox."

Lennox had no color left in her face. The servant gently pulled her away toward the exit. Lennox shuffled after her before stopping abruptly, facing Tylan.

"I am the daughter of Altheia, blessed by her light. This is not my new home. You are not my master, and by the Goddess, I vow to escape this place." Lennox's eyes sparked with resolve, her tone serious. For that fleeting moment, the priestess's exhaustion faded; determination radiated from her, as if the goddess had somehow chosen this moment to fortify her acolyte. The sight almost made Kezra believe. Tylan only smirked.

"You might want to be careful of making vows you can't keep. Altheia has no power here." Just like that, the light drained from the girl's face. Her shoulders slumped forward as she followed the servant, shuffling away. When she was gone, Tylan turned to face his servant, his blade. "You did well today, Kezra. Get some rest. You've earned it." Unbidden pride swelled in her chest. No matter how she hated Tylan, she couldn't help but feel pleased by the compliment. A pang of guilt flickered into her consciousness when she thought of Lennox. Kezra wanted to turn around and leave, enjoy a hot shower and a restful night of sleep, but the fate of this girl ate at her. Kezra felt a duty to keep her safe, or at least as safe as she could be in this place.

"My Lord, may I ask why the priestess is here? What are you planning on doing with her?"

"Are you questioning me?" Tylan's tone was amused for the moment, as he reveled in his victory. Kezra paused, calculating which words would elicit the best reaction.

"Of course not. You're so wise, my lord. I'm just looking for a glimpse into the grand plans you have for our guest." Tylan's expression softened.

"Ah, you're worried about being replaced. Don't worry, you'll always have a place here. As for our new houseguest, my plans for her do not concern you. Now go rest." She wouldn't press her luck further by asking more. As Kezra turned to leave, Tylan called after her.

"Oh, and Kezra, don't presume to question me again. You don't want to wake up in the belly of my pet. It's been a while since she's had a good meal." She scurried back to her room before Tylan could make good on his threat.

Despite sleeping in her own bed instead of a tree, she didn't sleep well that night. Thoughts of Lennox plagued her every time she started to doze off. Which was silly; Lennox shouldn't have bothered her. Tylan used her countless times to hunt down his bonded, and many had met worse fates than Lennox - those who were acquainted with the pet living in the mist outside the palace walls. Kezra listened as they pleaded for mercy, as the beast sunk its claws into their flesh, as their tortured screams faded to gut-wrenching silence, and she lost little sleep over their demise. This priestess shouldn't have been any different, but she was. Lennox didn't willingly bond herself to Tylan. She didn't reap any rewards for his magic, and still Lennox would suffer the consequences of a choice she never made. Trapped in Helica under Tylan's watchful eye, she'd have even less freedom than Kezra. The sound of Lennox's panicked scream, the look of absolute horror before it faded to steely resolve, played relentlessly in Kezra's mind as she tossed and turned.

Finally, the restlessness pulled Kezra out of bed. It wasn't like she was going to be able to sleep, anyway. Maybe she could get a glimpse of Lennox before Tylan gave her the next assignment. Yes, she thought to herself, seeing the priestess safe and unharmed would alleviate her guilt. Kezra dressed and set off on her search. Her boots kicked up a thin layer of dust as she wandered through the stone hallways. Even though Tylan occupied a castle, he had no need for all the space. He'd all but abandoned the west wing, and even the east wing, where Kezra stayed with the rest of the servants, was sparsely populated. The halls were layered in dust, and covers had been thrown over furniture in abandoned rooms. She watched the specks drift through the air, illuminated by the light glowing from her lantern. The corridor revealed no signs of habitation, only layer upon layer of gray dust. Opening door after door, empty rooms greeted her. The search turned increasingly frantic before Kezra had to admit Lennox wasn't in any of the abandoned rooms near the servants. That only left one alternative, one that made Kezra uneasy. Tylan had placed Lennox in one of the rooms closest to his own. It was the only stretch of the palace she hadn't searched. Not only would she be unable to get Lennox alone if she was positioned so close to her master, but Kezra couldn't make sense of the arrangement. Still, she should check in with him to see if there was a new assignment. Perhaps she'd get a glimpse of the priestess on her way there. Kezra stopped at her room and set down her lantern, then changed out of the dust-covered clothes, mentally bracing herself for a meeting with Tylan.

As she made her way up to Tylan's chambers, she noticed a few differences. Lanterns holding white, twinkling lights lined the hallway. They illuminated the stone, which was gleaming and gave off a soft, fresh smell. In this section of the palace, the floor had been cleaned well enough to sparkle under the white lights. It was clear Tylan had made an effort for the priestess, but why? Right before knocking on Tylan's door, she passed the priestess's new room. She stole a glance inside. Her room was spacious, with the same soft, white light from the halls glowing inside. Instead of fire, the lanterns placed around her room held small, bright white orbs that appeared to float inside the glass. In the corner, she had a fireplace, which had been lit for her. A small stack of wood sat next to it, along with her own fully stocked desk and two plush reading chairs. Kezra felt a longing to curl up in one and read for hours, letting her mind escape into a new world. A massive bed dominated the center of the room. An emerald color blanket lay on top with several matching fluffy pillows. It looked so soft and comfortable; she didn't know how anyone would get up once they lay down.

Between the study area and the bed sat a door, presumably leading to a private bathroom. Later, Kezra would steal inside for a better look. Lennox was curled in a chair with her knees to her chest, silently staring at the flames of the fire. Kezra glanced between Tylan's door and Lennox's curled figure, contemplating approaching her. It was too risky here. She knocked on Tylan's door instead; the sound echoing through the hall.

"Wait for me in the throne room, Kezra," he shouted. She'd expected as much. Never had Kezra been allowed inside Tylan's chambers. With one last look at Lennox, Kezra headed to the throne room. When she did, her eyes locked with Lennox's. The desperate, hurt look on her face was one Kezra knew would haunt her for the rest of her life. Kezra tried to hold her stare, to convey her regret through looks alone. Lennox just kept looking, her eyes pleading for help. Like the coward she was, Kezra broke her stare and scurried off to meet her master.

CHAPTER 6

Lennox

Where was she? Lennox curled into the chair to warm herself by the fire, squeezing her eyes shut. The last twenty-four hours flashed through her mind in a blur: the fight with Jasper, relenting to stay and take the Blessing, then everything exploding into a blinding white light, followed by a cloyingly sweet purple smoke. Now she was in this place, wherever it was. It had to be a test, a part of the ceremony. The Mother was trying to make sure she was dedicated to Altheia. Any moment now, The Mother would come out to tell her she'd passed, and they'd go back to the temple. She and Jasper would celebrate their successful completion of the Blessing, and everything would go back to normal. Except The Mother didn't materialize in front of her; no one came to lead her back to the temple. The fireplace was still to her left, quietly crackling in the corner. To the right, a door still sat open to the hallway. Lennox couldn't bring herself to shut it. Somehow the simple motion of shutting the door felt like acceptance of her circumstances, like closing herself into her cage.

She squeezed her eyes shut again, willing herself back to the temple.

It was just a dream, a nightmare. She would wake up in her own bed if only she believed harder. Using every ounce of hope, Lennox willed herself back home. When had almost convinced herself, she peeked out from behind her eyelids, half expecting to be in her own bed. Nothing had changed. Her vision blurred. The taste of salt hit her mouth as tears streamed down her face. Lennox wiped them away angrily. It was not the time to fall apart. She needed to find a way back home.

"Wait for me in the throne room, Kezra." The voice jolted her out of the bout of self-pity; her head jerked in the direction of the voice. That woman was standing there. The dark-haired girl who brought her here, who tried to stop her screaming and whispered a warning about *him*. Maybe she would help. Their eyes locked; Lennox silently begged for help. But before she could gather the courage to voice her thoughts, the woman was striding down the corridor and out of sight. Alone again, Lennox shut her eyes, trying to stop the tears welling behind them from falling.

Eventually, the door across the hall squeaked open. The man from last night stepped out, Tylan. His height caught her attention first. Lenox didn't see many men in the temple, but the few she'd met hadn't looked anything like this one. He would easily tower over her, as if he could squash her under his foot. He had strong, broad shoulders. His un-tied white hair grazed them. Amethyst-colored eyes glittered in the firelight. Lennox wasn't expecting the monster who'd grabbed her, the man she'd been warned about, to be so…striking. In her confused state the night before, Lennox hadn't really registered his appearance. Now that she did, Lennox forced herself to recall the night before, the way he'd spoken to her, the cruel, cutting remarks he'd made, and his height was no longer fascinating but imposing, terrifying. She curled herself into a ball in the chair, praying he didn't notice her. Thankfully, he marched down the corridor without so much as glancing in her direction. Lennox released a sigh, the tension leaving her body. At least for the moment, she would have some time to herself.

Right, it was time to stop sulking. If she were going to free herself, she'd need to learn more about her surroundings. Lennox looked around the room, really seeing it for the first time. It was large, much bigger than the space she'd been sharing with Jasper for her entire life. The chair she'd been sitting in was one of a set of two, each set around the fireplace. They were a lovely shade of pale green, and it was deliciously soft. Under different circumstances, Lennox would have loved to stay curled up in it for hours studying. A shiny new desk sat pressed against the wall, its cherry wood glossy and smooth. Paper and quills had been thoughtfully arranged on top, a perfect corner for copying texts.

Someone decorated with soft, luxurious items before arrival that she would never dream of having access to at the temple. A part of her wanted to throw herself onto the soft feather bed. She'd burrow under the lush, green comforter to pretend that none of this was happening, but stayed frozen in her chair, unable to move, afraid that if she did, she'd upset whatever forces were keeping Tylan away. The isolation was the only thing allowing her to keep up the fantasy that none of this was real. She wasn't sure how long she could stay curled in the chair, but eventually a servant wandered in. He carried a tray of food, which he set down on the desk. He then bowed at the waist and left without a word. Lennox refused to eat it. Who knew what slop they ate in this evil place? It was probably poisoned.

The smell of beef wafted through the air, causing her mouth to water involuntarily. The sudden assault on her senses brought her stiff neck into focus. She'd been sitting in the same position for so long that she could barely feel her legs. Lennox supposed it couldn't hurt to stretch them out. Then maybe examine the food while she was at it. Could one tell if food had been poisoned from looks alone? She edged over to the plate as her stomach gave an inhumane growl. Lennox picked up a vegetable and nibbled on the corner, then waited to see if she felt sick. Nothing happened; maybe the food wasn't poisoned after all. The thought was all it took for hunger to override caution. Like a starved animal, she started shoveling food into her mouth. Lennox had hardly swallowed the beef and vegetables before she greedily gulped down the cup of wine that accompanied the food. The Mother would have been appalled by her behavior.

"I would have thought a priestess would have better manners. What are they teaching you in that temple?" Lennox looked up from the massacred meal to see a figure leaning in her doorway. The woman standing there, the one from the night before, was dressed in tight black leathers, fitted to her frame like a second skin with a matching long sleeved top. She'd braided her long, dark hair back, away from her face. Even from where she sat, Lennox could see the glint of steel flashing as it caught the light. Looking at her made Lennox feel like a child caught stealing bread from the kitchen. Heat flooded her face as Lennox desperately swiped at the crumbs lining her chin. Her captor strode over from the doorway and stopped directly in front of her, looking her up and down skeptically.

"It's good to see your legs still working. I was beginning to worry you were stuck in that chair. Now, you need to get changed. That…dress isn't suitable."

"They're robes," Lennox said lamely.

"Robes then. You need to change out of them." The woman gestured to a wardrobe next to the bed, which Lennox hadn't noticed before.

"Changed for what? I always wear my robes."

"We're starting your training today, as per Tylan's instructions. And you simply can not train in that," the woman said. She waved her hand toward Lennox's flowing crimson robes with mild distaste. Then she stomped across the room to the wardrobe and pulled out a replica of the outfit she was currently wearing. Lennox used the moment to examine the woman who had captured her, the way the fabric molded itself around her legs, the tightness of the top around her chest. No, Lennox thought to herself, she would not be wearing that.

"No, thank you."

"It wasn't a suggestion."

"Regardless, I will pass. I do not wish to train; therefore, I see no reason to change. Even if I did, I'm content with my robes," Lennox said. The woman threw her head back and let out an exasperated sigh. She pinched the bridge of her nose, wearing a look Lennox had seen on The Mother's face countless times: the look of a parent dealing with a petulant child.

"It isn't up to you. Tylan wants you to train, so you will train. I don't know why he's demanding this of you, nor do I care. If you don't listen, there will be trouble for me. I will drag you to the training room myself if I must. As for the changing..." In a blur, the woman rushed toward her so fast Lennox's eyes couldn't track her. Lennox tried to turn around, to run from her, but was yanked back, hard. Then she was falling backward. Pain shot up her spine from landing on her back. The woman stood over her, peering down with a smug look, a foot firmly planted on the end of her robes.

"As I said, you can't train in those. I promise you'll already have enough bruises by the end of the session in the fighting leathers. Don't add unnecessary ones by wearing bad clothing. It makes you an easier target." Lennox got off the floor and gave her attacker the best scowl she could muster, but she snatched the clothes from the woman's hand anyway, relenting to the request.

"You have five minutes before I drag you out of there." Lennox stuck her tongue out at the voice from the safety of the bathroom.

She untied her robes, letting them fall to the floor, then pulled on the black pants and matching top. Unlike the woman's, Lennox's top had no sleeves, leaving her shoulders completely exposed, an odd feeling when she was so accustomed to her heavy, long-sleeved robes. A mirror hung in the room above the sink, and Lennox took in her reflection. She looked ridiculous. The face in the mirror had puffy, red-rimmed around her irises from crying; her hair stuck out in wild directions; her skin was sallow, the pale complexion amplified by the dark clothing. Lennox was a mess. A mess who was completely unprepared for whatever was about to happen. The door banged open to reveal her new trainer storming in.

"Let's go, it's been well over five minutes."

"I look ridiculous," Lennox said, her voice coming out in a whimper. The woman's expression softened a fraction.

"Not ridiculous, just different. We need to do something about that hair, though." Lennox's new trainer looked around the bathroom until she located a brush. She grabbed it, then brought it over and ran it through Lennox's hair, pulling it back into a braid. If she closed her eyes, Lennox could almost believe she was back at the temple with Jasper helping her get ready for prayers. All too soon, it was over. There was a light tap on Lennox's shoulder and the fingers left her hair. Her eyes fluttered open. The girl in the mirror looked foreign, older, more serious. The dark-haired girl laid her hand on Lennox's shoulder, leaning down to speak into her ear.

"See, you don't look ridiculous. You look like a warrior." She turned to leave, but Lennox stopped her.

"What's your name?" Lennox asked softly.

"Kezra. I'm Kezra. Now come on, let's get you into shape, little priestess."

"I'm Lennox," she answered, even though Kezra clearly already knew that based on the previous night, but it felt weird not to introduce herself. Kezra didn't respond, but started walking away, motioning her to follow. Lennox thought she heard whispered words - something that sounded like "I'm sorry", but she couldn't be sure she'd heard anything at all.

Training with Kezra was brutal. The first problem was the new clothing. Lennox had grown up wearing the heavy, flowing robes of a future priestess. In the leather, every movement made her aware of how the clothing molded to her skin. Somehow, not having anything to restrict her movements, being free of the robe's weight, made her actions clumsier. Lennox felt as though she was learning to move in a whole new way, one she wasn't particularly skilled at. The second, and perhaps most glaring, problem was her complete lack of combat skills. During the session, Lennox tried to pray Kezra away, begging the goddess to take her. She tried cursing her, promising Altheia's vengeance. None of it worked. Kezra shouted commands at her, not leaving a moment to breathe between one move and the next.

"Plant your feet! Don't lose your balance. Stop locking your knees!" The commands were relentless. Lennox tried to keep them straight, but they muddled in her head, making it difficult for her to concentrate. Exhaustion set in, and they hadn't even started fighting. They were simply practicing steps, movements that looked like a flowing dance when Kezra did them, but didn't feel natural when Lennox tried to mimic them. Each attempt at a step resembled the movement of a fish dropped on dry land when Lennox attempted them, each movement clumsier than the last. As someone who'd spent her life perfecting the steps of rituals, she was getting increasingly frustrated at being defeated by these movements, making it more difficult for her to do them correctly. Lennox tried to flow through the exercises without overthinking them, hoping her body would know what to do. Immediately, she could feel her foot placement was wrong again.

"What are they teaching you at that temple?" Kezra asked, shaking her head. She let out a sigh. "You might as well take a break. You look like you're going to collapse."

"Thank Alethia!" Lennox all but collapsed, leaning against the wall for support.

"I'm not sure why you're thanking her. I can't see what Altheia's doing for you here," Kezra quipped with an eye roll. She held out a skein of water, which Lennox snatched from her hands, gulping it down greedily. She finished the water and stared up at Kezra, who loomed above her.

"Why am I here?"

"It's not my business to know," Kezra answered, her tone gentle, free from her cocky swagger.

"Fine. Then why did you try to help me last night? It's not like you care for me." Kezra looked away, staring out into the hall. Seconds passed in silence, and still she didn't answer. Lennox assumed she was going to ignore the question completely. Instead, her answer came in a whisper so quiet Lennox had to strain to hear her.

"I know what it's like to be trapped and frightened. I wish someone would have helped me when I was at my worst moment." A smirk slid onto Kezra's face, a mask slipping into place; the moment of vulnerability vanished. "Get up, Lennox. Let's see if we can fix that footwork. Or maybe Altheia will hear one of your curses this time and she'll grant your wish to smite me."

They kept at it for hours, going through the motions again and again until the movements began to feel familiar to her body. By the time they were done, Lennox was dripping sweat. The taste of salt landed on her as perspiration poured down her face. It was punishing work, but Lennox appreciated having a task to complete. It kept her mind busy, stopping her from spiraling. There wasn't spare time or energy to wonder at the situation, or to wallow in self-pity. There was only Lennox, Kezra, and the complicated footwork that still eluded her. In the brief breaks, Lennox tried to puzzle out the mystery that was Kezra. She was Lennox's kidnapper. She was not a friend, could not be a friend. And yet…she had been mostly pleasant throughout the day, kind in her own way. Although Kezra made it clear that she would do what it took to protect herself, she hadn't attempted to be cruel while doing so. Lennox wondered if maybe she could convince Kezra to protect her too.

"What's going on here?" Lennox froze. Tylan sauntered into the training room, his violet eyes boring into her. Stopping made Lennox realize how tired she was. Her legs were shaking. She had to fight to keep herself upright, but she refused to fall down in front of him.

"We're training, My Lord. Just as you requested." Tylan sauntered in, circling her, eyes roving over her up and down like a predator circling its prey.

"She looks to be in one piece. No visible bruising or scratches. Did I train you so poorly, Kezra, that you're unable to best a scrawny, untrained priestess?" Even as he spoke to Kezra, his eyes never left Lennox as he waited for a response. Kezra's brows pinched together, a question forming on her face.

"We're practicing footwork," she said slowly. "As you said, she is untrained. I didn't imagine she would be ready to spar yet." Tylan rolled up his sleeves, revealing black ink wrapping around both arms from shoulder to wrist. He never so much as glanced up as he strode over to Lennox, pushing Kezra aside.

"I guess I will have to give her a lesson myself then." Humor edged into his voice. Kezra hesitated, and for a moment, Lennox had a moment of hope where thought Kezra might intercede. But whatever protests were forming in her head stayed there as she stepped out of his way, leaving nothing between Lennox and Tylan with his feral grin. Kezra retreated to the corner of the room.

"Remember to plant your feet. Don't lock your knees," Kezra said.

Tylan circled around her, assessing Lennox as she wobbled on her shaking legs, as he looked for the opportunity to strike. He tested out different movements to see how she'd react, a predator toying with its prey. Lennox tried to work through all the movements Kezra had taught her so far, which, to be fair, were not many. Her body was already exhausted, though, and it took most of her concentration just to stay upright. She steadied herself, bracing for an attack. In the end, it didn't matter. When Tylan struck, it was swift and savage. One moment, he was moving in her direction; the next, she found herself flat on her back, unable to comprehend what had happened.

"Get up. Protect yourself this time."

"I can't." The words came out in a pathetic whimper that she was ashamed of, but her body was spent, her back bruised, and even the idea of moving seemed painful. Tylan squatted down to look at her. He responded with measured patience, as if he were dealing with a small child.

"You will get up and you will defend yourself. I am not a patient man, Lennox. When I ask for something, I do not ask twice. Get. Up." He yanked Lennox up by the arm, dragging her roughly back to her feet. Gathering herself, she prepared to try again.

Over and over, Tylan struck with the same result. Again and again, Lennox slammed into the unforgiving stone floor. Her back, her ribs, her arms, her legs, all of them were in agony. Liquid iron dripped into her mouth as blood poured from her lip. She didn't recall biting it, let alone doing so hard enough to draw blood. Despite the pain, she peeled herself off the ground to face Tylan again.

"You are not even trying!" Tylan raged after she fell, yet again, without so much as stepping out of his way. Kezra began to edge out of her place in the corner.

"Maybe a break would help. Look at her, she can barely stand."

"Do not tell me what she needs!" Tylan whirled at Kezra in fury. She shrank back into her corner, afraid. Kezra would not save her.

"Again!"

"I can't," Lennox sobbed.

"Get up, Lennox."

Lennox tried. She really did. She simply couldn't stand up. Pain coursed through her with every movement. She'd never experienced anything close to that level of pain. Getting up again was not an option; she couldn't do it. Something abruptly snatched her off the ground. Then she was flying. Her head crashed into the wall as hands wrapped around her throat, squeezing. This was how she was going to die, which was very unfair because she wasn't ready to die yet. Lennox needed to find Jasper to take her vows, to prove to The Mother that she could be a perfect priestess. She had so much left to give.

Rage built in her chest at the unfairness of it all. Rage at being ripped from her home, at having her choices taken away, and most of all at having her life stolen away so pointlessly. A final, weak scream erupted from Lennox's throat with what little air she had left. Lennox raised her hands in a last attempt to push Tylan away. A dazzling silver light burst from her palms as the pressure squeezing her throat was torn away. Something forced Tylan across the room. He didn't lose his footing or fall as Lennox had, but he was pushed a few feet back. Tears were streaming down Lennox's face as she gulped down air, forcing into her lungs. When she looked at Tylan, he was beaming back at her.

"I think now is a fine time to take a rest." He didn't wait for an answer before disappearing down the hall. Lennox managed to stay upright, shock sustaining her until he left the room. Then she collapsed.

Lennox awoke in the softest bed she'd ever laid in. For a split second, she forgot her circumstances, even believing that maybe the improved accommodations were a result of her promotion to priestess. Lennox jolted up to find Jasper, but the movement sent a shock of pain coursing through her ribs. The images came rushing back - the temple vanishing in smoke, Kezra training her, Tylan knocking her to the ground, hands crushing the air from her lungs, the silver light rushing out of her body, forcing Tylan back. She held her hands in front of her face, examining them for any changes, but they looked the same. Smooth, white skin, unmarred by recent events.

"Finally, you're awake." Kezra strolled into the room, much too comfortably for Lennox's liking, chomping on a snack.

"Are those raspberries?" Lennox asked. Kezra snorted at her.

"You wake up from getting knocked on your ass, breaking a rib, and using magic, which no one but Tylan has done in years by the way, only to ask me if I'm eating raspberries?"

"Well, are you?"

"You're unbelievable."

"I'm starving." Lennox held her hand out expectantly, hoping Kezra would share. Kezra rolled her eyes and set three plump red raspberries in Lennox's open palm. Lennox bit into one, savoring the bittersweet juice spilling across her tongue, bringing a smile to Lennox's face.

"I heard magic was supposed to do that - before it disappeared, I mean. It was supposed to burn through you, make you tired and hungry. Gluttonous for other people's raspberries, apparently." Kezra said. Lennox's smile dropped.

"I don't have magic," Lennox whispered.

"No? Then explain what happened with Tylan."

"I don't know what happened! Nothing like that's ever happened to me. I can't explain it, but clearly it was something he did, a trick of some kind." Lennox tried to calm herself, but she started to panic, not knowing how to process the situation.

"He's going to want to recreate it. That's why I'm here. He wanted to know if you'd woken up." Kezra said it to her gently, as if the words might break her.

"I can't, though. I'm not even sure it came from me, whatever it was. Whatever he wants, he's got the wrong person. Before this, I'd never even left the temple. I can't possibly help him." Kezra didn't respond with words, only supplied a pitying look. She placed her last raspberry in Lennox's hand before moving to the door.

"I'll tell him you need some time to heal. You look like hell." Kezra turned to leave.

"Wait!" Lennox called out. "Why are you being so nice to me?" She didn't expect an honest answer, but she needed to know if Kezra could really be her friend. She was desperate for some form of companionship. Kezra just looked at her blankly with those deep green eyes, saying nothing.

"I'll get someone to send you something to eat." Then she walked out without another word, leaving Lennox alone and friendless.

CHAPTER 7

Kezra

Kezra couldn't stop thinking about it, about the light shooting from Lennox's hands, knocking Tylan back. It shouldn't have been possible. Magic didn't exist anymore, especially not in that raw, powerful form. Everyone knew Tylan controlled all that remained, and Kezra had stopped questioning how he'd obtained it. What did it mean? More importantly, how did Tylan know Lennox had magic? That must have been the reason he insisted on bringing her here. Kezra wondered if she could help the girl harness it somehow. Maybe with Lennox, there was a way to break her bond to Tylan once and for all.

It took a few days, but Lennox finally healed enough to continue with her training, and Tylan insisted they work on it for hours every day. Fortunately, he'd been too busy with his bonded to attend himself, so Kezra worked with Lennox alone day after day. She now realized that he wasn't looking to make Lennox a fighter, but to force the magic from her again. But after a week of training, they hadn't even been able to produce a spark. In fact, Kezra was beginning to wonder if she'd imagined the whole thing, or if maybe it was just some trick of Tylan's like Lennox claimed. However, the problem could have been Kezra herself. When they sparred, Kezra always held back, unwilling to injure Lennox like Tylan had on the first day. She needed today to be different. Without any progress to report, Tylan would be unhappy, and neither of them would be safe from his wrath.

Kezra walked to her door, ready to pull Lennox out of bed again. Instead, before she could knock, the door swung open, revealing Lennox dressed, hair braided down her back, ready for training. Kezra couldn't fight off the smile pulling at the corners of her lips at the quick transformation.

"Eager to earn your bruises today, I see."

"I'm ready to learn, that's all." Lennox looked serious; a steely resolve threaded through her voice.

"Why the sudden change of heart?" Kezra asked, curious. Getting Lennox out of bed and changed had been a daily battle up to now. She couldn't blame the priestess's reluctance to accept this new life, but her insistence on staying in bed, waiting for someone to rescue her, had been making Kezra's life more difficult.

"The sooner I learn whatever it is Tylan wants from me, the sooner I can get it done and go," Lennox said with a shrug. The casual answer stopped Kezra in her tracks.

"Lennox, you can't think... I mean, you must know..." Lennox whirled around, stopping her from completing the thought.

"I vowed to get back to the temple, and I meant it. Now let's get this over with." Kezra followed her into the training room without correcting her. Tylan was never just going to let her go, but Kezra wanted to let her hold on to that hope. It could be useful later for both of them..

The day's training session was not going any better than the previous ones. Lennox stood across from her, feet planted in the positions Kezra had shown her. Lennox held her left arm at an odd angle. It was visible she was still hurting from her last meeting with the stone floor. The two of them were well acquainted by now, much to Lennox's dismay. Kezra tried to push her harder this time, to get some spark of magic out of her. Tylan was expecting a progress report tonight, and Kezra had nothing to show him. She moved for Lennox again, her leg sweeping out to hit the back of Lennox's knees. Lennox was getting better at reading her moves, and spun away, but she was still too slow. Kezra used Lennox's movement against her and caught her bad arm, yanking the priestess toward her. The momentum left Lennox falling forward. Kezra moved out of the way so she could slam into the ground, hoping the priestess would use magic to catch herself first. Lennox put her hands out to stop herself from falling on her face, but that was all. Nothing else happened. The impact hit her hard, leaving her cradling the arm Kezra had pulled.

"We're not getting anywhere!" Lennox yelled, her voice dripping with pain and frustration. She stayed lying on the floor, looking either too exhausted or defeated to move. Kezra couldn't tell which. She crossed the room and sat down next to Lennox, searching for something encouraging to say.

"What if we try something different?" Kezra asked, her mind whirling. Lennox tilted her head up, paying attention. Kezra took it as a signal to continue. "We've been trying to force the magic out of you. Either you have no self-preservation instincts, or the magic doesn't respond well to being beaten out of you."

"What are you suggesting we do instead?"

"Maybe we can coax it out," Kezra said. Lennox looked at her as if she'd sprouted another head.

"I don't know what happened. I'm not even sure that the magic is mine. You want me to do what - ask it nicely to come out and play?"

"I don't know. Would you rather I keep throwing you on the floor and shatter your other arm?" As the words burst out, louder than intended, Lennox looked at her, stricken. Kezra sucked in air, trying to level out her tone. "Just close your eyes and try to concentrate." The skeptical look didn't exactly leave Lennox's face, but she closed her eyes.

"What exactly am I meant to be concentrating on?" Lennox asked. Kezra didn't know. With no magic of her own, it was impossible to say. But she just couldn't keep breaking this girl. Kezra knew they weren't friends; they couldn't be after she'd kidnapped Lennox, even if she'd done it unwillingly. But after spending the past week together, they had at least developed a kinship. They seemed to understand one another and, despite the circumstances that thrust them together, Kezra wanted to help.

"Concentrate on trying to form the silver light. Envision the light, form it in your hand." Kezra tried to coach Lennox as well as she could. A few painfully long seconds ticked by in silence, with nothing happening. Kezra waited, focused on Lennox, searching for any shred of magic. They stayed that way as the seconds turned to minutes, Lennox with her eyes closed, her brows knitted together in concentration, Kezra holding her breath, hoping against hope anything would happen. She would have taken a solitary spark, a flash of light, a hint of smoke, but nothing happened. Lennox's eyes snapped open. She shot up off the floor, then raced to the other side of the room.

"We're wasting time. If something's going to work, it's sparring. Go again." Kezra stayed seated for a moment after Lennox's outburst, reluctant to hurt her again. With her feet firmly planted, determination etched onto her face, Lennox waited for Kezra to move. Kezra let out a sigh before getting up to attack again.

Another day, another failure. Kezra left Lennox in her room and sent a bonded to tend to her wounds. Now, she would need to face Tylan and report that the past week hadn't yielded any results. It seemed odd he'd demanded Lennox to his side so urgently, then left Kezra to train her. But then again, she'd never known Tylan to handle anything himself. Her entire childhood had been spent training to be his blade, and he had no problem wielding her as he saw fit. He was in the throne room, seated on the swirling obsidian throne. Kezra had always wondered why he kept up this pretense as king of an empty realm, but it was beyond her to question it. The only court he kept were bonded servants Kezra brought to him and Kezra herself. It was rare to see the bonded around the castle though, as they scurried around in the shadows, avoiding Tylan's gaze.

He looked regal on his throne, white hair tied back, his purple eyes glinting in the light on his unlined face. Others probably found him handsome, but all she could see was the way his face twisted into a sneer before he unleashed his magic on her, sending it coursing through her veins with a paralyzing electricity, and how he watched emotionless as she screamed. Even now, Kezra could see the cruelty etched beneath the surface.

Tylan's eyes landed on her as she entered the room. His only greeting was a cock of his head, directing her to stand in front of him. Kezra knelt before him, hoping she wouldn't need to stay on the ground too long.

"You may rise. What progress have you made with Lennox?"

"Her footwork has gotten better. As for combat, her responses are still too slow. I wouldn't trust her with a weapon yet, and won't begin training her on them until I feel confident she won't kill herself accidentally." Tylan's stare bored into her. He raised an eyebrow, the rest of his face still, as if carved from stone.

"What about her magic?" He asked it far too gently for her liking; it felt like the calm before a storm.

"We haven't been able to reproduce the results you saw that first night. Lennox doesn't believe she was the source of the silver light." Kezra waited for a display of anger, tensing in preparation for yelling, for the painful feeling of magic coursing unchecked through her veins, but none came. Instead, he looked contemplative.

"Very well. I will train her myself. You may go now, Kezra. Be prepared to leave tomorrow."

"Leave, my lord? Where are you sending me?"

"You're going to make an appearance in my place. It seems I won't be able to attend this meeting, but I fear it would be rather impertinent of me to ignore it completely." Kezra waited for an elaboration, feeling her brows knitted together in confusion. Tylan often left to answer the call of those seeking magic, those who bonded themselves to him as payment for a magical favor; she wouldn't be able to attend one of those meetings in his place.

"Go now. You must get ready to meet the King of Osana. Long may he reign."

Hours later, she found herself back in the markets of Tesmerin. This time, she felt comfortable navigating the vendor stalls. Kezra walked past the fragrant foods and pastries, past the stalls selling luxury silks and fabrics, wandered through the neglected outpost where she'd met the fortune teller on her last visit, and into the shadow of the castle. The seriousness of the situation threatened to overwhelm her. The king made very few public appearances, so there was little information about him. Magic had been dwindling for years, but it completely disappeared shortly after his rise to the throne, creating a certain amount of unrest among the people of Oscana. Suspicious of assassins, he only let those he trusted into the castle. As far as she knew, he had a close circle of nobles allowed within the castle. It was their job to relay the king's decrees to the territories they governed. The army helped implement the laws. They also ensured the nobles didn't get out of line when settling disputes within their territories.

The one exception to the King's seclusion was an annual celebration held in honor of Altheia. Many other gods had a public holiday, but as the goddess of light and life, her celebration came at the beginning of spring when the sun peeked out from behind grey winter clouds, and the crops sprouted from the ground. It was the most important holiday in Oscana; hence; the king chose it to make his yearly appearance at the festival, giving a brief speech and blessing the coming year's harvest. He followed this with an exclusive feast for his nobles. However, it was still months away. Most of the kingdom had only glimpsed him before, and she'd never even gotten that much. Other than rumor, he was a complete mystery to her, made even more mysterious by Tylan's association with him.

Kezra walked up to the palace entrance, unsure of what to do. Tylan didn't give her an invitation or anything to show that she had a right to enter the castle in his place. On her walk up to the palace, Kezra wondered if she'd be sent back to Tylan empty-handed, barred from entry. The guards stood in their positions at the gate, their teal uniforms vibrant against the grey of the castle. Gathering as much confidence as she could muster, Kezra swaggered up to them, hoping to walk into the castle unhindered.

"Halt! What is your business in the palace?"

"I'm here at the request of the King, representing Tylan of Helica." The soldiers exchanged a glance, their eyes growing wide at the mention of Tylan, or Helica, or both. They came to a silent decision. The soldier on the left, the elder of the two, addressed her.

"May we see your arm?" Kezra tried her best not to let surprise show on her face, but she rolled up her sleeve to reveal the black band wrapped around her left forearm. The older soldier looked at his younger companion and tilted his head in the direction of the palace. He went running through the gate without another word. The soldier who had spoken to her waited in the center of the gate, clocking the entry–not that she would have tried to move past him. Whatever Tylan wanted her to do here, she doubted it would be accomplished by beating her way through the guards and demanding an audience with the King.

After a few minutes of silently observing one another, the young soldier came running back, followed by a middle-aged man dressed in servant's clothing. The midnight blue tunic and matching pants blended into the shadows, allowing the nobles to forget his presence as soon as they were served. He eyed the soldier with a look of reproach before turning to address her. Interesting, this man held some authority as the soldier shrunk beneath his gaze.

"I apologize for keeping you waiting, miss…" his eyebrows raised as he looked at her in question, his intelligent blue eyes boring into her.

"Kezra," she said.

"Miss Kezra then. I understand you're here on behalf of Sir Tylan Faine?"

"Yes, he sent me to meet with the King." Kezra lifted her sleeve again to show her black band, proving her bond to Tylan.

"Very good, then. Please follow me. I'll show you to your room."

"There's no need for a room, but I appreciate the courtesy. I'm just here to meet with the King and be on my way." A smirk caught the corner of his mouth at the response.

"There will be time for that later. The king keeps his own time. Besides, it's time to get ready for tonight's festivities," he said, giving a pointed look at her black leathers coated in dirt from the road. She wouldn't argue with a bath and a change of clothing, but she didn't like the idea of more activity tonight.

"Festivities?"

"Of course. Sir Faine didn't tell you? The King's nobles are meeting; that's why you're here. Of course, you're expected to attend the welcome feast."

The man led Kezra through the halls of the castle, much better lit and more brightly furnished than Tylan's palace in Helica. Servants scurried about their tasks, keeping their heads down, concentrating on arriving at their destination. Their clothes blended easily into the shadows cast by the torchlight. She assumed it made them easy for the nobles to ignore, but Kezra knew the advantages of passing unseen. She made sure to observe the quiet corners of her surroundings and didn't miss the puzzled looks the servants threw in her direction. New faces wouldn't be common in the palace of a recluse king. The servant stepped in front of the closed door. The man handed her an ancient-looking iron key.

"Your rooms, Miss Kezra. A servant will be back soon with some suitable options for tonight's feast. Your bath has already been drawn."

"Thank you. You know, I didn't catch your name."

"I'm here for whatever you need, miss." He bowed to leave without answering. Kezra opened the door to step inside, but the servant hesitated and turned back to face her. "If I may?" Kezra nodded before he continued. "I don't imagine the king will be pleased that Mister Faine didn't come himself. I would advise you to be cautious and to look your best. The king has a weakness for beautiful women. It may help you when dealing with him if he thinks you're no more than a demure maiden."

"I'll keep that in mind. Thank you for the advice, and for your kindness." He bowed again and left without another word.

Stepping into the room, Kezra tried to imagine Tylan occupying it. It was comfortable, but not grand, which didn't suit his usual tastes. The door opened into a sitting area, comfortably furnished with a burgundy couch and two reading armchairs. A modest bookshelf lined the wall. Kezra felt her heart skip a beat upon seeing it. She knew this mission wasn't meant to be a reprieve, but the idea of spending an evening curled on the couch, reading one of the books at her disposal, seemed like heaven. Adjoining the sitting room was the bedroom with an attached bathroom. She gave the bedroom little attention, taking a moment to slip the daggers hidden along her legs under the mattress before the hot bath beckoned to her.

The bath must have been made ready just before she arrived. Steam furled from the water invitingly. Scented soaps and oils lined the tub. Kezra picked one up, inhaling the rich scent of jasmine. She sank into the bath, taking time to soak in the luxury, to scrub the grime from her skin and oil her dark hair so it shimmered in the light. By the time Kezra left the bath, the water had started to cool, but she'd wanted to take as much time to luxuriate in the warm water as possible. Reluctantly, she exited the bath. As she finished drying and brushing her hair, a soft knock sounded on the bathroom door.

"Miss Kezra, I've laid your gowns out for you. Are you ready for me to help you dress and style your hair?" The door swung open, and a young girl entered the room. She couldn't have been more than fourteen. She had a soft, round face and heart-shaped lips lining a generous mouth, but the beginnings of adulthood had started to take some of the fat from her cheeks, showing the beginning of sharp cheekbones to come. Her dark hair was wrapped in a bun, and the servant's tunic clung to her beginnings of her womanly curves she would one day grow into. Her body clung to the vestiges of girlhood, but she would soon grow into a great beauty. Kezra felt a twinge of protectiveness for the young girl, surrounded by uncaring nobles who might want to take advantage of such looks.

The girl looked up at her meekly, long eyelashes framing startling golden eyes. Kezra's breath caught in her throat. Suddenly, she was back in the markets of Tesmerin, those golden eyes boring into her while she sat inside a patchwork tent. A voice foretelling doom, calling her daughter of the night. She'd tried to forget the whole encounter, tried to erase it from her memory, but the golden eyes were unforgettable, trudging the entire encounter back to the forefront of her mind.

"Miss, your dress?" Her voice brought Kezra out of the unpleasant memory. In a daze, she followed the girl to the bedroom and the selection of dresses awaiting her. Four dresses in various colors lay before her, each more beautiful than the last. Kezra briefly marveled at how these dresses had been acquired when she'd shown up unexpectedly without giving anyone the opportunity to take her measurements, but she forgot the concern the moment she picked up the dresses. Kezra's eyes snagged on one in particular. It was a dark forest green, matching her eyes. It would be held up by thin straps, showing off her bare arms. The back was open except for thin laces that tied in a bow where the dress would meet her lower back. The green of the dress morphed into an iridescent black at the bottom with a flaring silk train that would puddle on the floor around her feet, rippling like the night.

"This one." Kezra said to the girl, picking up the dress.

"Excellent choice, miss," the girl replied, taking the dress from Kezra's arms.

The girl helped her get ready for the feast, tying the dress, fixing Kezra's hair, and helping paint on makeup, something she had absolutely no experience with. Making conversation was not Kezra's strong suit after years of hunting down frightened bonded, but she attempted to speak with the girl regardless, to learn how she came to be at the palace at such a young age. But the girl either deflected her questions or neglected to respond. Eventually, Kezra gave up, sitting quietly while the girl threaded emerald-green pins into her hair, completing the ensemble.

"You look beautiful, miss," the servant whispered, gesturing for Kezra to look into the full-length mirror in her bedroom. When she did, Kezra didn't recognize the woman looking back at her. The girl had coated the exposed skin of Kezra's arms in a shimmering gold powder, so it glittered subtly, drawing attention to her arms and shoulders, toned from years of weapons training. It drew eyes away from the damning black band on her forearm, and for that, Kezra was grateful. With the bodice of the dress tightly laced, it clung to her like a second skin; the modest neckline was a stark contrast to her mostly exposed back. Part of her hair had been pulled up with glittering green pins woven through it to match the dress. The remainder of Kezra's hair hung down her back, lying in gentle waves resting on her shoulders. With dark makeup adorning her eyes, the green stood out like two jewels. The makeup mimicked the fading effect of the dress, bringing the whole look together. For a moment, Kezra felt like Niveran, goddess of death, herself. She didn't know a dress could do that, make her feel so powerful. Another part of her felt utterly ridiculous. Although she'd never hidden her body, Kezra's normal leathers fit tightly, allowing her free range of movement while leaving very little to the imagination. However, she'd never openly displayed it like this either. The goal was always to blend into the shadows, not to draw attention, and Kezra didn't feel completely comfortable flaunting herself in this way.

She felt a wave of sympathy for Lennox, wondering if she felt as out-of-place giving up her robes as Kezra did in this dress. The girl handed her a pair of matching heeled shoes, which Kezra instantly rejected in favor of a pair of plain black slippers. The dress was distracting enough. There was no need for her shoes to announce her presence. A knock sounded at the door, and the man who had led to her room entered. He shooed the golden-eyed serving girl away. With an appraising nod, followed by a curtsy, she scurried out of the room, her job complete.

"If you'll follow me, Miss Kezra, it's time for the feast to begin."

"Hello again. I believe you forgot to mention your name earlier. You know mine, but I don't know yours. I find myself at a disadvantage in this situation." A smile broke on his face, despite an obvious attempt to suppress it.

"You'll forgive me, miss, guests rarely care to learn the names of the staff. You took me by surprise. My name is Alec."

"It's nice to meet you, Alec. Thank you for your advice earlier. I could use a friend in the castle."

"You may not want to share our friendship with the nobles. They won't look upon it kindly. Now let's go. You don't want to be late for your first appearance at court."

"I'll be right out. Give me a moment, please. I just need to touch up my makeup." Alec didn't look as though he quite bought the excuse, but he left the room regardless, giving Kezra a moment to herself. As quietly as possible, she slipped out the daggers she'd hidden under the mattress upon arrival, strapping them to her body under the dress so they fit perfectly against her thighs. Kezra double-checked herself in the mirror, ensuring the outline of a hilt wasn't visible to lingering eyes. Giving the armchairs and fireplace one last look of longing, she walked out of the room and slipped her arm through Alec's, letting him escort her to the feast. Kezra wasn't sure what the evening had in store for her, but now she felt prepared to face it.

Chapter 8
Lennox

Kezra was gone. She was the one person Lennox could at least speak to, and now she'd left. In Kezra's absence, Lennox tried to befriend the servants, striking up conversations while on their way to meet with Tylan or when they brought her food, but they greeted her only with silence. Tylan must have instructed them not to speak with her. It made for a lonely few days, and she had no idea when or if Kezra would be back. It felt wrong to long for the company of her captor, but Lennox missed the sense of camaraderie they'd cultivated.

Most days belonged to Lennox to do as she pleased, so long as she didn't leave her room. Once, Lennox tried to wander the castle, and a frantic servant had quickly ushered her back to the room. So she spent her days resting and reading, or trying to heal because the few hours a day she spent with Tylan had taken a toll on her body - bruises, sore ribs, and a dislocated shoulder were her rewards at the end of the lessons. He'd taken over her training since Kezra'd been gone, showing none of Kezra's mercy or restraint. Instead of practicing basics like footwork or form,

Tylan used brute strength. He attacked, moving faster than Lennox's eyes could follow. When she finally learned enough of his movements to see an attack coming and avoid it, he changed tactics. The result was always the same: Lennox fell to the floor, or found herself pinned against the wall, battered, bruised and unable to breathe.

"Push me away, Lennox. Call on your magic. Defend yourself," Tylan yelled variations of this as they sparred, as Lennox failed to fight him off. It was useless. She could not feel her magic, if she had any at all. Lennox hadn't been able to reproduce even a spark of light since that first day, and she now felt certain the whole thing had been some trick of Tylan's.

Tylan grew more frustrated as their sessions produced only failure. His attacks became increasingly brutal, coming to the point where he bent her arms so they felt like they would snap. He choked the air from her lungs, punched her ribs hard enough to make them feel like they would crack. He hadn't hurt Lennox in a way that caused any real or lasting damage, yet, but she feared it was coming soon. The fear was an additional distraction, resulting in considerably worse performance day over day, expounding his frustration.

All of this was swirling through her mind when he came to collect her for another lesson. That itself was odd. Tylan always sent a servant; he never came himself. Even though her room was near his own, the task was clearly beneath him, or at least Lennox assumed that to be the case. She jumped up at the sight of him, already drawing her loose hair back into a braid. Lennox was ready for the lesson, dressed in the black pants and tunic Kezra provided for her. The wardrobe was full of them, and she hadn't been able to bring herself to put her temple robes back on, even though she'd be far more comfortable in them. They reminded her too much of Jasper, of the life she'd lost. Lennox hid the robes away, stuffing them into the back of the closet, and with them, the false hope someone would rescue her. Only when she could rescue herself and return to her friend, would she pull them out, worthy of wearing them once more. Involuntarily, Lennox winced as she reached back to braid her hair, her ribs still bruised from a previous sparring session, causing a shooting pain to course through them when she moved wrong. Tylan's violet eyes caught hers; he lifted an eyebrow in question.

"Is something wrong, Lennox?" Heat rushed to her cheeks. She shouldn't have been embarrassed; he was the cause of her pain. But she disliked showing weakness.

"Nothing I can't handle." Lennox tried to lace her voice with calm and cold, mimicking his own detached cadence. But instead, it cracked as she moved her arm down, sending another shock of pain through her body. Tylan was clearly unconvinced, able to see through the lie. He walked over to her slowly and held out his hand expectantly. Lennox instinctively cringed away. Tylan paused.

"May I?" he asked, reaching for her hand again. Reluctantly, Lennox held it out for him, curiosity getting the better of her. He grasped her hand tenderly in his own and shut his eyes, his face growing surprisingly peaceful. His white hair hung loose, skimming his shoulders. Lennox searched his face for a hint of the cruelty she knew lurked beneath the surface, but found none. Instead, he appeared vulnerable, his brows wrinkled slightly in concentration, leaving Lennox a moment to wonder what exactly he was concentrating on when she felt heat flood from her hand up through body. The warmth shot up her arm and over her shoulder before centralizing around her ribs; the pleasant warmth quickly evolved into a boiling heat. Lennox tried to rip her hand away, but Tylan held firm.

"Just wait," he muttered. The heat around her ribs built until she felt as though she'd been set on fire from the inside. Just when she felt like she couldn't take it any longer, the pain fled, leaving a relieving cool sensation in its place, like taking a dip in a cool spring on a hot day. Tylan opened his eyes, abruptly dropping her hand. "How do you feel?" Lennox ran her hands over her body, searching for a tenderness that was no longer there. Then she stretched out, expecting the motion to cause pain, but none came. Instead, Lennox felt refreshed, energized in a way she hadn't been since her arrival.

"I feel…wonderful," Lennox said, amazed. A smile broke out on her face. "How did you…?"

"Good," Tylan said, interrupting. "Come with me; we're trying something new today." He turned and left the room. Rushing to follow, a strange mix of apprehension and excitement overcame her.

Tylan didn't lead her to the darkly lit training room today. Instead, they wandered down an unused hall of the castle - the floors covered in dust; the walls caked in grime. It made her skin crawl. Lennox's eyes watered from exposure to the disturbed dust. By the time Tylan opened the door of their apparent destination, she'd moved from nervous to truly afraid. The servants wandering the castle hadn't tried to protect her, but the presence of other humans was a comfort, nonetheless. The location was completely isolated. Whatever Tylan meant to do, no one would be around to witness it.

Against every instinct, Lennox followed him into the room, her jaw dropping in shock as she did. Lennox had been expecting some form of prison; she'd briefly envisioned Tylan chaining her up, torturing her until she produced the magic he desired. The room held none of the horrors her brain had conjured, no chains on the walls or cages to lock her in. It was a large, open space, more expansive than the throne room Tylan favored using. In the center was a pool, big enough to fit her entire room inside it. Most astonishingly, the room was lit with the same orbs of light inside the lanterns in her room. Uncaged, they floated gracefully through the air. Not all of them were the soft white she'd grown accustomed to, rather, most of them were different colors. Yellows, blues and greens spun through the air surrounded by orbs of magenta, orange or violet. They danced together above them; the water below reflected their brilliant colors. It was the most magnificent sight Lennox had ever seen, rivaling the beauty of Altheia's temple.

"What do you think?"

"It's breathtaking," Lennox replied truthfully. Never in her wildest dreams had she envisioned something like this.

"It reminds me of home." Lennox didn't miss the hint of sadness lacing through his voice.

"Where's your home?" She couldn't help but ask, curious about a world in which a place like this just existed.

"Gone. I didn't bring you here for nostalgia." His demeanor changed, the wistful vulnerability replaced by a cold, businesslike exterior she'd become familiar with.

"This place, this castle, is ancient. Built by some of the strongest magic wielders in the realm, some of the relics still contain magical properties. This pool is one of those places."

"The water contains magic?" Lennox asked, fascinated. "But how? Does it grant it like the lunasha blooms were said to?"

"No. The pool doesn't grant magic to those without it. For that matter, neither did the lunasha bloom. It can help replenish magic, though, or in your case, help to strengthen it. It should call to your magic; help you guide it."

Lennox looked at the water doubtfully.

"I know you have magic," he said, as if reading her mind. "I've seen it. We just need to coax it out of you. Once you feel it, you can train it."

"So, you just want me to drink it?" Tylan looked appalled, almost offended at the notion.

"I want you to get in the water." As Lennox stepped toward the pool, Tylan was still muttering under his breath, shaking his head.

"Drink from the pool. Ridiculous." Lennox moved to step into the water, and Tylan reached out to stop her before she could.

"To be effective, the water must touch your skin." His eyes roved up and down her outfit, which covered her from head to toe. Lennox took a moment to process the implication.

"You want me to undress?" Tylan met her eyes, and an unexpected shiver ran down her spine. She ignored both the shiver and the hint of a smirk lighting the corner of Tylan's eyes.

"I'll give you a moment of privacy. Let me know when you're in the water." Abruptly, he turned away, allowing her to strip down to her underclothes in private. Lennox found stripping off the tight pants and tunic surprisingly freeing; as if her body had let out a breath she didn't know she was holding. On a whim, Lennox pulled her hair out of its band and shook it loose, so it fell in soft waves over her chest. For the first time since being pulled from the temple, Lennox felt like herself.

Tentatively, in only her underclothes, Lennox took her first step into the water. It washed over her feet, feeling like a warm bath, neither too hot nor too cold. After a few cautious steps, Lennox launched herself into the water, drawn into the delicious feeling of the warmth on her exposed skin. For a moment, she forgot to be self-conscious and let herself enjoy the moment as the pool wrapped her in its embrace. Pulling herself out of the moment of luxury, she waded deeper into the water until it covered her chest, leaving only her head and bare shoulders exposed. Lennox braced herself, mentally preparing, before calling out to Tylan, knowing she couldn't make him wait any longer.

He turned toward her, his shirt and trousers already unbuttoned. In one smooth, graceful motion that Lennox could have never hoped to replicate, he stripped them both off. She sucked in a deep breath on a reflex, trying not to notice him. He was a monster; she told herself. A monster with a broad chest and muscles rippling down his inked arms. Not that she noticed them. Lennox also pointedly did not notice his smooth stomach, or the toned outline of his abs. Nor did she admire the way his hips cut into a "V" above his underclothes. He repulsed her, this monster who kidnapped her from her home and brought her here unwillingly; Lennox was not attracted to him, or at least, this was the lie she told herself.

"Are you all right in there, Lennox?" he asked with a quirk of his lips, perhaps noticing her quiet embarrassment.

"Fine!" Lennox's voice came out in a squeak. She faced away from him, feeling her cheeks heat with embarrassment. Lennox focused on the feel of the water on her skin, the lights twinkling above, anything to distract her traitorous, wandering mind.

"Excellent, now, submerge yourself in the water." Panic rushed in, overriding the sense of wonder. Lennox had no desire to be helpless, fully underwater, with this man watching her. Had he really brought her to this beautiful place to drown her?

"What?!" Lennox whimpered. Tylan either didn't hear it or he ignored it.

"You will need to fully submerge yourself to really make it effective. Try to connect with it, feel the magic pulsing around you, drink it in, and harness it."

Then, before she could finish processing what he'd told her to do, Tylan ducked underwater. Lennox waited, watching for something magical to happen. An age passed, and he remained submerged. Finally, he broke the surface, holding out his hands with his palms up. A small ball of silvery light started forming in his hands. It grew, changing from the size of a small berry into that of an orange before stopping, holding its shape. The colors began changing - silver to red to magenta to violet and on, shifting between all the colors of the lights floating above their heads. Finally, it settled on a fresh spring green. It reminded Lennox of the temple gardens when everything was in bloom.

"Hold out your hands." Intrigued, she listened without question. He tilted his hands, and the ball of light lifted into the air, floating over her outstretched hands. She cupped the ball of light in her palms, entranced. It was beautiful up close. The light pulsed softly, glowing through the gaps in her fingers.

"Let it go." Imitating Tylan, Lennox tilted her hand gently, sending the glowing ball levitating in the sky. It kept traveling up and up until it joined those already dancing through the air.

"Now, you try. Under the water." He issued the order briskly, and convinced by his performance, she didn't hesitate to comply. Lennox's heart pounded with excitement as she took a deep breath and plummeted under the water. At first, she didn't notice anything unusual. She felt peaceful, serene in the water's embrace. Then memories came to her unbidden of afternoons spent playing in the river by the temple as a small child. She remembered wading in the water, splashing Jasper with every step. Those days with Jasper, playing under the summer sun, were where their friendship grew. Both given to the temple as babies, they were too young for the full training of an acolyte, only getting underfoot, so The Mother often sent them off together somewhere they couldn't pester the priestesses.

Lennox hadn't thought of those days in a long time, and the memories were strikingly vivid. In her mind, they had taken on a slightly sparkling quality, as if enhanced with magic. That was when she felt it, or at least, thought she did. There was a faint hum, running through the water, a subtle vibration she hadn't noticed before. Now that she heard it though, Lennox couldn't imagine how she'd missed it. The longer she stayed underwater, the more strongly she felt the resonance of it flowing through her, powerful, addicting. Someone grabbed her elbow, yanking her above the surface. Lennox emerged from the water with her hair dripping, clinging to her face and gasping for air.

"That's enough. I can't have you drowning on me when you could still be useful." The words were harsh, but Tylan's tone was almost tender. Usually, she would puzzle over this small intimacy, wondering what it means. But the power thrumming through her was too distracting. Finally, for the first time in her life, Lennox felt powerful. The magic Tylan insisted she held was pulsing against her skin, begging to be released. "Do you feel it?" Lennox gave a crisp nod as a reply, unable to speak while caught in the magic's thrall. Tylan rewarded her with a genuine smile. At that moment, she almost lost focus on the magic. The smile transformed his face, making him look kind and carefree - handsome even. "Good, Lennox. Now focus on that feeling. Command the magic to take shape. See what you want, and will it into existence."

Easy. Lennox was in control of the power coursing through her veins, and she alone commanded it. Envisioning a ball of light, grander than the one Tylan showed her earlier, Lennox held out her palms expectantly, pulling the formless magic into something real and beautiful. For a moment, nothing happened. The magic resisted her command. Lennox concentrated harder, pulling at the foreign beating she felt inside of her and shaped it into a ball. There, a speck of light, so small she might have been imagining it, flickered into existence. It quivered in her hands, blinking in and out of existence. Feeling encouraged, she told it to grow, trying to coax the magic out instead of forcing it through sheer will. The precious ball of light glowed even brighter, then winked out.

Lennox looked to Tylan, trying to gauge by his reaction whether her first attempt was a success or an utter failure. As usual, his face was back in an inscrutable mask, betraying no hint of how he felt. "Again" was his only feedback. And gathering up her determination, she tried again to master her new skill.

Lennox didn't know how long she stayed there, trying and failing to yield a more successful result. Her fingers pruned from hours in the pool, making her skin beg for warm, dry land. Her body shuddered with exhaustion, but still she tried. Lennox willed her magic to take shape. She tore at it with her mind, using force to create the light. When that didn't work, she resorted to begging it, pleading, screaming at it, anything to produce a different result. Each time, she only created the same pitiful spark, or worse, nothing at all. Lennox was ready to scream in frustration, but still, Tylan didn't comment. After yet another failure, her shoulders slumped forward in defeat, and she was fighting back tears of frustration.

"That's enough for today," Tylan said.

Lennox grunted her agreement, unwilling to speak for fear her voice would betray her frustration. She tried to drag herself out of the water, feeling even more exhausted than she'd been after Kezra's training. When she spotted Tylan out of the corner of her eye, looking refreshed and smirking at her, Lennox's mood worsened. Of course he wasn't tired; he hadn't done anything. He didn't look away when she noticed him, and she threw on the robes, feeling more annoyed at his smugness than embarrassed by her state of undress.

She stomped ahead of him, wringing out her hair, feeling grumpy, when she glanced back and caught the look on his face. He'd stopped to admire the swaying lights, the way they glittered off the pool. At that moment, he looked at ease, vulnerable. When his eyes lit on her, a satisfied smile spread across his face, and the look in his eyes was shockingly close to admiration. Although there was still a predatory gleam to them, he was looking at her…hungrily. A blush heated Lennox's cheeks as she became aware of how the wet underclothes clung to her body as she exited the water. She wrapped her arms around herself, embarrassed by her earlier immodesty. Her eyes alighted on a towel and robe, apparently delivered for her by a servant during her time in the water. Lennox snatched them up, throwing on the robe and wrapping her hair in the soft towel.

"Let's go," Tylan said gruffly. He trudged out of the pool, breaking eye contact and elbowed his way past her without so much as glancing back as he made for the room's exit. Lennox froze for an instant, confused by his abrupt behavior. Then again, from what she'd seen, Tylan ran between hot and cold often. Lennox followed him back to her room, leaving the moment behind and banishing it from her mind. She stood at the room's entrance, dripping water onto the floor in her soaked robe, waiting for Tylan to leave her in solace.

"A servant will be around shortly to help you dress and get ready for dinner."

"Dinner with whom?" Lennox asked in surprise. Every evening so far, she'd eaten alone in her room. The only exception being Kezra occasionally stopping in to steal a bit of her food or to lecture her about footwork.

"With me, of course. You finally conjured your magic today. A pitiful showing, to be sure, but the occasion deserves celebration, nonetheless. Besides, you must be starving." Now that he mentioned it, Lennox noticed how ravenous she was on top of being bone-weary. She wanted nothing more than to sit in the cozy chair by the fire and devour a feast fit for a king in solitude, but she assumed turning Tylan down wasn't an option.

"I'm looking forward to it," Lennox said instead, with as much false sincerity as she could muster.

True to his word, a servant showed up shortly after he left. She was a middle-aged woman Lennox had seen before as she usually brought meals. She had a crooked nose and a thin mouth that stayed in a perpetual sneer, and light brown hair streaked with gray and tied in a bun.

"Hello, lovely to see you again."

Ignoring her greeting, the servant went into the bathroom, soon followed by a parade of other servants carrying steaming water to fill the bath. Once it was full, the woman dismissed the others and gestured for Lennox to come over.

"Let's get on with it, girl." Lennox realized the servant meant to help with her bath.

"Oh, no thank you. I can wash myself."

"Tylan commanded me to help you bathe, so I have no choice in the matter. Now come here. We need to do something about that tangled hair." Thoroughly chastised, Lennox got into the bath without further argument.

The woman lathered her hair, scrubbing it with a lavender-scented soap as she worked out the tangles that had formed. It wasn't necessarily gentle, but she was effective, leaving Lennox's hair soft and free of the snarls that had plagued it. However, after her hair was done, Lennox insisted on finishing the bathing process on her own. The sneering servant seemed satisfied that what she'd already done fulfilled the terms of her command, and left Lennox to her own devices.

"I don't know why Tylan bothers with a scrawny young girl," the woman muttered to one of the other servants on her way out. "A sturdy woman, one with experience, is what he needs."

Lennox gave little thought to the whispered ramblings. Tylan saw her as an object, a tool to use and wield at his discretion, nothing more. Their sessions together in the training room had made his feelings toward her very clear. The glimpses of tenderness she'd seen today weren't going to make her forget about the brutality she'd experienced.

"It's time to dress for dinner," the servant said. Lennox guessed she hadn't been left completely alone then. Reluctant to spend more time alone with Tylan, she took her time getting out of the bath. By the time Lennox exited the room in her underclothes, the servant was tapping her foot with impatience.

"We have a schedule to keep. Hurry over and get dressed," the woman said. Lennox complied, walking over to her.

"Maggie," Lennox said. The woman raised an eyebrow at her in question. "If you don't tell me your name, I'm going to call you Maggie. I can't keep referring to you as "the servant" even if it's only in my head." Maybe Maggie sighed, bending to the floor to lay out a cream dress so Lennox could step into it.

"You really are an impertinent child," the servant grumbled. "If you must know, it's Anna," she said, her voice softening.

"Anna. It's beautiful. I'm sorry for any trouble I've caused you, Anna."

"My troubles are of my own doing, child. Don't take that burden for yourself." Anna had a faraway look in her eyes, like she was recalling another time, an unpleasant memory. "Come now; I don't have all day and the floor is hurting my knees. Get this gods-forsaken dress on."

Anna did more than help Lennox dress. Seeing Lennox's helplessness with the makeup brushes, Anna sat her down and lightly applied it to her face; having never worn it at the temple, she was grateful for the help. Anna gently dabbed powder onto Lennox's face, lined her eyes with kohl, and added a baby pink powder to her eyelids. Then they moved to Lennox's hair; Anna weaved it into a braid, wrapping it across the back of Lennox's head and pulling loose hair through so it cascaded in a waterfall down her back. Plucking small flowers of an array of colors from a vase, Anna pinned them into the braid. When she finished, she held up a mirror, and Lennox was stunned by the transformation.

The dress was magnificent. Made of cream silk, it was the most elegant garment she'd ever worn; the dress was designed with intricate flowers that matched those in Lennox's hair. With a bodice of plain cream silk, the flowers were sparsely added around the waist, then, further down, they began to cluster more tightly together. The dress's bottom slowly turned from cream to the fresh green of spring, the color of freshly budding leaves; the multi-colored flowers bunched together over the green, giving the illusion of a garden growing on the garment. Its sleeves were long and flowing, covering Lennox's wrists in cream silk. It was art. A fading of winter into spring on a dress. Even though she'd been taught to live without luxuries at the temple, she couldn't help but fall in love with this gown. In it, Lennox had never felt more confident and beautiful. And it was nice to wear something other than those terrible trousers Kezra gave her. Lennox beamed at Anna, ready to compliment her work. However, Anna gazed back at her sadly.

"I see it now. He's going to eat you alive, child." They were leaving the room before Lennox had a chance to ponder what she'd meant.

They walked to a formal dining room Lennox hadn't seen before, one that clearly hadn't been used in some time. The room was decorated with tapestries hanging on the stone walls, silver candelabras freshly polished and shimmering on the table. An amethyst rug sat under the table laced with a swirling black design. Despite the care taken to decorate the place, it lacked the warmth of a room well used, well loved. The trappings were too new, the room too immaculate. Despite the effort, the ghosts of memories shuttered away to be forgotten still lingered in the atmosphere.

The train of thought was abandoned though, when Lennox spied the feast laid out on the table: roasted duck with figs, a variety of cheeses and meats and fruits on a platter, crisp pies filled with beef, spices, and onions all laid out along the table. And in between them all sat a wonderful variety of desserts scattered among the food. There were fresh raspberry tarts with clotted cream, pies filled with fruits she'd never seen, and a chocolate cake with a creamy frosting Lennox wanted to dig her hands into and eat like a barbarian. Lennox wondered if Tylan was expecting other company; surely this wasn't all for them.

Tearing her eyes from the feast, she took the opportunity to look more closely at the tapestries on the wall. Lennox picked one at the end of the room, furthest from the table. It depicted a woman dressed in ancient, bronze armor. She sat atop a great black beast covered in scales. It had wide wings, stretched out as if ready to take off in flight. It has a long snout with slits for nostrils and beady eyes as black as its scales. The woman raised a silver sword above her head, the handle of which was carved to look like the head of the beast she rode. Her black hair flowed behind her, giving the impression it was blowing in the wind. Fog swirled all around them. Lennox recognized the woman as the goddess Niveran, the goddess of night and death. The beast was her dragon, Nithe. Legend stated she flew the dragon across the sky each day, bringing night across the land and guiding newly departed souls with her to her realm, Helica, where they awaited judgement. She guided the worthy, the good, to an afterlife beyond the veil. The wicked, she fed to Nithe.

They'd learned a little about Niveran in the temple while studying Altheia, as the two goddesses were opposites. They were sisters, twins, one light, one dark. Lennox had never seen Niveran depicted quite like this though, in armor, ready for battle. The ancient books did not speak of gods fighting in wars, at least, not in her studies. While she had occasionally found the temple a little stifling, Lennox always enjoyed her studies of ancient lore, imagining herself a scholar who traveled to far away lands, learning the histories of the world. This version of Niveran was never mentioned, but maybe she'd have learned about it in her studies after The Blessing. It made Lennox wonder where this piece had come from, what it was doing here of all places. Had someone imagined this version of Niveran, or did it depict a history she would have learned about had Tylan not stolen her future?

"Admiring my art collection?" Tylan sauntered up behind her. Lennox hadn't heard him enter the room, not that she'd been paying much attention, lost in thought.

"It's a wonderful piece. I've never seen its like, and I've studied Niveran a bit before."

"I suppose you would have, in a temple for Altheia. The Mother's have never been a fan of showing Niveran in her true form though," Tylan said, sounding bitter. He seemed to recover from the darkness that overtook him. "Come, let us eat before the food gets cold."

Acting as a gentleman, Tylan pulled out Lennox's chair, opposite his own. Once he was seated, a servant came around, cutting slices of meat, filling her plate with food and her cup with wine. The food was savory and rich, grease from the duck mixing with the sweetness of the fig, the wine strong and flavorful, the taste of the cherries and chocolate in the wine swirled on her palate. Lennox felt intoxicated from the combination of the two, leaving her feeling slightly reckless.

"You look beautiful tonight. The dress suits you."

"Thank you." Lennox blushed at the compliment. "It's the most exquisite gown I've ever seen. It makes me feel like I'm wearing a spring garden." She was aware of herself becoming more animated, unable to restrain her smile, drunk on food and good wine.

"It's good to see you smiling. I know this has been… a tough transition for you."

"I will admit, being confined to a palace and learning I have magic by having it choked out of me wasn't what I thought I'd be doing this week," Lennox said lightly. The wine had stolen her caution, letting the words free before she could think any better of them. Her words hit Tylan like a physical blow; any hint of joy vanished from his face.

"The incident in the training room was regrettable. I'd hoped; well, it doesn't matter what I'd hoped. Sometimes magic comes when you need it most. I went too far trying to force you to access it quickly. Please, forgive me." The apology stunned her. Lennox snapped her mouth shut to keep food from falling out as it hung open. He didn't strike her as the type of man who often admitted to being wrong, much less asked for forgiveness.

"Time will tell whether you are worthy of my forgiveness." Lennox tried to keep her tone joking, but missed the mark, the conversion too serious. They went back to eating in relative quiet, both trying to figure out how to navigate the awkward tension still hanging in the room. Gathering the courage granted by the wine, Lennox decided to ask the questions that had been bothering her since the day she'd arrived. With a long drink of wine, Lennox fortified her resolve.

"What do you want with me, with my magic? I have seen you use your own. Even the small things I've seen you do are more than I could accomplish in years of training. You can heal, make objects out of nothing, bond souls to you. What use could one, untrained priestess, be to you?" The words tumbled out of her, hardly coherent for the speed at which she'd delivered them. Tylan sat for a moment, unmoving as he contemplated the question.

"What do you want, Lennox?"

"To go back to the temple and finish my vows. I want to become a high priestess of Altheia and serve her will." But the answer had come out too stiff, too rehearsed. It rang false even to Lennox's ears.

"No, I don't think you do. I think yours is a wild heart, one that doesn't wish to be trapped in a cage, even one as beautiful as the temple is Tesmerin. What do you truly desire?"

"Freedom," Lennox said before she could stop herself. The answer flew from her mouth, unable to be bottled inside her any longer. "I want to travel, to have an adventure, to see the world beyond the temple, from Tesmerin to Kitsummit, to Nalathay. I want to eat exotic foods and dance in festivals under the moonlight, to experience all life has to offer without restraint or worry of what others think. That is what I want."

A weight lifted off her heart as she spoke. Even to Jasper, Lennox had never admitted aloud that she didn't want to be a priestess. To do so would have been dishonorable, ungrateful. The declaration left her breathless as the words poured out, leaving her raw, vulnerable. Waiting for Tylan to say something was painful. Finally, he stood, moving away from the table.

"Come with me." He started walking away from the room. It took Lennox a second to process what was happening and move. "And bring the duck," he yelled. Not thinking about what she was doing, or what she'd just admitted, Lennox grabbed the whole roasted duck and sprinted after him.

He led her to an ancient-looking stone door. Carved into the frame were unfamiliar squiggly symbols. Looking more closely, Lennox recognized some from the old language, the language of the gods. However, she didn't know what they meant; they weren't words she recognized. It sent a pang of loss through her; Lennox might have learned them had she stayed at the temple.

Tylan placed a hand on the center of the door, whispering an incantation too quietly for her to hear. The symbols on the frame glowed a faint blue, and the door creaked open. The heavy door raked across the floor, making an awful scrapping noise. Tylan led her through the door into a thick red fog. It was so dense, Lennox could only see a few feet forward. She couldn't make out any of the landscape. Terrified of being lost, she clung to Tylan's side. He casually turned his head in her direction, looking calm.

"Did you bring the duck?" Lennox held it up, dumbly, grease dripping down her fingers and coating the sleeves of the beautiful dress. "Excellent. Now we wait. Don't worry, it won't be long." She recalled vague threats Tylan made to feed Kezra to his pet. Lennox's nerves kicked up as she pictured a beast waiting for them in the fog.

It didn't take long. Whether it was the smell of roasted duck or the work of some unforeseen force, Lennox found herself faced with an impossibly long, white claw surrounded by fog. Frightened, she cringed back, dropping the duck. Two more joined the lone claw, attached to a massive paw big enough to crush them both with one ill-placed step. The claws wrapped around the duck and dragged it back into the fog. There was a sickly crunch. Lennox could imagine the beast's enormous teeth cracking the duck's bones in a single bite. Her survival instincts kicking in, Lennox turned to flee, no longer caring if she got lost in the fog, but Tylan held her back.

A form took shape as it crept from the fog. Steam rolled over Lennox's face, then a long, black snout, covered in scales, greeted her. A face emerged, showing two beady eyes, dark as night. The beast's body was the size of the temple. Black scales covered every inch of the creature's body, except for two leathery wings tucked at its side. The lethal claws stopped feet in front of her. Its snout bent down inches away. Then the creature emitted another round of steam, uncomfortably hot as it furled around her skin. There was no stopping the inhuman scream that erupted from Lennox's throat. Tylan's pet was a dragon, and it was staring at her like she was its next snack.

Chapter 9

Kezra

Despite Alec's efforts to rush her along, they arrived at the feast already in full swing. Lords in colorful tunics and finely made surcoats walked about the room, chatting happily. Tables lined the walls, filled with different arrays of food on each, so one could choose what to eat, put it on their plate, and continue about the room. There was an entire table filled with cheeses and fruits, some of which Kezra was familiar with, but others were foreign to her. A bowl of red grapes sat next to a platter of exotic fruit, bright pink, shaped like a star. The next table was meat of all varieties: beef, roasted pheasant, chicken, pork slathered in a syrupy sauce, lamb with mint jelly. But it was the last table that truly made her mouth water. A four-tiered cake sat in its center. The cake was sky blue, the king's color, and bore his crest as a decoration, a golden lion mid-roar. Kezra wondered how the bakers achieved such a color, or how they created the animation in the lion's face. Pastries, pies and puddings surrounded the cake, with chocolate-covered fruits filling the gaps between. Kezra eyed a particularly scrumptious-looking lemon tart and made her way over to it. Before she could grasp it, a hand reached out, stopping her. The hand was surprisingly soft, considering its size and heavy weight. It was a gentle grab, not meant to harm, but Kezra didn't appreciate someone coming between her and her dessert - something she intended to make known.

"The King wouldn't be happy if you start without him," came a husky voice from behind her. He released her hand as he spoke. Kezra's face flushed with embarrassment, the anger fading. She hadn't thought anything of the untouched tables, despite the busy room.

"I hardly think he would have noticed one missing pastry," Kezra mumbled, still annoyed.

"Forgive me, My Lady. I was only trying to come to your rescue, although maybe the attempt was misguided." He held out his hand for her own. Kezra placed her hand in his, assuming it to be the proper greeting. He brought her hand to his lips, giving it a soft kiss. Kezra's cheeks flushed again at the intimate moment. As Kezra tried to beat down the fluttering of her heart, she took the opportunity to study his appearance.

He was wearing a midnight-blue tunic and a matching surcoat with silver stitching. Underneath, he wore silver leggings to match the stitching. Tiny, matching blue swirls were embroidered along the side. His black leather boots looked worn, but of good quality and well cared for. Soft brown curls covered his ears, and one curl hung over his forehead, almost covering brilliant grey eyes. His face was round, but soft, and kind, handsome in a subtle way. He had light, pale skin that looked like it would burn easily in the sun, making Kezra's look even darker with her hand in his. He bowed low after kissing her hand. Even bent over, she could tell he was uncommonly tall, almost as tall as Tylan.

"I don't remember reading of any knights who saved a maiden from pastries."

"Ahh, but I was saving you from the potential wrath of the king, much more knightly. I hear lemon tarts are his favorite after all. He may have noticed one out of place. Especially if it was in the hands of a beautiful maiden such as yourself." Kezra rolled her eyes, unwilling to fall for the first bit of charm thrown her direction, but intrigued enough to follow when tried to pull her away from the tempting tables. "I don't believe I've seen you at court before. Such a lovely face would have stood out."

"This is my first time at court and my first time seeing the king. So, thank you for saving me from an unpleasant first meeting."

"It's no trouble, my lady. Perhaps, as a show of gratitude, I could get your name?" Kezra debated lying, but didn't see the point in this situation.

"Kezra."

"Do you have a last name, Miss Kezra?" she smiled, shaking her head, hoping it came across as coy. Though truthfully, she'd never taken a last name, nor had the need for one. Kezra couldn't take Tylan's name, and having been with Tylan since she was a child, Kezra didn't know the identities of her birth parents. The bonded she captured had started to call her the amethyst assassin, named for the smoke left behind as she disappeared with her victims. Kezra hated the ridiculous name. Her new acquaintance didn't appear inclined to press the matter further.

"Very well, Miss Kezra. You may call me Peter. What brings you to court?"

"I'm here on behalf of Tylan."

"Tylan Faine?" His gray eyes widened with shock, but he quickly smoothed it over. "Well, this evening just became more interesting. Let's find some wine, Kezra. I have a feeling we're going to need it."

Peter linked his arm through hers, steering her toward more nobles. Someone thrust a cup into her hand, red wine sloshing precariously close to its edge. Peter clinked his cup against her own, a devilish grin on his face.

"Cheers, Kezra. To a night to remember."

"To a night to remember," she echoed. After a moment's hesitation, Kezra drank half the glass. It was not a good time to lose her wits, but the atmosphere was intoxicating, and for once, she wanted to let loose. It felt so good to be seen, to feel free and unrestrained, nice to share a moment with this stranger as if she were a normal woman flirting with a man seeking her attention. Kezra was drunk on the jealous looks from other women who were staring at her with Peter, from nobles vying for an introduction to the newest member of court. Peter and Kezra wandered around the room and listened to nobles tell stories of their diplomatic trips to Ocana's neighboring country, Nalathay. Kezra laughed along with everyone else at nobles' bad jokes, sipping her wine, paying no attention to how often someone refilled her cup. Eventually, her stomach rumbled, but no one could eat until the king appeared, and it seemed he enjoyed a late entrance. Giving the tables one longing look, Kezra decided to drink more to curb the hunger.

Eventually, the king arrived, looking strangely bleary around the edges. He entered with a procession of guards, and the conversation stopped; the room stilled as everyone watched the king make his way to the podium at the head of the room that held his throne. The king looked younger than she had imagined. Kezra expected a hardened man, wise in his later years of life. In her mind, she pictured a man with a wrinkled, kindly face. Maybe it was his unwillingness to appear in public that made her envision him as a sweet but reclusive old man. However, in reality, he didn't look much older than Kezra. She would have placed his face somewhere in his late twenties, although it occurred to her that she might not be able to trust her vision at the moment. If she didn't concentrate, the king seemed to have two faces. Kezra squinted to focus on him. His face was rather plain, with brown eyes and matching chocolate-brown hair. He seemed handsome, but forgettably so. Not too tall, or too short, not someone who would stand out in a crowd.

His outfit, though, was extravagant, as expected. He wore an all-white tunic and trousers, with matching tall white boots adorned with enormous gold buckles. The outfit was stitched with gold thread that glimmered when the light caught it just right. On his shoulders sat a cape, despite the heat of the room, also white. A roaring lion was embroidered in gleaming gold thread on the back of the cape. Completing the ensemble was a delicate crown, solid gold and carved to resemble twisted tree branches. He stood on his pedestal in front of the lion throne to address the silent crowd of nobles.

"Thank you all for coming. I know many of you travelled far and rode hard to be here. As many of you know, we have been seeing peasant revolts across the nation as our rivers dry and crops fail. Nalathay has sent spies along our borders, looking like they may attack. War continues to threaten the nation, but you, my loyal followers, have come together to seek a solution to our growing problems and to find a path forward." Murmurs broke out among the crowd, sharing whispered rumors of villages already invaded and burned by Nalathay. War wasn't on the horizon; it was here, and the peasants were getting desperate. Kezra had seen it firsthand tracking down Tylan's bonded. The king lifted a hand, silencing the crowd once more. "We have sent priestesses throughout the country to bless the harvests and perform the sacred rites of Altheia. I am also doubling the guard along the border. But we must discuss a plan should the worst happen." The king held out a glass of wine, which he tilted in the direction of the crowd. "Although this is a somber occasion, we won't let it mar tonight's festivities. Tonight, we celebrate our reunion and good health. Let the feast begin." A cheer rose from the crowd as the king took a sip of wine, and the serious air evaporated, the worries of those outside the castle walls forgotten.

The crowd dispersed, finally tucking into the food laid out on the tables and taking a seat where one could be found. Throughout the chaos, Peter stayed by her side. He sat next to her while Kezra bit into the lemon tart she'd been craving. It was worth the wait, the buttery pastry crust melting on her tongue. Kezra licked a piece of lemon off her lip, savoring the sweet, acidic flavor.

"The King will visit each noble one on one throughout the evening. It is a show of appreciation, but more importantly, it allows the king to see for himself which nobles didn't show up tonight. Judging by the turnout, I think the only noble missing is Sir Faine." Peter talked between bites of pheasant. Kezra thought about looking for a plate of her own.

"Tylan isn't a noble," Kezra remarked. Peter didn't acknowledge the comment but continued on.

"While that's happening, there will be some form of entertainment, definitely a little dancing and likely a few fistfights."

"What happens when the feast's over?" she asked. Petter shrugged.

"Everyone returns to their room, some with their wives, some with an ambitious woman who is not their wife, and some alone. It does pain me to think of you all alone and cold in your bed." Kezra rolled her eyes, ignoring the last remark.

"That's not what I meant. When will the king discuss this plan with everyone? How long am I - are we expected to remain?"

"Until the king is satisfied or we can prove we are needed elsewhere. Sometimes he calls on nobles for a few days, others for months. We're here at the king's pleasure, and it can be a long journey. The King takes care of his nobles, though, and it's essentially one big party the entire time they're here. People rarely complain about remaining in court. Many even find a reason to stay." Kezra's mouth went dry. She couldn't remain in court indefinitely. As much as she was enjoying the opportunity to act like a normal person for once, leaving Lennox entirely alone with Tylan for an extended amount of time felt wrong. Kezra knew that she shouldn't care, but she undeniably did, at least a little bit. Not to mention, feasting and dancing at court was just a distraction from discovering a way to break her bond with Tylan.

"Are you alright? I don't agree with the way the court is run either. Although I wouldn't complain about a few months in your company."

"I'm fine." Kezra tried to force a smile. "This is all a bit overwhelming." She waved her hand generally around the hall, trying to indicate the enormity of the situation. "I just need to sit for a minute." Peter took her to a table and handed her a cup of water, which Kezra took gratefully. She plopped down on the bench, only now realizing how unsteady she'd felt on her feet.

"Don't sit for too long. The dancing is about to begin." He bowed, winking at her, and then strode away, melting into the crowd and giving Kezra a moment of peace.

As promised, musicians entered soon after, taking seats on the far side of the room, away from the feast. Music filled the room, sweet, vibrating notes that slid through Kezra's ears and wrapped around her heart. Her missions for Tylan didn't offer much opportunity for music, so Kezra only heard songs played in passing. A single lute played on a street corner, a solitary serenade, the passing notes from a band, were the only hints of music she was exposed to, and she hadn't realized how much her heart longed for it. The king had hired a full orchestra to play, and she'd never heard anything so sweet. The notes crescendoed through her soul, the notes filled with a longing that Kezra instantly connected with. She understood the other's desire to sway to the music's beat; she felt it too.

Standing up, Kezra brushed off her dress, determined to find Peter for a dance. Even if she didn't know the steps, she felt confident he could lead her. However, Kezra's plan was quickly derailed by an approaching soldier. She recognized him as the young guard from the gate. He stood in front of her, blocking her movement.

"We have to stop meeting like this." Either the soldier didn't hear the joke, or he didn't find her funny, because his face stayed serious, his mouth a flat line.

"The king will see you now." He stood behind her, vigilant of every step she took in the direction of the king. Kezra couldn't help but feel like he was an executioner, walking her to her death.

Up close, the king looked older than he had from a distance, but the aging seemed to come from stress, rather than from time. Dark circles sat under his eyes, indicating many sleepless nights. His face carried the weight of days spent worrying, his posture was slightly hunched, as if he was carrying an invisible burden. He eyed Kezra up and down apprais- ingly before he deigned to speak, as if assessing the value of a good he was about to buy.

"I don't believe we've been acquainted," he finally said, once his eyes had finished roving over her body. Given his appearance, she shouldn't have been surprised by his brusque demeanor, but it still took her aback. Kezra immediately disliked him, but reminded herself to remain calm.

"We've never met. It's my first time at court."

"Your Highness," the soldier spoke up from his place behind them. "You will address the king as Your Majesty or Your Highness." The king waved him off.

"We can forgive a breach in etiquette. It's the lady's first day in court after all. Who are you here with? Did one of my lords marry in secret? I can understand why anyone would be tempted by such a beauty. Still, I don't recall anyone requesting a priestess or receiving the marriage tithe. We must rectify that at once. Which lord was it?"

"I'm not married, My Lord."

"Your Highness," the guard corrected her again. Kezra swallowed.

"Your Highness. I'm here representing Sir Tylan Faine." His demeanor changed instantly. Emotions rolled across his face in a wave: disappointment, desperation, settling on anger, which turned to a sly calm.

"Interesting, he saw fit to send a girl in his place. Are you a gift, perhaps? I wouldn't be opposed. However, it doesn't excuse his absence." He licked his lips as his eyes again drank in her body. Suddenly, Kezra felt all too exposed in the dress she'd admired so much earlier. The dagger concealed on her thigh burned; her fingers twitched. If they tried to harm her, Kezra would grab it, kill the soldier and make a run for the exit.

Kill him. The words appeared quietly in her mind. Then a second time, louder, *kill him.* The voice she heard sounded like Tylan's, but she couldn't be sure if it was real. Was he instructing her to do it here, in front of the entire court, or was she just imagining things in her current state? Before she had time to think through the situation, the king was already dismissing her.

"I'll figure out what to do with you later. For now, go, enjoy the party." He waved her away, but Kezra stood there, confused. Likely misinterpreting her hesitation for drunkenness, the guard ushered her off the pedestal, away from the king, as if she was incapable of following the command on her own. Walking back into the crowd, Kezra tried to sort through her thoughts. Tylan had never spoken to her through the bond before, and as far as she knew, it wasn't possible to do so. The wine and the stress were probably playing with her mind. Kezra shook it off. Yes, it was definitely just the wine. Giving the subject no more thought, Kezra went in search of Peter. Wandering the hall, she weaved between dancing couples, men packed in groups, and women giggling into their fans, determined to find Peter for a dance.

No matter where she looked, though, Kezra couldn't find him. Kezra glanced back toward the king's throne, trying to see if Peter was there, but guards blocked her view. He must have been with the king. Kezra decided to for him, grabbing a bit of cheese to snack while she waited. At least there was plenty of good food to keep her occupied. Kezra plucked the odd, star-shaped fruit from the table, closing her eyes to savor the taste. It was sweet, like candy, before turning sour enough to make her lips pucker. As she was reaching for another piece, an arm threaded through her own.

"I see I've lost your attention to the sunder fruit. A worthy foe." Peter smiled down at her, leading Kezra away from the food and onto the dance floor.

"The sunder fruit was easier to find and infinitely sweeter," Kezra quipped. Peter held his hand over his heart, pretending to be wounded. The music started up again, and he wrapped a hand around her waist, grabbing her hand with his free one.

"Ah, but you can't deny that I'm more irresistible." He spun Kezra around as he spoke. She twirled back into his arms, smiling. This was just as she'd imagined. They moved as one, spinning effortlessly around the dance floor. She could feel others' eyes on us as they danced.

"Where were you? I looked everywhere for you." He bent close to her ear.

"Later, Kezra. There are too many ears here for me to going around spilling my secrets." She could feel his breath on her neck as he spoke, sending shivers down her spine. "Besides, the show's about to begin." They stopped swaying as the music stopped and stood, breathless in the middle of the dance floor, all eyes still on them. A circle had formed around them while they danced. The entire room was silently holding its breath, watching them. The king stood, giving us a slow clap, although anger seethed behind his eyes, and the spell was broken. A few nobles joined in, giving a round of light applause. Peter bowed theatrically, nudging Kezra to do the same. She gave a clumsy curtsy, unsteady on her feet now that the music had stopped. Peter pulled her off the floor, blending back in with the crowd.

"What a delightful and unexpected show from our newcomer." The king's voice boomed across the still, quiet hall. "Thank you for the display, Kezra. I'm sure you'll find yourself battling off suitors in no time, that is, if Sir Faine doesn't claim you himself. Now for the main event." Whispers broke out at the mention of Tylan's name.

The king clapped his hands twice, and entertainers flooded the room. Women scantily clad in silk outfits danced between groups of men. Magicians entered in a puff of smoke, laddies already clambering after them, craning their necks with interest. Following behind them was a fortune teller; her wild, curly brown hair escaping from a red patterned scarf. Her patchwork skirt swished around her ankles as she walked through the crowd. One lone woman should have been lost among the allure of the dancers, the wonder of the magicians, but she had a commanding presence that drew eyes to her. She scanned the crowd, her golden eyes meeting Kezra's. The blood drained from Kezra's face. There she was, the woman from the markets at Tesmerin, the only person besides Tylan to make her flee.

The golden-eyed woman sat down at a table covered in red velvet cloth and pulled out a deck of cards. The crowd was already dispersing, forming circles around the dancers and magicians. A line formed behind the fortune teller's table, made up of young women, barely out of girlhood. They chatted excitedly about things like marriage proposals, who would attend what upcoming party, or what they would wear to said parties. Kezra had little interest in standing among them, she hadn't come from their world and no matter how much she tried to fool herself tonight, she would never be one of them. But she needed to talk to Yelena. Standing with young women her age, who giggled amicably with one another, was a painful reminder of how different Kezra's life had been from theirs. It was strangely lonely to standalone in line among so many people familiar with one another. Conversations hushed around her, replaced by whispers and giggles. Kezra told herself it didn't matter. But still, she felt her face flush at the knowledge that they were talking about her.

Kezra's purpose in meeting the fortune teller again wasn't to find out if she would meet the love of her life or come into great fortune, both things these girls were undoubtedly hoping to hear; it was to continue their odd conversation from a few weeks ago. As much as she'd tried to forget the interaction, those golden eyes still haunted her; the husky voice whispered a strange prophecy in Kezra's dreams. They would clear up this "daughter of night" nonsense once and for all. Then she would finish up this meeting with the king and go back to searching for a way to sever her bond.

The line moved quickly, some women letting out excited squeals at their readings, others shedding a quiet tear. When it came to Kezra's turn, she took a seat across from the fortune teller, holding the woman's unwavering gaze, unwilling to shy away as she had last time.

"Welcome to my booth. I am Madame Yelena. Tell me, child, what answers do you seek?"

"We've met before, Madame Yelena. It's not my fortune I seek, just answers."

"I remember you well, daughter of night. I've been expecting you." It took effort to stop herself from rolling her eyes.

"Let me guess, you foresaw this meeting," Kezra said, sarcasm dripping from her voice. Yelena smirked.

"No, my daughter told me you were here." Yelena shuffled her cards.

"Your daughter?" Kezra's mind wandered to the serving girl from earlier who was unwilling to speak to her. She wondered if that was Yelena's daughter. The girl's mother filling her head with stories of some demon of the night set on dooming everyone would explain her hesitancy to speak. Yelena must have seen the realization on her face. She gave Kezra a small, sweet smile, probably for her daughter.

"Yes, Shondra. She's been assigned to you during your stay in court. I trust you'll treat her kindly. Not all nobles do." She stopped shuffling the cards and set the deck on the table. "Ask your questions and cut the deck, daughter of night. For that is all my fortunes are, answers to the questions lying heavy on your heart."

"I told you, I'm not seeking a fortune. I just need to talk about our last conversation," Kezra answered. Yelena shook her head and lowered her voice.

"We can not speak openly here." She cleared her throat and raised her voice again. "Ask you questions, we must get through the line. Think of your question, daughter, and cut the deck." The air felt thick with possibility, as if she might really be able to answer the question that had haunted Kezra, the one that wouldn't leave her mind.

"Can I break my bond? Will I ever be free?" The questions came out in a whisper, betraying her fear to ask. Kezra was afraid. She tried to tell herself she didn't believe in this nonsense, but Kezra feared the answers the cards would give more than she cared to admit. Without further hesitation, Kezra cut the deck. Yelena turned over the first card. It depicted a storm: big gray clouds, lightning strikes and pelting rain. Three tornadoes swirled in the background.

"The storm card. It foretells great change coming in your life very soon. It looks ominous, but storms are not always a bad thing. Sometimes, a storm brings a fresh start with it." Kezra eyed her skeptically but kept her opinions to herself as Yelena flipped the next card. The next card depicted a long, winding road with a fork in it. The road was surrounded by green grass and rolling hills on a sunlit day.

"The crossroads. You will make an important, life-changing decision, followed by a great journey. Bear in mind, it may be an emotional journey, not a physical one. It's not possible to know." Yelena bit her lip, as if considering something before continuing on. She flipped the last card; it was split down the middle by a thick, jagged black line. One side depicted the sun, surrounded by the stars and moon. They seemed to glimmer on the card's surface. The other side showed nothing. Just a grey, empty void.

"This is a card of uncertainty. Your journey's outcome is uncertain. It will either be fulfilling, or leave you with nothing." Yelena shut her eyes, rubbing her forehead with her hand. "It is as I feared, daughter of night, there may be doom at the end of your path." Kezra gulped; she didn't know what any of that had to do with breaking her bond, but it left her feeling defeated.

"Thank you for my reading, Madame Yelena. I'll go now; others are waiting." Before she could get up, Yelena grabbed her hand.

"There's still hope for us yet. The cards are uncertain. All they show are decisions and changes. With some help, things could go in the right direction." Yelena paused for a moment and bit her lip again, clearly wrestling with an internal decision. "I will help you. Meet me back in the market tomorrow night, under the castle's shadow. Come to my tent alone. I can give you what you seek." Stunned, Kezra could only nod before walking away, as Yelena plastered on a smile for the next customer.

After having her fortune told by Yelena, the rest of the party passed in a blur. Kezra couldn't find Peter again, and the conversation with Yelena left her disturbed, so she determined the best way to soothe herself would be with more wine and tasting as many new foods as possible. When she started back to her room, she was possibly swaying a little, bleary-eyed, and so full that she couldn't eat another bite. Exhausted, Kezra stumbled into bed, barely managing to get herself undressed, leaving the beautiful gown in a heap on the floor. Then she fell into a dreamless sleep.

Kezra woke the next morning to the sound of metal clanging on the floor. She bolted up, searching the room for a threat, and immediately regretted it because her head throbbed. Kezra hadn't bothered to take the pins out of her hair before going to sleep, and now they dug into her scalp. Her head pounded as if it had a heartbeat. Kezra glanced around the room slowly, trying not to move too fast. The source of the noise was a dark-haired girl, kneeling on the floor to retrieve a fallen spoon. She sat frozen under Kezra's stare, a dark blush blooming on the girl's cheeks. Slowly, Kezra racked through her hazy memory searching for the girl's name, knowing Yelena had given the name of her daughter. Shauna. No, that wasn't right. Shondra. That was it. Placed on the table next to the bed was a tray containing a teapot along with some fruit and biscuits, presumably for Kezra's breakfast.

"Would you mind helping me with these pins? I forgot to take them out, and I fear they're rather stuck now." Kezra tried to keep her voice even, hoping she sounded kind. Shondra hurried over, gushing an apology for waking her and hastily removing the pins from Kezra's hair. The stabbing sensation relented a little. Her head still pounded, but at least she no longer felt like thorns were digging into her head as well.

"Would you like some tea, Miss?"

"Yes, please. Could you bring me the whole tray? I think I spied some biscuits."

Shondra poured some tea, adding a few spoonfuls of sugar and some milk. Kezra's stomach immediately lurched, trying to bring some of the previous night's feast back up. She fought to keep it down. Something about the tea's heat and steam helped her aching head. Kezra took an experimental bite of the biscuit. It melted in her mouth, buttery and soft. Shondra was busy fluttering about the room. The discarded dress had been picked up and replaced by a new one for the day, laid out on the armchair.

"Would you like one?" Kezra held out a biscuit, already begrudging the loss.

"I've already eaten, ma'am. Thank you," Shondra said sheepishly. But she eyed the biscuit hungrily. Kezra shrugged.

"It's yours if you want it. I can't eat all of this by myself." It was a physical challenge to set down the biscuit, but she made herself do it, knowing she could absolutely eat the whole breakfast on her own. But she wanted the girl to stop being afraid of her, and I had promised Yelena she'd be kind. Plus, Kezra knew from experience that unnoticed people like Shondra heard the most. People generally forgot to watch what they said around the help, and servants talked. Kezra hoped Shondra could help fill her in on palace gossip, anything useful when trying to find her footing in this unfamiliar territory.

Shondra edged closer to the bed, unsure. Patting the space next to her in invitation, Kezra waited with bated breath for Shondra to sit. Making up her mind, Shondra snagged the biscuit and settled on the bed, with one foot on the floor, allowing for an easy escape. The action brought to mind an animal in danger, sending a surge of anger through her. Even though the girl was young, she imagined the other nobles Shonra'd served had feigned kindness such as this for much more sinister reasons. Some of them may have even been tempted by the fact Shondra still held such girlish features. Imagining what she might have been through filled Kezra with white hot-rage, and the girl shied away from her, thinking Kezra's anger was directed at her. Kezra adjusted her position to shift away from Shonra and tried to cool her temper in order to make a more comfortable space. Shonra's relief was immediate.

"I promise I won't hurt you." Shondra's face wasn't completely trusting, but Kezra saw some of the tension release from the girl's shoulders. She let Shondra finish her treat in peace, then handed over another when it was gone. This time, the girl took it more readily, seeming at ease. "I was hoping for your help, though." In an instant, Shondra's guard went back up, and Kezra fought back a flinch, guilty for having caused it. Shondra's face smoothed over, emotionless, and her body went rigid. Already, Kezra regretted asking. She should have just let the girl eat in peace.

"What do you need?" Shondra asked, her tone devoid of any warmth.

"You don't have to do anything you don't want to, I swear. It's just, I'm new to all of this," Kezra said, gesturing around the room, hoping Shondra understood that she meant the court as a whole. "I could use a friend to fill me in on the gossip." Shondra still looked skeptical, but a smile snuck onto her face.

"That's all you want? Just a friend?" Shonda asked flatly.

"That's it. You don't have to do or tell me anything you don't wish to. Friends don't force each other to do things. But I'd be grateful to have someone on my side." Kezra watched as the girl warred with herself, weighing previous hurts against her desire for the offer to be real. Slowly, the smile settled on her face.

"If I'm your friend, can I keep eating your biscuits?"

"Well, I suppose friends share."

"Then we can be the best of friends," Shondra said, beaming. Kezra smiled back, but guilt nagged at her, wondering at the last time someone had offered Shondra true friendship.

It turned out Shondra could be an excellent friend and an even better gossip. She had started serving the nobles when she was twelve and had now been in her position for a little over two years. A select bunch of nobles lived at court, acting as advisors to the King. These returned to their lands only occasionally, usually to help oversee the harvest. The others were rarely invited to court and were mixed of two types: those who were vying for the King's favor and a more permanent position within his palace, and those who came and left as swiftly as possible. Kezra hoped to copy the latter bunch, wanting to get out of the palace as soon as possible. Regardless, Shondra had gossip about them all. Kezra learned who was in the King's favor, and which overly ambitious nobles hoped to present their daughters as marriage prospects, about the petty feuds and quarrels common among the upper class, and about those who had fallen from grace. Shondra also had access to the more lurid details, such as who was involved in long-standing affairs, which lord had a secret vice, and more practical details like who was likely to abuse the servants. Those ones Kezra made special note of, so she could visit them another time and show them the consequences of such abuse.

Unfortunately, Shondra didn't know much about Tylan's affiliation with the King. Evidently, he showed up once or twice a year, and when he did, the entire court was on edge, simultaneously trying to shun him but unable to stop competing for his attention. Tylan flaunted his magic, doing tricks and granting favors, stacking them for later use, but without the bond he inflicted on others. It made the court edgy, more prone to violence. Shondra seemed relieved he hadn't shown up, but sent Kezra in his place. Apparently, he also kept to himself, throwing out any servants sent to help him, and always requesting the same room, which he kept locked at all times.

As she went on, Kezra realized that she'd been listening for one name she hadn't mentioned at all.

"What about Sir Peter?" Kezra asked, trying to fight the blush heating her cheeks. Shondra was quiet. She bit her lip, looking confused. Kezra felt bad for interrupting her. Relaying gossip had been the most lively and animated Shondra had been. Kezra wondered if she had many friends in the palace, if she ever had the opportunity to talk this freely in her daily life. Now, the color had started to drain from her face, and she'd stopped talking altogether. "Oh no, do you not want to talk about him? Did he do something to you?" It was hard for Kezra to imagine the kind, affable man she'd met the night best hurting someone, but over the years, she'd learned that sometimes the ones who seemed the kindest could inflict the worst damage. Shondra shook her head quickly.

"No, nothing like that," she took a deep breath, and Kezra waited patiently for her to continue, "it's just that I've never heard of Sir Peter; there's no one at court by that name."

Chapter 10

Kezra

The answer hit her like a bucket of cold water being dumped over her head. Maybe, in her intoxicated state, Kezra had misremembered his name. She tried describing him,his soft brown curls, dazzling gray eyes, the tallest man in the room, his dimples when he smiled. Kezra kept going, recalling details that would stick out like his midnight blue tunic with the beautiful silver stitching or his boots with the oversized silver buckles. Surely Shondra had noticed him, but she only shook her head.

"I haven't seen or heard of anyone matching that description." It seemed impossible. She'd danced with him; he'd introduced her to other nobles, who had laughed with him, including him in their stories. How could it be that Shondra didn't know of him? "But I can ask around for you," Shondra said quickly, her mouth turned down in a tiny pout as tears formed in her eyes.

"It's fine, don't worry about it." Kezra forced a smile, giving the girl's hand a gentle squeeze. "Thank you, truly. You've been so helpful. I'd be lost without you." Her smile brightened again before she got up in a rush.

"Oh no! I need to go. I have much more to do and Alex will be cross I've spent so long here." Shondra glanced over at the discarded dress, then at Kezra, taking in her disheveled state. "I could spare a few more moments though," she said carefully, "if you need help getting ready."

"No, no. I can handle it. Go, I wouldn't want you to get in trouble on my account." Taking the empty tray and making her way to the exit, Shondra appeared to be holding back a rebuttal.

"I'll see what I can find out for you about Sir Peter."

"Thank you. I would appreciate it. You've been a good friend, Shondra." With that, she left, and Kezra was alone.

Officially alone, Kezra's mind started reeling with all she'd learned. Peter's reputation, or rather his lack of it, bothered her more than it probably should have. He'd acted as if he'd known his way around. The other nobles had been at ease with him, laughing at his jokes with an air of familiarity. It would have taken time to build up that kind of intimacy; after all, she'd experienced first-hand how unwelcoming court could be to newcomers. Or perhaps they just hadn't been welcoming to her. There was no way he could build that type of familiarity with people and remain unknown to the servants, but that mystery would need to wait a little while. Shondra had spoken at length about Tylan and how he was insistent about having this specific room to the point he refused to stay elsewhere. In fact, Shondra had even apologized, saying they would have prepared something grander for her had they known he wouldn't be attending himself, which meant there was something specific he needed access to. Yesterday hadn't provided much opportunity for exploration, so she intended to take advantage of any downtime the day offered.

First things first, Kezra needed to clean up. She scrubbed the smudged makeup from her face with cold water. The large tub in the bathroom called to her; Kezra would have loved a hot bath, but she didn't want to take the time. Kezra needed to move quickly, aware the king could summon her at any moment. Next came the decision about how to dress. Kezra had brought her normal black tunic and pants, which would be ideal for slinking about the shadows of the castle. But Shondra had also laid out a new dress; one the King likely expected her to wear. This one was simple but beautiful. The gown was all ivory with long, flowing sleeves and a scooped neckline. The dress would be tight through the bodice, then flare around the hips, the hem kissing the floor. Accompanying the gown was a simple belt of interlocking gold hoops that hung dramatically to the floor. Kezra couldn't imagine a worse garment for going unnoticed.

Reluctantly, she put her normal clothes away in favor of the dress. Although she certainly wouldn't fade into the background in it, Kezra reasoned that if anyone saw her creeping about the castle, they'd be far less suspicious of her dressed as an innocent maiden than as a spy, and she fully intended to use the helpless maiden act to her advantage. There would be plenty of time to sneak about more comfortably once everyone went to sleep. Kezra got dressed and ran her fingers through her hair, letting it hang loose in its natural dark waves. Unbidden, the image of Lennox's golden hair came to mind. Lennox was a lighter mirror of Kezra in so many ways: golden where she was onyx, eyes fresh spring green instead of dark, emerald pools, Lennox's skin a light ivory instead of Kezra's toffee coloring. Even in captivity, she had a lighter air compared to Kezra's stormy nature. It felt like Lennox represented what Kezra could have been, had the darkness of Helica not infected her for so long. She banished the fanciful thought' there was far more important work to accomplish today than daydreaming.

Dressed and ready for any unexpected visitors, Kezra decided to look around the room. If Tylan insisted upon having this room, there had to be a reason, the most likely one being a hidden escape somewhere in the room. A secret way to sneak around and spy on others was absolutely the sort of thing Tylan would insist on having access to. Pulling up rugs, Kezra began her search, looking for a trapdoor or an entrance to a tunnel. No such luck. She tapped on the bricks of the stone wall, looked behind the large tapestries adorning the walls; nothing. Kezra even crawled under the bed, looking for a hidden door, only to be rewarded with itchy red eyes and a very dusty dress, which she desperately tried to scrub clean. Kezra inspected herself in the full-length mirror, looking for any missed dirt, hoping it was at least clean enough to avoid suspicion. Her hair was a disheveled mess, and her eyes were still puffy and red, but hopefully she could pass that off as a result of too much fun the night before. While staring in the mirror, wondering how she could make her hair more presentable, she saw it: a paper-thin hinge, artfully crafted as a gilded mirror edge, shining in the light of the morning. If she hadn't been looking for such a thing, it would have blended right into the mirror, making it nearly impossible to see. Even though she'd been looking intently for something like this, Kezra still almost missed it.

She ran her fingers over the opposite edge of the mirror and gently pulled, praying the mirror didn't break. With a soft click, the mirror swung open to reveal a narrow, dark passage. It was low and cramped; she'd need to hunch to fit through it without hitting her head, and it was only about an arm's length wide. Although Kezra was confident she could fit through it, it was hard to imagine Tylan squeezing into such a small space. Intrigued, she resisted the temptation to crawl into the dark space to explore now, reason overpowering her curiosity. There was no way the king would leave a new guest unsupervised all day, and her disappearance would draw unwanted attention. Besides, Kezra had no idea where the passage led. It could drop her into an occupied room or a particularly busy corridor, leaving her stuck with the awkward task of explaining exactly how she'd gotten there. It would be better to wait until the castle's occupants were asleep to risk such a thing. Gently, Kezra shut the mirror with another quiet click.

Encouraged by the discovery, but deflated by the prospect of waiting to investigate; Kezra sat in one of the chairs near the fireplace, debating what to do next. It was too bad she hadn't thought to bring the priestess's book. There hadn't been much time to examine it since Lennox's arrival, and from the brief times she had looked at it, Kezra knew the language was one long dead. However, the royal palace also contained a royal library. Maybe there was a book in it that could help her translate, one no one would miss if it were to accompany her back to Helica. That seemed as good of a place to start as any. Kezra found the key to the room, determined to go find the library instead of waiting for the king's summons, when the plan was derailed as she walked straight into Alec. Luckily, he wasn't carrying anything, and their run-in seemed to stun him rather than cause any harm. Kezra scurried back, realizing she'd stomped on his foot in her haste, and nearly tripped again. She had exactly two friends in this castle, and she'd started the day out by trampling one of them.

"I'm so sorry," Kezra gushed, rushing to make sure Alec was alright. Alec straightened his jacket after the collision.

"Don't worry about it, Miss Kezra. May I ask where you're headed in such a rush?"

"I was on my way to look for the royal library. That's alright, isn't it?"

"Of course, you're free to roam the castle. Although I'm afraid you'll have to wait. I was actually on my way to collect you."

"What for?" Kezra asked wearily.

"The king has requested you join him for lunch. If you'll follow me, please."

"But I -" Alec put up a hand and stopped her.

"I'll have someone show you to the library later. Come, the king doesn't like to be kept waiting, and I'm afraid our little incident has us running behind."

Alex led her to a room far smaller than the feast hall everyone had gathered in last night. This setting was more intimate, but no less opulent. A table was set for eight people, with four teapots placed in the middle of the table between every two plates. The teapots, cups, and saucers were all made of matching teal-blue china. The table and chairs were hand-carved mahogany with edges gilded in gold. Chairs at the head and foot of the table had the head of a roaring lion carved into the back, inlaid with gold which sparked in its mane. Across from the table was an enormous window shaped like an arch, which started at the floor and went all the way up to the ceiling, taking up an entire wall. The window gave a view of the royal garden, which had a small stream running throughout the lush greenery. White marbled bridges crossed over the stream at different points along a grassy trail. Flowers of every variation and color bloomed along the sides of the path. Kezra imagined what it would feel like to walk along that path, feeling the sunshine on her face and the breeze blowing through her loose hair. The more she indulged in the fantasy, the more real it became, as if she could take a step forward and be there.

Kezra moved to take that step, picturing herself on the sunny lawn, when a cough came from behind her, shattering the fantasy. A chair scraped against the wood as Alex pulled out a seat. Embarrassed, Kezra moved away from the window with no memory of getting so close to it, and sat down. The other lunch guests filed in shortly after. None seemed as enchanted by the view as she had been. In fact, they all looked a bit bored. A man and woman entered together, arms linked. Their skin the color of toffee with raven black hair and amber eyes; they were clearly from the southern city of Versa. The city bordered the Barrens, and many of its inhabitants were descendants of the once great Asulan Kingdom that had ruled the lands. It was said to be the greatest of all nations, built by the most talented architects. It was the height of societal power, with the brightest scholars and the most talented craftsmen residing there. But the kingdom collapsed centuries ago, leaving only crumbling columns and barren lands in its wake. Now, nothing grew there, and the land was overrun by fearsome creatures. Any surviving residents had long ago fled to Versa.

A few faces Kezra recognized from the feast entered the room - an older gentleman in a pristine grey ensemble; a young, fair-haired man who looked how she felt upon waking up this morning; a lone woman, likely in her thirties, with long, intricately braided hair and a heavy, plain wool dress lined with fur. They were followed by an elderly woman with the same fair straw hair as the young, very hungover looking, man. She sat across from him and gave him a stern look, accompanied by a few cross words. He sat up a little straighter and made an attempt at smoothing his wrinkled tunic, but it did nothing to help the paleness of his complexion. Last, the King walked in, wearing a teal to match the china. His pants were a smoky grey color with matching boots. His twisted gold crown sat on his head, a reminder of his authority. Everyone stood as he entered; Kezra scrambled to follow suit.

"Thank you all for gathering at such short notice. As my most trusted members of council, we have much we need to discuss." The older woman glared at Kezra, making it clear that she was not included as one of the trusted members of the council.

"Are you sure we should be discussing such sensitive matters in this company?" The woman asked without taking her eyes off Kezra. Around the table, the others nodded in approval. The king cleared his throat.

"Lady Kezra is here representing Sir Tylan Faine. I trust he has filled her in on the situation and given her leave to speak on his behalf. We should treat her with the same respect we would afford him, had he deigned to join us." With that, the king took his seat. The room followed his lead. Kezra sat down, feeling dazed. Tylan had certainly not filled her in on anything, let alone given permission to speak for him. Despite the lingering headache, Kezra suddenly wished for something stronger than this tea.

Seated to her left was the king at the head of the table; the fair-haired lord sat to her right. The position seemed to be coveted based on the looks thrown her way by those further down the table. Tension hung in the air; Kezra felt the contempt and curiosity radiating through the room. She took a large drink of tea, racking her brain for something clever to say.

"So, Kezra, what can you tell us about the mysterious Tylan Faine?" The question came from the young man next to her, the only one who seemed oblivious to the tense atmosphere, his light-hearted tone so at odds with the environment. "I'm Quinn, by the way. Quinn Darlington."

"Yes, what can you tell us about Sir Faine? You must know him better than anyone else. We've never seen Sir Faine with a companion, let alone one he trusts enough to send in his place." An elderly woman who Kezra assumed to be Quinn's grandmother chimed into the conversation. Her inquiry seemed decidedly less friendly than her grandson's.

"I can't tell you much," Kezra replied honestly. "Tylan - err, Sir Faine,

I mean, doesn't share much with anyone. He told me I needed to come here on his behalf, and so here I am."

"I see," said the king, "then I presume you have some way to access his magic, or somehow have magic of your own, perhaps?" He asked softly, barely above a whisper, but the words rang out in the stillness of the room.

"No. As far as I'm aware, Tylan is the only person with access to magic, and before you ask, I've no idea where it comes from. I'm not sure why he sent me here, or what I'm supposed to do for any of you." Anger flashed across the King's face, but he smoothed it over quickly.

"Well, it seems Tylan is playing a bit of a joke on us, sending a little girl in his place. No matter. The grown-ups will discuss our plan, and you can relay the message back to your master," his voice dripped with venom, his previous speech about treating her with respect forgotten. Kezra was rarely afraid of anyone other than Tylan, but the king scared her now. "Now, to get this mess over with."

With that, the nobles lost all interest in her, continuing as if Kezra weren't there. She wanted to disappear, not that they would have noticed her lack of presence, anyway. The king had effectively dismissed her as an irrelevant inconvenience, and nothing more, so they discussed the situation amongst themselves, never looking for her input. Setting aside her embarrassment, Kezra listened intently while she sipped her steaming tea. The nobles didn't think she was a threat; which was just fine. That was how she could learn the most, and she would take advantage of the information later. From what she gathered, Oscana was struggling even more than she'd thought, which was saying something considering the number of desperate people flocking to Tylan for favors.

Oscana had relied heavily on the trade of lunasha blooms, their magical properties highly desired by all countries, but for whatever reason, those had disappeared along with magic years ago. Alongside this, the year had been dry, and crops were failing, leaving the river city Corlon, Oscana's center of trade, with no goods to export and starving citizens to feed. People had already started going hungry, and it looked like another poor harvest was ahead. As they starved, people grew desperate and resentful, resulting in a small outbreak of riots. Citizens whispered that the king was to blame for the disappearance of magic, that maybe things would be better if someone else took his place. And with the unrest, the neighboring kingdom of Nalathay was growing bolder, sending scouts further into Oscana's territory. Rumors had started that soldiers were lining Oscana's borders, waiting to strike. In short, the king and those who shared his power needed to find a way to protect themselves before Oscana was in full-blown rebellion.

It made Kezra wonder why Tylan stayed in the shadows. Those who dealt with him whispered his name in hushed conversations held in the dead of night, as if summoning a demon. His bonded tended to be only the most destitute, the most reckless. His name had turned into a horror story used to frighten children into obedience. The truth of his existence, of his magic, became so twisted that many assumed he wasn't real. Those who had called him knew better. Why would he not come out of seclusion, fix these problems, and let the people worship him as a god when he was the world's last remaining source of magic? Kezra wondered if he couldn't or if he just preferred his devilish reputation. Lost in her own thoughts, she didn't realize the conversations had ended until chairs began scraping across the floor as the king stood.

"We will reconvene tomorrow to formalize our commands for Sir Faine in writing, Kezra. You will deliver them, sealed, to your master. Understood?" Kezra nodded in reply, too caught off guard to respond.

"Good. After that, report back to the castle. I'd like you here while our plan is completed." He raised his eyebrows, waiting for a response.

"Yes, Your Majesty," Kezra said through gritted teeth, suddenly furious. She hated being ordered around by Tylan, but to have another man, even if he was the king, try to dictate her life, to take away her freedom, set her blood boiling. Kezra clenched her hands into fists, barely restraining her fury. Satisfied, the king left, and the nobles followed; only Quinn's grandmother lingered. She gave Kezra a long stare, but whether it contained suspicion or disappointment, Kezra couldn't say. It felt as though this lunch had been a test of some sort, and judging by her expression, Kezra had failed.

After the disastrous lunch, Alec took her straight to the library. Kezra fell in love the moment the doors opened. The room had two levels, both filled with shelves of books. It looked like the library was housed in one of the castle's circular towers, as the room was round. Shelves twisted around the open space, filled with every book imaginable. Another enormous window, reaching from the floor almost up to the ceiling, sat on the far wall, allowing sunlight to warm the room. Several comfortable-looking chairs and desks with reading lamps had been scattered throughout the large space. Roaring fireplaces adorned both levels of the library, keeping it cozy and warm.

However, her awe melted into a prickling panic. How could she possibly find what she was looking for in such a massive space? There must have been thousands of books. Alec had left her at the library's entrance, claiming he had other duties to attend. Now, Kezra wished she'd asked him to stay for a while longer. Kezra scanned the room for an attendant, but it looked like she was alone. In fact, now that she looked closer, it didn't appear as though anyone had cared for the library in some time. Cobwebs hung in the corners of the shelves; a thin layer of dust coated the books. Some chairs showed signs of wear and were moth eaten. Kezra felt a rush of appreciation for Alec, realizing he must have had the fires lit just for her.

Trying not to feel overwhelmed, Kezra decided to dive right in and search through the books in front of her, then make her way through the room shelf by shelf. She spent hours pulling books from shelves, climbing ladders, getting covered in dust, and had several run-ins with a couple of nasty looking spiders. In short, Kezra was tired, dirty, and exhausted, with very little to show for her efforts. So far she hadn't found anything in the odd language from the priestess's book. Slumping at the desk, Kezra put her head in her hands. This was hopeless. She could search through these books every day for a year and still wouldn't get through them all. She needed help, but couldn't ask Alec or Shondra for it. They had other tasks to do, and Kezra wouldn't risk either of them getting in trouble for her. She stayed there for a while, letting herself feel defeated, unable to get up and leave. Kezra didn't want to face the king or his nobles again, or admit that she had no idea what she was doing.

"Are you planning on hiding in here during tonight's dinner?" She recognized that voice, that teasing tone. Kezra looked up to see Peter standing across from her, smiling. He had dimples when he smiled; she hadn't noticed them last night, but certainly did now. "I wouldn't blame you. The books are better company."

"That's probably true. At least the books don't care if you show up in a filthy dress," Kezra said, wincing at the now grey-tinged dress. Ivory was not a suitable color for her on a normal day, let alone one spent searching through a forgotten library. She couldn't imagine how wild she looked right now. This was closer to her true self than the beautiful gown-wearing girl from last night. But for some reason, Kezra wanted

Peter to remember her as the glamorous girl, not like this. "To be fair, the dress was clean when I arrived."

"Ah yes, blaming the books. How rude when they can't defend themselves." Peter said. Kezra looked away, feeling a blush trying to creep onto her face. "Either way, you look lovely. The cobwebs in your hair suit you. In fact, if you showed up to dinner right now, I think it would become the new trend." Kezra rolled her eyes at him.

"Stop it, I'm a mess. But thank you for trying to make me feel better." Peter only shrugged.

"It's true, though. So what brought you to this forgotten corner of the castle?" With no one else to turn to, she told Peter about the book. Kezra described the worn leather cover, the curl of the writing, repeating what she could remember of the words that bonded Jasper to Althia's temple. The color drained from Pete's face. "The Book of Light," he whispered. "Where did you say you obtained this again?"

"In the market, outside of Altheia's temple. They were selling loads of them on the road leading to the temple," Kezra lied. Peter searched her face, looking for the lie as Kezra tried to keep her expression blank, hoping she wouldn't give anything away in her exhausted state.

"I suppose it's a copy then, but still..." he trailed off, lost in thought. "The Book Light is in the old language of the gods. It's been missing for decades. I'm surprised the publisher knew enough about it to get anything right." Skepticism slid into his voice, but she kept her face stilled.

"What's in the book?" Kezra asked, trying to sound as innocent as possible.

"Spells. Some very dangerous ones. It's not likely anyone would be able to use them now, and with the book missing for so long, I'd imagine the replica is mostly made up. Although the spell you just repeated is a very real bonding spell." Kezra perked up, trying not to seem too excited. Maybe she wouldn't need to find a book to translate after all. Peter seemed to know the language. Although she worried Peter would recognize the book as the original and not the replica she claimed. Deciding this was a worry for the future, Kezra pushed ahead, making the most of the situation.

"How do you know all this?" Kezra was practically bouncing with excitement now. "Can you read the language? Would you be able to translate the book?" Peter shook his head, although he thought before answering, choosing his words carefully.

"I've studied the gods quite a bit. I've always found them fascinating and could give you some history about them and their artifacts, but I wouldn't translate the book. Do you have it with you? I'd love to see it." All the excitement she'd been feeling fled in an instant.

"No. I didn't bring it to the castle. I just thought maybe I would recognize the language in one of these books and find a way to translate it."

"And then you'd steal the book?" Peter asked with a mischievous grin.

"And then I'd have borrowed a book. I would have returned it. Eventually."

"Do you know stealing from the king is considered treason? I didn't know you were such a criminal. Why are you so interested in this book, anyway?"

"Borrowing. Not stealing, so there would be no crime involved. This seemed like a better way to spend my evening than with a bunch of stuffy nobles."

"Well, I don't think you're going to find it tonight. Let's get you out of that dusty dress and ready for dinner."

"I'm not sure if I'm up for dinner tonight, actually. I'll be sending my regards in a note saying I'm not feeling well."

"At least let me walk you back to your room then. A gentleman wouldn't let you wander the castle alone. Who knows what could happen."

"Oh, so you're a gentleman now?" Kezra teased.

"Truly, Kezra, your wit's beginning to sting." He feigned a pout, but the warmth never left his eyes.

They chatted and joked all the way back to her room. Their banter flowed naturally, and Kezra enjoyed the feeling of being someone else for a moment. It was easy to pretend to be a normal woman, possibly being courted by a handsome man. This must be what normal life felt like. She was having such a wonderful time that Kezra forgot what Shondra had said about him until she was back in her room, alone. Kezra didn't know what she meant to ask Peter as she threw open the door and rushed back down the hallway in search of him. Maybe she would have invited him into her room for tea, and asked about where he came from, his family, if he's been to the castle before - anything to try to justify the fact that Shondra hadn't heard of him. Maybe another glimpse, a confirmation that her mind hadn't conjured him up in lonely situations, would have been enough. Peter had just left; he should still have been in the hall. But as she fled into the hallway, desperately searching for any trace of him, he was gone, as if he'd vanished into thin air.

Kezra went back to her room confused and upset, not needing to fake it when she told Shondra she felt unwell. Instead of helping her dress for another lavish dinner as intended, Shondra returned with a bit of soup and bread. Kezra felt a little guilty as Shondra lingered in the room, probably wishing to stay and talk. Instead, she took the soup and bread gratefully, asking for a bit of privacy to rest. Her encounter with Peter had left her feeling rattled, and Kezra needed a clear head for what came next. It was time to meet with Yelena.

She lay in bed for a while after Shondra left, just in case someone came to check on her. Having asked to be left undisturbed for the night, Kezra expected to be left alone. But while she trusted Shondra, Kezra wasn't sure one of the King's men wouldn't want to verify the story personally. When dinner should have been well underway, Kezra changed into her black trousers and tunic, happy to have them back. After ensuring the door was locked and retrieving her daggers from their hiding spot, she was ready to go. The mirror's hidden door opened easily, revealing the dark tunnel beyond. With a deep breath to gather her courage, Kezra set off.

The tunnel was pitch black and, without knowing exactly where it led, she wasn't willing to risk carrying one of the candles from her room. Trying to ignore the things that crawled up her arms, Kezra made her way through the dark, cramped space. A few times, the tunnel forked off, but in both instances, she could hear music or catch a glimmer of light which helped guide her. Kezra's goal was to get out of the castle, not to sneak around inside it, so she moved away from the light and delved further into the darkness. As she went, Kezra pushed down the growing concern for how she would manage to find her way back to the room.

Finally, Kezra felt a cool breeze blowing through the tunnel and saw a glimmer of dim light. As she got closer to the exit, she heard people laughing and talking excitedly. The tunnel dumped her right outside of the castle's walls on the outskirts of Tesmerin's market. Kezra felt her way along the walls, which were rough, scratchy. Poking her head cautiously out of the tunnel's opening, she gasped. Kezra was inside a very large tree. In front of her, a couple was laughing together, stealing a moment of seclusion in a secluded space under the moonlight. Further ahead, market stalls were illuminated by the moonlight. She crouched low, moving quietly to avoid the couple's detection. The tree she'd come out of was one of the many that sat along the castle walls. Kezra turned to examine it, expecting to see a clear hole, roughly the size of a person. Except when she looked, the tree appeared whole. If she hadn't just come through it, there would be no reason to suspect it was different than any other. Not quite believing her eyes, Kezra crept back up to the tree, feeling around in the general area she remembered the tunnel being. The more she thought about it and pictured the tunnel in her mind, the clearer the outline of the entrance became in the tree.

Kezra stepped back through the blurry entrance to the tunnel, the darkness enveloping her. The moment she crept back out, the entrance disappeared again. If she concentrated, the tunnels' outline reappeared, but it was never completely clear. A glamour. Kezra had heard of glamours, of course, the ability to use magic to disguise something, but she'd never actually seen one. Glamours were said to be a difficult magic, and while Tylan could do many things, she doubted that crafting a glamour this strong was possible for him. It must have been very old. Taking out her dagger, Kezra carved a discrete symbol into the base of the tree so she could find it again. Then, she headed for the market.

Madame Yelena's tent stood exactly where she remembered it being from their last encounter, even though she'd looked everywhere for the patchwork tent in the weeks following their first meeting with no luck. Kezra assumed Yelena had simply moved, but after her recent experience with a glamour, she wondered, or maybe hoped, there was more to the story. Standing in front of the tent's entrance, Kezra debated what to do next. She didn't want to barge in unannounced, but knocking on cloth was hardly an option.

"Are you going to keep standing out there all night, or will you come in?" Yelena yelled, making the decision for her. A little embarrassed, Kezra walked into the tent. Madame Yelena sat at the table again, gesturing for her to take a seat. "Have you threatened anyone else at knifepoint lately? Cut any throats since we've last seen each other?"

"No one who didn't deserve it," Kezra muttered, crossing her arms. "Well, I'm here."

"So you are," Yelena sighed, dropping her joking attitude. "Part of me had hoped you might stay away."

"But why? What's going on? Does it have to do with Tylan breaking my bond?"

"There is much to tell you and not enough time."

"Please, just tell me what you know," Kezra said through gritted teeth, becoming frustrated with Yelena's evasive manner.

"It is not what I know,child, but what I see. Magic hasn't completely vanished as people think. Small things are still possible, such as brewing a potion, casting a small spell, or glimpsing into the future. The days of grand magic have passed, and normally there's very little I can actually see when I read a person's future. Noble ladies are easily fooled, and it's better to tell them what they want to hear regardless of what little I see. But when I touch you, I see…more." She paused, as if deciding to go on.

"What do you see?" Kezra asked as she dropped into the chair across from Yelena, drawn into the show. In the back of her mind, she knew Yelena was putting on a performance, but against her better judgement, Kezra still wanted to believe.

"I see darkness surrounding you, a red haze tethering you, although I cannot say to what. Two figures reach for you, bathed in light, but their faces are hidden. Another figure searches for you in the darkness. Both sides call to you in equal measure. You are freed from your shackles, the haze dissipates, but I do not see what you do next. I don't know if you choose the light or if you're led into the darkness, only that you choose it willingly."

Kezra's heart stopped; she couldn't breathe. She wanted so badly to believe the fortune. Not the nonsense about the light and the darkness, but about being freed. The red haze that tethered her must have been Tylan and Helica; Kezra was shackled to him through their bond.

"Why did you ask me to come?" Yelena finally asked once Kezra grabbed ahold of herself. Again, Yelena paused, looking like she was having an internal debate. It didn't last long, but Kezra wondered if the woman was about to send her away.

"I think I can help you."

"How?"

"As I mentioned, magic isn't truly gone, just greatly weakened. I can't break your bond, that would be nearly impossible even with the strongest magic. I'm afraid something that strong can only be broken willingly by the two who entered into the agreement." Kezra's heart dropped. She knew it was a stretch, but still, after hearing the prophecy, her hopes had grown. "I can't break the bond for you," Yelena continued, "but I can give you something to dampen it."

"What do you mean?" The spark of hope reignited.

"There are potions and artifacts, things that still hold power even though magic has faded. I have come to possess a few of those items over the years, and I have something that will dampen your bond."

"Thank you," Kezra gushed. "Truly, you have no idea what this means -" Yelena held up a hand, silencing her.

"I have only 3 vials. They last only 1 moon each. This is not a permanent solution. You will need to find your own way to break it completely, and my help does not come free." The happiness fled. Kezra's hand darted toward the dagger hidden on her thigh. Of course Yelena's kindness was not given freely. Even now, Kezra could taste the blood that would be required for her services, for favors were always paid in blood.

"What do you ask in return?" Kezra's voice was cold, devoid of emotion. Lesser beings usually flinched under her gaze, but to her credit, Yelena showed no signs of backing down.

"My daughter, Shondra. She serves in the castle against her will and against mine. Circumstances prohibit me from getting her out. The path you're about to go down will cause great change, unsettling the kingdom. I only ask that you do your best to bring my daughter back to me, to keep her out of harm's way." A lump formed in Kezra's throat; whatever she had expected the request to be, this wasn't it.

"I swear I will get her back to you. You have my word."

Kezra took the vials, which were filled with a clear liquid that gave off a faint phosphorescent glow. Doubt crept into her mind looking at such a small amount of mundane liquid. What could this possibly do against the power she'd seen Tylan exert? It could be water for all she knew, tainted with something to make it glow. Yelena had no reason to trick her, at least none that Kezra could think of. But someone could have lied to Yelena about what was in the vials. There was no use worrying about it now. They would work or they would not, and Kezra would be right back to where she started. She shoved them into her tunic, next to her heart where Kezra knew they'd be safe.

"Thank you," Kezra said, turning to leave.

"There is something you should keep in mind. Those potions are old and may not be as potent as they once were. Once you drink one, you have enough to go for three months on your own, but it could be less. Use them wisely." Kezra thanked Yelena again, both for the potions and for the advice. She decided to wait to use the potions until she'd had a good night of sleep and a clear mind to plan her next move. Feeling more confident and hopeful than she had in a long time, maybe ever, Kezra made her way back to the glamoured tree, unable to believe her luck.

That's when she felt it, the sharp tug in the back of her mind, more powerful than ever before. Purple smoke clouded her vision. Unprepared for such a powerful tug on the bond, Kezra was unable to resist it. Instead of resting comfortably in her bed back at the palace, Kezra found herself sprawled on the hard floor of Tylan's lair. He looked surprised to see her.

"You're here," he said bluntly.

"Of course, my lord. You called."

"Where were you?"

"You sent me to Tesmerin?" The statement came out as a question, but she was puzzled by his question when he had sent her to a specific place. Tylan let out a low growl.

"I know where I sent you. But where in Tesmerin were you precisely? In the palace or the city?" Kezra briefly considered lying, but abandoned the thought after a moment of consideration.

"I was in the markets. I wanted to explore the city, and the King gave me leave to do so after today's meeting."

"You should have stayed in the castle," he muttered under his breath, but he didn't sound angry. "Did you hear anything, feel anything through your bond while you were in the castle?" She thought of the voice whispering to her in the king's presence, but Kezra still wasn't sure if she had imagined it after too much wine, so she didn't mention it.

"No, my lord. The bond was silent."

"The wards are still in place then." He was talking to himself more than her, pacing the floor. "Well, you're here now." He grinned widely. "The king won't be pleased you've gone missing. Tell me everything that happened. I want a full report."

"If I may, it's quite late. Perhaps I could give a better report in the morning?" It was a bold ask, but Kezra was exhausted and still reeling from the events of the day.

"You do look a little worse for wear," Tylan said, taking in her appearance. "Fine. Rest for now, but I expect you to recount every detail in the morning."

"Yes. Of course, My Lord. Thank you for your generosity." On her way back to my room, her heart beating so heavily she expected it to break the vials concealed against her breast. Kezra let out a sigh of relief, but it was short-lived. There wasn't much time to figure out her next move. Kezra didn't know what was going on, but she had a feeling something big, something dangerous was brewing and she needed to be gone before it exploded.

CHAPTER 11

Lennox

Hours after Lennox got back to bed, she could still feel it: the rush of soaring through the air. At first, she'd been terrified by the sight of the enormous, scaly beast making its way out of the red fog. The dragon watched her with its beady eyes, appraising its new meal. Her instincts screamed to run, but she remained frozen in fear, unable to move. Not that running would have helped anyway; most likely, the beast would have been upon her after a few seconds. She replayed the memory in her head, standing there with the remains of the duck fat dripping down her arm.

"Hold out your hand," Tylan had said.

"Why? Was the duck not enough?"

"Just trust me." Lennox didn't. But their time at the pool had shown her another side of Tylan. Besides, he possessed healing magic. Maybe if the dragon ate her arm, he could fix it, although she didn't think there would be anything he could do if the dragon swallowed her whole. Also, she didn't see any choice but to go along with whatever Tylan wanted. She held out her hand, palm facing up. Steam billowed from the dragon's nostrils. Her instinct was to yank her hand away in terror, but it was as if Tylan could read her thoughts.

"Just wait. Be steady." Exercising every fiber of restraint she possessed, Lennox kept her hand steady, outstretched to a beast that could swallow it in one bite. She shut her eyes, bracing for the impact of razor-sharp teeth cutting into her flesh.

Instead, cool, smooth scales rested gently on her fingertips. Lennox's eyes fluttered open to see the dragon's muzzle resting against her open hand. Vibrations rumbled through the dragon's body, bringing to mind a purring cat.

"I knew she'd like you," Tylan said, beaming.

"What if she hadn't?"

"She would have eaten you, of course. Which would have been a shame; we were just starting to make progress. Don't look at me like that. It all turned out fine, didn't it? Come on." Tylan grabbed her hand, guiding her toward the dragon's leathery wing. He placed a hand reverently on the dragon's side. A moment later, the dragon stretched out her wing, allowing it to act as a ramp for them to climb. Before Lennox had time to think about what they were doing, Tylan was pulling her up the outstretched wing onto the dragon's back. He seated himself in front of her and placed both hands on the dragon's hide.

"You're going to want to hold on." That was the only warning Lennox received before the dragon launched into the air. The scales were slick underneath her, sending her sliding back. Lennox let out an ear-splitting scream and wrapped her arms in a death grip around Tylan. He chuckled softly.

"I told you to hold on."

"You didn't specify what to hold on to. A little warning would have been nice."

"Relax, priestess. You wanted adventure, right? This is an adventure. How many people can say they've soared through the sky on a dragon's back?"

"Not many," Lennox admitted, begrudgingly.

"That's right, priestess. Enjoy the ride."

"I'm not really a priestess, you know." She felt Tylan's shoulders stiffen. "I probably never will be now." Lennox didn't expect a response, so the following silence didn't surprise her. Lennox let herself enjoy flying through the air, an experience she never would have gotten as a priestess, loathe as she was to admit it. With closed eyes, she savored the feeling of the wind on her face, blowing through her wild, loose hair. When she opened them, Tylan was looking back at her, smirking.

"Do you want to have some fun?" Lennox nodded. Tylan patted the dragon three times.

"Hold on tight," he called back, the wind stealing his words, making them barely audible. This time, she didn't hesitate. Lennox clung to him. The dragon banked right, hard, then started a magnificent series of twists and somersaults through the air. Lennox didn't know how Tylan stayed seated. Without him to hold on to, she surely would have fallen to her death. As they soared, Lennox let out a little whoop of joy. Whatever else had happened, whatever may come next, she knew this was a feeling she would cherish forever.

Eventually, the dragon landed. Light-headed and breathless, Lennox allowed Tylan to help her down. He bowed to the dragon before turning to leave, thanking her for the ride. He walked with Lennox back to her room in comfortable silence. They stopped just outside the door.

"Thank you for today. I never thought I'd see a dragon, let alone ride one. It was…incredible." Something shifted between them at that moment. Tylan almost seemed vulnerable, more human somehow, when he clasped her hand and looked directly into her eyes.

"It was my pleasure, Lennox. I haven't had a day like that in, well, a very long time." His hand lingered on hers as though reluctant to leave. "I'm sorry for the pain I've caused you. You're meant for greater things than to serve in someone else's temple." He bowed, abruptly letting go of her hand, before hurrying off to his own room. Left at her front door, Lennox stood with her hand hanging lamely at her side, pondering what had just happened.

Now, hours later, safely in bed, Lennox was still in awe of it all. Tylan had an actual dragon. She'd thought they were just a myth, a relic from a time long gone at the very least. And now, she had actually ridden one. A wave of sadness washed over her. It was times like these she missed Jasper the most. Jasper would have loved to hear all about the adventure, even while quietly begging Altheia for her forgiveness at Lennox's rash actions. They could have talked about Tylan and Lennox's tangled thoughts toward him. He'd caused her too much pain for her to like him exactly, but today he'd shown a different side of himself. Behind his cold, emotionless mask was a vulnerable, funny person who wanted to be kind. Lennox hoped that with more time, she could dig that person out of him. She smiled at the thought; maybe he would give Kezra the freedom she desired.. And just maybe, he'd let Lennox go back to the temple.

The temple - thinking of it brought back his parting words. What possible "greater things" could he be referring to? Her mind played through the possibilities as she drifted to sleep. Perhaps he meant nothing by it. Perhaps he was just trying to make her feel better about the current situation. Lennox drifted to sleep, pondering the words as they played through her head. She awoke to a hand over her mouth.

"Don't scream," said a familiar, husky voice. Telling her not to scream didn't help calm Lennox's nerves, and one almost erupted from her throat against her will.

"Kezra? When did you get back? What's going on?"

"You need to get dressed. We're leaving."

"What do you mean we're leaving? To go where?"

"Lennox, we don't have time for this right now. I'll explain later, but now I need you to get dressed. Hurry, we need to go before one of the bonded comes and sees me here." Lennox started to put on the black pants and tunic Kezra had thrown her direction.

"Here, take these." Kezra handed her a pair of leather boots. Bleary-eyed and still confused, Lennox struggled to put them on. They were made for travelling, making her wonder once again where they were going. Lacing the boots as quickly as she could in the darkness, Lennox watched as Kezra paced frantically across the floor. Kezra's eyes darted to the corner of the room, searching for people who weren't there. The Kezra while toward Lennox.

"Show me your arms."

"My arms? Why?" She didn't wait for Lennox to listen, but yanked Lennox's uncovered arms toward her, examining them. She let out a sigh, apparently satisfied with what she saw.

"He didn't bond you?"

"I don't know what that means."

"The servants, they're all bonded to Tylan. They request use of his magic and in return, he bonds them." She pulled up the sleeve of her jacket to show a black tattoo around her forearm.

"The bond leaves a mark, like this," she explained. "If you had one, it could complicate things."

"Then how can you leave now? Is the bond broken," Lennox asked.

"No, I have another way. Like I said, I'll explain later. We need to go. Now. Are you ready?" Lennox looked around the room once more, surprisingly sad to leave it for the unknown. It had started to feel a little homey.

"Do you have another cloak?" Lennox asked.

"Yeah, here." Kezra handed over one identical to the one she wore. Long and black as night, perfect for hiding in the shadows. Kezra grabbed her hand. "Come on, let's go."

"Wait, what about my robes?" Lennox asked, remembering them shoved into the back of the cabinet.

"Leave them. They won't fit into my pack and carrying them will just slow us down." She thought about protesting more, but Lennox decided she could get new robes at the temple now that they were leaving. She grinned stupidly, realizing this meant she could get back to the temple. Lennox couldn't wait to see Jasper again and tell her everything.

"Alright, let's go." Kezra pulled a vial out of her tunic. It appeared to hold a smoky purple substance. She grabbed Lennox's hand, holding it tight. "Whatever you do, don't let go, okay?" Lennox gripped her hand in response, having learned her lesson from nearly falling off a dragon earlier. Kezra pulled the cork off the vial and tilted it back, inhaling the smoke as it curled around her lips. For the second time, purple smoke clouded Lennox's vision; it clogged her nose and throat as it ripped her from the room and unceremoniously tossed her somewhere new. Lennox landed on soft grass, startled by the abrupt departure.

"Where are we?"

"The markets of Tesmerin," Kezra answered.

"Why? Wait -" A revelation dawned on her, "do you mean to tell me you could have gotten us out of there this whole time?"

"Yes. Well no. Sort of. It's complicated."

"Explain, please." Lennox tried to keep her voice level, but she could hear the anger seeping through. Evidently, Kezra did too because she winced at the tone.

"Technically, yes. I always have access to that particular potion. It's the most efficient way for me to travel on Tylan's behalf." Lennox reared up to yell at her, but Kezra held out a hand. Lennox waited for her to continue. "But, Tylan only let me access it because of our bond, which makes it impossible for me to run from him."

"You should have still gotten me out," Lennox muttered.

"What good would that have done? He would have made me hunt you down and bring you back again - that's if he didn't kill me outright for disobedience and bring you back himself." She had a point, but Lennox wasn't completely willing to let go of her anger yet.

"Well, what's changed now? Did you break the bond or something?" Lennox asked, pointedly staring at the spot where Kezra's arm was marked with one of those awful black bands.

"Yes, or something." Kezra hesitated, debating on sharing the "or something". She must have decided there wasn't a risk in trusting Lennox with the information, because she pulled out another vial, filled with a thick, clear liquid that gave off a subtle glow. Kezra cradled the vial with all the care of a mother holding her newborn baby. "This is supposed to dull the bond so that he can't use it. It won't break it, but I shouldn't be able to feel it either - at least, I don't think I will. It won't last forever, but it should give me time to find a more permanent solution."

"What do you mean you think?"

"Well, I haven't actually tried it yet. And just like that, the anger came flooding back.

"So you risked dragging us out here for something that might not even work?" Lennox was yelling at this point, but she didn't care. This was stupid, dangerous even.

"I can get us back if I need to," Kezra said defensively. "I'm not sure if Tylan will be able to feel it once I take the potion, so I wanted to put some distance between us before I took it and if I'd left without you, I wasn't sure if it would be safe for either of us if I went back for you after taking this..." She sighed. "I'm not sure I would have been able to go back there for you," Kezra said more quietly. She hung her head as she said it, unable to meet Lennox's eyes. The anger Lennox had been holding onto fled.

"You got me out, and that's all that matters now." She didn't know much about this girl, but Lennox couldn't imagine what kind of life she led working for Tylan. It must have taken an act of courage for Kezra to come back for her at all, and Lennox was grateful. "Well, what are you waiting for? Let's see if this mystery potion works and get out of here."

"I'm scared," Kezra whispered. "What if it doesn't work? I've wanted this for so long, and while I wait, there's still hope. I'm too scared to shatter what little hope I feel."

"I'm right here if it doesn't. Then we'll go back, and I'll help you find another way. We'll be in it together at least. Apparently I have magic; maybe we can find a way to put it to use and make Tylan regret showing me how to use it." It was a bolder claim that Lennox was used to making, but it was worth it when a ghost of a smile graced Kezra's lips.

"Let's get this over with," Kezra said as she popped the cork off the vial and gulped down the potion. When it was done, she sat very still, waiting for something.

"What does the bond feel like?"

"It's hard to describe. It's like Tylan is always there, in the back of my mind, as if some invisible cord is connecting us. Sometimes it gets tight and I feel a tug on my brain, pulling me away. Then I end up back with him; no matter how far the distance, he can always summon me back in an instant. It's why he has no problem giving me the travelling potions. He knows I can't escape him." Lennox had about a million questions, but she fought to keep them back, assuming Kezra wouldn't appreciate them right now.

"What about now? Do you feel any…different?" In response, Kezra closed her eyes, her face lined in concentration.

"It's so quiet," Kezra said finally.

"What do you mean?"

"The bond has always been there, as long as I can remember. I didn't realize how loud the constant hum of magic was, how much pressure I felt from his presence in my mind. Now it's silent. There's only me."

"And that's a good thing, right? It worked?" Lennox asked. Kezra shot up from the ground and gave a little whoop.

"It worked! It really worked. I'm free. We're free!" Kezra pumped her fist into the air as she beamed. Her antics were drawing glances from some of the people still out, and Lennox realized then that it must be quite late. The onlookers were scowling at the noise, but Kezra didn't pay them any attention.

"So what's the plan now?" Lennox asked, hoping there was one.

"Now, we find somewhere to sleep for tonight. We can figure out the rest tomorrow." With Kezra in the lead, they walked through the quieting market with confidence. Many shops had shut down for the night, but a few remained open, and Lennox gazed at them in wonder. Tesmerin's market district wasn't far from the temple. In fact, many villagers who came to the market often made the trek up the steep hill to pay tribute to the goddess at Altheia's temple. However, as an acolyte, she'd been forbidden from venturing down the hill and into the markets herself. It may as well have been a whole new world down here. At night, the markets would be a shadow of what they were during the day, but even still Lennox was in awe.

People shuffled between stalls, packing up for the night. A man sold fragrant pastries to a couple and Lennox's mouth watered in response, even though she wasn't hungry. Men filtered in and out of the inns scattered throughout the district, giving odd looks to the pair as they wandered the streets. Kezra glanced back at her, taking in Lennox's unbound golden hair.

"Pull up your hood and push your hair back into it," Kezra said, doing the same. They attracted far less attention with their hoods drawn, although it was still more than Lennox would have liked. The eyes of men were a physical presence as they roved over her cloak, perhaps evaluating the worth of what she carried, or thinking far darker thoughts. Both were tall for women, and in the dark, with their hoods drawn, they might pass as men at a glance. Even so, the look of the men still roaming around this time of night made Lennox nervous; a confrontation with them likely wouldn't end well.

"How much further?" Lennox hissed.

"There's an inn just up ahead that should take us without asking too many questions." She had no choice but to trust Kezra and hope that they made it there without incident.

After a few more minutes, they arrived at the inn, The Broken Crown. The sign was old and hanging at an odd angle, but the building itself looked stable enough. Although it was older and less pristine than some of those they'd passed along the way, Lennox was just grateful to be off the streets. They walked inside, an opening dining area greeting them. Rows of long tables sat mostly empty, save for the few groups of men still drinking and gambling. It appeared to be winding down for the evening and Lennox was both relieved and disappointed not to be in a raucous crowd of people. A woman with a broad build and round face greeted them near the entrance. Lennox's jaw dropped against her volition.

She'd never believed in giants, but if anything could change her mind, it was the woman in front of her, standing at least seven feet tall with thick legs and a broad, ample chest. Her light brown hair curled in wild directions around her face. She wore a simple day dress with an apron tied at the waist, embroidered with tiny, lifelike hummingbirds in vibrant colors. Lennox was simultaneously fascinated and intimidated by her. She turned her gaze to Lennox.

"Close your mouth before you catch a fly," the woman said. Lennox's jaw snapped shut.

"Hello, Greta," Kezra smiled up at the giantess.

"Oh, it's you. What do you want? Did Aiden get himself into trouble again? I swear that boy, I'll wring his neck." Greta craned her neck, looking around the room for the aforementioned Aiden, but Kezra stopped her.

"No, nothing like that. I'm cutting ties with my previous associate. My friend and I find ourselves in need of rooms for the night. Would you be able to help with that?" Greta nodded, looking relieved.

"I can't say I'm not surprised, but I'm glad to see you out on your own. I always knew you were a good girl. Only one room's available.

We're filling up with the festival around the corner, but you're welcome to it. Here, you and your friend have a beer while Aiden gets it ready."

Greta handed them each a pint of watery looking beer and instructed them to sit at a table in the corner of the tavern where they wouldn't garner too much attention. Lennox took an experimental sip and fought to get it down. The few times she'd had alcohol, it had been the mild, sweet wine from the temple stores. The beer was not similar. It reminded her of bread left out in the sun all day, overwhelmingly yeasty and a bit stale, yet somehow, watery as well. Kezra watched her, and from the amused look she gave, Lennox could only imagine the face she'd pulled.

"There's no beer in that temple of yours, eh priestess?"

"There is not. A glass of wine might be better instead," Lennox said, pushing the beer away. Kezra gave a dramatic eye roll.

"You're not likely to find that here. Come on, drink up. You get used to the taste after a while." Lennox doubted that, but obediently took another small sip so as not to appear rude to their host. Her nose wrinkled in distaste. Kezra watched with eyebrows raised as she took a healthy drink, but didn't say anything else.

"So what's next?" Lennox asked. Kezra just shrugged.

"I've been thinking of trying Kitsummit." Sipping her beer, Lennox contemplated our situation. She wouldn't ever tell Kezra, but the beer really was getting better. In theory, Kitsummit was the closest large city to Tesmerin. However, it was deep in the heart of the mountains. People rarely went up the mountain path. Instead, traders brought things from the nearest port town, Alara, into the markets selling thick, expensive furs, winter berries and salted fish from the mountain streams. Boats loaded back up with preserved fruits, vegetables, breads and spices and took them back to Alara for the people of Kitsummit to collect. The people of Kitsummit were reclusive, and few had ever seen them at all, creating rumor and mystery about what exactly happened in the mountains. So they never visited the temple to pay tribute to Altheia. The Mother had tried sending priestesses there in the past, but they'd all come back dejected, complaining they'd been unable to make it up the mountain at all. Some said the people of Kitsummit still worshiped the old gods, and had no need for beings like Altheia or Niveran who had walked among us for so long. So, while Kitsummit was technically close, it was hard to get to, and I wasn't sure how welcoming the people would be to outsiders if they could make it there at all.

"Why, what's in Kitsummit?" Lennox asked. Kezra responded with a shrug, taking a long drink from her cup.

"The potion is temporary. I need to find a more permanent solution. People say that the villagers in Kitsummit still practice the old magic, that it's been given to them by the old gods. I've also never seen anyone from the mountains bond to Tylan. Maybe they know something that can help me. It's worth a shot at least."

Lennox nodded along, drinking as Kezra talked, then noticed that at some point, she had finished the entire mug. A pleasant warmth was spreading from her stomach through her body. She was starting to see the appeal of this drink.

"Why not use your potion to magic us to Kitsummit?" Lennox said this a little more loudly than intended and drew some sideways glances from a few of the gamblers. Luckily, their own conversations were loud enough they hadn't heard what she said, but were likely more interested in the pitch of her voice. Kezra shushed her and waited until everyone was soundly engrossed in their conversations before continuing.

"You need to be more mindful of your surroundings," Kezra scolded. "As for the potion, it doesn't work that way. I have to be able to visualize a place to go there. I've never been to Kitsummit, so the potion can't take me there. Maybe one it could have, before magic was weakened. But now, it's not strong enough."

Lennox wondered faintly if she could do it, if her weak magic could somehow help fuel the potion to make it stronger. But she kept her mouth shut. Now that she was free, her goal was to return to the temple tomorrow, and she didn't want to give Kezra any reason to stop her. Clearly, whatever she'd drunk to suppress the bond had worked; she wouldn't need anything from Lennox. More questions burned on her tongue. Before Lennox could ask them though, a scrawny, curly haired teenager stood in front of them.

"Your room is ready, Miss Kezra."

"Thank you, Aiden. It's nice to see you again."

"You as well, Miss Kezra," he said. He couldn't meet her eyes and instead stared resolutely at his feet. Kezra took a key from him and moved to get up.

"Staying out of trouble, are you?"

"Yes, Miss." His cheeks and neck flushed to a deep red.

"Good, we wouldn't want to worry your Mother." The boy muttered a response. Kezra stood, waiting for something.

"Right, will you show us to our room then?"

"Oh, right. Yeah, if you'll follow me then."

Aidan led them up a winding staircase until they reached the top, then down a cramped hallway, forcing them to duck as they went. Lennox couldn't imagine the giantess, Greta, even attempting to walk through. The hall contained a single door, which Aiden promptly handed Kezra a key to before scurrying away without another word. Kezra unlocked the door and Lennox promptly followed her into the room. Two beds sat shoved against the wall. A small window hung on the opposite wall, giving us a glimpse at the darkened streets of Tesmerin below. Under the window sat a small desk with two lit candles. After growing accustomed to the magic orbs of light she'd had at Tylan's the candle light seemed dim, disappointing. Kezra threw her bag on the desk and looked out the window with a smirk.

"Oh, Greta, she really gets me," she said. Lennox wandered over to the window to see what Kezra was talking about, but didn't see anything remarkable. In fact, their view, if one could call it that, was largely obstructed by rooftops, blocking the streets below.

"She knows you love rooftops?" Lennox asked, confused. Kezra snickered at her.

"Yes. Look at the size of this window. It's small, but we could fit through if we needed to. If you look down, you can see it's a short drop to the landing. If, for some reason,we needed to make a quick escape, we could shimmy out the window and be gone. She also made sure to give us a window that locks." Kezra jangled the keys in front of her. "It would be hard for someone to break in, there are no grips unless the window's open and you can snag the ledge, but we can get out. Greta gets me."

Lennox eyed the window skeptically. Maybe she could probably squeeze through it if needed; however she lacked Kezra's athleticism and grace. Escape across rooftops seemed like more of a death sentence to her, but Lennox kept the thought to herself.

Kezra left the window and claimed the bed closest to the door by loudly throwing herself on it. Not seeing an attached bathroom, Lennox carefully undressed, trying not to draw attention to herself. Thinking Kezra had already fallen asleep, she blew out the candles and climbed into bed. Her eyes heavy and her body limp from the beer, making the bed feel heavenly. Lennox closed her eyes, wavering between the waking world and sleep. They hadn't discussed a plan yet, but surely she would go back to the temple tomorrow. It was just up the hill after all. As excited as she was to see Jasper and to rejoin her old life, Lennox felt a pang of loss at leaving this behind. Not the inn, but Kezra, the adventures she would have, ones a part of Lennox's heart longed to be a part of. No, Lennox told herself firmly, she belonged in the temple and that's where she would go first thing tomorrow. Lennox was nearly asleep when she heard Kezra's whisper.

"Lennox. Psst. Lennox, are you asleep?"

"Mmm," Lennox groaned in response. Kezra giggled. The sound was light and airy, like chiming bells. She wouldn't have imagined such a sound could come from Kezra.

"I just wanted to say thanks, for sticking by me after we escaped. You could have run before I took the potion, but you..." Kezra trailed off. "Anyways, just thanks. It's nice to have you." She rolled over without another word and seemed to fall immediately to sleep. Lennox tossed and turned all night, her sleep plagued by wild dreams. She saw mountains, felt the cold of the snow as it landed on her cheek, there was a bright, blinding light, a woman with wild hair and golden eyes, a black shape hovering above the clouds, watching them. Lennox woke covered in sweat and unable to shake the feeling of that dark presence, watching her every move.

Chapter 12

Lennox

Golden light streamed in through the window, giving the room a comfortable glow. Lennox stretched out lazily in the bed, enjoying a day without the temple's constant rush or the plague of anxiety present in Tylan's castle. She spared a glance at Kezra's bed, half expecting to see her sprawled out and snoring. However, the bed, though in a tangle of sheets and bedding, was empty. Before Lennox had time to get herself out of bed and fully wake up, Kezra burst into the room carrying two steaming mugs. Kezra handed her one without comment, which Lennox accepted gratefully, letting the rising steam swirl under her face, inhaling the smell before taking a sip, basking in the smell of rich spices like ginger and cinnamon emanating from the mug. She glanced up at Kezra to see her smirking, looking amused.

"Is this the type of discipline they teach you in the temple?" Kezra asked, her tone light, joking.

"I've never been good at following the pillar of discipline." Lennox threw her head back into the pillow, unwilling to give up the comfort of the bed for the brisk morning air yet.

"Lennox..." Kezra started, but trailed off. Lennox peered back at her, raising her head slightly to look at her savior. Kezra was biting her lip, tapping her fingers in a rhythm on her mug. In their limited time together, Lennox hadn't seen her so uncomfortable. Honestly, it was unsettling. Kezra was always so confident, so self-assured that her nervousness put Lennox on edge.

"What is it?"

"It's about the temple." Kezra started, haltingly, as if searching for the words and unable to find them. Sipping on her tea, Lennox waited in the uneasy quiet for Kezra to finish the thought, "It's just, do you really want to go back?"

"What do you mean, do I want to go back? My whole life's there, of course I want to go back." But even as Lennox shouted the words, they rang false to her ears. Her voice sounded too loud, too forceful, like she was trying to convince herself. Kezra must have heard the traitorous tone, giving away the lie.

"I just mean, we've started something, maybe we need to finish it together. I know that sounds silly, but I can't get rid of the feeling that you're supposed to be with me. When I think about going on my own, I get this sense of doom. Don't you feel it too?" Lennox considered lying, telling Kezra that she had no idea what she meant, but in truth, Lennox felt it too. Every time they were together, there was an energy shift in the air, like something was beginning. And if she was being honest with herself, she also wanted to explore her newfound magic more, and she wouldn't be able to do that as a priestess. Magic was reserved for the gods, The Mother would simply die if she saw Lennox using it.

"I won't deny it. But I can't go with you. My life is at the temple. I've been training to be a priestess since I was a child. If I don't go, if I don't finish this, then who am I?"

"Whoever you want to be," Kezra said. She rushed over, gripping Lennox's free hand with her own. "You can make your own future instead of settling for the one laid out for you. Come with me, Lennox."

"To where, Kitsummit?"

"For a start, yes. But then, who knows? We won't be attached to anyone or anything. We can go wherever we want."

"But I am attached to someone; what about Jasper? We're like sisters. I can't leave her. I won't."

"Lennox, you have to know you can't stay there," Kezra said in a whisper.

"What do you mean?"

"Tylan will realize we're gone anytime now. In fact, he could be searching for us already. Where do you think he's going to start? He'll come for you, and he won't let you go." Lennox's heart sank into her stomach as her eyes filled with tears. She didn't bother to hold them back this time, knowing that Kezra was right. Going back would not only be pointless but potentially dangerous.

"I guess you're right," Lennox said reluctantly. "I'll come to Kitsummit with you, but I won't leave without at least saying goodbye to Jasper." Kezra grimaced.

"Going back to the temple at all is a mistake. As I said, Tylan could already be looking for us."

"I won't go without seeing Jasper one more time. I won't abandon her," Lennox said, steeling herself for a fight. They glared at each other, battling wills, neither one willing to look away first. The stale air burned Lennox's open eyes. They watered under the strain, but Lennox refused to blink it away. Eventually, Kezra looked away first, turning to look out the tiny window down, glimpsing the slice of sunlit street.

"Fine. We will go to her tonight and you can say your goodbyes. You'll need to be quick though. We can't stay here long. Wait here today while I get us some supplies for our journey. We'll go up to the temple when I get back, then head straight to the docks."

Lennox nodded in agreement, afraid to speak in case Kezra changed her mind. Unwilling to push her luck, Lennox bit her tongue about accompanying Kezra into the city, even though she was desperate to go. Besides, she wouldn't have been much help. Lennox was completely inexperienced in the art of haggling down prices, and had no idea where to go to find the best supplies. She'd be no better than a child, and she didn't want Kezra to look down on her for getting in the way. Kezra seemed to calm down now that they'd agreed. Any remaining tension released from her shoulders, and the crease along her brow smoothed out.

"I'll be back in a few hours then. Stay here, Lennox. I mean it. You don't know who we can trust out there. Tylan has many bonded, and he's certainly noticed we're missing by now. It's best to stay out of sight." Lennox rolled her eyes, bored by the lecture. If she was going to stay behind while Kezra gallivanted around the market, she didn't need a speech about remaining hidden on top of it; Lennox wasn't an idiot.

"I know, I know. I'll stay here."

"Promise?" Kezra asked. The intensity of her glare would have been enough to send people running in fright, but after so many years enduring The Mother's withering looks, Lennox failed to find it intimidating. Instead, she sighed and threw herself down onto the bed, committing to the drama.

"Yes, I promise. Now go. I'll be fine here, out of sight, out of mind and out from under your feet like the good priestess I was trained to be." Kezra chuckled at the biting tone, but she walked out of the door.

The quiet felt oppressive now that Lennox was alone, leaving a gnawing anxiety growing in her stomach. Not only was she abandoning Jasper, but Lennox would be useless, unable to even do something as simple as accompany Kezra for supplies. The thought made her both furious and unbearably sad. Pushing the thought aside, Lennox tried to enjoy her morning as the sunlight streaming in through the tiny window warmed her face. But in the absence of anything to do, her mind kept wandering back to Jasper. She kept picturing the look of hurt etched on Jasper's face the night before the blessing. How would she react when she learned Lennox was leaving for good? Lennox wished Jasper could come with them, but she'd be bound to the temple after completing the blessing.

Thinking back to the pool with Tylan, Lennox wondered if maybe there was a way. Sitting up, she held up her hands, palms facing upward just as they had that day. She kept her eyes squeezed shut, searching for the quiet beat of magic thrumming through her veins. Maybe the magic could break Jasper's bond. Just maybe, the power Lennox held would be enough to bring her sister with them. There, if she concentrated, Lennox thought she could feel it, the tiny pulse beating alongside her heart. Giving the magic a tug, Lennox willed it to move down her arm and through her fingertips, mentally shaping it into a ball of light. She opened her eyes, already grinning with the knowledge that a ball of light awaited her. But when she glanced down, there was nothing. Not even a flicker of that silvery light.

The disappointment crushed her. Suddenly, Lennox felt so alone in this brightly lit room. The sunlight streaming in no longer lent a warm, comfortable feeling she'd been basking in just a moment ago; instead, it felt like a mockery. How could the world outside be so normal when she felt such turmoil inside? Lennox tried to reason through it. Maybe the magic had worked and she simply couldn't see it. The soft, silvery glow would be almost impossible to see when the sun was shining so brightly.

Yes, that must have been the case. Lennox flew out of bed to shut the curtains and tried again. She poured her heart into conjuring the light, but still, nothing happened. In the darkness she tried again and again to conjure any hint of the magic she'd used before. Still, nothing. Lennox threw her hands up, exasperated and angry. If she couldn't conjure a simple ball of light, how could she possibly free Jasper? It felt so impossible. Lennox couldn't stay, but she couldn't bring Jasper with her, and yet leaving her again was impossible. What was she supposed to do?

A loud rumble drew her out of her thoughts. Lennox's stomach made another ungodly growl, making her realize she hadn't eaten yet today. Opening the curtains. Lennox saw that the sun had travelled across the sky, driving away the morning and giving way to the afternoon. She must have been practicing for hours. The thought brought another wave of disappointment for how much energy she'd wasted without a result. Lennox stared out of the window, contemplating her next move. Kezra hadn't given an indication of when she would return, and Lennox had no desire to upset her, but there wasn't anything to eat in the room. She could venture out in search of food, but Kezra might be upset to come back and find the room abandoned. But her stomach rumbled again, making up Lennox's mind for her. She pulled on her borrowed clothes and threw her hair into a messy braid, resolved to go downstairs and beg for something to eat. After all, Lennox reasoned, she'd told Kezra she wouldn't leave, but had never specified if that meant the room or the building. Surely she couldn't be mad if Lennox at least stayed in the tavern and ate that delicious smelling stew she'd spied last night.

Going downstairs was like entering a new world. At midday, the tavern was bustling with people looking for their afternoon meal. A server wove between tables, skillfully setting down cups and bowls while avoiding any overly friendly men. Groups of people sat together laughing and chatting as they enjoyed bowls of stew and bread. Lennox found herself frozen on the staircase, taking in the scene. It was so unlike meals in the temple with the acolyte's subdued chatter, always making sure they were paying reverence in the home of the goddess. She felt a pang in her chest. Jasper would love this; she should have been here to enjoy this openly joyous atmosphere. Lennox could practically hear her gushing over the food, and see her slotting herself into one of these conversations as if she belonged, asking any of these strangers where they were from.

"Are you planning on standing there all day blocking the staircase, or would you like something?" Her head whipped around toward the voice. The woman from last night stood next to her, and Lennox racked her brain for the woman's name, coming up empty. "Well, come on, girl. Quit standing there with your mouth open. You're spooking the customers." With a snap, Lennox shut her mouth as she followed the giantess to a small table in the corner. As she walked, Lennox felt eyes following her, and noticed that the conversations in the room had hushed. It seemed her staring had indeed made them uncomfortable. Once she settled in, they hesitantly turned their attention back to their own meals, picking their conversations back up. The woman left her without another word, only to return moments later with a bowl of piping hot stew, a hunk of bread, and a pint of beer. Her name suddenly popped into Lennox's mind - Greta. Greta sat down in the chair across from her, somehow graceful despite her size.

"Does Miss Kezra know you're down here?"

"Not exactly. She told me not to leave, and I didn't." Lennox's tone picked up an edge of defiance as she spoke and her cheeks flushed with embarrassment at Greta's question. Why should she defend her choice not to sit in that room and starve, waiting like a dog for her master's return? "I don't see how she can be upset at me for eating. Besides, Kezra doesn't control me." Greta smirked at the cool tone, neither threatened nor offended by it.

"No, I don't suppose she can. I don't know what the pair of you are running from, and I don't want to. Goddess help you both if you've betrayed that master of hers. I'm just here to warn you not to draw attention to yourself. You never know who could be watching, especially in a place like this."

Greta got up from the table, about to leave. Lennox wanted to reach out to beg her to stay. She wasn't used to being alone, and the separation from Kezra was becoming more unsettling the longer she was gone. Greta turned to look back at her. "Eat up. I'll bring you another bowl once you've finished. You're too scrawny for whatever Kezra has planned." Lennox shook her head in protest, becoming acutely aware that she had no money to pay for one meal, let alone two. "On the house, of course. I won't have it being said that Greta doesn't repay her debts."

Lennox wolfed down the bowl of stew and the hunk of bread, not tasting anything. The severity of her hunger was a surprise, but then she remembered how little she'd eaten since her feast with Tylan had been interrupted. And with how exhausted she felt each time Tylan had forced magic out of her, the hunger made sense. The serving girl brought over another bowl of stew and two more pieces of crusty bread, as promised. She ate those more slowly this time, savoring the richness of the stew. Now that her hunger was moderately satisfied, Lennox's thoughts drifted back to Tylan. Caught up in the chaos of their escape, she hadn't given him much thought. Kezra was right; he must have noticed their departure by now. Lennox wondered if he was out there, searching for them; if he had spies doing it for him. What if one was here right now, ready to report back to his master?

Lennox slunk down in the chair, unable to stop herself from picturing every customer in the tavern as one of Tylan's henchmen. She peered around the room, looking for anyone who seemed out of place. No one immediately stood out. Suddenly, her paranoia felt absurd. There was no way he would know to send a spy here of all places. She was perfectly safe under the watchful eye of Greta and her delicious stew.

Finished with her food, Lennox decided to head back to the room to wait for Kezra's return, which was when she saw her. There was a woman sitting alone by the door, her food untouched. Her golden eyes were locked onto Lennox; she didn't even bother to pretend to look away when Lennox spotted her. The woman just continued staring intently without shame. She wore a patchwork dress made of squares and stripes, and faded blocks of color. Between the unusual dress and her wild, curly hair, she should have looked ridiculous, but instead, she looked almost powerful and serene. Without noticing, Lennox had gotten up and taken two steps toward the woman, caught in her hypnotic stare, making the unconscious decision to approach her. Something was telling her that they needed to speak. Just as she was about to approach the golden-eyed woman, the door was thrown open, breaking her trance.

Her attention turned to the doorway where Kezra stood, surveying the room - her muscular body highlighted by the fading sun, her dark waves floating gently around her face, and her green eyes blazing. For a moment, she looked like a goddess standing there observing her people. Then she shut the door, and the illusion cracked. The golden-eyed woman stood to leave. Her eyes once again locked with Lennox's, then flicked to Kezra. She could have sworn the woman gave her a subtle, reaffirming nod before drawing up her hood and leaving.

"What are you doing down here?" Kezra hissed in her ear as she settled into the adjacent chair. Lennox rolled her eyes, exasperated by yet another lecture.

"You've been gone for ages. You can hardly expect me to sit in the room and starve waiting for you to come back." Kezra let out a huff.

"Fine. I see you've eaten now." Kezra gave a pointed glance at the empty bowl and the bread crumbs littering the table. "Come back upstairs so we can talk." She glided across the floor and up the stairs, making her way through the crowd with ease. Lennox sat for a moment longer, not wanting to follow like a lapdog, but with the food gone and no one to talk to, she felt silly sitting there on her own. Reluctantly, Lennox followed her upstairs, taking her sweet time so Kezra didn't think she'd won too easily. Once they arrived at the room, Lennox could feel some of the anger melting away from Kezra as she shut the door. Lennox silently waited for a scolding that didn't come. Instead, Kezra made her way to the bags of supplies, organizing them.

"Did you leave the tavern?" Kezra asked, continuing with her task, not looking at her.

"No, Mother," Lennox joked. "I stayed inside and was extra careful not to draw any attention." She walked over to help Kezra with the supplies, but there was little left to do. Kezra had laid out all the supplies on the bed by category and split them in half - one side presumably for Lennox and the other for her. Kezra glanced at her as Lennox moved to her side, her expression still stern, clearly unmoved by the joke.

"You're sure you didn't see anyone suspicious? No one who paid too much attention to you. Was there anyone alone, observing the crowd and seeming to blend in?" Lennox shifted her weight from foot to foot and bit her lip, a nervous habit. She thought of the woman watching her earlier. Her gut instinct was that the woman was harmless. She didn't know how to explain it, but Lennox felt like the woman was on their side. On the other hand, she didn't want to endanger them over something as trivial as a feeling, nor did she want to cause Kezra any undo panic. In not making up her mind though, Kezra had gone on high alert - Lennox's body language giving her away. "Who was it?" Kezra's voice was ice, cutting through to the bone. She instinctively took a step back, her body recognizing a predator.

"There was a woman by the door when you walked in. She had this curly brown hair, a very distinctive patchwork dress and golden eyes; I didn't speak to her, but I wanted to. There was something about her that felt almost familiar." Recognition lit on Kezra's face, and her expression thawed.

"Yelena."

"Who's Yelena?"

"She's no one for you to worry about," Kezra said frostily. Her mood changes were starting to get under Lennox's skin. Were they partners or not? Lennox wasn't a child who wouldn't understand.

"Maybe I could trust you if you would just listen instead of doing whatever you want whenever you want to do it." Kezra rounded on her and threw her hands in the air. "I am trying to keep us safe from Tylan, and all you think about is visiting the temple and sating your stomach!"

"Well, if you would include me in your plans instead of wandering off alone, then I would have something else to focus on! I want to help, Kezra, not be treated like a child."

"Then stop acting like one!" Kezra sat down on the bed, putting her head in her hands. "Were you even going to tell me about the woman you saw today?" Now that she'd calmed down, Lennox ventured to sit next to her. Gently, she placed her hand on Kezra's back to comfort her.

"I don't know," Lennox admitted, biting her lip. "I didn't want to worry you. Who is she?" Kezra was quiet for so long Lennox thought she was just going to ignore the question.

"I don't really know. A friend maybe. I've met her a handful of times, and she's always been kind, helpful even. But I don't know what she wants or if we can trust her."

"Thank you for trusting me." They sat in silence as Kezra gathered herself..

"You need to trust me. It's just going to be us out there on our own and Tylan will be hunting for us. I know I've put you through a lot, but if we're going to make it, we have to rely on each other," Kezra said.

"I'll do my best." It wasn't the response Kezra was looking for, but it was all she had to give. Lennox wanted to trust her companion, but she wasn't ready to put her complete faith in a woman who had already hurt her so greatly.

They finished packing together in relative peace. Kezra seemed to be lost in her own thoughts, and Lennox was too anxious about seeing Jasper to speak. Packing their meager belongings didn't take long, but by the time they were done, she was exhausted. Her nerves were frayed from worrying about Tylan and wondering what she'd say to Jasper. But Lennox was also buzzing with anticipation to see her friend, and even though she was tired, there was no way she could sleep. Lennox pulled on her pack, ready to say goodbye to her best friend, her sister, and get out of here. Kezra lay on the bed, watching her.

"Where are you going?"

"The temple?" The answer came out as a question, even though Lennox didn't mean it to be.

"I was thinking, what if we stayed here for another night?" Kezra rushed on seeing her puzzled expression and the argument forming on

Lennox's lips. "Would you even be able to see Jasper this late? It might be best to go at dawn during her morning walk in the gardens."

"I guess you're right." Lennox put down the pack, sinking into the bed. Her emotions were in turmoil: she was relieved to put off this goodbye a little longer but ashamed of her cowardice. Facing Jasper shouldn't have unsettled her, but it did, and part of her was happy for the delay.

"That's settled then. Get some rest; tomorrow's going to be a hard day." Kezra blew out the candles and closed the curtains, but Lennox didn't sleep. Instead, she lay awake wondering for the first time where they were going and how this journey ended. She tossed and turned endlessly, pondering whether Kezra would stay or if she was about to end up alone and friendless in the mountains of Kitsummit. Finally, exhaustion overpowered her nerves, and Lennox drifted to sleep.

She woke the next morning to Kezra's loud grumbling. As usual, Kezra was already dressed, her hair in a pristine braid, ready to go before Lennox had even opened her eyes.

"Come on, Lennox. You can't sleep all day. We need to get going," Kezra said. Lennox peered out of the open window, propping herself up on one arm to look out.

"The sun hasn't even started to rise, why should we?" Kezra rolled her eyes at the question.

"We need to leave now if we want to make it to the temple by dawn and before morning prayers. Aren't you used to waking up at this hour, or did you only participate in holy duties when it suited you?"

She hurled a pillow at Kezra's head in response. Kezra snatched it out of the air before the pillow made it close to its intended target. Lennox let out a heavy sigh, but swung her legs around to get out of bed, admitting defeat.

"To be honest, morning prayers never really agreed with me. I never would have made it on time if not for Jasper." Lennox's heart tightened as she uttered the name, reminding her of the way she was about to break her best friend's heart. Would it be kinder to leave without saying goodbye at all? No, even if it was selfish, Lennox couldn't leave without seeing her one last time.

"And were you always this hostile toward Jasper when she saved you from Altheia's wrath by waking you at dawn?"

"Sometimes," Lenox smirked to herself while lacing her boots. "She put up with a lot from me, but she never complained." She looked up, raising an eyebrow at Kezra. "Unlike some people I know."

"If you think this is me complaining, you haven't seen anything yet. Lucky for you, I'm still in a good mood."

"You wouldn't know a good mood if it bit you in the ass." Kezra scowled at her.

"Being bitten in the ass would put anyone in a bad mood," Kezra muttered. Lennox finished with her boots. The bags were packed and ready. There was nothing left to do but set off for the temple and face the unknown lying ahead.

The crisp morning air bit through her skin. Freezing wind whipped the stray strands of hair into Lennox's eyes and cut through her cloak, chilling her to the bone. The last vestiges of summer were quickly fading into fall. She tried very hard not to think about what that would mean for her and Kezra on their journey. Lennox hoped she had a plan. They trudged up the hill, frozen and breathing heavily by the time they made it to the temple. The path to the temple's entrance ran directly through the gardens. They'd just started walking down the path when Lennox saw her. Jasper's bright red hair was a beacon among the fading green of the dying garden. She was sitting on the ground, stroking the petals of a wilted lunasha bloom. At first, Jasper didn't hear her approaching. Lennox's throat was thick with emotion, strangling her voice. She wanted to call out, but found she couldn't get the words out. Instead, Lennox sat down next to her. Jasper startled, looking as though she'd seen a ghost.

"Lennox?" she said softly. Tears streamed down Lennox's face; emotion choked her voice. Lennox could only nod and held out her arms to embrace her friend. "Lennox!" Jasper threw herself into Lennox's open arms, and they tumbled to the ground. Then they were both crying and laughing at the same time. Jasper's tear-streaked face was muddy from the ground, and leaves stuck out of her hair, but none of that could mar the beauty of her happiness.

"What happened to you? After my Blessing ceremony, I went back to the room. But I ran out when I heard The Mother screaming. I saw some strange smoke, and one moment you were there and the next you were just gone. The Mother won't talk about it. She won't talk about you at all. It's as if you never existed."

"It's a long story." It's all Lennox could manage to get out, fighting all the emotions running through her. Jasper squeezed her arm.

"It's all right. You can tell me all about it later. We should go see The Mother. I'm sure she'll be excited to see you." Jasper gave her a once-over, fully taking in the tunic, soft trousers and sturdy boots, all surely covered in dirt and leaves from their reunion. She wrinkled her nose. "Although we should probably get you changed first. What in the world are you wearing?" She took Lennox's hand, no doubt to lead her back to the temple, back to her old life, and Lennox almost let her. It would be so easy to follow, to let Jasper take her back to their old room and don her robes, to fall back into the role of a priestess, as if the past few months had never happened. Everything in her rebelled as Lennox pulled her hand from Jasper's grasp.

"Jasper, I can't."

"Don't be ridiculous, Lennox. Of course you can." Jasper reached for her again. The hope in Jasper's eyes broke her. Lennox stepped toward her friend, clasping Jasper's outstretched hand. "I can't stay here. I'm so, so sorry." Jasper's face crumpled.

"What do you mean you can't stay? Where would you go?" Her eyes scanned Lennox's face, looking for answers, a clue to the reason for the betrayal. Jasper's eyes landed on Kezra. "Who is that? What's she done to you? If you're in danger, The Mother can protect you; Altheia will protect you! Please, Len, just stay." Jasper's voice broke in a sob. Lennox pulled Jasper into a tight hug, knowing it might be the last one she ever gave her.

"There's so much I wish I could tell you. Maybe one day I'll get to. For now, I have to go. I'm in danger, but not because of Kezra. She saved me. I'll -"

"What is going on over here? I swear, Priestess Jasper, half the temple can hear your hysterics. I expect better out of someone of your station." The Mother strolled into the gardens cutting off anything else Lennox had to say. "No matter, it's lucky I found you. I have a man here who'd like to ask you some questions." Her instincts screamed at her to move, but shock rooted her in place. As The Mother came into view, so did her companion. He walked with an easy, confident gait. Looking respectable in his black trousers, green tunic, and with his white hair braided back, Tylan came into view, and he was heading right for them.

CHAPTER 13

Kezra

"Lennox! Lennox, get down!" Kezra hissed. Instead, Lennox stood, staring down the path, frozen in place. There was no time for her to grab the priestess before she was seen, so Kezra crouched down in the bushes, waiting for the right moment - she knew this trip was a bad idea. Tylan smiled as he saw Lennox, the feral grin of a predator snaring its prey. The old woman, on the other hand, looked as if she might faint.

"Lennox! Is that really you? Dear child, what a blessing the goddess brought you back to us, and just in time to meet your relative. Altheia's light shines upon you brightly."

Lennox just stood there, her mouth gaping open, like a fish. As quietly as possible, Kezra slid the pack from her back, trying to find one of the few vials of smoke. Jasper glued herself to Lennox's side, grasping her hand. Lennox shrank back as Tylan continued to approach.

"Lennox, my dearest niece, you can't imagine how relieved I am to see you. My beloved sister passed away giving birth to you. I was forced to bring you here, knowing you'd be cared for since I couldn't afford to raise you on my own. But I always intended to come back. I'm sure this must come as quite a shock after so many years. I came here to take you with me, so I can answer all your questions. I can't wait to learn all about you." The Mother had been nodding along to Tylan's speech, but her face tightened at the last line.

"Yes, well, she is still an acolyte of Altheia. I'm sure there is much to discuss, certainly, but she can't leave the temple grounds yet. Especially so soon after her miraculous return." Tylan ignored her, approaching Lennox. He held out his hand to her in invitation. She took a cautious step back, glancing around for an escape. Kezra fumbled through the bag, becoming increasingly desperate to find the stolen potion. She needed to get out of here, and the window to bring Lennox with her was rapidly closing.

As Lennox continued to back away, Tylan advanced on her. Kezra couldn't let him touch her; if he did, it was all over. He would whisk her away and Kezra would never see her again - never build up the courage to save her again. And worse, then he's come after her. Lennox knew Kezra's plan, and there was no doubt he would find a way to get them out of her even if she didn't tell him willingly. Kezra's thoughts started to spiral just as her fingers closed around a smooth glass edge. She yanked the vial free, relieved to catch a glimpse of the purple smoke swirling inside. Shoving everything back into the pack, Kezra slung it around her back and prepared to run.

The next few moments were pure chaos. Tylan lunged toward Lennox, brushing her arm. And as Kezra thought all hope was lost, Jasper yanked Lennox away, out of his reach. Murmuring a prayer to Altheia, hoping it might bring her luck, she ran full force toward Lennox. Kezra hooked her around the waist, getting ready to disappear.

"No, we can't leave her! Jasper! Come with me, please!" Lennox's eyes were frantic as she tried to claw from Kezra's grasp. She let go of the frantic priestess, afraid she'd knock over the vial and, along with it, ruin their chance at escape. Jasper grabbed Lennox by the shoulders, giving her a fast embrace.

"I love you, my friend, but my place is here," Jasper said before turning to Kezra. "Take care of her." Then Lennox let out a feral cry as Jasper pushed her out of the embrace directly into Kezra's arms. With Lennox's cry came a surge of energy, radiating out of her. Jasper, Tylan, and The Mother were all thrown back. Kezra used the distraction to open the vial and tilt it back, picturing the docks in her mind. The last thing she saw before the magic swept them away was Jasper on the ground clutching her chest and a look of shock and frustration etched on Tylan's face. With that, they tumbled onto the hard stone road leading to the docks, Lennox sniffling softly. Kezra shot up from the ground.

"What was that?"

"I don't know what you're talking about," Lennox said glumly.

"That surge of energy you released. The one that knocked everyone down and had your friend clutching her chest - you don't know what it was?"

"I don't know! It wasn't me!"

"Like Helica, it wasn't! What did you do? It almost looked like -" Kezra's voice trailed off.

"Like what?"

"Like magic," she whispered. Lennox's face blanched.

"You know that's not possible."

"I think it is. I don't know how, but this isn't the first time something like this has happened around you. The first time I thought maybe I had imagined it. But now...well, how else do you explain what just happened?"

"I don't know. But it wasn't me. It couldn't have been. The only time anything magical has happened is when I've been around Tylan. It must have been him somehow."

"I don't know, Lennox. I don't think he would have done that." Lennox just shook her head in response.

"It couldn't have been me," Lennox whispered. "I thought maybe I had magic too, but I've tried to use it a couple of times, and I just couldn't. Whatever that was, it wasn't me." Kezra wanted to argue more, but she took in Lennox, still seated on the ground with her knees clutched to her chest. She looked so helpless; Kezra didn't think now was the time to push it further.

"Ok. It wasn't you. You stay here. I'll see if I can find us a ship headed toward Kitsummit. There's bound to be something this time of year." She thought again of Lennox's scream as Jasper shoved her away, of the burst of pure energy that followed. Having some time to process everything by herself might do her some good.

Tesmerin's docks were small, but bustling. The city had been built inland, safely tucked away behind mountains to the north and guarded by its smaller cities to the south. Paved roads led to the city center throughout the continent, but the only way for a foreign nation to reach the city would be to sail to the mountains and hike down them, nearly impossible as the terrain was rocky and treacherous with no set paths. Or, they could use the river, where the water flowed to the Oscalian Sea, known as one of the most dangerous bodies of water for sailors. Storms formed out of thin air on otherwise cloudless days. The waves were sometimes taller than ships and the winds blew hard and haphazardly. Only the bravest of merchants sailed on it, bearing goods to Kitsummit. This was the path she sought to sail with Lennox.

Again, Kezra questioned the wisdom of her plan, of taking such a treacherous journey for no guaranteed reward. But something about Kitsummit called to her. Kezra just knew there was something waiting for her in those mountains; there had to be. But if she was wrong, and her weakened bond was restored before she could find a way to sever it for good - well, Kezra wasn't going to focus on the consequences right now.

As she approached the docks, workers bustled around, loading and unloading cargo. People mostly ignored her, although her trousers were occasionally given the odd look by those who noticed her more feminine features. Kezra resisted the urge to draw her hood and hide behind it, not wanting to look untrustworthy when approaching a potential partner. At a quick glance, most strangers assumed she was a man, an assumption that suited her just fine. Kezra scanned the crowd, looking for the people delivering orders as opposed to moving the cargo. One group of men stuck out. They were scattered around a shabby table, under a ramshackle awning. They sat far enough from the docks not to be caught in the work, but close enough to keep an eye on the merchandise.

There were four men seated around the table, throwing dice and taking swigs from a bottle of wine. Kezra fingered the bag of gold coins tied to her waist. She'd taken more than enough to procure passage for her and Lennox on one of these ships, but she knew the captain would press for whatever he could get. Drawing her cloak around her chest to hide her figure and adopting the confident swagger she'd seen Tylan use, Kezra went to strike a deal.

"I have a proposition for any captain sailing toward Kitsummit. Do any of you gentlemen know where I could find such a man?" Kezra pitched her voice lower, knowing she was more likely to get a better deal as a man than a woman. The group barked out laughter. A man with shaggy, shoulder-length hair and a matching full beard answered without looking up.

"Aye lad. What would you want to go there for? That's a madman's journey, that is."

"Nothing there but mountains and snow," his bald-headed companion added.

"Look at the lad, he'd lose his lunch at the first sight of a storm."

"Maybe he's off in search of a woman."

"I hear the women there are harrier than the men."

"At least the hair would keep ye from freezing yer balls off lying with them." More laughter peeled out of the men. However, one was looking at her in a way she didn't like. He was younger than his companions, with blonde hair pulled back from his face, piercing blue eyes and a full mouth. He should have been beautiful, but his face was marred by a thin red scar that ran across the corner of his eye to the top of his mouth. Worse still was the expression of open hostility he wore. The man continued staring while taking a long sip of his wine. Unwilling to be the one to break eye contact, Kezra glared back with equal intensity.

"Yes, *lad.* What business could you have in Kitsummit? Not looking to smuggle out a wife, I hope? You'll be disappointed if you think you'll get a young, docile woman like you'd find in the city. Those mountain bitches are feral, trained from birth to fight, the lot of them."

She kept her expression neutral, not letting on the disgust his words made her feel. This man was vile, but better temporarily working with him than remaining bonded forever. Kezra kept her tone bored.

"I have matters to attend to and am willing to pay for passage. If you know of anyone with authority more interested in gold than crude taunting, please point me in their direction."

"Calm down, lad, we're just having a bit of fun," the black-haired man said. "I might be heading that way myself. But I'll be bringing a load of cargo with me. It's hard to grow crops up in those mountains. I wouldn't want anyone to starve because I had to make room for one little lord and his belongings." Kezra refrained from rolling her eyes at the clear extortion attempt. He must have thought her naive, but she could use that to her advantage.

"All I require is a cabin for myself and my travelling companion. We only intend to travel with the packs we carry. I assure you, there's no need for anyone to go hungry."

"A travelling companion, eh? Seeking a bit of adventure, are ya? Or running away from home, maybe?"

"As I said, I'm looking for someone interested in gold, not a life story. If that's not you, I'll find someone else." Her voice turned cold. The captain bristled.

"My apologies, lordling. We didn't mean to offend ye. It's no matter. I don't care why you're running, only for the coin ye carry." He examined her clothes, appraising her seriously for the first time. "Yer sure you wouldn't prefer Versa? Better weather there."

"Prettier women too. Not bundled up under all of those furs," the bald man said.

"I'm sure. I only need a cabin for two to Kitsummit if you're going that way." The captain begrudgingly nodded. "I can't take you all the way there. I dock in Alara, and that's as far as I can get you. You'll need to find your own way through the mountain path to Kitsummit. Ten gold crowns for a cabin for yourself and your companion." It was an outrageous sum, and he knew it. Ten gold crowns were more than many would see after a year of work.

"I'll give you two. One crown for each of us."

"Now listen here. You'll be expecting food, won't ye? I'll need to provide you with food and water. Plus, I'll have to kick poor Greg here out of his cabin for ye." The bald man nodded, pulling a frown, presumably the Greg who would be losing his cabin space. The captain opened his mouth to haggle again, but Kezra stopped him.

"It's more than the voyage is worth, and you know it. I'm not running away from anything and I have no problem lodging in Tesmerin until a more reasonable caption comes along." The man grumbled under his breath, but finally let out a sigh.

"Aye, fine. Ye drive a hard bargain, ye do. Be here in an hour, or I'll leave without ye."

"Deal." Kezra stuck out her hand to shake on it.

"What's your name then, lad?" he asked, giving her hand a firm shake. Kezra only smiled, avoiding the question.

"I'll gather my companion and be back in an hour, Captain. We'll get acquainted then."

"We'll see you around, *lad*," said the man with the scar, his tone unfriendly. Kezra kept up the slow, confident gait on the walk back. But the whole time, her instincts screamed at her to run from that man and never return.

Lennox was right where Kezra had left her, sprawled out on the ground next to the stone road. She didn't turn to look as Kezra approached.

"Have you been lying here the entire time I've been gone?" Lennox remained mute, staring up at the sky. Kezra crouched down beside her. "I'm surprised no one bothered you in plain sight of the road." She slowly rotated her head, her gaze finally meeting Kezra's.

"I would have moved if I'd heard someone coming. I'm not an idiot."

"You didn't move for me."

"I knew it was you. I wasn't too concerned about your desire to rob or kill me," Lennox said. Kezra rolled her eyes at the foolish girl.

"There's no way you knew it was me; you didn't even look up."

"I didn't have to. I knew it by the sound you make when you walk."

"And what sound would that be?"

"You sound like a dragon clomping through the woods."

"I do not clomp," Kezra said, offended by the comparison. It was an insult to the years she'd spent training to stalk Tylan's victims undetected. Kezra was very good at it, and she didn't appreciate the insinuation otherwise. "Anyway, you need to get up. I found us a ship, but we'll need to hurry. The captain said he wouldn't wait, and I believe him."

"Help me?" Lennox lifted her hand. Kezra let out a loud sigh, but grabbed her hand and stood, pulling Lennox up with her.

"The money I gave you, where is it?"

"Tied to my waist, hidden inside my cloak."

"Good, keep it out of sight. I don't trust our dear captain. Oh, and he thinks I'm a man, so if you could try keeping up with that ruse, it would be helpful." Lennox looked offended.

"No one would mistake me for a man," she sniffed.

"Dressed in trousers, with your hair pulled back and with the right walk, they probably will. People see what they want to see, even if a contradiction is staring them in the face. Use it to your advantage."

"Is that why you're stomping about? Because you're pretending to be a man?"

"I do *not* stomp. But yes. Spread your feet apart and try to walk as if you own the road. Let's go."

"A priestess doesn't stomp," Lennox mumbled.

"For the last time, I DO NOT STOMP!"

They hustled down to the docks with Lennox practicing her new swagger. Kezra winced while watching it, trying to give her some tips. But every time she did, Lennox would only roll her eyes and exaggerate the steps to annoy her. Lennox looked ridiculous, but that might work in their favor. Young noblemen often walked with a swagger that bordered on comical, and with their fine clothing, they would certainly be taken for nobles. Whatever else he had done, Tylan had never given her low quality clothes. To him, Kezra's image was a part of his, and having his assassin dressed in rags would have reflected poorly on him. Therefore, their clothing looked expensive enough for them to pass as the sons of some minor lord, which might just be enough to help them get through this without being caught. As they approached the dock, Lennox still stumbled around with exaggerated steps, not yet perfecting her walk.

"Draw your hood, and let me do the talking," Kezra said. "Let me do the talking for now." Lennox sighed, but complied with the instruction.

The captain waited for them at the end of the dock, arms crossed. His black hair looked even more unruly under the sunlight. His skin was tan and weathered, probably from hours spent in the sun and exposure to constant sea spray. He wore brown breeches and a loose white tunic with a burgundy overcoat. The colorful piece was impressive; it stood out among the sea of white and tan fabric; he must have been doing well for himself. His scowl deepened when his eyes landed on the pair of them.

"Yer late, lad."

"Apologies, captain. It took my friend here some extra time to get down the road. You see, he overindulged last night; now he's suffering the consequences." The captain's eyes shifted to Lennox, taking in her expensive clothes and hidden face. His eyes narrowed further.

"I've been known to have too much fun on a night myself; nothing to be ashamed of. No need to hide unless; are ye disfigured, man? Why keep your hood up on such a glorious day?" Kezra opened her mouth to answer, but Lennox beat her to it.

"The sun pains my eyes, my lord. If you'll indulge me, I'd like to lay down, preferably somewhere dark." Lennox's voice came out cool and smoky. Kezra tried not to look surprised by her acting.

"I'm sure ye would, lad. But first, there's the matter of those gold crowns. I'll be liking payment up front," the captain said. Kezra snorted.

"I'm sure you would. We'll give you half now, half upon arrival." The captain started to turn the exact crimson as his coat.

"Now listen here, lad, I've given ye a fine deal on yer cabin. Ye can't expect me to take ye on without payment."

"I don't," Kezra said, ignoring the part about the so-called "deal" he'd given them. "I need some assurance that you'll be motivated to take us the whole way. Half now, half upon arrival or I'll wait and find someone else." He threw his hands up in defeat.

"Fine. Fine. One gold crown now. Hand it over and get on the ship. We don't have all day." She pressed the coin into his palm with a smile. The captain lit up upon seeing it, clearly not having fully believed they had the money.

"Welcome aboard the Devina; Captain Dallos at your service. My first mate, Asher, will show you lads to yer cabin. Oi! Asher, come show our guests to their room." As Lennox and Kezra hustled onto the ship, the blond man from earlier slunk out from the shadows of the ship.

"Aye, captain," he said with a grin. "It'd be my pleasure."

Asher led them below deck into a tight, dark hallway. Sunlight trickled in through small, dirty windows, making it difficult to see exactly where they were being led. Kezra's senses were on high alert though. There was something about this man that set her edge. Her hand slid down her thigh, resting on the spot where her daggers were hidden. Kezra was acutely aware of how easy it would be for Asher to kill and rob them now that they were out of sight of the streets. Captain Dallos seemed alright, but she knew better than to trust him implicitly, and she had even less faith in Asher.

"The mess hall is down below and to the right. Chef rings the bell twice at meal times. You'll need to come down and eat with the crew; no fancy room service like you little lords are used to. You'll find the crew's bunks to the left. I recommend staying away from there if you're attached to your coin or your clothes. You'll find things have a way of disappearing around that lot." Asher led them to a door at the end of the hall. "This will be your cabin. We don't have enough room to give you separate rooms, so you'll have to share. The captain's office is across the hall. Do not go in there without an invitation. I'll be two doors down to keep an eye out for you." Kezra didn't like the way he looked at them when he made the last statement. The hairs on the back of her neck prickled, and she tensed, ready to strike. They opened the cabin door and went into the room. Asher stood in the doorway, simultaneously observing them and blocking her from shutting the door.

"Thank you for showing us to our room. Now, if you'll excuse us, my companion needs to rest." Kezra grabbed the door, ready to slam it, but Asher lingered in the doorway as if deciding what to do. He finally relented, moving back.

"Of course. The dinner bell will ring in a few hours. Make sure to come straight away. We won't save anything for you if you miss it."

"Thank you. We'll be there." Asher stayed for another moment, scanning her face as if he were looking for something.

"I don't believe I caught your names, *lads*." It was her turn to smirk at him.

"That's because we didn't give them to you. Now, if you'll excuse us, my companion could really use some rest." Asher grunted, but moved out of the doorway, finally making enough room to close it. Kezra slammed the door in his face the moment she could, not bothering with a goodbye, but she could hear Asher chuckling in the hallway.

"Rest while you can. I'll be watching," he said. The door muffled the words, but Kezra still heard them clearly enough to send a shiver down her spine, making her grateful for the thick wooden door between them.

"Where is the gods-forsaken latch?" Kezra muttered. Her shaking hands groped the door in the dim lighting, searching for a lock. Finally, she found it and threw the latch shut with a satisfying click. Kezra scanned the room, taking it in. The cabin was larger than expected, so at least the captain was honorable enough not to put them in a broom closet. There was a large bed pushed against the wall immediately in front of her. Small dressers sat on either side, and she was pleased to see a lantern sat on top of the one furthest away. Otherwise, the cabin contained little else. There was a small, rather rickety looking desk sitting under a circular window, also with a lantern on it, and a small wardrobe sat next to a desk. Everything had a layer of dust on it, already tickling Kezra's nose in the enclosed space.

"So much for poor old Greg."

"Who's Greg?" Lennox asked. She'd flopped herself down onto the middle of the bed and already looked half asleep.

"A damn liar, that's who he is."

"What?"

"It doesn't matter." Kezra let out a sigh. This room clearly hadn't been occupied for a while. "Let's see if we can get that window open, let in some fresh air." She busied herself with the window while Lennox lay there, sending a wave of irritation through her. Kezra understood it had been a hard day for her, but some help would have been nice.

"Asher was nice," Lennox said, breaking the silence. Kezra laughed.

"Do you honestly have no self-preservation instincts?"

"What do you mean?"

"I mean, Asher is most certainly not nice. I don't like the way he looks at us." She left out the bit about him watching them for now, not wanting to spook Lennox.

"You're being paranoid."

"For good reason. We are on a ship, surrounded by men we don't know, while we're pretending to be something we are not." Kezra pushed at the window harder and felt it budge, giving her enough motivation to keep trying. "Honestly, a little paranoia would do you some good. We shouldn't trust anyone, least of all -" The window finally sprang open, letting sunlight stream into the room and sending the dust swirling. The forward momentum broke off her thoughts, and Kezra inhaled deeply in surprise as she lurched forward, breathing in a mouthful of dust. "AH-CHOO". Kezra let out a loud sneeze. Her nose started running and her eyes watered. It was going to be a long trip. "As I was saying - you can't trust anyone, least of all Asher." Lennox sat up and studied her. With her dripping nose and likely puffy eyes, she was sure that she no longer looked very authoritative.

"I still think you're just being paranoid. It'll all be fine. You'll see."

Kezra approached the bed and sat down beside her. Lennox scooted over, making room. Kezra found herself surprisingly touched by the thoughtfulness. No one ever made space for her unless they were backing away in terror. She was used to needing to fight for every inch of space she took up. Not wanting to lecture Lennox any longer, she decided to let it go and move on.

"Right. Whatever you say. What do you want your name to be?"

"My name's Lennox?" She looked at Kezra, puzzled. Kezra couldn't help but roll her eyes. This girl wouldn't have lasted a day on her own.

"Yes, but I can't call you that in front of the captain. We can't refuse to give him a name; it's incredibly suspicious, and he thinks you're a man. Pick a man's name, but something similar enough to your own that you'll answer to it. I'm going to go by Kieran."

"Oh. That makes sense." Lenox thought for a moment.

"I'll go by Tavius," she said definitively.

"Where did that come from? You can't choose Tavius." It was incredible how little the priestess listened.

"It was a man I met at the temple once. He came looking for a priestess to say a blessing over his newborn daughter. There was so much love in his eyes as he gazed down at the little baby girl. If I have to be a man, I want to be like him. I choose Tavius."

"That's not going to work," Kezra replied with a shake of her head.

"Why not?"

"Because you'll never remember to answer to it. You need to pick something close enough to your own name or that you're familiar enough with that it'll get your attention, even when you're not expecting someone to call."

"You're no fun. Do you know that? But fine, I see your point. Let me think." She sat in silence, trying to think. Closing her eyes, Kezra embraced the quiet.

"Can't you just pick something for me?"

"It would be better if you chose it yourself, but I can try. What about Lenny?"

"Ew, no."

"Nolan?"

"That's not even close; I won't remember it."

"Well, I don't see you coming up with any suggestions," Kezra said, keeping her tone flat. This was getting irksome.

"Jasper," she said quietly. "It can be a man's name too. I want to use Jasper."

"Are you sure that's a good idea?"

"Why wouldn't it be?" Lennox asked, body tense. Kezra was careful with her answer, sensing that Lennox was on edge.

"Because it's a name you're familiar with, but it's not close to yours. And I know today's been…hard., but you shouldn't make an emotional decision right now. Are you sure this wound isn't too fresh for this? No offense, but it's going to look strange if you tear up whenever someone calls your name."

"Jasper and I are - well were - always a pair. Yelling her name was as good as yelling mine. Trust me. This just feels right. Trust me, I'll be fine." She looked at Kezra so earnestly that it broke her heart. Kezra didn't love the idea, but she supposed the decision wasn't really hers to make anyways.

"Fine. Jasper it is. What's my name?"

"Kezrin." Kezra shook her head.

"It's Keiran." Lennox scrunched her nose.

"Are you sure that's what you want to settle on? I quite like the sound of Kezrin," Lennox said.

"This from the person who liked the name Tavius."

"Tavius is a perfectly respectable name."

"Yes, if you're roughly fifty years older," Kezra snorted.

"Well, I suppose dear Tavius did have his daughter rather late in life." They both laughed, all the tension momentarily melting away. Kezra closed her eyes to savor the moment, almost able to imagine that they were long-time friends as they lay on the bed together giggling. This was the first time in her life she'd felt content. It was nice to have a companion on this adventure, even if Lennox wasn't truly her friend. She knew they could never truly be close, not after all Kezra had put her through. But still, she couldn't help the hope that sparked in her chest that just maybe, after she'd broken this bond, after they both felt safe from Tylan, Lennox would still want to stay with her.

"I'm going to try to clean up some of this dust before the dinner bell, but why don't you try to get some rest," Kezra said.

"I could use some rest; I really didn't sleep last night. Do you want some help? We could clean together after dinner, and both rest up."

"No, that's okay. I don't want to risk missing the bell. I believe Asher would let us starve in here for the fun of it. Besides, I don't think I could sleep in all of this dust. You rest, I'm going to see if I can scrounge up a bucket of water and a rag," Kezra said. Lennox shrugged.

"Suit yourself. Wake me up for dinner?"

"Of course. I've seen what trouble you'll get into when you let your stomach guide you. Letting you go hungry is not a mistake I'll not be making again."

Lennox let out an indignant sniff, but she rolled over and covered up without further retort. Kezra smirked, reveling in the feeling of companionship and freedom washing over her. She left Lennox lying in bed and exited the room, determined to find some cleaning supplies. Locking the door behind her, Kezra tested the handle, making sure the room was truly secure. It was always possible that Asher or the captain had another copy of the key, but that was out of her control. As she walked down the dim hallway and up the stairs, Kezra absent-mindedly reached for the two phosphorescent vials in her pocket, reassuring herself they were still there. She estimated it would take roughly two weeks to reach the port town leading to Kitsummit if the winds favored them, more like three if they didn't. The warm feeling that had taken root inside her fled. She would only have two months to find a solution once they reached their destination. She had just gotten free from Tylan, had barely had time to savor the sweetness of independence and already - time was running out.

CHAPTER 14

Lennox

Days on the ship rolled together as nothing eventful happened. This was most likely due to Kezra's insistence that they stay holed up in the dingy cabin. Lennox could understand why she'd want to be cautious, but she still thought Kezra was being a little paranoid. They'd taken all their meals in the mess hall with the other sailors, and nothing bad had come close to occurring. Although they were mostly left to eat on their own now. At first, a few of the bolder crewmates had tried to come chat with them, some looking for the stories they'd have to offer, others trying to tempt them with games of dice, hoping to make a few crowns. Personally, Lennox didn't see the harm in indulging them. They could give a background story without revealing too much about themselves, and they had the crowns to spare for a bit of gambling. But Kezra had scared them all off by telling them the sea was not agreeing with Lennox's stomach and firmly suggesting they find other forms of entertainment with a loosely veiled threat that they may lose a finger or two if they didn't. So between fear of being vomited upon and of Kezra, or Keiran as they called her, the crew had learned to keep their distance. Even Asher hadn't bothered to check back in on them.

Kezra seemed relieved, but Lennox was disappointed. What was the point of being free if she was just going to be trapped in a cabin? At least at the temple, she'd had Jasper; at Tylan's lair, Lennox could cling to the hope of seeing her again. Now though, even if she could travel back to the temple, she didn't know if Jasper would want to see her again. With nothing to do, Lennox would lie in bed for hours, running their goodbye through her head over and over again. She tried to tell herself that the wave of energy didn't come from her; it wasn't her magic. Surely Lennox hadn't hurt Jasper, had she? Jasper had to be okay. If Lennox told herself the lie enough times, maybe she could believe it, despite the pressure that had been building in her body, despite the glorious, powerful feeling coursing through her when that pressure released. It was her imagination. Lennox would never do anything to hurt Jasper, so that rush of energy had to have come from somewhere else.

Lennox released a dramatic sigh, hoping to catch Kezra's attention, but she didn't so much as look up from her book. Lennox wondered which it was: the one she studied with a creased brow, or the one Kezra read again and again. Lennox decided it didn't really matter. Another loud sigh escaped her.

"Is there an echo in here? Maybe a discontent ghost?"

"I wish. At least a haunted cabin would make things interesting." Lennox sat up on the bed to get a better look at Kezra. Kezra was seated at the desk studying her book by the light of the afternoon sun. The room was much brighter since Kezra had cleaned up all the dust and grime. Lennox felt a little guilty about not helping her clean, but not guilty enough to sit in this room a moment longer with nothing to do but count the wooden beams on the ceiling over and over again. There were four. Kezra hadn't even looked up at her when she spoke.

"You can borrow my book if you'd like something to do."

"It's too dark in here to read." Which wasn't exactly true, as Kezra was doing just that, but Lennox wanted to leave. "I need to get out, stretch my legs, get some fresh air."

"Dinner will be in an hour or so. The walk from here to the mess hall is just thrilling, more than enough for a nice stretch." "I need to see the sun." Lennox's voice started to take on a whiny tone that made her cringe, but she couldn't help it.

"Good thing someone cleaned the window for you then."

"Kezra. You know what I mean. I want to go on deck, see the ocean, and back in the sunshine. We haven't stepped foot on the deck. It would be good for one of us to make an appearance, right?" Now Kezra did turn to look at her, or glare at her, rather. Kezra took a deep breath, like a mother finding patience for their child.

"I don't think you'll understand the danger we're in here. What if one of the sailors presses you about where you're from? What if someone corners you on the way back and tries to rob you? Or, if the captain decides the journey's easier without us and throws us overboard?"

"You're being paranoid again. If anyone asks what I'm doing, I'll say I thought the air would help my seasickness, but that I'm still not feeling well. But everyone has left us in peace so far. It's been nearly a week. Surely if anyone meant us harm, they would have tried something by now. I'll be fast. I just want to see the ocean, please? I've been trapped in that temple for my entire life. I'll go up to the desk, look around, and come right back. I promise. Besides, if I say here, I'm just going to keep bothering you while you try to study that book. You won't get anything done with me here. What are you reading anyway?" Lennox asked. Kezra snapped the book shut, her shoulders slumped in defeat, and Lennox knew she'd won.

"Fine, a quick trip up, and then come straight back. Try not to talk to anyone if you don't have to. And stay away from Asher." Excited, Lennox jumped up to grab her cloak.

"I'll be fast, I promise. No unnecessary interactions and no Asher, got it."

"I mean it, Lennox. Something's off about him. I just don't know what yet, and hopefully I never have a reason to find out."

"Yes, yes. No, Asher. I swear. It'll be fine." Lennox didn't wait to see if she'd respond. She burst through the door as soon as she fastened her cloak, before Kezra could change her mind.

Getting close to the deck, Lennox made an effort to slow her feet, mindful not to attract attention by running. Act like a lord, she reminded herself. Lennox adopted the confident swagger Kezra used, or at least tried. The salty air hit her nose as she made her way up the steps. The sun was blinding as she walked aboveboard and it took her eyes a moment to adjust after becoming used to the dim lighting of their cabin. When her eyes finally adjusted, Lennox saw several crew members stopping to stare at her.

"Get out of the way, lad," came a booming voice from behind her. Lennox scuttled up the stairs and to the side, making room for the voice's owner. The man was large, broad-shouldered and full-chested. He had bright red hair cropped close to his head and wore a simple outfit of light brown trousers with a white tunic. A bucket of foaming water he carried sloshed around as he walked, the water precariously close to splashing over the sides. As he elbowed past her, he let out a loud "hmph" noise, then continued down the deck without another word. After he pushed past her, the rest of the crew either lost interest in her or were too consumed with their work to pay much attention.

Lennox, now more confident, walked over to the railing, letting out a gasp. The ship was surrounded on all sides by crystal-clear blue water as far as the eye could see. A bright turquoise sky was overhead, free from clouds. In the distance, the sea and the sky met, creating a barely visible white horizon that divided the two. Sea spray splashed her face. Lennox groped the railing and looked down to see white foam churning and crashing into the side of the ship. It was glorious, the whole scene. She excitedly scanned the water, hoping to spot a creature popping its snout above water, or a stray fin. But all she could find were unbroken waves of dazzling blue.

"Feeling better then, are you? The crew was taking bets on how long you'd stay holed up down there." Lennox froze, too startled to respond. She hadn't heard Asher approach, but he had sidled up beside her at some point. Recovering, she cleared her throat, trying to pitch her voice lower as Kezra did.

"I thought the fresh air might help settle my stomach." Lennox forced a cough and focused on the waves, not looking at Asher, but his eyes burned into the back of her neck.

"You are looking rather pale. Then again, who wouldn't be after days without sun?"

"It's a spectacular view," Lennox said, changing the subject. "You must never tire of being at sea."

"Aye, it's pretty enough now, but you should see it when there's a storm. The sea's vengeance comes without warning. Waves aren't so pretty when they're the size of the ship and threatening to knock you overboard."

"Still, the freedom to roam, to see the world must be exciting." She tried to keep her longing from her voice, but it laced through her words. Asher must have heard it too, as he gave her a strange look.

"Surely a little lordling such as yourself must be free to travel. You're going to Kitsummit after all, and few travel there." She cursed her stupidity for revealing too much accidentally and arousing his suspicion.

"My father liked to keep us at home; he's a strict man," Lennox said, trying to feign neutrality.

"And where was home, exactly, little lord? Come on, don't be shy. You're a long way from home now; there's no harm that can come from telling me about it."

"No, where special. We have a small estate on the outskirts of Tesmerin. My father liked us to be home, not wander into the city where he claimed temptation waited, so this is my first time away." Asher simply nodded.

"I guessed as much. You don't have the look of a traveler about you. Your friend, though - that's a mystery I'd like to solve. Where's he from again?"

"You'd have to ask him. It's not my story to tell." Lennox expected anger, or for him to pressure her further, but Asher barked out a laugh.

"A loyal man, I like that. Very well, there's plenty of time for me to inquire later." She ignored this and looked out over the waves, taking in their beauty and hoping Asher would take the hint and leave. Instead, he stood next to her in contemplative silence.

"Say lad, I was thinking - what's your name again?"

"Jasper," Lennox replied, proud she hadn't hesitated, "I don't think we've been properly introduced yet."

"No, we haven't. Well, Jasper, I was thinking, why don't you join me and a few friends later for a game of dice?" Her body stiffened.

"I don't know that I'll feel up to it." Lennox placed a hand on her stomach. "I'm still feeling a little seasick and I wouldn't want to ruin your night."

"Come on, you don't have to ask that friend of yours permission, do you? You seem well enough to me. Try your hand at a few rounds. What's the harm?" The harm was Kezra would snap Lennox's legs before letting her go, but she couldn't say that.

"I'll think about it." Asher clapped her on the back, hard. Lennox stumbled forward, using the railing to steady herself.

"That's a good lad. Meet me on deck after supper." He walked away without waiting for a response. Feeling unsettled, Lennox started back toward the room, preparing to face Kezra's anger. When she walked in, Kezra was still seated at the desk where Lennox had left her. She didn't look up from her book as the door banged shut.

"How was the deck? Was it everything you hoped it'd be?"

"It was wonderful!" Lennox answered, not needing to fake enthusiasm. Despite her encounter with Asher, she'd enjoyed every minute aboveboard. In fact, Lennox planned ongoing for another stroll tomorrow, making it a daily occurrence, but there was no need to bring that up now.

"Good, I'm glad you got that out of your system. Did anyone speak to you?" Great. Now Kezra turned to look at her, eyes blazing into Lennox's soul. She couldn't have lied even if she'd wanted to; truth was written all over her face, and Lennox knew it. "Who was it? What did they want?" Kezra's voice went cold. Lennox hated when she did that. The switch in Kezra's demeanor from friend to killer always left her feeling rattled and afraid.

"Asher may have come over to keep me company."

"And that's all?" Kezra's eyes narrowed in suspicion.

"He had a few questions as well."

"What exactly did he ask, and how did you respond? Tell me everything." Lennox recounted the conversation, and Kezra's face grew redder and redder. She wasn't sure if Kezra took a single breath during the story. "Absolutely not," Kezra said when Lennox mentioned the game of dice Asher had invited her to. Lennox's face grew hot as Asher's words echoed through her head. Kezra did not control her; Lennox didn't need her permission to go. Other people had been in charge of her decisions for Lennox's entire life. That ended now.

"I'm going."

"What do you mean you're going?"

"I mean, I'm going and you can't stop me. My life isn't yours to control, and I want to go. I don't plan on staying imprisoned anywhere else for a moment longer, not even this cabin."

"Lennox, I'm sorry, I didn't…" Kezra trailed off. She stopped, contemplating her next words, but there was no point. Her apology, her stricken face, had already sucked the anger out of Lennox. Kezra sounded like she genuinely meant it. "I didn't think about how it might feel to you, having me tell you that you can't leave. I'm just trying to keep up safe, but that's no excuse for how my actions have made you feel. I'm sorry if I made you feel like a prisoner again; that's the last thing I would ever want to do." Lennox raised an eyebrow.

"You are quite literally the one who imprisoned me in the first place." Lennox laughed as she said it, hoping to convey that she didn't hold it against Kezra.

"The irony of what I just said is not lost on me. But still, I really am sorry, Lennox." The last bits of fight melted away.

"Apology accepted. I know you were just trying to protect me." Kezra patted her shoulder, giving an awkward smile. Lennox smiled back, an easy camaraderie falling into place.

"Good, now that that's out of the way, we need to practice our story."

"We do?"

"Of course. The more we practice, the easier it will be for us to recount the details convincingly. You didn't think I'd let you go alone, did you?" Kezra asked. Lennox ran over, throwing her arms around Kezra.

"Thank you, thank you, thank you!" Kezra's arms hung temporarily at her side before she gently wrapped hers around Lennox, returning the embrace.

"Shh, quiet. Your girlish screams will give us away," Kezra scolded.

"Nope, you're not going to ruin this moment by being grouchy. I refuse to let you." Lennox let her go, releasing Kezra from her discomfort.

"Come on, let's get started. The dinner bell will ring soon and we have a lot to cover before then."

They headed toward the mess hall about an hour later. Lennox's head was ready to burst from repeating their story back so many times, but she felt confident they wouldn't forget it. The two had decided to say they were the sons of minor lords on the outskirts of Tesmerin, a detail Lennox had already mentioned to Asher. She wanted to be a scholar and would be travelling to Kitsummit in hopes of learning about the culture of the reclusive mountain folk, and Kezra was her escort, meant to keep her safe and out of trouble. It was close enough to the truth of the matter that it would be easy to remember. Lennox did want to explore the mountains of Kitsummit, and in her heart, she had always wanted to be a scholar, but never thought she'd have the chance. Kezra played the part of her brooding, overprotective cousin well, and it was unlikely anyone would question the ruse. Lennox was ready to burst with excitement at the charade. Never had she imagined she'd have the opportunity to sail across the sea to Kitsummit while disguised as a man. It was exactly the sort of adventure Lennox had always dreamed of.

Lennox hardly tasted the food as they ate - not that there was much to taste. Dinner typically consisted of fish or some other unidentifiable meat boiled into a stew. Unlike the stew she'd eaten at the tavern, which had been richly spiced and flavorful, this one was watery and bland with scant vegetables floating around. Lennox guessed there probably wasn't too much to work with while trapped on a ship. Still, for a lot who traveled the world specializing in trade, it seemed the chef had miraculously never heard of spices. As usual, the two ate in peace, the rest of the crew giving them a wide berth. As the meal progressed, it became evident Asher didn't mean to approach them at dinner, leaving Lennox both relieved and disappointed. It would have been unusual, but she thought maybe her encounter on the deck would put an end to their solitude. Kezra rarely spoke while they ate, afraid the crew would overhear something that would give them away. So Lennox ate the watered-down stew in silence, focusing on the night ahead.

They waited for the mess hall to clear out before turning in their bowls and venturing up to the deck. At night, there were few people roaming around: one a few sailors scanning the waves for potential threats, and a couple of men by the ship's wheel, supposedly navigating by the stars. Gone was the day's normal hustle and bustle, leaving peaceful stillness to the night. It wasn't difficult to spot Asher and his companions. They stood on the far side of the ship by the railing, smoking and laughing. Kezra looked at her, giving Lennox a firm nod, and together they walked over. Asher was the first to spot them. If he was upset by Kezra's presence, he didn't show it.

"Well, look who's decided to come out and play. The little lords have arrived. I see you brought your minder along, Jasper."

"It's Kieran," Kezra said. "I couldn't let my cousin here have all the fun." It came out lightly, but Kezra smiled her predatory grin that sent shivers down Lennox's spine.

"I don't care who he brings as long as they've got some coin," said a man with red hair. Lennox remembered him from the deck earlier that day. He laughed loudly as he patted Kezra on the back, like she were part of the group already.

"We've brought some coin alright," Kezra laughed along, jingling her bag to make a point. The crowns they'd brought with them for gambling clinked together, and the red-haired man eyed them with more interest.

"So you have, let's get to it then." The man gently put a hand on each of their backs, guiding them below deck.

"We're not playing out here?" Lennox asked, disappointed. Asher just laughed.

"The deck's no good for cards, too windy out here. We're out for a smoke before playing a few rounds."

"I thought you said we were playing dice?" Asher shrugged.

"Cards are better with the four of us. Here, have a smoke on me. You'll need it after we're done cleaning you out." Kezra eyed the cigarettes suspiciously, but let Asher hand them over along with a match to light them. Excited for the new experience, Lennox eagerly lit the cigarette and inhaled the smoke, imitating Asher's friend. She gagged. The smoke burned her eyes and clogged her throat, making it impossible to breathe. She coughed until she was red in the face, clawing for breath. Asher and his friend both roared with laughter. Kezra just gave Lennox a pitying look.

"You've never had a smoke before, lad?" Asher wiped a tear from his eye.

"Poor little lordling. Your father's not here to stop you now. Try again, but maybe not so much this time, eh?" Lennox tried again and took a small drag before immediately letting out the smoke. The red-haired man thumped her on the back, like that might stop her from choking. Lennox managed to hold back a cough, and Asher nodded in approval.

"He's got the hang of it now. I'm Bear, but the way. Now let's go relieve the two of you of your coin; those purses look mighty heavy, better for a big man like me to carry them." Bear threw the rest of his cigarette into the ocean, and Lennox followed suit. She spared the waves one more look, trying to capture the sight for her memory. The ocean was pitch black and endless under the night sky. Away from the lights of Tesmerin, millions of stars lit the sky with the crescent moon hiding in the middle of it all. In the darkness, the sea and the sky blurred together, creating a vast expanse of open black.

"Oi, lordling. Are you coming?" Reluctantly, Lennox turned around and followed their new companions down the stairs.

They went to the room Asher had pointed out as his own. It made their cabin look shabby by comparison. Where Kezra and Lennox had a bare floor, a rich crimson rug covered Asher's. Lanterns hung in to four corners of the room, giving the space a warm, comfortable glow. His bed was tucked into the far corner of the large room, leaving plenty of space for the seating area to the left. He had a couch and two chairs surrounding a coffee table. His desk sat next to the bed, the oak looking brand new and well made, where ours was old and falling apart. The table held a bottle of wine and a deck of cards. Asher cracked open the bottle and poured for glasses. Kezra pulled Lennox close.

"Don't finish that glass. He's going to try to get us drunk," Kezra hissed in her ear. Asher passed around the glasses filled to the brim with burgundy liquid.

"A toast to new friends," he said. They clinked the glasses together and everyone drank. Lennox took a small sip, savoring the taste of plums and spices. Asher sat in the chair, and Lennox scrambled to get onto the couch with Kezra, not wanting to end up next to Bear.

"Everyone knows how to play King's, I assume? Surely even a sheltered lordling such as yourself has played cards." Lennox thanked Altheia. Kings was one of the most common games on the continent. While acolytes weren't technically supposed to waste their time with such frivolities at the temple, almost every priestess had learned to play Kings while seated around the dining table. The Mother usually turned a blind eye as long as it didn't keep them from their studies. Lennox nodded her confirmation. Asher passed around the cards. Lennox took another small sip of her drink, noticing his was already halfway gone. Asher's eyes landed on the drink as he dealt.

"Drink up, lads. There's plenty of wine to go around."

"We don't want to impose. I'm sure you paid handsomely for such a fine vintage," Kezra said. Ashe chuckled in reply.

"Oh, I'm sure the two of you will more than pay for it tonight. I'm feeling lucky. Aren't you, Bear?"

"Aye, I wore my lucky socks and everything." Lennox snorted a laugh, but noticed Bear looked serious.

"I don't mind a challenge," Kezra picked up her cards. After examining them, she laid down two copper crowns. "It makes it more satisfying when I win. Place your bets, and be prepared to taste defeat."

The first rounds passed smoothly. Kezra won the first hand, Asher the second, and in a stroke of luck Lennox took the third. Bear grumbled all the while about his socks not working. Asher kept everyone's drinks topped off, making it difficult for Lennox to keep track of how much she'd had to drink. But she sipped from the glass slowly, mindful of Kezra's words. She appreciated Kezra relenting to coming tonight; Lennox wouldn't tarnish it by getting drunk and revealing their secrets. She began to relax as the evening went on, feeling a little smug at being right. There had been nothing to worry about. Kezra won another round. As she scooped up her winnings, she tilted back the rest of her drink.

"Well, we should call it a night. Breakfast comes early, and you don't want to run into Jasper when he's missed a meal." Kezra laughed and started gathering up the handful of coppers she's won.

"Already? Stay another round. Give Bear a chance to earn back some of those coppers he lost." Bear hadn't won a single hand. He kept frowning at his feet.

"Must have put them on inside out. It's bad luck to wear your clothing inside out, you know." As Asher refilled Kezra's glass while keeping his gaze pinned on Lennox.

"What do you say, Jasper?" Lennox just shrugged.

"I guess one more round couldn't hurt." Kezra shot her a look to communicate that they'd be having a conversation about this later, but she sat back down.

"Fine," Kezra huffed. "One more round. Then bed."

"Excellent. It's your deal." Asher smiled widely and handed the cards to Lennox.

"Why don't we get to know each other a little better now that we're friends?" Kezra raised an eyebrow.

"Are we now?"

"Aye, we've shared a bottle of wine and played a friendly game. Now that you've relieved us of our coin, I'd say we're friends. Bear even told you about his lucky socks. He's usually secretive about those." Bear nodded in confirmation.

"Higgins, the slimy bastard, he'd try to steal them if word got out.

You know he would, Ash." Asher nodded along gravely.

"See, now that you've learned one of our secrets, I think it's fair to know more about you in return. Where did you say you're from?"

"Nowhere special, just a small estate outside Tesmerin. Where are you from, Asher?" Kezra leveled her stare at him; daring Asher to answer. Asher smirked back, unbothered.

"Dallos picks us up from all over, doesn't he, Bear? The sea has been my home since I was a boy. I've travelled far and wide, and met many people, and know of many families throughout the region. Maybe I've heard of you. What's your surname again?"

"Emerett," Lennox answered quickly. "Both of us, we're cousins." Kezra glared at her again for going off script, but Lennox didn't see any harm in providing the detail. After all, the Emeretts really were a family who lived on the outskirts of Tesmerin. They likely weren't wealthy, or they wouldn't have needed to give Jasper to the temple, but there was no reason for Asher to know that. In fact, Kezra should have been thanking her for thinking on her feet. Lennox would tell her so later. Kezra placed a few coins on the table, raising the bet. Bear folded, grumbling about his socks again. Lennox followed suit, leaving just Asher and Kezra in play. Asher matched, raising the tension in the room between them. Lennox laid down the next card.

"Aye, I can see the family resemblance between the two of you now, something about the eyes. You sure have deep pockets for a minor lord. How did you come by such wealth?"

"As you can see, we're lucky. We've made a little money here and there on our way to the coast." Lennox laid down another card; Kezra raised again. Asher matched.

"Right, and that luck is carrying you all the way to Kitsummit. It's a strange place for a couple of young lordlings. Nothing there for you but rough terrain, snow and an unwelcoming population. It's a curious place for you to travel."

"Curious indeed. My cousin here wants to be a scholar. I'm escorting him there for his studies." Asher's gaze flicked Lennox's way.

"I wouldn't have pegged your cousin as the studious type." Asher's gaze bore into her while Lennox flipped over the last card. All the money Kezra had won during the evening was now in the pile. "What's your work about, little lordling? What are you searching for in the mountains?" Before Lennox could answer, Kezra flipped over her cards, diverting Asher's attention. She revealed a pair of threes, a losing hand if Lennox ever saw one.

"Well, lordlings, looks like your luck's run out." Asher revealed his hand, showing he had four of a kind. He scooped up his winnings. Bear let out a whoop.

"It seems it has. With that, we'd better get going before we lose our travelling money. Thank you for the excellent drink and company." Kezra rose to her feet and made her way to the door, not bothering to see if Lennox followed. Lennox mumbled her thanks and scrambled to follow. As she stood, Asher rolled up his sleeves, and Lennox noticed a tattoo wrapped around his arm. A black band. She'd seen something like that before, but where?

"Good night, little lords," Asher called after them, "it was an enlightening evening."

When Lennox caught up with Kezra, she'd already unlocked the door to their cabin and was holding it open for Lennox to follow her inside. Kezra did not look happy. She slammed the door closed as Lennox stepped inside and bolted the lock. Lennox couldn't take the hostile silence any longer.

"So, I think that went well. Right up until you lost all of that money. What were you thinking making such a bet on a pair of threes?"

"What was I thinking? What were you thinking, giving him a surname to follow up on? He will ask around now. You could have just ruined everything."

"So what if he finds out we lied about a surname, which is unlikely by the way? No one on this ship is going to have heard of the Emeretts, and even if they have, we'll be gone in a week, anyway."

Lennox lay down on the bed, suddenly exhausted by the night's events and possibly a little intoxicated. Kezra stormed over to the desk, as if trying to put as much space between them as possible.

"The problem is you've left a trail to follow now. Tylan was at the temple. You used your friend's real name. When the sailors wind up back in Tesmerin, speaking of Jasper and Keiran Emerett, you don't think Tylan will put that together?" Kezra stared at the desk and cocked her head to the side. Lennox slunk under the covers, hoping Kezra didn't turn to look at her again. Lennox hadn't thought of that, but she was determined to stay positive.

"If Tylan even hears from the sailors, we'll be long gone. It'll take weeks for them to make it back to Tesmerin. Everything's going to be fi-." Kezra spun around and looked about the room, searching. The abrupt motion stopped Lennox from finishing her thought. Kezra threw open the wardrobe.

"Someone's been in here." All of her anger melted away, and her face had turned white with panic.

"What makes you think that?" Lennox asked.

"The book, it's not in the same place I left it. And come here, look."

At first, Lennox didn't see anything out of place. But when she looked harder, their packs appeared jumbled. Stray items had been left spilling out of the sides, like someone had tipped the contents on the floor then tried to shove it all back in a hurry. Lennox never would have noticed, but now that Kezra had pointed it out, it seemed obvious.

"But..how?" Lennox stammered. "You have the key."

"There must be a copy." Kezra emptied the packs. She went through every item, searching for anything missing. Lennox was grateful now that Kezra had made her carry the rest of their money, hidden in her cloak. At the time, Lennox told Kezra she was being ridiculous but now…

"Is anything missing?" Kezra shook her head.

"I don't think so. We didn't leave much of value behind."

"What do you think they were looking for?"

"I don't know. Maybe just money. They could have left when they didn't find anything of value. But they put our things back. Whoever it was didn't want us knowing they were here." Kezra tucked the packs back under the bed, satisfied all the content was accounted for.

"So what's it mean?"

"I don't know; I don't think it was a common thief looking for money. I think Asher wanted us away from the room to look for something. I told you, we can't trust him." Even with the evidence laid out in front of her, Lennox wanted to deny it. She didn't want to admit that she'd been wrong about him. Lennox felt manipulated, used.

"I'm sorry. I should have listened," Lennox said. Kezra seemed to soften.

"It'll be okay. But we need to be more careful. No more card games - okay?" Lennox nodded. They went to bed, but as tired as she was, Lennox couldn't sleep. She'd seen something in that room, something she wanted to tell Kezra about, but no matter how much she tossed and turned, Lennox couldn't remember what it was.

CHAPTER 15

Kezra

After the night playing cards, the rest of their journey passed without further incident. They mostly had the weather to thank for that. Storms rolled in, turning the sea violent. The waves grew larger, and the crew fought to stop them from toppling the ship. Wind and rain pelted the deck. No one wanted to slip on the slick wooden surface of the deck and be caught off guard when a powerful wave crashed into the boat. They no longer needed to fake Lennox's bout of seasickness. She'd been looking green ever since the storm started; she clung to a bucket for dear life, waiting for the next round of turbulence to upend her stomach. The storms cost them a few extra precious days at sea, but Kezra felt it was worth it as it kept unwanted guests from their door.

By the time they landed in Alara, the port town outside Kitsummit, Lennox had lost all of her swagger, along with a slightly alarming amount of weight. She clung to Kezra's side for support as Kezra helped carry her off the ship while Lennox's legs wobbled beneath her. Captain Dallos waited for them at the end of the docks. Kezra deposited Lennox on the shore, making sure to place her away from the crew unloading the cargo. Still, they snickered at her as she passed, not impressed by the lordling's ability to handle the life of a seafarer. Satisfied Lennox was safe, Kezra made her way over to Dallos, pulling a gold coin from her purse. As she did so, Kezra let her fingers linger over the two remaining vials of potion, confronted by their presence. She was glad she'd thought to bring them with her the night of the card game because whoever searched their cabin certainly would have taken them. Anything rumored to contain magic was increasingly valuable, and the phosphorescent glow of the liquid screamed of a spell. It would be so easy to sell them as a love potion, or a brew for good fortune without knowing the actual effects. Dallos tapped his foot, impatiently waiting.

"Captain!" Kezra raised a hand in greeting. "Thank you for the passage on your lovely vessel. We'll sing praises of the Devina's fine lodgings and disciplined crew far and wide." Dallos fought back a smile.

"Aye, well, I wouldn't mind taking a few of your lordling friends as passengers, granted they paid the same as you. Speaking of which, I believe three gold crowns are in order."

"You'll have the one crown I still owe you." Kezra handed it over, placing it in Dallos's awaiting palm.

"I had to try. You could throw in a little something for Bear. He's still sore about some coin he lost; won't stop talking to anyone who will listen about the dangers of wearing your socks inside out."

"He can ask his friend Asher about that. They cleaned me out. If anything, you should be paying me for the additional services I performed. Dear old Greg's cabin was particularly filthy. It's hard to believe he was staying there." Dallos pocketed the coin and looked over at the crew, suddenly seeming very busy.

"Aye, well, you'd have to take that up with him, you would, not while he's busy unloading, mind you. Can't take him from his work over a dirty cabin."

"And where is he? I don't think I've had the pleasure of seeing him on the ship at all, not since the port in Tesmerin in fact. I'd love to share my gratitude to him for letting us have his room."

"Oh, he's over there somewhere." Dallos waved his hand in the general direction of the busy crew. "Now, I have to go. I have a group of bone-headed crew to supervise, and they've already put the barrels on the wrong end of the dock. Oi! Not there, you idiots!"

"Of course. Goodbye, Captain. Until our paths cross again," Kezra said. Dallos nodded in her direction and scurried off, back to the crew, barking out orders all the while. With that handled, Kezra started back toward Lennox, who was looking better already. Some color had returned to her face, and she was standing up, holding her pack. Kezra threw her arm around Lennox's shoulder.

"Come on, Jasper. Let's go find an inn for the night. I think we've earned a night of rest on solid ground." Lennox turned a little green again, perhaps remembering trying to sleep on the rolling sea; she stumbled a little as Kezra led her toward town.

Although, town was perhaps a generous term for the collection of buildings surrounding the docks. In Tesmerin, a collection of stalls sat directly outside the docks as vendors tried to haggle with incoming sailors for inventory or tried to sell their wares to those passing through. The streets of Alara, on the other hand, were empty. The crew unloaded their goods in relative silence, broken only by grunts or muttered curses from a lone worker. A rough dirt road led from the docks into town. The main center of town consisted of a small square. Kezra only saw a few signs; a blacksmith and a fabric store sat next to each other. The buildings were all small stone houses with thatched roofs. Smoke billowed out of the chimneys of the rows of homes. They didn't have any trouble finding the inn, one of the few buildings with multiple floors. Next to it sat the town pub, already filling up with the lucky crew who weren't needed for unloading. The thought of the drunken crew members trying to pull them into conversations and card games filled Kezra with dread, so she steered Lennox straight into the inn, where Kezra hoped to find a hot meal, a nice bath and a clean, warm bed.

Heat washed over her as they stepped into an empty room. Kezra hadn't realized how cold she'd been until she'd entered the warm room. Summer was fading into fall, but Tesmerin was still warm this time of year. So far up north, fall had come harder, giving the air a chill. Kezra made a mental note to check the fabric store later to see if she could find them some warmer clothing. For now, the fire roaring in the hearth warmed them, the only sign that the inn might be open.

"Hello," Kezra called out to the empty room, "is anyone here?"

"Don't be daft, of course I'm here. Seat yourselves; I'll be out in a moment." A woman's voice yelled back at them, thick with a northern accent. It was difficult to understand, but Kezra got the gist and sat herself as close to the fire as possible. Lennox plopped down across from her and slung her bag on the bench. Lennox's teeth chattered as she tried to warm herself. A woman strode into the room. She wore trousers as they did, but hers looked thicker and much warmer. Tall brown boots adorned her legs, stopping at her knees. She had on a cream-colored long-sleeved top and a brown vest that appeared to be made of the same material as her trousers. Pale hair flowed down her shoulders and framed her face. Even under her layers of clothing, Kezra noted the woman's muscular arms, probably a result of the laborious lifestyle that mountain life demanded. The woman snickered at their thin clothing, shaking her head. "The docks are straight ahead. Go down the dirt road, opposite the direction of town. You can't miss them."

"I'm sorry?" Kezra asked, taken by surprise at the instructions.

"I assumed you two must be lost, walking around dressed like that. Go back to wherever you came from. You won't last long here."

"We were actually planning on sticking around a while and hiking up to Kitsummit. Although I can see now, we're not prepared. You wouldn't happen to know where we can get some more suitable clothing, do you?"

"And maybe something to eat?" Lennox asked. "What? I'm starving and it smells divine in here."

"That would be my cake. I've been baking for days as we've been expecting a ship to come in. This place will fill up with sailors soon enough once they're done at the tavern. The food I can help you with. As for clothes, well, I suggest you eat and return right back to the ship you came in on. Kitsummit is no place for you, especially this time of year. Winter comes early in the mountains. You'll freeze to death or get lost in the snow before you even get close to Kitsummit." Kezra looked her straight in the eyes.

"Going back isn't an option. We need to make it to Kitsummit. Please? Do you know of anyone who could help us?" The woman examined their faces, scrutinizing them before nodding to herself, drawing a silent conclusion.

"Jessa's going to kill me. She hates being rushed. But you won't last a week dressed like that. Stay here. I'll get you something to eat and see if Jessa can help you." The innkeeper walked away from them, disappearing from view as she muttered to herself about taking in strays. Lennox stretched out, seemingly unthawed at this point.

"Well, that went well," Lennox said.

"I guess so. You don't find it strange how she tried to scare us away?" Kezra asked. Lennox just shrugged.

"Maybe she was just trying to look out for us. It is pretty cold out there. What did you even buy when you were at the markets in Tesmerin? You were gone all day and didn't think to get some clothing with some fur?"

"You didn't think of it either," Kezra grumbled. Honestly, she hadn't thought it'd be so cold yet. She'd been so anxious to get away from Tesmerin, away from Tylan, that Kezra hadn't really thought this through. What were they going to do? Waltz up to a notoriously reclusive mountain tribe and say: "Hi, have you been hiding magical solutions to breaking a bond forged with magic?" No, that probably wasn't going to work and then she'd be completely screwed. And worse, so would Lennox because Kezra had insisted on dragging her into this like the selfish person she was, just because it felt better to have Lennox at her side. Yelena's prophecy kept playing through her mind; she wondered if Lennox could be the light force Yelena had alluded to, especially since she was now convinced that Lennox possessed magic.

"You ok over there?" Lennox bumped her shoulder into Kezra's.

"Fine. Why?"

"You've gone a whole five minutes without lecturing me to be careful or about the dangers of the mysterious cake-making innkeeper. The change in character is genuinely concerning." Lennox examined her fingernails while she spoke, frowning at them. "Broken already. I really miss basic self-care. I'd kill for a nail file."

"Are you actually worried about your nails right now?" Kezra blurted out. Lennox scowled at her.

"Altheia demands her followers be well-groomed. Just because we're on the run doesn't mean we have to neglect good hygiene." Her eyes settled on Kezra's calloused hands and the absolute mess of her nails with their broken cuticles. "I suppose you've never been acquainted with a nail file."

"Would you keep your voice down?" Kezra hissed.

"No need to stop on my account." The innkeeper came back carrying a full platter. She set the platter down between them, along with two steaming mugs. The scent of wine, heavily spiced and warm, wafted in the air. Food enough for a family filled the platter: warm cake, dried fruits, freshly baked bread along with meat and cheese. Kezra forced herself to turn away from the food and look the innkeeper in the eye.

"Thank you for your hospitality..." Kezra trailed off, not knowing her name.

"Celene," she supplied.

"Thank you for your hospitality, Celene. I'm sorry for my cousin's outburst. You see, he's avoiding an arranged marriage. He wants to be a scholar instead and hopes to show a study of Kitsummit as evidence of the path's merit."

"Right, he's getting married, you said? To a woman?"

"That was the arrangement." The words came out garbled through Lennox's mouth full of food, and Kezra fought off the impulse to shoot her a disapproving look.

"Right then. And you are in the same position?" Celene asked.

"I'm not getting married, I'm just here as an escort."

"That's not what I mean."

"Well then, I'm not sure what you're referring to." Celene raised an eyebrow in response, but Kezra didn't waver under her stare. Celene sighed, throwing back her head.

"Look, it's no business of mine what troubles the two of you, but

I did ask Jessa to make you some more suitable breeches and she takes pride in her work." Celene took a deep breath and glanced around the room, which was still empty, and lowered her voice. "There are some, shall we say, stylistic differences between how she makes them for lads and lasses. Right now, she's making breeches for two stray girls I seem to have taken in. Would you prefer I change the order?"

"You knew?" Kezra's jaw hung open and she tried to snap it shut. As far as she knew, no one had ever caught her while playing Keiran before, and she wasn't sure what gave them away. Celene snorted.

"Of course I knew. It takes more than some binding a pair of breeches to fool me. You wouldn't be the first pair to decide it would be safer to travel as a man. So, shall I change your order?" Lennox and Kezra exchanged a look. Lennox gave a subtle shake of her head.

"I don't think that will be necessary," Kezra said. She took a gold crown out of her purse and slid it to the end of the table. "This is for the food and a room for the night. Also, your discretion while the crew remains in Alara would be appreciated."

Celene picked up the coin and turned it around, playing with it. She smacked the coin back on the table and pushed it back.

"I'd recommend hanging onto that. There's no telling what Jessa will charge you for a rush order, but I hope you have plenty more where that came from, or she'll be coming after me. Now, eat up while you still can. It seems your cousin has quite the appetite." Sure enough, Lennox had already helped herself to a slice of cake, two pieces of bread, a thick slice of cheese and was currently working through the dried apples.

"What the hell?" Kezra snapped.

"What?" Lennox looked at Celene with her big, green doe eyes. "You should have seen the slop we've been eating these past few weeks. I was starving. This is truly delightful, food fit for a goddess. I don't suppose it would be possible to get another slice of that cake?" Celene was about to answer when the door clanged open, revealing several crewmates stumbling into the room. Kezra cursed under her breath, recognizing the man at the front with blazing red hair.

"Hey look, we found the little lords," Bear shouted, smiling. Celene plastered on a dazzling smile.

"I'll see what I can do about that cake." Kezra returned her smile with an uneasy one of her own and muttered a thanks. She didn't like that Celene hadn't taken the bribe. What if she was planning on selling them out later? Kezra still wasn't sure what Asher wanted with them, but Kezra was confident he'd pay this woman for what little information she had. She doubted he'd hesitate to attack two runaway women when the threat of insulting a minor lord no longer hung over his head. Celene squeezed Kezra's shoulder, seeing her unease.

"Your secret is safe with me," Celene said, low enough for only Kezra to hear. Bear slid into the open seat next to Kezra and gave her a hearty slap on the back, as if greeting an old friend. Lennox hastily shoved more food into her mouth as she gave Bear a wary look.

"Fancy seeing you two here. Though you'd be too good to settle for a pint in a place like this."

"Well, options were rather limited." Kezra took a sip of wine, letting the spices wash over her tongue and settle her nerves. She knew the crew was bound to come in eventually, but she'd hoped they would be settled into their rooms by the time they did.

"What are you drinking?" Bear peered into her mug, turning his nose up at the warm, spicy drink. "I knew you lot wouldn't drink a lowly pint." Lennox rolled her eyes.

"This was just a warm-up before the real fun begins. I'll bet I can drink one faster than you. Loser buys the next round." She gave Bear a mischievous smirk, and Bear threw his head back laughing.

"You're on, lordling. What about you, Kieran, isn't it? Think you can beat me?"

"No thanks, I know when I've met my match. Someone's going to need to be coherent enough to get that one up the stairs tonight." Kezra tried to copy Lennox's easy charm, but it fell flat. She was more accustomed to delivering threats or cutting remarks than winning someone over, and it showed.

"Ah, suit yourself, ye old mum." Bear laughed again at his own joke and summoned Celene back for the requested ale.

Kezra watched as Lennox heartily drank the ale, trying with her might to gulp it down before Bear and failing miserably. He finished before she was even halfway done. Undeterred by the loss, she finished chugging down the pint without stopping to breathe, which earned an appreciative round of cheering from Bear and his friends.

"I guess I was wrong about you two. You're alright, as far as lordlings go. The next round's on me," Bear gave Kezra a pointed look. "And that includes you too, Mum. It'd be rude to turn down a free drink."

"Alright, alright. One pint," Kezra consented. This elicited another round of cheering from the group, who had clearly started working on their intoxication before arriving. She sipped the ale, marvelling at Lennox. For all Kezra had lectured her about being cautious, it was her spontaneity that bought them the most security. Now that she'd been drinking with Bear and the crew, they started to see her as a friend, not a stuffy, rich outsider like they'd first assumed. Kezra wouldn't need to worry as much about them trying to attack or rob them now that Lennox had ingratiated herself to them. Kezra would have thought after a life in the temple that it would have been difficult for her to adjust to the outside world, but Lenox fit right in wherever she went.

Now Lennox was nodding vigorously as Bear told a story involving a lady's dress, capturing a pig, and presumably putting said pig in the aforementioned dress. She asked all the right questions to keep the story going, and for a moment, Kezra felt a pang of jealousy. When was the last time she had fit into a group that easily? When had Kezra last had a friend, or even a companion to grab an ale with, or share a ridiculous story? Never. Working for Tylan didn't afford her many opportunities to get close to people. In fact, stories of the amethyst assassin made their way across Oscana, making people terrified of her. How could Lennox slip into this group of hardened sailors so easily? Kezra studied her, hoping to find the secret. Kezra drank the rest of her ale and wiped her mouth with her sleeve, chasing the bitter thoughts away. She stood up, pushing back the chair.

"Well, it's been good to finally share a drink together. If you'll excuse us, it would be good to get some sleep on a bed that's not lurching side to side." Bear looked at Lennox and raised his eyebrows.

"Us, eh?" Lennox threw back the rest of her pint and slammed the glass on the table hard enough to earn a stern look from Celene and a laugh from Bear.

"I know when I've been beaten. It's time to call it a night. I'll get you next time, Bear," Kezra said, attempting to join in on the joke.

"Whatever you say, little lordling. I'll be waiting." Reluctantly, Lennox joined her as they walked toward Celene together, Lennox stumbling occasionally. Kezra rolled her eyes. Had she really just been jealous of the drunken girl?

"If you're going to start breaking my glasses for your little show, I'm going to have to ask you to leave."

"I didn't break it!" Lennox exclaimed. Celene just held her stare, not responding to the outburst. "Fine, I'm sorry," Lennox slurred. She stumbled forward, as standing seemed to be too much for her to manage.

"It won't happen again," Kezra said. She took Lennox's arm and hooked it around her shoulder, helping to steady the drunken priestess. "Would you mind showing us to our room, please? Before this one hurts himself?" Celene led them up the stairs to a simple room with two small beds pushed up against the wall. A fledgling fire burned in the hearth, not yet hot enough to warm the space.

"It's not much, but it's what I can do when we're expecting an inn full of sailors. You do have your own washroom, though." Kezra nodded appreciatively, starting to feel the strain of supporting Lennox as she leaned on Kezra more heavily. Celene handed Kezra the keys and moved out of the doorway so they could get in. She slowly maneuvered Lennox to the bed, where she fell with a loud thump. It was honestly impressive how quickly the alcohol had hit her. Kezra thanked Celene again, moving to close the door. Celene met her eye before leaving.

"Lock that door and don't leave the room tonight. Not all the crew are so friendly."

"I will. Thank you for looking out for us."

With a final, stiff nod, she turned and left the room. Kezra appreciated the advice, but she wasn't too worried now that they were on land. It would have been easy for Asher to rob them on the boat and throw them overboard. But here, there were witnesses; it would be more difficult for him to cover his tracks in a town he needed to return to regularly. They would be fine. Still, Kezra made sure the door was locked and bolted, just in case. She checked on Lennox, who was now snoring softly. Kezra removed Lennox's boots, then covered her up. Once Lennox was taken care of, Kezra went to the washroom ready for a much deserved, and if she was being honest with herself, much needed bath.

Blessedly, this town, or at least this inn, had running water. Kezra let the hot water soak through her skin. Finally, after weeks of being alert, on edge, she let herself relax. They could do this; they would make their way to Kitsummit; they'd find a way to break her bond for good, then they would...what exactly? Lennox couldn't go back to the temple; that life was over for her. Going back to Tesmerin wasn't an option either. Maybe they could stay in the mountains after breaking the bond? Or go further afield, out of Oscana altogether. Kezra had heard that Nalathay was beautiful. Tylan's reach didn't seem to extend that far. Yes, Kezra decided; she would talk to Lennox about it on their way to Kitsummit. They would start a new life in Nalathay, maybe use the money Kezra brought to open a little shop, a bookshop. It was as good a dream as any. She came out of the bath feeling refreshed, both mentally and physically. Kezra lay in bed, exhausted, ready for a solid night of sleep, and started dozing off.

"Kezra?" Lennox's soft voice was startling loud in the quiet room where the only other sound was the crackling of the fire.

"Mmm?"

"Thank you for taking care of me. I'm glad I came with you." The drunken words came out slightly slurred, but they still warmed Kezra's heart.

"I'm glad you came too." Kezra's voice was thick with emotion. Then, unable to deal with the emotional mood in the room, she added, "Even though you seem determined to cause trouble for us." Lennox let out a quiet giggle. In the following silence, Kezra's eyes fluttered closed. She was almost asleep, calmed by the bath and the cozy atmosphere, when Lennox spoke again.

"It'll be alright, Kezra. I promise. We'll find a way to break your bond. I won't let you down." Lennox rolled over and went to sleep, not expecting a response. Kezra wasn't sure if Lennox knew she was awake, or if Lennox would even remember saying that in the morning, but Kezra's heart cracked, nonetheless. She had helped ruin this girl's life; Kezra didn't deserve her kindness. She fell back into a troubled sleep, feeling like a fraud. As she drifted to sleep, Kezra promised herself that she wouldn't let Lennox down. Together, they would build a better life than the one Kezra had helped destroy.

After what felt like only a few minutes of sleep, a scraping sound jolted her awake. The door scraped across the floor as it opened. In her tired state, it was difficult for Kezra's brain to make sense of the chaos unfolding in the dim firelight. Three men burst into the room. One grabbed Lennox and was trying to bind her with a rope. Kezra grabbed for the knife she usually kept under her pillow to go help Lennox, only to come away with nothing. Damn it. Exhausted from the journey and content from a warm bath and good food, Kezra hadn't prepared for an attack, something she always did. Stupid, stupid Kezra. She needed to help Lennox, but first, she had to take care of the two men coming toward her. Unlike the man who'd rushed Lennox, these two came at her slowly, circling Kezra on both sides, looking for the best moment to strike. The door was still wide open. Kezra knew that if she ran now, she could make it, maybe run and get help. But what if they took Lennox? Kezra didn't think she could live with herself if she ran away and Lennox was taken. Besides, someone must have heard the noise these men had made breaking in, but no one had come. Which meant they were on their own. Celene had betrayed them. The thought hurt, but Kezra would deal with it later.

For now, Kezra needed to take down the men circling her. She launched herself at the man by the door, thinking she might be able to knock him off his feet and grab his weapon. As she dashed toward him, his features came into focus. Blond hair glinted in the firelight, a scar cut across his cheek, just below his eye; Asher had come for them. Kezra grinned. She knew something was off about him. Taking him down would be fun. Bracing herself for impact, Kezra hurled toward him, but the impact never came. At the last moment, he stepped out of the way, leaving Kezra off balance as she tried to slow her momentum. Kezra stopped herself from falling, but quickly realized that she was in trouble. The man who'd been wrestling with Lennox had her subdued with her feet and wrists bound. Now all three of them were approaching Kezra.

Normally, this wouldn't be an issue. She could last long enough against them to at least get away. But Lennox presented a problem. It was unlikely Kezra could rescue her while weaponless. For one awful moment, she thought about leaving Lennox there. After all, Kezra hardly knew the girl. Was she obligated to sacrifice her freedom for Lennox's sake? Kezra shook the intrusive thought away, giving her full attention to the oncoming attackers. She had just vowed to herself to help Lennox build a better life, and she wouldn't be so quick to break it. The odds weren't in her favor, but she would try to handle them one at a time. Asher would be her first target. Kezra threw herself at him again, kicking at his legs to knock him off balance. This time, he didn't evade the attack, and Kezra knocked him off his feet. Not stopping to enjoy her success, Kezra turned to the man approaching her and spun out of his grasp. With one hand, she thrust up at his face, and with the other, she twisted his wrist until he dropped the dagger in his hand. Snagging the weapon, Kezra began feeling more confident about her odds when a pair of arms grabbed her from behind, lifting her into the air.

Without hesitation, she snapped her head back, smashing it into the man's nose, then drove the knife back blindly, hoping to hit his thigh. He let out a string of curses, roaring in pain, and released her. Unfortunately, Asher had recovered and was prepared for her this time. He caught Kezra's wrist, twisting it roughly behind her back, parroting the move she'd just made to steal back the weapon. Kezra threw her head back, as she'd just done to his companion, but he moved aside, maintaining hold of her wrist.

"Oh, no you don't!" Asher shouted. He kicked Kezra's feet out from under her, bringing Kezra to her knees. She felt his weight on her back, pushing her face down onto the ground. Panicked, Kezra started flailing, trying to break free. Distantly, Kezra heard Lennox's muffled screams. They'd gagged her, those bastards.

"Quick, Huck, bring the rope," said a voice Kezra didn't recognize. The rope circled her hands and feet, then another kick hit her in the ribs.

"Enough! Tylan wants them back alive. Do you want to be responsible for damaging his captives?" Asher said.

"He never said we couldn't rough them up a bit."

A groan escaped Kezra's lips as she tried to clear her head. They mentioned Tylan. Real fear started to take over; Kezra had to fight it down. How had he possibly found us? Worse, what would he do once he got ahold of her after she'd betrayed him. Kezra raised her head, searching for Lennox. She looked just as terrified as Kezra felt, but was mercifully uninjured. At least they didn't seem interested in harming her. The three of them stood in front of the fireplace, having a quiet discussion. Kezra had to strain to listen since her ears were still ringing from the kick in the head. One of them was tearing apart the room, searching for something.

"There's nothing here, boss," he said, rummaging through their packs. "Just some food and clothes, nothing that looks like what you described." Concern flickered across Asher's face.

"No matter. We just need to sneak them onto the ship and keep them in the hold. Huck, go look out for the caption. He can't see us."

"Make Kael do it. Let me take that one," he said, pointing at Kezra.

"I said go." Asher's tone didn't invite further argument. Grumbling, Huck left the room. Finally, Asher turned his attention back to Kezra and smiled.

"You thought you were clever, didn't you? Trying to pass yourselves off as some backwoods lords of a small estate. I knew who you were from the moment I saw you. Tylan passed your description to us as soon as you escaped. It's a shame you didn't bring any of that purple potion with you though. It would have made this easier. Oh, don't look so surprised, sweetheart. He has a way of communicating with those of us loyal to him." Kezra glared at him. Asher wore a coat to keep out the cold, but she'd bet anything that his arm sported a thin, solid black band. How had Kezra missed that? For all the time she'd spent worrying, Kezra had somehow missed spotting one of Tylan's bonded.

She tried to shove down the anger and self-loathing she felt so Kezra could clear her head enough to find a way out of this situation. Asher couldn't get us on that ship. If he did, everything they'd done would be for nothing, and they'd never escape again. Kezra's mind whirled, trying to find a way out, but she kept coming up empty. Lennox seemed to have calmed, or at least her muffled screams had stopped. Kezra wasn't sure if that was a good sign or a bad one. She debated screaming for help, but decided against it. Everyone in the inn had to have heard the struggle, yet no one had come. They were on their own. If she yelled, they'd only gag her too; it was better to remain quiet and hope Asher stopped paying so much attention to them.

It would help if Lennox would stop moving so much; that was bound to get their attention at best. And at worst…Kezra shuddered to think about it. Turning her head in Lennox's direction, Kezra tried to convey a message to her to stop. What she saw almost made her let out an involuntary yelp. Lennox was glowing. It was very faint, almost imperceptible, but Kezra had seen her use this magic before, so it was easy to recognize. The man named Huck scurried back into the room, still holding his nose, which was swelling rapidly. Kezra grinned, satisfied; at least she'd broken it.

"The coast's clear. The captain retired to his room for the night. Grab them and let's get out of here before someone comes looking," Huck said. Asher nodded.

"Kael, you get that one," he said, pointing to Lennox. "I'll grab the troublemaker. Huck, you scout ahead, make sure no one sees us." Huck started grumbling in protest, but a gasp from Kael shut him up.

"Boss, what is that?" Kael pointed at Lennox, backing away from her; his whole body shook.

"Impossible," Asher said in a whisper. "This is impossible!"

"Witchcraft!"

Lennox glowed brightly; the silver light radiated out of her and grew brighter and brighter. Her green eyes glowed with it, and her long hair steamed out behind her, caught in a wind no one else could feel. The ropes binding her snapped, falling to the ground. Their captors were frozen, stunned by the impossibility of seeing magic with their own eyes. Asher came out of the trance first.

"What are you waiting for, men? Get her!"

Lennox glowed brighter still. Kezra had to look away from the blinding light. Kael fell to his knees.

"Forgive me, goddess." He started sobbing.

"Get up, you dolt. She's no goddess, just a girl playing with forces she doesn't understand." Asher's voice wavered as he said it, as if he wasn't convinced by his own words.

Kezra spared a glance at Lennox, and she did indeed look like a goddess. The silver light swirled around in her green eyes, glowing. Her hair fanned out around her, and silver wisps of light floated off her skin.

"Enough of this," Huck growled, charging at her. Lennox slowly swiveled her head toward him. As he came at her, she held up her hands in defense. And then Huck was gone.

"Huck! You'll pay for that, you bitch." Asher pulled out his dagger.

"Lennox, look out!" Kezra screamed. Lennox flicked her fingers at him, and Asher was gone too. In the firelight, Kezra saw specks of silver float through the air where he'd been standing. Kael stayed on his knees, head on the floor, bowing to Lennox. His sobs were the only sound in the room.

"You, get up." Lennox's voice echoed through the room, taking on a rich, otherworldly quality. Reluctantly, Kael sat up, sniffling. "You will not tell anyone what you saw here, or try to harm us ever again. If you do, you'll meet the same fate as your friends. Am I understood?" Kael started sobbing again, but nodded his head vigorously. "Good, now untie her." He crawled over to Kezra, and with shaking hands, started sawing through her binds. Once her hands were free, Kezra took the dagger and pressed it to his neck.

"You will tell the captain that Asher and Huck ran away. You don't know where," Kezra said. Kael nodded again, still unable to speak. "Fine. Then go. And remember, don't tell anyone about what you saw here today, or she'll know." Kezra inclined her head toward Lennox, still levitating in her strange silver wind. Kael scrambled toward the door, bowing to Lennox as he went.

"As the goddess commands. I won't forget her mercy," Kael said.

With that he bolted out of the room, shoving past three people who appeared in the doorway. Celene stood still, gawking at the scene in front of her. She was flanked by a very short woman wearing a crimson robe and the large, husky form of Bear. Lennox's glow started to soften, the silver fled from her eyes, and the wind surrounding her died down. Then, the light vanished completely, bathing the room in darkness. It took a moment for Kezra's eyes to adjust to the faint glow of the fire. Lennox's round, clear green eyes met hers.

"What just happened?" she asked. Kezra started to reply, but was cut off as Lennox crumpled to the floor.

CHAPTER 16

Lennox

"Lennox! Lennox!" Kezra's panicked voice bled through the fog clouding Lennox's mind. She tried to sit up, but the pounding in her head knocked her back down.

"What happened?" Lennox tried to say the words, but they came out as garbled mush.

"Help me get her into bed, please?"

Large, gentle hands pulled Lennox from the floor, carefully cradling her head. She let out an involuntary moan as her body hit the bed; why did everything hurt? As she laid there, her head began to clear. Memories came flooding back, a sweeping silver light, wind swirling around her, a man with a dagger turning into harmless flecks of glittering dust. Lennox darted up, panicked. What had she done? Another bout of dizziness tried to overtake her, but she fought it back. Kezra hovered over Lennox, chewing her nails. Lennox had never seen her do that before, Kezra must have been really worried.

"What happened?" The words came out clearly this time.

"I'm not completely sure. Asher and his men tried to kidnap us, and then…" Kezra trailed off, glancing at the doorway as if unsure about whether she could continue.

"I think," calm a soft, steady voice, "that we could all use a warm drink to process this and discuss what comes next. Can you stand?" Celene looked at Lennox, expecting an answer. Whatever had happened, Celene looked completely unfazed, unlike her companions. Lennox was surprised to see Bear standing in the middle of the room, his face scrunched like she was a puzzle he was trying to figure out. A short, petite woman stood next to Celene. She wore a thick, crimson cloak, made of expensive looking material. Her hood was up, shadowing most of her face, but Lennox could just make out a gleeful smile, the whites of the woman's teeth reflecting the firelight. Celene pointedly cleared her throat. Right, she was still waiting for an answer. Lennox swung her legs around the side of the bed, taking care not to move too quickly. Her head still spun from the movement, but it was no longer overwhelming.

"I think so. I just need a minute."

"Good. Jessa, Bear, come with me. We'll give you two a moment; meet us downstairs when you're ready. I'll warm up some spiced wine." Celene left the room, the other two trailing after her. The woman she'd called Jessa legged behind, giving Lennox a wink before shutting the door behind her.

"Is that the woman making our clothes? Does she seem a little off to you?" Lennox asked. Kezra gaped at her, open-mouthed.

"She seems off to you?"

"I mean, a little. What's she so happy about?"

"I have no idea. But we just watched you start glowing and turn two men into powder with a wave of your fingers, so I'm not sure what a normal reaction to that would be."

Lennox winced. So that had been real? The memories were hazy, it felt like a dream. Part of her had hoped it was an elaborate fantasy she'd made up. The reality of it started to sink in. She'd killed two people and thoroughly traumatized a third. And even though Asher had been trying to hurt them, it was difficult for Lennox to wrap her mind around the fact that she'd taken his life. Lennox gasped for air, suddenly unable to breathe. Her thoughts started racing. Those three people downstairs had seen her. Who would they tell? What happened when Dallos started looking for his crew? Would she go to prison, be executed? What would happen to Kezra? Air, she needed air. Kezra grabbed Lennox by the shoulders, giving her a gentle shake.

"Breathe with me, Lennox. Three deep breaths in and out." Lennox followed along with her until her heartbeat slowed to a reasonable rate and she could get air into her lungs.

"You ok now?" Kezra asked. Lennox nodded. "Good, let's get down there before Celene comes looking for us. I don't know about you, but I could use a cup of that spiced wine."

"What are we going to tell them about…" Lennox waved her hand in the general direction of the silver dust still layering the floor. Kezra shrugged. For the first time, Lennox really looked at Kezra. There were bags under her eyes from the weeks of not sleeping; her shoulders slumped forward slightly; the careful braid she usually kept was a mess, stray strands of hair sticking out everywhere. Kezra looked exhausted, and Lennox couldn't help but feel guilty knowing she had helped cause it.

"I really don't know. I guess we'll think of something." Kezra held out her hand to help Lenox stand. Together, they went downstairs to face the unknown.

Celene had been busy while waiting for them. The table was filled with snacks to choose from: meat and cheese, salted nuts, a couple trays of freshly baked scones filled with fruit that sat next to small jars bursting with fresh cream, jam and butter.

"When did you have time to do all of this?" Kezra asked as she looked at the table, eyes wide with awe. Celene just shrugged.

"I like to feed people. I find conversations are easier on a full stomach. Besides, Jessa thought that one might need something to eat," Celene said, inclining her head in Lennox's direction. In response, Lennox's stomach growled loudly. Celene was right; despite having eaten a full meal just hours ago, Lennox was absolutely starving. Requiring no further invitation, she hurried over to the table and started filling a plate. Kezra looked at the rapidly filling plate, specifically eying the scone in Lennox's hand, which she had added a generous amount of butter and cream, then Kezra pointedly rolled her eyes before joining the table. Jessa and Bear were already seated, but seemed to be waiting before helping themselves. Honestly, how anyone resisted the fresh, yeasty small of these scones was beyond her.

Celene ladled out five mugs of steamy, spiced wine, then set them down in front of each of them before taking one herself. There was an awkward silence where no one seemed to know what to say, so Lennox used the opportunity to bite into the scone. She closed her eyes, and was pretty sure a small moan escaped her lips, but Lennox didn't care. It was soft and sweet; the fruit balanced perfectly with the scone's flaky layers. She devoured it, savouring the flavor and feeling the contentment that came from eating home-cooked food. When she looked up, everyone was staring at her. Kezra looked both appalled and embarrassed all at once, but the other three seemed amused. Jessa broke the silence first.

"I knew it," she said.

"Knew what?" Kezra asked. Celene took a gulp of her wine before replying.

"Jessa believes the old magic has awakened in the two of you."

"What do you mean, the two of us? Obviously something just happened with Lennox, but I'm just me. I've never done anything like that. What makes you think I have magic?"

"I can see it," Celene said simply. She took another sip of wine before continuing. "Or at least, I think I can. Magic has been gone for generations, so I wasn't sure what I was seeing at first. There's a faint glow surrounding both of you. When I asked Jessa to make your clothes, I talked to her about it and she agreed." Lennox stopped eating long enough to ask a question.

"How do you know it's magic you're seeing though? Can everyone see it?" Lennox stared at Kezra, looking for the glow Celene spoke of, but all she saw was Kezra's scowling face. Jessa laughed.

"No, child. Celene is a seer. One of the last of our people. Our seers have powerful connections to the earth, separate from the old magic, though there are few of them left." Lennox nodded, accepting the answer, even if she had trouble believing it. For her entire life, she'd been told the Gods controlled all magic; they alone had the power to bless humans with it, even though they rarely did so anymore. At the temple, The Mother retained old artifacts that still held Altheia's magic, which allowed the priestesses to perform their rituals. The idea of magic as a living thing, something that could be awakened without divine intervention, contradicted everything she'd learned in the temple.

The food started to churn in her stomach. Lennox tried to catch Kezra's eye to see if she felt the same, but Kezra appeared deep in thought; ignoring her entirely. Lennox sipped her wine, hoping the warmth would soothe her. She had meant to take slow, lady-like sips, but instead ended up drinking the whole thing in an attempt to calm her nerves, making her feel worse. A scraping sound echoed through the room as Kezra pushed a full glass of water toward her, shaking her head. It lifted Lennox's spirits a little to know Kezra was looking out for her.

"There's no denying she has magic. What I saw, what we all saw, can't be explained otherwise, but you're wrong about me."

"Our seers are never wrong. If Celene says you have magic, do you," Jessa said.

"I don't doubt what she sees. Only, I don't think the magic is my own. Have you ever heard of Tylan Faine?" Kezra asked. Jessa hissed. Celene drew back, and even Bear looked uncomfortable.

"I would have thought you smart enough to avoid such company," Celene replied coldly.

"Even most of the crew stays away from him," Bear added. Kezra accepted the criticism without flinching.

"He bonded me when I was just a child. I'm sure Celene sees magic, but it's his. If I had any of my own, I would have broken this bond already." Celene studied Kezra, then shook her head.

"I don't know. I'm not practiced enough to see anything more than the glow of magic around you. That could be the cause, but it might not." Kezra turned away without responding. Lennox wondered if anyone else could see the hopeful gleam in Kezra's eyes. Maybe breaking the bond wouldn't be as difficult as she'd thought.

"Tylan is why Asher was after us. I left Tylan's lair without permission, but somehow, he managed to get our description out. Asher was trying to take us back." Kezra leveled a scowl at Bear. "So I guess not all the crew had the sense not to work with Tylan Faine." Lennox glanced at Bear, who appeared to be muttering a half-hearted quip to Kezra. The card game popped into Lennox's head, how close Beara had seemed to

Asher, and she grew suddenly uncomfortable. What was he doing here? For the first time, the thought occurred to her that maybe they couldn't trust Celene. Maybe they were in danger.

"Well," Celene said, "that explains what they were doing here, but not what happened to them."

"I think it's pretty clear what happened. Somehow I turned them to dust. I don't know how I did it, but I won't apologize for protecting us," Lennox said, defensive. Jessa reached across the table, patting her hand.

"No one blames you, child. We're merely wondering how it happened and what it implies for the rest of us. The return of magic like that, it changes the world."

"I really don't understand how it happened. I've used such small amounts of magic in the past, I wasn't even sure I had it, but that…nothing like that had happened before. It was unexpected to say the least," Lennox said. Celene sighed.

"It's no use grilling her about it, Jessa. If the girl says she doesn't know, maybe she doesn't. Regardless, I don't think we'll get anything useful out of her tonight." Lennox winced as Celene spoke about her as if she weren't there. "What we need to figure out is what to do next."

"We won't be doing anything. Lennox and I will be going," Kezra said.

"Where?" Celene asked.

"That's none of anyone's business." Kezra scowled at Bear again.

"What did I do?" He practically yelled.

"Shush, we don't need to attract any more attention." Jessa said.

Bear folded his arms and sat back in his chair, frowning. Kezra looked exasperated.

"You're part of the crew. You were Asher's friend. How can you be here?" Kezra leveled a stare at Celene. "How could you let him in after what you just saw? In fact, we've stayed too long. Come on, Lennox, we're leaving." Kezra pushed herself up from the chair and slammed her hands down on the table, looking ready to throw Lennox over her shoulder and make a run for it. Bear started yelling a reply, but Celene cut him off.

"Would you sit down and stop with the theatrics, please?" Celene rubbed her temples. "Lennox clearly isn't going anywhere; she could barely walk down the stairs. And as for Bear -"

"Yeah! If you think I'd -" Celene glared at him, and Bear snapped his mouth shut without finishing his reply. She took a deep breath.

"If you think I would really allow Bear in this inn tonight if he'd aligned himself with that maniac, you're dumber than I thought. Asher has always been a problem in this town. Well before he met you, he used to terrorize my patrons every time that blasted ship docked here. Bear only joined the crew and befriended Asher so that he's leave us alone."

"And why would he do that?" Kezra asked, looking skeptical.

"Because Bear is family. And once Bear was in his inner circle, Asher wouldn't bother us anymore."

"They only gave you so much shit because of me," Bear said, his voice straining with guilt. "Asher wanted my muscle, wanted someone to enforce his threats, and so he harassed you until I joined. I'm so sorry, Celene." Bear was teary-eyed. He and Celene exchanged a look that spoke of a history together. She laid a palm gently on his face.

"You have nothing to apologize for. It wasn't your fault. It's always been his." Celene removed her hand and turned her gaze Lennox's way. "I should thank you for getting rid of that problem for us. Now, Bear can take his life back. Still, the captain's going to start looking for his missing first mate soon. We need to get our story straight."

"I don't think Kael will tell anyone the truth if that's what you're worried about," Lennox said. Jessa nodded, thoughtful.

"He did seem convinced he was in the presence of a goddess. Not that I can blame him, considering what he saw."

"Even if he did, the crew wouldn't believe him." Bear said between bites of scone. Now that Kezra wasn't actively hostile toward him, Bear seemed to have settled in. "The crew are a superstitious lot, but the captain is not; a few might bite on the story, but not enough to arouse any real interest. The captain won't have it on his ship. And they saw you play cards with us and lose. It would be difficult for them to imagine a goddess wouldn't be able to win a round against the likes of us, no offense."

"None taken, I'm certainly no goddess." Lennox replied, using her sleeve to wipe away the crumbs from her face.

"So it's business as usual then. We saw nothing. If the captain comes around asking questions, we'll tell him we didn't see anything."

"I still think we should leave," Kezra grumbled.

"You'll just look guilty if you run," Celene said.

"And you'll freeze to death in those mountains without proper clothing," Jessa added. "Let me finish your order. I need one week. Then you can go on your adventure to Kitsummit."

Relief coursed through Lennox; they were right; she wasn't in a state to run. The food helped her regain a bit of her strength, but now that it had settled; Lennox was exhausted.

"A week! We can't stay for an entire week! For your sake and for our own. Tylan knows we're here now. What do you think he'd do to you for harboring runaways? He'll make whatever Asher did look like child's play," Kezra exclaimed. Celene and Jessa exchanged a look, contemplating something. They arrived at a silent conclusion. Jessa spoke for them both.

"I'll do my best to get your order done faster. But if it comes down to that, we'll help you escape. You have our word."

"Why would you do that? What's in it for you?"

"Maybe nothing. But I believe there's something bigger happening here. Now, go, this one has practically fallen asleep at the table, and apparently, I have some sewing that needs to be started urgently. Although, I'd like to get a few hours of sleep before I start." Celene was up first, clearing the table. Kezra offered to help, but Celene waved her away.

"Help your friend upstairs and get some rest. I have a feeling none of us will be getting much sleep in the coming days." With that, Kezra held out her hand to help Lennox up, but Lennox shooed her off. As tired as she was, Lennox wanted to make it up on her own; she didn't know why, but it felt important. Once they were out of earshot, Kezra pulled her close.

"I still don't trust them. I know you're probably tired of hearing this, but we need to be careful, Lennox." Lennox just nodded, too exhausted to argue. But really, what was there to be careful about? Everyone downstairs knew all of their secrets: who they were, that Tylan was looking for them, where they were going, and about Lennox's magic. They had nothing left to hide, and Lennox had no energy for secrecy.

"Jessa is a little off," Lennox conceded. "But I like Celene. And if Bear wanted to harm us, he would have done so already. He's the size of a mountain; if he's hauled us off to Tylan, no one could have stopped him," Kezra grumbled something in response, but Lennox wasn't listening. She rolled over in bed and let exhaustion take her as she entered a dreamless sleep. Hours later Lennox woke up with Kezra hovering inches from her face.

"AHHH!" Lennox screamed. "What are you doing?"

"Making sure you're still breathing. Honestly, you looked dead. I've never seen anyone sleep so deeply or so still. It's horrifying."

"How do you think I feel waking up to your face inches from mine? Talk about horrifying," Lennox quipped. Kezra scowled. "See, never even a smile in sight."

"I see you're feeling better this morning. Too bad, I preferred the version of you that was too tired to talk." Now it was Lennox's turn to frown at Kezra.

"Whatever. I'm starving. Do you think Celene has made any breakfast yet?"

"I don't know when she would have had the time to sleep and bake, but I suppose we can go find out."

As they descended the stairs, the sweet, floury smell of freshly baked goods wafted through the air. Lennox's mouth watered and her stomach growled loudly. Following the smell, she practically floated down the stairs. They'd only been at the table a moment before Celene was over with an assortment of muffins and mugs of coffee. The coffee's distinct aroma instantly made Lennox feel more awake. Coffee had only been available on special occasions in the temple, but sometimes she'd been able to sweet-talk the cook into slipping her a mug before one of her many early morning punishments. Lennox had developed a small obsession with it, and couldn't believe something so rare was readily available in this little town. She took her time picking apart a muffin, using all of her restraint not to shove the whole thing into her mouth. Kezra slowly sipped her coffee, eyes closed, as if savoring the taste.

"So…" Lennox started, trying to break the silence. "What's the plan for today?"

"I've been thinking about that. We need to go out into town; we need to be seen. The whole crew knows where we're headed, so we might as well go out and prepare for the trip. We'll get some supplies and look for a guide."

"Sounds like a good plan for you. I was thinking I could stay here and taste test more of Celene's baked goods, and then take a nice, long nap."

Kezra gave her what Lennox thought of as her signature scowl.

"Your whole plan is to let me do all of the work while you nap all day?"

"Not all day. I was also planning on eating. Maybe I could even find Bear and have a pint. You know, relax a bit. You should try it out; you look a bit stressed."

"Unreal."

"Or, I could go with you, I guess. I'll help you find a guide and all that, make sure you don't scare anyone away by scowling at them," Lennox said, enjoying riling Kezra up. Kezra rolled her eyes.

"I don't scowl. At least not that much."

"You're literally scowling right now." With enormous effort, Kezra turned her expression neutral.

"No, I am not. See. I wouldn't scare anyone away."

"Whatever you say," Lennox said, biting into another muffin.

"I'm thinking we should drop into Jessa's first and check on the -"

The door banged open. Captain Dallos strode in with a pale-faced Kael trailing behind him. Kael spotted Lennox and Kezra, and any remaining blood drained from his face. Celene came rushing out from the kitchen at the noise, dusting flour off her shirt. The captain zeroed in on her and strode over, Kael practically shaking behind him.

"Can I help you, Captain?"

"Maybe, maybe." Dallos ran his fingers through messy, black hair, taking his time to look around like he'd lost his sense of purpose. "I'm sorry to bother you, Celene, but I seem to have lost my first mate. Kael here seems to think he and one of the other crew members have made a run for it."

"I'm sorry to hear that, Captain. But I'm not sure what I can do about that."

"Oh, no, yer not. I know you and Asher had your differences, but did you hear anything from him last night? I don't know that I believe he'd just disappear." Celene's gaze turned cold.

"I can't say anything comes to mind. And I don't appreciate what you're insinuating, Captain." Dallos's face grew red.

"Oh, come on, Celene; I don't mean anything by it. Just check with that cousin of yours for me, aye?" Celene's shoulders relaxed, and her expression softened slightly.

"Fine, fine, I'll ask him. But for the love of Altheia, Dallos, don't storm in here like that, you're scaring the customers away." Dallos looked around, noticing them for the first time.

"The lordling? The lads seem fine to me, aren't ya, lads?" Kezra and Lennox both just nodded.

"See, they're just fine. Send Bear my way when you see him. Please." Celene waved him off, and the captain strode out. Kael gave Lennox a slight bow of his head, then went scurrying off. Celene came to collect their mugs and tidy the table. Celene leaned close to them as she cleaned and brought her voice down to a whisper.

"It doesn't look like Kael will be a problem; he looks terrified of you. Keep an eye on Dallos though."

"Is Dallos dangerous? He seemed honest enough," Kezra asked. Celene thought for a moment before she replied.

"Dallos is a good enough man, but you don't stay Captain of a ship that long without making it know you're not to be crossed. Just be careful, yeah?"

"We will be; thanks for everything, Celene."

"Yeah, well, my help's not free, nor are my muffins. Don't forget to leave a nice tip." Celene gave them an uncharacteristic smile and wink, her voice light. Lennox turned to Kezra as Celene walked away.

"So she's funny. Who would have guessed? Are you taking notes?"

"Notes on what?" Kezra asked.

"On how to have a personality outside of being serious and brooding. You can have fun sometimes too, see?"

"Shut up," Kezra said without any heat.

"I'm serious. You should ask Celene for tips on how to turn off the grouchy part of your personality."

"I'm leaving. Why don't you just go take that nap?"

"No, no. I'm committed now. Lead the way." They left Celene's and walked out into a sunlit morning. Kezra stopped and surveyed the town square.

"Which shop do you suppose is Jessa's?"

"Probably one with lots of fabrics in the window, if I had to guess. Why are we going there anyway? Don't we have other supplies to get first?" Lennox asked. Kezra let out a long suffering sigh.

"Jessa needs our measurements to make the clothes. Besides, there's something she's not telling us. I'd like to talk to her."

"You mean aggressively questioning her while giving her hostile looks? Yes, just like that one."

"Are you going to do anything helpful today, or are you just planning on pestering me?"

"I can do both," Lennox said, flashing her biggest smile. "And I am helping. Jessa doesn't strike me as the type of woman whom you can intimidate easily. All I'm saying is we might want to try being polite. Let me do the talking."

"You might actually have a good point for once. Fine. I'll let you lead," Kezra relented.

As they walked into Jessa's shop, a little bell rang, announcing their arrival. Jessa emerged from behind a pile of fabrics that were haphazardly piled on top of one another. She seemed to have a little bit of everything: silks, velvet, cotton, thick furs in cream, tan and blue, everything one could want. There was a fur dyed a deep navy blue Lennox was instantly drawn to. She drifted over to it, running her fingers along the soft fur.

"Good, you're here. Come on back and let's get your measurements."

Jessa waved them back to a room hidden behind a mound of fabrics. The room was small with a single full-length mirror in front of a pedestal. A baby blue arm chair sat in the corner with a matching round pillow in the middle.

"You first," Jessa said, pointing at Kezra, who groaned, but obediently stomped up to the pedestal with her arms crossed.

"Uncross your arms, dear." Jessa pulled out a measuring tape and got to work, jotting down notes in a little notebook. Kezra huffed, but did as Jessa said. She looked in the mirror, catching Lennox's eye with her reflection, and raised an eyebrow. Right, time to get some answers. Lennox cleared her throat, trying to think of what to ask.

"You have such a lovely collection of fabrics, Jessa. How did you come by it all?" Jessa didn't look up from her work as she answered, continuing to make measurements and record her notes, but a proud smile crept across her face.

"I have to say, Bear's been most helpful in expanding my collection; the boy has an eye for fabrics. Before he joined Dallos's crew, they brought in the most dull collections they could find on the continent. Bear helped find some of the rarer items and some I acquired myself while travelling."

"Oh, have you travelled much then?"

"All over, before the King cut Oscana off from the world and started this damned war." Jessa's voice took on a wistful tone. "Alright, all done. Down you go." Relief washed over Kezra's face as she stepped off the pedestal. Lennox giggled. It was hilarious to see someone so tough and capable upended by attention. As Lennox traded places with Kezra, her mind finally processed what Jessa said.

"What war?" Lennox blurted out. Jessa's jaw dropped as she looked between Lennox and Keza.

"What do you mean, what war? How can you not know?" Jessa asked, practically screaming.

"We've been somewhat sheltered the past few years," Lennox admitted.

"Can you really have no idea though? Well, I suppose you're both young. You wouldn't remember the world before."

"Before what?" Lennox asked.

"Before the war, of course, before magic disappeared."

"Can you tell us what happened?" Lennox asked. Jessa set down her measuring tape and pulled up a stool.

"It would have been about twenty or so years ago now. You see, a tea made with lunasha blooms could help awaken magic in humans. Nothing too strong, like what happened the other night, but enough to help with small things: encouraging crops to grow, creating light, doing some light housework. Lunasha plants only grew in Oscana, so we sold them around the world. At one point, we were the wealthiest, most envied nation in the world. But then, it all just stopped. Even though lunasha continued to grow, the teas stopped working. People who had been using magic for decades lost access. We could no longer sell the blooms, and so the kingdom withered. Worse, Nalathay accused us of hoarding magic for ourselves. Their King is convinced that we are still using magic in secret to take over his kingdom, and so he has spent years trying to invade ours to take the lunasha for themselves. Our king closed the borders, and trade died, the economy has been on the verge of collapse ever since."

Lennox sat in silence, enraptured by the story.

"There are some whispers of people like Tylan Faine, those with old magic from the gods themselves. Magic that doesn't depend on the lunasha blooms to sustain it. But Tylan is the only one I know of with such power, and he uses that magic to bond desperate people to his will. He's even gone to Nalathay in search of more people to bond, which has only strengthened their king's suspicion that we're hoarding magic. His soldiers surround our borders, invading and burning the towns along the border, inching closer to Tesmerin. That is the war we find ourselves in. How could either of you possibly not know any of this? Even here, we've gotten news of the towns burned to the ground; we've seen the occasional refugee who escapes the wrath of Nalathay."

"Like she said, we've been pretty sheltered," Kezra said. But she looked troubled, like she was hiding something.

"That is why your magic is so important. Maybe it's the start of magic returning, or at least a new force to rival that of Tylan Faine. It might even help turn the tide of the war."

A heavy silence descended on the room as they let the words digest. Lennox felt the color drain from her face, though. Jessa was pinning too much hope on her. Lennox didn't have the slightest idea how to do any of the things Jessa wanted from her, nor did Lennox know if she wanted to try. When they didn't respond, Jessa went back to measuring, letting them go after a few more minutes. "Give me a few more days and I'll have everything ready."

"I thought you needed a week?" Kezra retorted. Jessa shrugged.

"It turns out your measurements are exactly the same. I can use the same patterns for both; it really cuts down on the work. Now, off with you. I've already wasted too much time this morning."

"Told you I could get her to tell us something," Lennox said, feeling smug. Kezra rolled her eyes.

"We could have found out about the war from anyone. There's still something she's not telling us."

"Did you really not know about the war?" Kezra looked off in the distance, not meeting Lennox's eyes.

"I could see the signs, and I might have overheard a bit about it on an assignment. But I didn't know all the details." Kezra bit her lip. "I guess it was easier that way. If I ignored what was happening in the world, I could think of everyone who I hunted down for Tylan as greedy or arrogant, foolish enough to make a deal with someone of Tylan's reputation. But if I had paid more attention; seen how desperate people were because of what was going on, I don't think I could have lived with myself. I'm still not sure how I can." Her voice cracked on the final words.

"Why did you have to hunt people down, anyway?" The question burst out of Lennox before she could stop it. Kezra glared at her, but she plowed on before Kezra bit her head off. "I only mean that you told me Tylan could summon you back through your bond. Can't he just do that with everyone he bonds? Why does he need you to go hunt them down?" Kezra shook her head, looking much less murderous. She rolled up her sleeve, displaying her forearm, where two interlocking black bands were woven together on her skin.

"Most only have one solid band to signify their bond. Mine is different somehow, stronger. It gives Tylan more control and lets him summon me. I don't know how he managed to forge this bond, or why he hasn't done it again since. But I can't resist him when he summons me. And if I try, if I disobey him, he makes the magic…hurt." Lennox squeezed her hand.

"You don't have to tell me about it if you don't want to, but I'm here to listen if you do."

Kezra nodded and kept walking, pulling away from her. They continued down the street like that for a while, just walking with no particular destination. After days cooped up in that tiny cabin, it was nice to roam around, breathing in fresh air.

"It's hard to describe," Kezra said. Her voice was so quiet Lennox had to strain to hear her. "The magic seeps through my skin, my muscles cramp, and my lungs constrict. I can't breathe and for a few seconds, everything just hurts. Then he rips it away, and I can breathe again. But the worst part is the ache of the magic leaving my body. As much as it hurts, I'm always left feeling empty when it's done because, for one second, through all of that pain, I can feel the power it offers, taste it. Some sick part of me relishes the punishment just for a taste of the magic. I feel so twisted. Maybe that's why I've never tried harder to break my bond, because deep down, I'm afraid I'll never feel the magic again." Kezra looked winded after the admission, like she'd been wrung out.

"Nothing's wrong with you. When what happened last night happened," Lennox paused, looking around to make sure there was no one to overhear them, "it terrified me, being able to do that. But at the same time, it was the most exhilarating thing I've ever felt. All that terrible and horrible power coursing through my fingertips, I felt like the goddess Kael thought I was, like Altheia herself. A tiny, wretched part of me wanted it to happen again, to feel that power. So if you're twisted, so am I." Kezra smiled.

"Then we can be twisted together."

"Oh no, I broke you," Lennox said, bringing her hand to her mouth in shock.

"What do you mean?" Kezra asked, her smile fading.

"You're actually smiling. Here I was, worried those muscles had atrophied from lack of use." Kezra rolled her eyes, but her smile reappeared.

"Has anyone ever told you that you're profoundly annoying?"

"Thank you, I've had years of experience honing the skill. Jasper could hardly stand me most days," Lennox said.

"I'm sorry you had to leave her." It was Lennox's turn to shrug off the emotions flooding through her.

"It's for the best for now. She's safer without me there. If Tylan wants me that badly, he might use her against me, and I'd never forgive myself if something happened to her."

"We'll get you back to her. I promise. Once we break my bond, we'll find a way to stop Tylan from hurting anyone ever again."

"Alright, I'll hold you to that." They started toward Celene's, their other tasks temporarily forgotten.

Lennox let Kezra go hunt for supplies and a guide on her own over the next few days, preferring to spend time at Celene's. Occasionally, Lennox helped her bake, being sure to taste-test the blueberry muffins before Celene served them, just to make sure they were perfect. Other days, she would hang around, drinking with Bear. Captain Dallos was delayed a few days, waiting for his first mate's return, so Bear had some free time on his hands. Lennox hadn't beaten him in a drinking contest yet, but she was getting closer, or that's what she told herself. It turned out Bear and his friends were at least an entertaining crowd, even if they weren't the most responsible bunch.

Jessa promised she was almost done with their clothes, which meant they would be ready to leave any day now. But as much as Kezra asked around, she still hadn't found someone to guide them through the mountains. The bell chimed, and Kezra stormed into the room, slamming her things down on the table.

"No luck today, huh?" Kezra stole Lennox's ale in response, throwing it back so fast Bear raised his eyebrows, impressed.

"No one wants to go up that blasted mountain with us," Kezra finally said.

"Is it because they're scared of you? As charming as I find your scowling face, others get intimidated."

"It's not my face!" Kezra snapped. "Apparently, the journey would take too long. Everyone's worried about missing any time at home, preparing for winter."

"Aye," Bear chimed in. "Winter lasts a long time, even down here. We start jarring and pickling food for the winter in the early summer months. It's the only way to make sure there's enough food when the shipments get unreliable."

"I guess that makes sense. Although I'm not entirely convinced Kezra didn't scare someone away. We might be on our own then."

"It's fine. A guide would have been nice, but we'll manage on our own. After all, the route to Kitsummit is an established path. How hard can it be?" Bear snorted at Kezra's comment, choking on his ale. "What," she asked.

"No offense to the two of you, but you won't last a day up there on your own."

"Why is that? Now that you know we're not "little lordlings" you think we aren't tough enough to survive on our own? Just because we're women, we need help?" Kezra asked Bear, trying to keep her voice down so other patrons didn't overhear.

"Not at all. Celene's been up that mountain a dozen times on her own. Some of this town's most capable people are women."

"Damn right they are." Celen said, coming to collect the empty glasses. "Bear's right. You need to know the mountain to climb it. Most of us have travelled to Kitsummit and back since childhood. We know when the wind is changing, when to forge ahead, and when to hunker down. Our eyes are trained to spot the paths. The two of you on your own wouldn't stand a chance. It would be best to wait until spring for the snow to clear."

"You know we don't have that long to wait," Kezra said. Celene shrugged.

"Maybe, maybe not. In the past few days, everything's been quiet. Perhaps you were wrong." Kezra shook her head.

"No, he'll come for us. And there are other reasons I can't wait that long. We need to go, soon." Celene and Bear exchanged a long look. He broke the stare first, sighing and throwing up his hands.

"Fine. Captain Dallos won't be happy though."

"He'll be fine. He'll welcome you back on board in the spring," Celene said.

"If the ship gets here," Bear countered.

"Oh, it will. Eventually. Nothing stops Dallos, not even a war," Celene said.

"Um, what are you two talking about?" Lennox asked.

"I'll be your guide," Bear answered. Before Lennox had a chance to reply, the bell chimed as Jessa walked in with a pile of clothes stacked up to her nose. The tower swayed precariously as Jessa made her way up to the table.

"I did it. In record time, might I add." She set the clothes down on the table, beaming at them.

"What are you sitting around for? Go, try them on, although I already know everything will fit perfectly. And then we can settle up the bill. Such fine work deserves a few gold crowns."

Lennox grabbed the clothes on the table where five different outfits were set out for both of them. While most of the tops and pants were the same, it was still an impressive amount of work in such a short time. One piece in particular caught Lennox's eye. The set of vest and trousers were leather, dyed a green so dark it was almost black. The inside was lined with soft, tan fur and it was paired with a deep brown tunic to go underneath. Jessa had also somehow managed to make them each a pair of boots. Furry brown things that came up to mid-calf. Lennox ran her fingers over the smooth leather of the vest, eager to try it on.

"Jessa, this is beautiful," Lennox said. Jessa smiled, smug.

"I saw you eyeing the blue version in the store, but I thought the green would look nice with your eyes. Mind you, the material was expensive; so is good tailoring," Jessa said. Kezra snorted at her.

"I'm sure it was. How convenient for you to choose the most expensive material for us." But Kezra's remark lacked heat. Kezra was also eyeing the clothes longingly. Kezra sighed. "Sorry Jessa. They're lovely. What do we owe you?"

"Ah, we'll work it out later. Go, try them on." Jessa shooed them away. Before taking the clothes upstairs, Kezra looked at Bear.

"Can you be ready to leave tomorrow morning?" Bear nodded, getting up.

"Aye, I can. Celene, will you grab me a bottle of ale? I'd better soften Dallos up enough to think my leaving was his idea."

"That's it then. Tomorrow, we head for Kitsummit." With that, Kezra strode upstairs. Lennox trailed after her, unable to determine if the feeling in her stomach was excitement or dread.

CHAPTER 17

Kezra

They woke up at dawn the next morning since Bear said it was better to get an early start on the hike up. Kezra dressed in the olive green outfit from Jessa, running her hands down the front of the vest's smooth leather as she looked in the mirror. Kezra loved the way it fit. Jessa had tailored it perfectly to her body, the fabric flexible enough to move freely, like wearing a second skin. And she could admit to herself that she liked the way she looked. No one would mistake Kezra for a man with the way the pants and vest hugged the curves of her body; she felt fierce and feminine all at once. It was so different from the boring clothing Tylan provided for her.

Lennox had just finished getting dressed when a knock sounded at the door. Celene barged in without waiting for them to answer. She had a full tray with coffee for each of them and the blueberry muffins that Lennox had been inhaling since they'd arrived. Lennox grabbed two, immediately biting into one of the freshly baked muffins. Kezra shook her head at the priestess.

"What? We need our strength for the hike, and it would be a crime to let Celene's baking go to waste."

"I didn't say anything. But you could have at least let them cool first," Kezra said.

"Well, I, for one, will be very offended if you don't eat something. And you wouldn't want to hurt my feelings, would you?" Celene asked, a teasing note in her voice.

"I would never." Kezra grabbed a cup of steaming coffee from the tray. Celene scrunched her nose.

"That's not food."

"I'm not much of a breakfast person." Still, Kezra picked up a muffin from the tray and began picking crumbs off the top. A blueberry popped in her mouth, warm and sweet, while the muffin itself was buttery and delicious. She could see why Lennox had been raving about these.

"Don't worry. I'll take hers." Lennox had already grabbed another off the tray as she spoke.

"Of course you will," Celene snorted.

"One of us needs to make sure there's food for the journey," Lennox said as she took three more muffins, wrapped them in cloth, and stuck them in her pack.

"I did bring food. Actual supplies that will keep for more than one day," Kezra said. Lennox shuddered in response.

"I saw what you bought, and those hard crackers are barely edible. You should eat real food while you can." Lennox handed her the last muffin, which Kezra was about to reject, but then realized she'd finished the one she'd been picking at. Kezra accepted it, figuring maybe Lennox was right after all. Celene crossed her arms with a satisfied smile.

"Right then, Bear's waiting for you downstairs. I bought you some time, distracting him with coffee, but you should get going."

"Thanks, Celene," Kezra said, draining the last of her coffee; it was truly magnificent coffee. "We'll be down in a minute." With that, Celene took the empty mugs and left the room.

"I'm going to miss those muffins," Lennox said, flopping down on the bed.

"I'll miss her coffee. Altheia knows when I'll be able to find a decent cup again. And what are you doing? Didn't you just hear Celene tell us we need to hurry?"

"I'm soaking up my last few moments of comfort," Lennox retorted.

"I'll have you know, I packed very plush sleeping bags, very luxurious." Lennox raised her eyebrows, as if she didn't believe it.

"Your definition of luxury probably means they're small and easy to travel with, not that they're actually comfortable."

"If they happen to be lightweight and travel efficient, it's just an extra perk. You'll thank me for it later when you're hauling your pack up a mountain," Kezra said. She triple-checked their packs, satisfied they had everything they needed.

"Are you done basking in the condor or whatever? I'd rather not start off the trip by making our guide grouchy." Lennox rolled her eyes, but got up and reached for her pack.

"It's Bear, I don't think he gets grouchy. He only gets louder the more you make him wait."

After a final survey of the room, they went downstairs. Kezra fingered the two vials kept safely in her vest pocket, a reminder that she was on a clock, one that was possibly shorter than she'd been told. It had only been three weeks since she had first taken the potion to block her bond, and already, Kezra could feel it wearing off. There was a tugging sensation in the back of her brain, constantly pulling her somewhere else. For now, the sensation was weak enough for Kezra to fight it off, but she didn't know how much longer she would last. She would have to use that vial sooner rather than later, limiting her time even more. Kezra whispered a silent prayer to Altheia that she'd find answers in Kitsummit. This had to work.

"Hey, are you alright?" Lennox asked. "You're breathing really fast." Kezra nodded, just now realizing that she'd been going into a full blown panic.

"I'm fine, just anxious to get going."

She shouldn't have worried about Bear being impatient to leave. He was finishing a mug of coffee, and telling what Kezra suspected was an embellished story about how he'd gotten Dallos to agree to give him some time off.

"I swear on Althia, the big sap had a tear rolling down his cheek, he did."

"Was he just that happy to be rid of you?" Lennox sidled up next to Bear, teasing him as though they were old friends. Kezra felt a pang of jealousy watching them.

"Bah, no. I'm the Captain's favorite. Told me I was his first choice to replace Asher as first mate, but he wouldn't stop me from going to see my sick mother one last time."

"You have a sick mother in Kitsummit, eh?" Kezra asked wryly. Celene chuckled.

"Bear's mother is very unwell, but I don't think a visit will do her any good seeing that she died three years ago, just before he joined the crew."

"See, like I told the Captain, she can't get any worse."

"We should get going then," Kezra said. "We wouldn't want to keep your Mother waiting."

"Wait!" Jessa burst into the room, bells clanging behind her. "Good, I caught you in time. I have one last surprise for you." Jessa pulled out two men's coats, both in a rich, coffee brown, and the inside lined with fur. Thankfully, the coats were bulky enough to hide their shape if they needed to pass as men again. They were perfect for two minor lords, but more importantly, Kezra could see the care Jessa had put into them, lined into every stitch. These must have taken her hours. Kezra reached for their pouch of gold crowns, which had grown substantially lighter after her last encounter with Jessa. These coats were going to be expensive, and they needed to be mindful of spending as Kezra was unsure when or if she'd be able to replenish their supply of money.

"They're exquisite, Jessa." Kezra slipped the coat on, luxuriating in the warmth it provided. Somehow, the thick material was light when worn, and it had nice, deep pockets that women's coats often lacked. Maybe she could just splurge on them - no. She needed to be responsible. Reluctantly, Kezra made herself take off the coat, handing it back to Jessa. "Really, they're perfect, but we can't. I'm so sorry, they're beautiful, but -" Jessa gently pushed the coat back into her hands, cutting her off.

"Consider it a gift for my favorite customers."

"Oh, no! We couldn't.

"Speak for yourself. I could." Lennox already had her coat buttoned and her pack slung over it. "You'd have to pry this coat off my corpse. I mean, have you seen the pockets, Kezra? I fit two muffins into each one and there's still room!"

"Did you take muffins out of the kitchen?" Celene chimed in.

"They were just sitting there for anyone."

"No, they were put away in the kitchen for me to serve to the other guests. No, no, they're yours now." Celene rolled her eyes as Lennox took her crumb-covered hands out of her pockets.

"Thank you," Kezra choked out, taking the coat and shrugging it on.

She had just been jealous of Lennox, but had failed to see that somehow, Kezra had forged friendships too. Because in the past few days, Jessa, Celene, and Bear had really become her friends.

"It was a pleasure getting to make such beautiful things again. Now, you should go before that one steals any more of Celene's baked goods." Kezra turned to Celene, emotions knotting in her stomach. No matter what she had told Lennox, Kezra knew that she wasn't good with people. How could she ever say enough to thank this woman who she barely knew, and who'd gone out of her way to help them at her own risk? Kezra didn't have the words to relay her gratitude for such genuine kindness. Celene caught her eye, and must have known what she was thinking, because Celene pulled her in for an unexpected, tight hug. It took Kezra a moment to process what was happening, and her arms hung limply by her sides before she hugged Celene back. She put all the words she didn't know how to say into the embrace. Celene let her go, giving her a smile as she gently pushed a bag into Kezra's hands.

"Lennox told me how much you love coffee, and she might have mentioned that it temporarily removes that scowl from your face. So for both of your well-being, I made you a batch of something I've been working on. You just mix some of the powder with hot water, and you'll have coffee. It won't be as good as what I make here, but it's better than nothing and it travels well."

The words flew from Celene's mouth in a torrent, as if she couldn't get them out fast enough. Seeing Celene lose her composure ruffled Kezra, and so did this final gesture of kindness. This bag of powdered coffee might have been the most thoughtful thing anyone had ever given her. Kezra opened her mouth, but instead of words, she emitted an embarrassing choking sound. Celene wrapped her hand around Kezra's and guided the coffee into one of the coat's many pockets.

"Have a safe journey, Kezra. May Altheia's light guide you back to my door. Know that you are always welcome in my home." With that, Celene turned on her heel and walked back to the kitchen. Taking that as her cue, Jessa gave them one final wave before trailing after Celene.

"If ye both had enough crying, let's get going while the sun's still on our side." Bear slapped his hands on his thighs, stood up, and strode out the door without another word.

"This is it, Kezra. Let's go get your freedom." Together, they took the first steps toward a new life.

As they started toward the mountain, Kezra found herself instantly grateful for Jessa's coat. Kitsummit was a village nestled on a plateau between two mountain peaks. To get there, they would need to hike up to the top of one peak and make their way down the other side. They'd hardly begun the ascent before the winds kicked up. What had at first been a gentle, refreshing breeze turned into a biting wind that tried to worm its way through the layers of clothing and seep into Kezra's skin. Bear kept a steady pace that started as manageable, but after an hour or so of steady climbing, it was starting to make Kezra's calves burn. She looked behind her to check on Lennox. While Lennox hadn't fallen behind, her cheeks were bright red with exertion, her breathing heavy and rapid.

"Maybe we should rest?" Kezra shouted so Bear could hear her over the gusts of wind. He stopped abruptly, turning around.

"You want a break already?"

"I just", huff, "need", huff, "some water." Lennox plopped down next to them, catching her breath.

"Don't sit down yet." Bear scooped Lennox up under her arms, hauling her to her feet. "It's harder to get going again once you've stopped, and we've barely gotten started. Get some water now, then we'll break for lunch in a few hours. Until then, we need to keep moving."

"Why? I know I wanted to get there quickly, but what's so urgent?" Kezra asked, using the moment to take a sip of water.

"The mountains are not safe, especially at night. There's a cave we can get to today, near a mountain spring. We need to get there before sunset. So no more stops until lunch." Bear started walking again. Lennox and Kezra scrambled to put away their water and hurry after him.

"Do you really think the mountain's that dangerous?" Lennox asked. She walked next to Kezra, matching her stride so they could talk. Bear was in sight, but too far away to hear them.

"Who knows. Probably not, you know how Bear likes to exaggerate." Lennox bit her lip and nodded, contemplating.

"He seems so serious though; Bear's never serious."

"Well, he has to sell the story, doesn't he?"

"Yeah, I guess he does."

"Right. Let's hurry up. The least we can do is humor him," Kezra said, hoping her answer put Lennox at ease. Lennox nodded and fell into step behind her. Bear kept up the brisk pace until it was finally time to stop for lunch. The whole way up, his steady gait never slowed, while Lennox and Kezra slowly fell further and further behind. The only plus side was the clear trail running up the mountain, making it easy to follow if they lost sight of their guide. So far, the path up the mountain was relatively easy to spot, having been stomped into a clear trail by those who had come this way before them, so even when she lost sight of Bear, Kezra knew where to go. She was beginning to think he really had been exaggerating about the dangers of the mountain. The way forward seemed clear enough; why did they need a guide?

They came around a bend in the trail to find Bear slightly off the path with a blanket laid out on a flat surface. Drops of sweat coated his red hair, which gleamed in the sunlight. He smiled, seeing the two of them stop to take in the scene, leaning on each other to catch their breath.

"Wow, Bear," Lennox said, "this looks fantastic. How did you have time to get this set up?"

"And why? I thought we were in a hurry," Kezra couldn't help but ask. Bear chuckled.

"There's always time for a proper meal. Besides, we're almost to the cave. You lot managed to make better time than I anticipated, although you were still slow enough to give me enough time to set this up. We need to walk about three more miles that way, and we'll be there." Bear pointed to the right, where there appeared to be a valley, an easy walk. It was also the opposite direction of the dirt path leading up to Kitsummit.

"But the path is that way." Kezra started standing, pointing back to the trail they'd just left.

"Aye, it is. But there's nowhere to rest for a good twelve miles in that direction. We won't make it before nightfall. Trust me, the cave is our best bet. It's an easy, flat walk. We'll be there in no time." Kezra opened her mouth to continue arguing, but Lennox stopped her.

"Just listen to him, Kezra. He's the guide. He knows what he's talking about." Now, can we please eat? I'm starving." Lennox practically threw herself down onto the blanket Bear head laid out, and dug through her pack, giving a delighted squeal upon finding some bread. With one last look at the trail, Kezra joined her. It was three miles to the cave in the wrong direction and then twelve miles up the path to shelter. They had fifteen miles to hike tomorrow, and who knew how much further after that? Her instinct was to press on, ignore Bears warnings and hike those twelve miles to their next stop. They could make it if they kept on through dusk, giving them plenty of time to rest.

Kezra looked at Lennox, cheeks still red and puffy, hair glistening with sweat, and she had to revise her assessment. Lennox wouldn't make it twelve more miles today; Bear was right about that. Maybe Kezra should continue without them and have them meet her at Kitsummit? It felt wrong to leave Lennox, but she wouldn't be alone. If Kezra left now, she could -

"Kezra, I swear on Altheia, if you don't take this bread in the next ten seconds, I'm going to eat it myself." Lennox's voice shook Kezra from her thoughts. She took the bread, still distracted by the possibility of continuing on her own.

"Are you allowed to swear on Altheia?"

"Why can't she swear on Altheia?" Bear asked, joining them. Kezra bit her lip, having forgotten that Bear didn't know about Lennox's past. She didn't want to reveal it without Lennox's consent, and cursed herself for the stupidity. Kezra met Lennox's eye; Lennox gave her a subtle nod.

"She's a priestess of Altheia's temple. Swearing on the goddess must be against the rules."

"You're a priestess?" Bear nearly spit out his food at the revelation. "Hells, if I knew priestesses were this much fun, I'd have spent more time in temples. Where's your funny dress?"

"I was training to be a priestess - I'm not anymore, and I wasn't a very good acolyte to be honest. I was always stealing wine from the kitchen, showing up late to prayers, and generally doing anything in my power to upset The Mother. And they're robes we wear, not dresses. I couldn't take them with me when we…left. Not that I need them anymore, I can't go back." Her voice hitched on the last sentence. "This is better anyway. Who wouldn't want to be stuck in the middle of a freezing mountain with a burly, lying drunk and a grouchy violence prone companion?" Bear barked out a laugh.

"You love my stories, and not a word of them is made up. As for the drunk bit," he pulled out a flask, shaking it so they could hear the liquid sloshing around inside, "I'll work on that once we make it to the cave."

Kezra rolled her eyes, about to make a remark about how ridiculous he was, when it hit. Pain, searing pain split through her head and flooded her muscles. Kezra doubled over, cradling her head in her hands.

"Kezra, are you okay? What's happening?" Lennox's frantic voice cut through the pain. Kezra struggled to reply. The tugging feeling on her brain was too consistent; the pain too strong. She wasn't going to be able to resist it much longer. Tylan would get her back, and he'd never let her go. Kezra swallowed, fumbling for the vial in her pocket, but her hands shook so violently she couldn't grab the vial, even when her fingers brushed against it. She felt as if she were fading.

"It's okay, Kezra. Concentrate on my voice. It will be alright. You can fight this."

"What the hell was that?" Bear's alarmed tone registered through Kezra's pain.

"Kezra just needs a moment."

"Not her. That sound. You didn't hear that scream?" Kezra tried to shove down the pain and concentrate on listening for the noise he was so worried about. Then she heard it, and her heart started pounding. A high-pitched wail cut through the air, followed by a deep, bellowing roar. Genuine panic set in

"Run! We need to run! Now!" Kezra fought to her feet, struggling to stay upright. She willed the adrenaline coursing through her system to take over. Why weren't they running?

"What is it?" Lennox sounded far too calm, but Kezra could see Bear had quickly started gathering their things. The roar came again, closer this time.

"That is Tylan's beast. If you want to live, we need to run. Now."

"How? You can barely stand."

"I'll be fine. Just go, run!" Another roar came, closer behind, and Kezra stumbled forward in the direction of the cave, hoping it would spur Lennox into action.

"You go, we'll be right behind you." No sooner were the words out of Bear's mouth than Kezra found herself being scooped into the air by a pair of strong hands. Bear had slung her over his shoulder like a sack and took off. Kezra wanted to argue that they should just leave her behind since they'd have a better chance without her, but it was hard to argue from over Bear's shoulder. Another ear-splitting roar pierced the air, and Kezra's head felt like it split from within.

"Just a little further," Bear road. Kezra bobbed up and down, strung across his back. A fresh wave of pain cleaved through her head with every movement. It felt like they'd been running for ages, but Kezra couldn't imagine how they could outrun the beast chasing them. She could have sworn she heard its wings beating the air around them, but in her current state, it was hard to say if it was real or just conjured from her terror.

Suddenly, she was plunged into darkness. Kezra felt herself being lowered down onto a cold stone floor. The pain was still all-consuming at this point, and worse, she could hear the roar coming closer. It was over. The beast would find them, and either keep them captive in this cave until Tylan came for them, or eat them before he got here.

"Where is it?" Lennox's gentle hands were riffling through the pockets of Kezra's coat. "Come on Kezra, you can do this. Where's the potion?"

"My vest...the right pocket."

"There are too many damn pockets." Lennox muttered. Gently, she removed one of the two remaining vials. Kezra smiled as she heard the cork pop.

"I thought you liked all of the pockets."

"Not right now. Sit up, I need you to drink this." Kezra grimaced as Lennox cradled her head. She forced herself to gulp down the potion, making sure not to waste a drop. Gently, Lennox lowered Kezra's head back down on the stone. She closed her eyes, savoring the feeling of the cool ground against her cheek. Slowly, the pounding in Kezra's head faded, the feeling of being pulled elsewhere disappeared.

"I think we're safe." Lennox whispered. Kezra strained her ears, listening for the roar of Tylan's pet. When it finally came, it sounded further away than it had before. Kezra nodded.

"I think it lost track of us. It seems to have passed right over the cave."

"How in Helica did it find us at all?"

She sat up, glancing at Bear. His face was drained of color. Sweat dripped down his forehead and coated his shirt. Kezra gulped, feeling guilty and so grateful that he'd saved her without so much as being asked.

"I think it was tracking me through my bond. But you don't have to worry, the potion I took dampens it, so the beast shouldn't be able to find me again, at least not for a while." Bear shook his head.

"What in the Helica did I sign up for?"

They all sat in the quiet for a while longer, listening to the best get further away until they could no longer hear its roar. Bear broke the silence first.

"Alright then. There's a stream straight out of the cave and to the left. I'm going down there to clean up and get us some fresh water. When I get back, the two of you could use to do the same. I don't suppose either of ya lasses could get a fire going can ye?"

"I can do it. We'll gather some firewood while you're out," Kezra said.

"Good. If you can do that, I'll get us a proper meal cooked. We could all use it after today."

"I'd take a stiff drink." Lennox chimed in. Bear raised his eyebrows at her.

"I'll be taking my stash with me. I'm not sure it would be here when I get back otherwise." With one last weary look at Lennox, he turned and left. Kezra pried herself from the floor, her body still stiff from the bond's magic searing through it just moments before.

"Well, there's no use in waiting. Let's see if we can find some firewood." Lennox stared at her, unmoving. Kezra turned, walking toward the cave's mouth. "Come on. I don't think Bear really believes we can start a fire. I can't wait to see the look on his face when we prove him wrong."

"Are you seriously not going to talk about it?"

"Talk about what?" Kezra continued out of the cave, scanning the ground for twigs. Leaves rustled as Lennox rushed out after her.

"About that! How you were just laying on the ground with your head in your hands while a dragon chased us down."

"I'm not sure what there is to talk about. It happened, and now it's over." She spotted a few dry twigs and one piece of wood that looked ideal for keeping a fire going. "Have you found anything yet, I might have enough to get something started, but we need more to keep it from going out."

"Kezra. What just happened? Are you ok?" Kezra whirled around, dropping the wood.

"You know what just happened! That potion wore off early and everything was almost ruined. Tylan would have gotten me back, and he never would have let me go. He'd have made me hunt you down again, and I wouldn't be able to free us this time. I messed up. That's what happened."

"You didn't mess up, Kezra." Lennox's voice softened. "I'm not angry with you. I was worried. That pain you were in, it was terrifying. I knew he could summon you back but that… I thought you were dying." Lennox gathered a few pieces of firewood and they headed back toward the cave.

"It's the magic. Sometimes when it floods into my system like that, it hurts. And when I try to resist it, to push it down, the pain is unbearable."

"Do you mean that's happened before?" Kezra nodded, unwanted emotion clogged her throat.

"Sometimes. When Tylan was unhappy with me, he'd use it as a punishment. He'd just flood my body with magic, and it just left me incapacitated. He's never laid a hand on me, but he's also never had to. The feeling of magic cramping my muscles and pulling at my brain is enough torture to keep me in line. I feel like I'm being ripped apart from the inside out."

"I'm so sorry, Kezra. That's just awful. No one should have to grow up that way."

"Do you know the worst part? In a way, I craved it. Magic isn't just pain, it's power. Through the ache, I always felt like I could do anything, be anything, if I could just harness the magic for myself. Then when it's gone, I feel hollow inside, like a piece of me is missing. Sometimes I would anger him intentionally, just to feel it again. I knew the potion was wearing off; I have for days. I've been telling myself I waited to take the next dose because I was being practical, buying us more time. But…" Kezra trailed off.

"You don't have to finish, Kezra. I understand." Lennox dropped her firewood and wrapped her arms around her. Tears leaked from Kezra's eyes, and she tried to blink them away. What was happening to her? When had she become so emotional? It was ridiculous; Kezra had never cried so much in her life as she had the past few days.

"I'm sorry, Lennox. That dragon finding us was my fault; I think it could sense me through the bond."

"You don't know that though. And Asher did say he passed a message to Tylan before I, well, took care of him. Maybe the dragon was just scanning the area."

"Maybe." Kezra shuddered, unconvinced by this theory. "I need to know how he did that though. It could make things much more difficult for us."

"Difficult how? He's done. Asher's not a danger to us anymore."

"True, but it means Tylan has more power than I thought, that he isn't limited in the ways I believed him to be. He is somehow passing messages to his bonded without being there in person, I didn't know he could do that. We need to be more careful."

"That's not much of a change for us." Lennox unwrapped her arms from Kezra and started picking through the fallen firewood.

"Right - enough of that. Let's get this fire started before Bear gets back. He'll be unbearable if he gets here and we haven't done anything."

They got to work in silence, Lennox going out to gather more firewood while Kezra tended to the tiny fire they'd started, letting it grow. By the time Bear came back, the fire was roaring. He pretended not to be impressed, but Kezra could tell he was.

Lennox and Kezra left, finding the stream he'd mentioned without issue. They washed off and filled their canteens. Although Kezra loved the peace of being at the spring, dusk was falling so they hurried back to the cave. When they got back, Bear had somehow rustled up fresh meat to cook. They settled in for the night, eating a small but satisfying meal, joking around by the fire. No one brought up her bond, or the dangers they'd faced. Lennox didn't act resentful or blame Kezra for what happened, and Bear didn't seem to question his decision to help them. For the first time in Kezra's life, she'd found friends, people who cared about her, would sacrifice their own safety to protect her.Kezra promised herself that she would protect them at all costs, and she would make Tylan pay for ever endangering the people who she'd quickly come to love.

CHAPTER 18

Lennox

After that first day, the trek to Kitsummit passed without further incidents. The mountain got steeper as they continued up to the peak, and the conditions became harsher. At this height, the mountain was no longer subject to the rules that governed the rest of the world. Despite the warmth of the season they'd just left below, the mountain continued to blast them with an icy wind that swept away their will to speak. Snow blinded them, thick enough to obscure the person in front of them, even when they were close enough to touch. Bear had tied everyone together with rope as they climbed higher, an action Lennox had laughed at just days before, but now she could hardly keep up.

The only reprieve was the nighttime. They always stopped hiking before dusk set in, and Bear seemed to know every secret cave and every overhanging ledge that they could shelter beneath along the way. Bear's familiarity with the mountain was that of an intimacy with an old lover. Without him, Lennox was certain they'd have died while wandering the cliff-side, searching for a path that was right in front of their face, yet completely undetectable. During the day, the conditions didn't allow for much conversation, only the occasional yell from Bear, giving them the encouragement to keep moving until they reached the next resting place. Kezra and Lennox trudged along, tethered to a man they barely knew, yet trusted with their lives.

Nights though, nights almost made the treachery of the day worth it. They spent many nights huddled together around a fledgling fire built from wood they'd gathered that first day and carried with them on their hike up. They used only a small amount at a time; the fire was hardly enough for cooking and too meager to provide any real warmth. But any warmth the fire lacked was made up for by the company. On hard stone floors, aching and freezing from long, arduous days, they listened to Bear tell his stories and were transported to wherever they took place.

First, he told them what it was like to grow up in Alara, but then he talked about his family and his life. His mother was a trader from Kitsummit, who had come down to Alara during the harvest to celebrate the moon festival, which was the first night of the year, the night the planet's third moon peaks into the sky and stays for harvest season. Over six feet tall with shining red hair, and the muscle of a woman accustomed to climbing the mountain, Bear's father thought her a goddess in disguise. They'd shared a fiery, magical love that Bear spoke of in awe, but after the festival, she explained that she needed to leave him and go back to her people.

Love-struck, his father wanted to plead for her to stay, but Bear's father knew he couldn't control something so wild and free, and so he let her go back, deep into the mountain, carrying a piece of his heart with her. Each moon festival, he hoped for her return, and each year, his heart broke a little more when she didn't. After three years, she reappeared with the largest toddler Bear's father had ever seen strapped across her back. He had his mother's startling red hair and her large build, but his eyes, his nose, the way his eyebrows quirked up in surprise at the world around him, those were the spitting image of his father. His goddess had returned to him, bearing him a warrior to raise.

The warrior's mother named him Bear, claiming she'd once found him wrestling with a small bear cub as soon as he'd been able to walk. The two became unlikely friends, and thus she named him after his childhood playmate, the bears who ran wild around the mountain together. She left Bear with his father before returning to the mountains, proclaiming it was time for a man to guide him. Happily, Bear's father took on the challenge of raising the unruly boy on his own. Luckily, his neighbor had a little girl of the same age named Celene. Celene's mother cared for both children while Bear's father worked, and the two grew close, like siblings.

Every harvest, Bear's mother returned, bearing a gift for her little warrior. And when Bear turned fourteen, he hiked the mountain back with her to see the home where he'd lived as a baby. But homesick, he traveled back to Alara after a few short weeks. He continued to visit, splitting his time between the mountains he had grown to love and the town where his family belonged. That is, until Dallos recruited him years later, just after his mother had died.

When he finished his story, Lennox had tears in her eyes. She couldn't stop thinking of that boy with his heart split between two homes, never truly content in either. Even Kezra's eyes seemed to glisten, but it could have been a trick of the firelight.

Most nights though were filled with more light-hearted stories. Some about all the trouble Bear and Celene had gotten into as children. Others about adventures he'd been on with Dallows and the crew. Kezra joked that each one was certainly embellished, and some were probably made up entirely. She was probably right, but it didn't matter. His stories drove away the cold and exhaustion better than any fire could have. More importantly, it helped Lennox bury the loneliness that gripped her heart tighter and tighter the further they ran away from the temple in Tesmerin and from Jasper.

The pain was a weight in her chest that became more difficult to ignore every day. Instead, she'd tried to distract herself with the task of controlling her magic. Lennox had accepted its reality. It was difficult to deny its existence after what happened with Asher, and now she wanted to learn to command it. So far, Lennox hadn't even been able to reproduce the tiny sliver of light she'd created with Tylan, let alone summon the type of power that had eviscerated her attackers. She was trying now, half of her brain concentrating on taking methodical bites of the dried, chewy jerky Kezra gave her, and the other half working on summoning a dazzling orb of silver light. So far, all she'd accomplished was gnawing on half a stick of jerky.

"Thank the goddess!" Kezra's exclamation broke through her concentration. Lennox decided to give it a rest for the night.

"What are you so excited about?" Kezra quirked an eyebrow at her.

"Didn't you hear what Bear said? We're almost to the top. Tomorrow, we can start heading down to the valley where Kitsummit lies."

"Oh! Thank Altheia! Does that mean I don't need to be tied to you anymore?"

"You're lucky you were tied to me. I practically drug you halfway up the mountain. Have you walked at all in the last two days?" Kezra asked. Bear nodded in agreement.

"Aye. I've felt like a sled dog the past two days pulling you behind me."

"I have been walking," Lennox sniffed, indignant. "It's just that the two of you are hard to keep up with. You have such long legs."

"We are literally the exact same height. Jessa measured us," Kezra said, throwing a piece of cheese at her.

"Hey, don't waste food," Bear scolded. Then he looked on, horrified as Lennox plucked the piece of cheese from the ground and popped it into her mouth.

"There you go. No wasted food." Lennox gave Bear her most charming grin, but he still looked queasy.

"We could have let that piece go to waste. Surely you're not so hungry that you need to eat food off the floor."

"Lennox isn't picky about what she eats," Kezra quipped. Lennox studied Bear's pale face. He looked like he might be sick.

"Did my eating off the floor bother you, Bear? Oh my god, it did, didn't it? Are you scared of a little dirt?"

"Of course not. I just have standards. You have no idea who or what's been on this floor and you just put it in your mouth." Bear was turning a little green as he spoke. "Disgusting."

Kezra and Lennox both got a good laugh out of it, and they all sat around eating in companionable silence, too tired from the day's hike for anything more. After she thought everyone was asleep, Lennox used the quiet to try again, concentrating on forming that glowing orb of light. She thought she saw a sliver of silver peaking into existence and tried to feed more magic to it.

"What are you doing?" The light winked out as her concentration wavered. Or perhaps, it hadn't been there at all. Lennox couldn't be sure.

"It's nothing," Lennox lied. She didn't want to admit her failure. But also, knowing she had magic and seeing the reality of it were two different things. Lennox didn't know how Bear would react to it. She didn't want him to fear her or treat her differently. He moved from his place by the dying fire and sat down beside Lennox.

"It's not nothing. Your gift, you are trying to train with it, yes?" Bear asked. Lennox bit her lip and nodded, looking over toward Kezra. She didn't know why, but having Kezra see her fail to summon magic mortified her. Kezra was so strong and capable; whereas Lennox couldn't even provide a light. What happened when Kezra realized she didn't need her? "Don't worry about her; she's sleeping." It was difficult to make out Kezra's huddled form in the dim light, but when Lennox listened carefully, she could hear her soft snores.

"Fine, yes. I'm practicing…or at least trying to, but I haven't been very successful." Bear just shrugged.

"Perhaps you should try something else."

"What do you mean?" Lennox asked, genuinely puzzled.

"If what you're doing isn't working, try a different way."

"I don't know a different way." Lennox huffed in frustration. She liked Bear, she really did, but this was a distraction, and if she concentrated hard enough, she'd be able to control the magic. All she needed was some peace and quiet, and maybe some privacy, as impossible as that was to ask for in such a small space.

"Think about how you felt that night with Asher. You were glowing; you yielded magic like a goddess. It is in you; you just have to find it," Bear said, coaching her. Lennox knew he was right, but she grimaced. He had a point, one she'd thought of before and shoved aside. Those memories were still tender, painful even. Lennox didn't want to embrace that kind of emotion. Instead, she wanted to shove it down, hide it, forget they ever existed. Besides, that use of magic hadn't been controlled; it had been wild, all-consuming. Lennox had been so out of control she hardly remembered using the magic, and that terrified her. Still, Bear was right; this wasn't working. "Go ahead, try again," he encouraged.

So Lennox listened. This time, she recalled how it felt when that man had grabbed her wrists and tried to bind her. She embraced the terror that had seized her body and pictured that orb of silver light. Using all of that horror, all of that pain, the overwhelming loss of leaving Jasper, Lennox used it as fuel for her magic, feeding the light with pieces of each memory. Out of the darkness, a starburst of brilliant light appeared. She gasped in surprise, losing control of the thread of magic entirely. And just as quickly as it had appeared, the light winked out of existence. Bear's giant hand thumped her on the back.

"I knew you could do it. Now let's get some rust. We have a long day ahead." With that, Bear left as Lennox still gaped at the space where the light, her light, had appeared out of nothing. As she settled into sleep, Lennox smiled to herself. She'd done it. Sadness mingled with a sense of pride. Lennox longed to tell Jasper; she wanted to run to Jasper's room and shake her awake to show her what she could do. Someday Lennox would go back and find her. Together, they would see all the world had to offer. The three of them would be unstoppable. The plan made Lennox feel warm and fuzzy inside. Holding onto that feeling tightly, she fell asleep.

"I thought - you said - we were almost there." Lennox struggled to get the words out with the thin mountain air making it almost impossible to draw breath. Kezra looked back over her shoulder as Lennox struggled behind the group, trying and failing to pull her own weight. Today was blessedly clear, so she could make out every line of Kezra's judgmental expression. Lennox didn't have the energy to tease Kezra about her grumpy face.

"We are almost there. The peak is just ahead, then we can take a rest and make our way down."

Lennox climbed for what felt like hours, but Bear insisted the journey had been short, less than an hour after she'd issued her complaint. She plopped down on the frosted mountaintop, taking in the beauty of the scene below. Although winter was setting in, the autumn blooms were reluctant to fade completely. A few flowers still peeked up from the ground, and bushes began to bear the red buds of bittersweet snowberries. Looking down the mountain, Lennox saw places where the frost had settled in patches of soft-white settled among the green grass and between the changing yellow-gold leaves. For a moment, she was transported back to the temple gardens. Even though the views were entirely different, she was filled with the same sense of serenity here as when she was sitting among the temple's lunasha blooms.

Placing her hands on the ground, Lennox swore she could feel the threads of life running through the soil. Closing her eyes, she imagined the lunasha blooms, their silky silver petals budding from the green stalks, blooming under the moonlight.

"What did you do?" A breathy voice came from behind her. Lennox opened her eyes to see Kezra standing over her, eyes wide and mouth agape. She looked around, confused by Kezra's expression, and found the source of her shock. All around her, green stems had shot up from the earth. Some of them bore the closed silver bud of the lunasha plant in its fledgling form. "How did you do that?"

"I don't know. I was just thinking about the temple gardens and the lunasha blooms and then - well," Lennox gestured to the ground around her, "then this happened."

"It's amazing." Kezra shook her head. "You should try to be more careful about it when we get to Kitsummit though, we don't know how the people will react to your magic." Irritation surged through Lennox at the comment.

"Aren't we here looking for magic?" Lennox snapped. Kezra sighed, taking a deep breath before replying.

"Yes, but I'm acting on a hunch, and we're strangers. We don't want to scare them away," Kezra said. Lennox wilted a little. She was so proud of herself for finally, and it hurt that Kezra's first instinct was to scold her. Perhaps reading her expression, Kezra's voice softened. "It's not that I'm not proud of you for this. I think you're amazing. But I don't know how they might react to this, and I couldn't live with myself if something happened to you because I drug you along with me." Lennox's cheeks heated as guilt ate at her for snapping at Kezra.

"You didn't drag me along. I wanted to come."

"Still, if something happened, it would be my fault."

"It wouldn't. I can be responsible for myself. But I'll try my best to control it, I promise."

"I didn't mean to upset you. I'm sorry. This really is amazing, Lennox." Kezra nudged her shoulder. "Let's get going while the sun's still out. Bear says if we hurry, we can make it to Kitsummit before dark."

"You mean I could sleep in a real bed tonight? What are we waiting for then?" As they started down the mountain, Lennox looked back at her flowers one last time. It was comforting to know she could create something beautiful - not just destroy.

The walk down to Kitsummit was far easier than the hike up had been. It helped that Lennox could breathe properly again, and the thought of a warm bed and a proper meal propelled her down the mountain at record speed. When they finally arrived, the sun was setting and her mouth was practically watering in anticipation of hot food. It probably wouldn't be a match for Celene's cooking, but one could hope.

Kitsummit looked warm and inviting in the golden glow of sunset. The homes all appeared to have thatched roofs. The streets were made of flattened dirt, not surprising as Lennox couldn't imagine how difficult it must be to haul large quantities of stone here. Smoke curled in the air from chimneys, and the glow of a hearth fire lit the windows. They were low enough now that the winter's frost hadn't quite reached the area yet, and the red-gold leaves of fall still hung from trees and red ivy grew up the sides of homes. The town struck her as strange somehow, but Lennox couldn't put her finger on what felt different.

"Welcome to Kitsummit, the heart of the mountains," Bear said.

"There's no wall," Kezra said, coming up to stand beside her. That was it. Even the temple in Tesmerin had a wall and a gate, guarding them from outsiders, bandits, or the dangerous creatures that lurked in the surrounding forest. Here, the homes were exposed; nothing stood between them and the outside world.

"We've no need of it here," Bear said with a shrug.

"But what about the creatures? The dangerous ones you warned us about? Surely the town needs to keep them out?" Lennox shuddered, suddenly feeling exposed in this town despite the nights spent in the wilderness. Bear laughed, a full-belly laugh that echoed through the open valley.

"You think a wall would keep out the creatures if they wanted in?" He shook his head. "They simply keep to themselves unless threatened. But believe me, if a shadow wolf wanted into your twins in Tesmerin, a mere wall would not stop it. The people of Kitsummit don't waste resources on such unnecessary things. The mountains deter bandits, and the people here live in harmony with nature." Kezra absorbed the information, pondering it for a moment before nodding in acceptance. Lennox swallowed, her throat tight. No matter what Bear said, her mind was having trouble accepting the lack of a wall having been behind one for her entire life.

Bear claimed to know of an inn nearby with soft beds and excellent food. A sense of foreboding grabbed hold of her as Lennox followed him, and she fought back the urge to run back to Alara and take a ship back to the temple. Lennox knew she was being silly. They had made it; nothing bad was going to happen. But with each step forward, the feeling that their lives were about to be altered forever grew stronger.

The inn Bear took us to seemed to be a large tavern where the whole town had gathered for their evening meal. With few travellers venturing up this way, she'd expected the Kitsummit inn to be a reflection of Celene's - quiet, but tranquil and homey. Instead, they walked into a scene that reminded her of the temple's dining hall during the harvest, when they opened the doors to the public and the hall was packed with revelers. Tables were crowded with people chatting happily, throwing back pints of ale. The tables held plates full of savory meat cradled in a bed of red berries. That looked interesting. Lennox practically floated behind Bear, imagining the way the berries would pop in her mouth.

"Who do we have here?" A man popped up from the table in front of them, approaching their group. Lennox's eyes bulged at the size of him. He was a head taller than Bear, his body bulging with muscle. His hair and beard were the same brilliant shade of red, but streaked with silver, showing his age. The others in the group grew quiet once he spoke, halting the merriment in the room. As one, the crowd turned to look at us, noticing us for the first time. "It can't be Helena's boy, back so soon? I thought you'd had enough last time?"

"That's funny, old man. You couldn't beat me with one hand tied behind my back," Bear retorted.

"I could be you with both my hands tied."

"Don't make threats you can't back up, Coran." Tables shifted, squeaking as they were moved aside. Kezra tensed, her stance changing as her hands slipped to her thoughts. Lennox felt magic beginning to pool under her skin. As though she could sense it, Kezra turned and gave Lennox a subtle shake of her head.

"Don't," Kezra hissed. So for the first time, Lennox tried to smother the magic building in her body.

"I don't make threats, Bear. Come on and fight. Yer not afraid of an old man, are ye?" Bear launched himself at the man. It was difficult to keep track of who was winning, they moved so fast. All of her concentration was focused on silencing the thrumming Lennox felt in her veins. Her skin felt too tight; her muscles throbbed. Lennox tried to ignore the agony and instead focus on the mass of flailing limbs in front of her. It looked like Bear was beaten, on the ground with the older man holding him down. Then Bear reared his head back and, using it as a weapon, bashed it into the other man's nose. Coran let out a howl, reflexively letting go of Bear. In a flash, their positions reversed, and Bear was pinning Coran down, twisting his arm into a position that made Lennox wince with sympathy.

"Alright last, I yield. Get off me." Bear extracted himself from on top of Coran and extended his hand to help him up. "Altheia's tits, I think you broke my nose."

"Now it will match the rest of your face," Bear said. Something twirled in Kezra's hand, glinting as the metal caught the firelight. She drew her hand back, poised to throw the dagger if Coran attacked. Instead, the man broke out in a hearty laugh, patting Bear on the back.

The crowd dispersed, moved their tables back into place, and went about their conversations as if nothing had happened. Kezra's hand slipped back to her thigh, the gleam of her dagger vanishing. Bear sauntered over to the two of them stood, his arm thrown around the shoulder of the man whose nose he'd just broken.

"Lennox, Kezra, I'd like to introduce you to my uncle, Coran."

"Nice to meet ye, lasses. I'd shake yer hand, but alas, mine are all bloody."

"This is your uncle?" Lennox sputtered. "What was that all about?" She waved her hand in the direction of their battleground.

"I had to make sure he hadn't gone soft in the lowlands. Too hot down there, makes everyone soft and lazy."

"Not too soft to beat yer old ass."

"Ah no, that's the mountain blood in ye. It runs strong. Now tell me, what are you two young lasses doing this far north? Come to find some real warriors, have ye?"

"Nothing like that, uncle, so don't let Aunt Isla play matchmaker just yet. They're here to see Senga." Coran raised his eyebrows, slipping his arm from Bear's shoulder.

"Senga? What do you want with Senga?" His demeanor shifted. The good-natured grin was replaced with a weary expression. Lennox thought about the way this massive hand had pinned Bear down in mere seconds. If he decided he wanted them gone, Lennox doubted there was much she or Kezra could do to stop him. Lennox reached for the magic still itching beneath her skin. For one glorious second, she thought she'd wrangled it, but then it slid from her grasp. Kezra's hands twitched toward her thighs and the dagger Lennox now knew she concealed there.

"I don't know who Senga is, but my friend here is in a bit of trouble. Maybe Senga can help." Lennox plastered on her friendliest smile, hoping to put this stranger at ease.

"What kind of trouble?" He asked, raising an eyebrow. Bear looked at Kezra, who gave a subtle nod.

"It seems she's been bound to Tylan Faine - against her will." Coran reared back; whatever he'd been expecting, it wasn't that.

"Everyone knows you must enter into a bond willingly. The old magic can't be forced upon someone, the balance does not allow for it." Kezra took a step toward Coran.

"I have been linked to Tylan for my entire life, since I was a child. Perhaps at one point, I accepted willingly, seeing no other choice, but I don't remember doing so, and I would have been too young to understand the consequences. Regardless, I don't want to be bound to him any longer."

"The Amethyst Assassin, you're her, aren't you?" Coran whispered. "The one sent to do his bidding."

"I've always hated that name," Kezra grumbled. "I despise it and wish to be her no longer."

"Will he come looking for you here? Either of you?" The three of them exchanged a look, but Kezra answered.

"I don't know. It's possible. We were betrayed in Alara, but we... took care of the situation. We should be gone before he finds us though; we mean you no harm."

"And yet, your presence puts us all in danger." He turned his gaze on Bear. "You should not have brought them here, little cub. But now that you're here, nothing's to be done. Take them to Senga in the morning. If anyone can help them, it's her." He looked back at them, lowering himself down to look them directly in the eyes. "Tell no one else why you're here. The fewer people who know of this, the better." They both nodded, neither of them wanting to expose these people to any harm. "Curse your soft heart, Bear Cub; let us hope it's not the end of our people."

"It won't be. I will not let him hurt you," Kezra spoke with steely determination. Coran smirked.

"No offense, lass, but you can't free yourself. How could you hope to protect my people?" With that, he walked away, rejoining his table.

"Ah, forget about the old geezer. You made it up the mountain! Come, let us find Isla so you can both get cleaned up. Then we'll give you a proper welcome." They found Isla in the back of the inn, ordering kitchen staff around with precision. She was Coran's opposite in every way.

She stood at least a head shorter than Lennox with pale skin and a mass of curly blonde hair so pale it was almost white. Lennox wasn't sure what she thought Coran's wife would look like, but this wasn't it. Everyone in Kitsummit, or at least at this inn, seemed to be unusually tall. Among them, Isla looked like a child, albeit an old one with an oddly wizened face. However, the staff clearly respected her and were possibly even a bit frightened of her. A girl who she'd spoken to sternly for messing up the dough for tomorrow's bread looked close to tears. However, the scowl melted off Isla's face when she spotted Bear.

"What brings you here, little cub? I hadn't thought I'd see you again until next spring." She threw her arms out to embrace him, and Bear scooped the woman up into a crushing hug.

"It's good to see you too, auntie. Still terrorizing the kitchen staff, I see." He set her down with a grin splitting his face ear to ear. Isla frowned.

"Yes, well, I swear that girl would lose her head if it wasn't screwed on. It's the second time this week she forgot to add yeast to the bread. Yeast! Silly girl. I ought to fire her." Isla smoothed her dress, and her eyes snagged on Lennox and Kezra.

"Who do we have here? Have you come to introduce us to your new wife and her kin? Our cub is all grown up! Tell me, darling, which one did you wed? The one with the dark hair, I hope. No offense, you're both lovely, but the blonde one could use some bulking up, not a shred of muscle on her." Looking down at herself, Lennox wondered how the woman had come to the conclusion when she was covered head to toe in Jessa's outfit and bulky coat. Lennox started to reply, but Bear beat her to it.

"I've not wed either one of them, auntie. I met the cousins in Tesmerin, where they told me of their dream of seeing Kitsummit. They needed a guide, so I helped them, nothing more." Isla clucked her tongue.

"What a shame; you're both such lovely girls. Where are my manners? You must be roasting in those coats and longing for a nice bath. Bear, show them up to the guest rooms, would you? I'll have some water and a change of clothes sent up, then we can get acquainted over a meal. Yes, that will do; off with you." She turned her attention back to the kitchen. "Agnes, the yeast needs to sit in water before you add the flour you foolish girl! How many times must we go through this? If you'll excuse me, I must go help the staff. We'll chat soon." She rushed off, leaving us baffled. Bear's face was as red as his hair. He cleared his throat.

"Sorry about erm, that. Isla means well, but she can come on strong." Kezra just shook her head.

"She's right about the bath; I'm dying to wash the dirt off of my skin. Where are those rooms?"

Chapter 19

Kezra

"I can't wear that." Kezra stared at the lavender, frilly garment sitting on the bed, mocking her.

"Don't be so fussy, Kezra. You'll look amazing." Lennox swirled around in an identical rose dress. Kezra had helped tie the laces on the embroidered corset top without knowing a similar monstrosity awaited her. Lennox's skirts swirled around in a dramatic arc as she walked. How impractical. "You can't tell me the notorious Amethyst Assassin is scared of a little dress." Kezra leveled her finest glare at Lennox. Such a ridiculous name, Kezra loathed it, and now that Lennox had learned it, she'd never let it go.

"I'm not scared; I just don't like it. It's impractical. There's nowhere to conceal a dagger." Lennox rolled her eyes.

"It's not meant to be practical; it's meant to be pretty."

"Things can be both. I don't see why I can't wear the clothes Jessa gave us," Kezra asked, aware she was whining.

"Because our host went to the trouble of providing us something beautiful for the evening. So as a guest, suck it up and wear the dress. We don't want to be offensive."

"Fine," Kezra grumbled, giving the black leather pants and vest one last longing look. "Help me with the back." Lennox squealed and started excitedly jabbering while lacing the dress. A dull ache began to form behind Kezra's left eye. She massaged it idly, ready to get the night over with.

"Now, what to do with your hair?"

"Leave it; it's fine," Kezra said, tired of all the fuss. Lennox frowned.

"At least re-braid it; it's a mess. I bet it would look so pretty down though." Kezra sighed.

"Impractical," Kezra muttered, but she took her hair out of its tight braids, letting it fall in waves down her back.

"Gorgeous." Lennox beamed. She pulled Kezra to the mirror. "Look. We make quite a pair." The woman who stared back at her was so…soft, with dark hair in gentle waves framing her round face. The lavender dress complimented her skin, and Kezra had to admit, there was something satisfying about the way the dress swished around her calves when she moved. Lennox shone, her golden hair shiny and her cheeks flushed a pink that matched her dress. "Come on, let's get something to eat; I'm starved."

"Hang on, one last thing." Kezra hiked up the dress, strapping a dagger to her thigh. It was good to be prepared. Lennox shook her head, then took Kezra's hand and led her downstairs.

"There you are. Don't you both look gorgeous? Here, have something to eat." Isla greeted them the moment they walked down the stairs and herded them to a table. On it sat two pints of ale and the spiced meat Kezra had spied walking in. Her mouth watered. Isla settled in next to her. As they ate, Isla peppered them with questions about their journey. Kezra let Lennox do most of the talking, content to quietly enjoy the food.

"Shame Bear didn't wed either of you. I've been hoping that boy would settle down instead of gallivanting off to sea." A smile spread across Isla's face. "No matter, there are plenty of eligible young men here who would love to meet you. I'll make the introductions."

Lennox got up and motioned for Kezra to follow. So much for enjoying a quiet meal. Kezra gulped down the dregs of her ale and followed Lennox into the crowd. It turned out Isla knew many young men, and she introduced them to every one of them. The men flirted shamelessly, kissing their hands and complimenting their dresses. Eventually the tables were pushed aside and someone began playing music. Lennox found a partner and twirled about on the makeshift dancefloor. Kezra would have been content to just watch, but eventually, someone grabbed her hand and pulled her into the revelry. Cups of ale were passed her way. She drank and danced and laughed with Lennox at her side. By the time they made their way back to the room, Kezra's cheeks hurt from grinning all night, her feet were sore from dancing, and her head swam from the ale. Her last thought before drifting into a blissful sleep was to wonder if maybe she could stay here after all.

Morning arrived, and Kezra's nerves came back with it. Today, they were going to meet Senga. Today, Kezra's life would change. She'd find a way to sever her bond from Tylan; Kezra knew it in soul. A knock pounded on the door, eliciting a moan from Lennox, who pulled the blanket up over her head. Kezra climbed out of bed and opened the door to reveal Bear standing there, dressed for the day. His expression turned to a smirk as Bear took in her appearance. To her horror, Kezra realized she hadn't changed out of the ridiculous dress from the night before. She scrambled to grab a blanket and drape it over herself, embarrassed.

"I'm glad to see you can have some fun, storm cloud."

"Storm cloud," Kezra asked, not bothering to hide the sarcasm lacing through her voice.

"Yes, if that one's sunshine, you're a storm, ready to blow at any moment. Ah, see, your stormy expression has returned." Kezra rubbed her temples, last night's headache resurfacing.

"Can I help you, Bear?"

"Aye, I was only letting you know I'm leaving soon to meet Senga, if you'd like to come." Kezra's palms started to sweat.

"Give me twenty minutes and I'll be ready." Bear nodded and walked down the steps. She slammed the door more forcefully than intended as anxiety grabbed hold of her. Senga. Twenty more minutes and Kezra's fate could change. Lennox set up, startled by the door.

"Gods, what time is it? Why are you slamming things?" Lennox exclaimed. Kezra's hands fumbled with the laces at the back of the dress. Her hands were shaking so badly she couldn't grab them. Kezra tried to settle herself. She'd killed men, powerful ones, hunted them down, dragged them to Tylan and slaughtered the ones he no longer had use for. Why was she so nervous about meeting one little old woman?

"I'm going to meet Senga."

"Oh. I'll come with you." Lennox swung her legs around the side of the bed, starting to get up.

"No, it's fine. I can go alone. You sleep." In response, Lennox bit her lip, looking uncertain.

"Are you sure? I really don't mind."

"I think this is something I should do alone. Can you help me get out of this ridiculous dress though?" Kezra turned around, letting Lennox unlace the strings at the back. She hurried to throw on one of Jessa's outfits, immediately feeling more like herself in the trousers; then ran her fingers through her tangled hair, braiding it back the best she could.

"I'll be here for you when you get back, no matter what happens."

"Thank you, Lennox, for coming all this way with me." Lennox only shrugged.

"That's what friends are for. I can't wait to hear all about it. Now go," Lennox said, shooing her away, "don't keep Bear waiting." Kezra nodded, unable to voice the words of gratitude she felt. Then she bounded down the stairs toward her new life.

Senga's home sat in the middle of town, just a short walk from the inn. As a respected village elder, her home sat in a place of prominence, easily accessible to members of the community. All day, people filtered in and out of her home, seeking advice, or asking her opinion on their new lemon tart recipe, or to know the best way to get rid of ethelrot. Kezra didn't hear the advice, but the lemon tarts could use a pinch of lemon zest, and more butter in the crust, an opinion with which Kezra agreed, and ethelrot could be fought by burying leaves of the jessop tree in the corners of the home where the rod had infiltrated. Apparently, this not only kept the rot from spreading, but could cure the rot entirely if caught early enough. All of this she learned while waiting for her turn to visit Senga. Finally, it was Kezra's turn. Bear let her into the room alone, promising to wait.

Senga sat in a chair near the fireplace, where a small fire was smoldering. She had knitting in her lap and didn't look up from her work as Kezra entered.

"Take a seat, dear. Can I get you anything, tea perhaps?" Kezra took the seat across from her, trying to stay as far as possible from the fireplace. Whether it was from heat or nerves, she couldn't be sure, but Kezra was already sweating.

"No, thank you. I'm fine."

"You're sure? It's no trouble. Astrid here helps me; I'm sure she wouldn't mind." A young woman around Kezra's age emerged from the kitchen with a mug for Senga.

"Really, I'm fine. Thank you, though."

"Very well, dear." Senga turned her attention to Astrid, setting down her knitting to accept the steaming mug. "Thank you, Astrid. Could you give the young lass and me a moment of peace, please?" Astrid nodded and scurried back toward the kitchen, never having emitted so much as a squeak. For days, the entire journey to Kitsummit, Kezra had been rehearsing exactly what she might say in this situation. But now that she was here, in front of a woman who might actually have some answers, her mind was blank. She racked her brain, looking for a way to start.

"What are you knitting?" Kezra blurted out. The old woman smiled.

"One of the women in the village is having a baby soon; I'm making some sweaters for the little one. But I doubt you climbed all the way up here to ask me about my hobby."

"Erm…no. You see, I was hoping you might be able to help me." Kezra paused, wishing she'd accepted that tea, if only for something to do with her hands. Senga waited for her to continue, letting the silence hang in the air. Kezra gathered her courage and plowed on; this was it.

"I was wondering, well hoping really, that you might know of a way to break a bond." Senga set down her knitting, meeting Kezra's eye for the first time. She kept going, the words spilling out. "You see, no one from Kitsummit has ever bonded to Tylan Faine, and there are rumors that you, or your people rather, still have magic. And if anyone knows how to break a bond, I thought that maybe they'd be here. Then Coran told me to meet with you. So, can you help me? Please?" Kezra winced at the desperation in her voice.

"Let me see your marker." Unsure what that had to do with the questions, but willing to oblige, Kezra rolled up her sleeve to reveal the linked bands on her forearm. Senga inhaled sharply. "Child, how are you here?"

"I came with Bear, he guided me and my friend up the mountain," Kezra answered, puzzled.

"No, not that. This marker represents a strong bond. You should not be able to ignore the wishes of the one who placed it. How have you evaded its pull?" Kezra pulled the glowing vial from her pocket after a moment of contemplation.

"I used this. Does that mean you know about the bond then? Can you help me break it?" Senga twirled the vial in her fingers, then popped it open. Kezra rushed to stop Senga before she drank the precious liquid. If Senga couldn't help her, Kezra couldn't afford to waste it. Senga sniffed at the contents and grimaced, replacing the stopper.

"Ashwart." Senga muttered, handing the vial back. Kezra's heart settled once the vial was back in her hands; she hadn't realized how hard it had been hammering in her chest. "I'm so sorry, dear, I can't help you." Despair gripped her, but Kezra shoved it aside, trying to hold on to hope.

"But the bond, you must know something that can help?" Kezra's voice cracked. "What is ashwart?"

"I've seen the bond markers before, yes. But the only way I know to break the bond entirely is to be released from it willingly. My people do not seek Tylan for favors because we have never dabbled in the old magic. We have the knowledge of our ancestors to help us survive, and that is all we need. Is this what you're using to suppress your bond?" She gestured to the vial.

"Yes, I got the potion from a friend," Kezra said. Senga gave her a sad smile.

"It's not a potion, dear, or at least not a magic one. Ashwart grows by mountain streams. It glows when you crush it and can suppress magic, but it can also be toxic."

"But if it's a plant, I can get more, right?" Hope flared in Kezra's chest. Maybe she couldn't break the bond, but she could suppress it, at least for a little longer.

"Foolish girl. Didn't you hear what I said? The plan is toxic. The magic builds in your blood; without an outlet for it to release, it poisons you. Continually taking this will kill you. You must stop taking it at once."

"Please," Kezra whimpered. "I feel fine, tell me where to find more. I need to buy myself more time." Senga sighed.

"It's your life, I suppose; I won't make your choices for you. There is a river outside the village, about an hour's walk east. There you will find tall plants with broad leaves that grow inside the river. Pull them out from the stalk and squeeze out the sap of one plant, then mix it with a small amount of water. The mixture will glow like this, but do not drink more than the sap of one plant in a moon cycle. There are signs when the toxin begins to set in. Your legs will tingle, then cease to function. Eventually, it will work its way to your heart. If you feel a tingling sensation in your hands or feet, you must stop immediately. Even then, it might be too late."

"Do you know how long I have before that happens?" Senga shrugged.

"I have seen those foolish enough to suppress a bond this way last more than a year before the effects begin." Some of Kezra's tension loosened; a year, surely that would be plenty of time to find a more permanent solution. "But your bond marker is a sign of powerful magic. You may only have half that before it begins poisoning you. I cannot say." With that, her heart dropped. Six months, that could be all she had. And Kezra had already wasted one precious month getting here. She fought the depression threatening to overtake her. It hadn't been a total loss. Senga told her how to get more ashwart. Kezra could buy herself some time at least.

"Thank you, Senga." Kezra choked out. "I appreciate the help." Senga only shook her head.

"Be careful, child. It is not a kind death. Maybe it's better if you go back to your master." Tears gathered in Kezra's eyes as she shook her head.

"I can't go back. I won't. I'll die first."

"I see. I wish you luck. May you find a way to free yourself of this burden." Kezra shoved her way past Bear as she exited, unable to meet his eyes. Blessedly, Bear left her alone, sensing her poor mood. Twice she saw him open his mouth to say something, but he snapped it shut without a word, and they walked back to the inn in silence.

"How did it go?" Lennox popped up as soon as Kezra entered the room. "Oh no, not well then?" Lennox asked after a look at Kezra's face. Kezra shook her head, finding the strength to be positive.

"It didn't go as expected. But I did find a temporary solution," Kezra said, lacing false cheer into her voice. Lennox waited patiently for her to continue. "It turns out that the so-called potion I've been drinking isn't magic at all, just the sap of a plant, and one that grows not far from here. Isn't that great news?" She smiled at Lennox, but it felt forced, and Kezra knew she could tell.

"So then, what's wrong?"

"It won't work forever." Kezra cast her gaze downward, tears prickling her eyes again. "The plant will buy us some time, but eventually, it won't work anymore, and Senga didn't have another way to help me."

"How long do we have?" Lennox asked. Kezra shrugged.

"Maybe a year, maybe less." Lennox sat on the bed, digesting the information. Her face turned serious; Kezra recognized signs of a plan forming in her head.

"That's fine. We can gather the plant and talk to Isla about staying here while we figure out our next step." Lennox started lacing up her boots.

"Where are you going?"

"I just told you, we're going to gather that plant for you." Kezra smiled in spite of herself, and this time it was genuine.

"It's an hour's walk east of here to the stream. Possibly up a hill." Lennox groaned.

"Of course it requires more hiking. So be it. Let's go."

"You really don't have to come. I know you hate hiking."

Lennox turned to Kezra, looking her squarely in the eyes.

"We're in this together, Kezra. I meant it when I said I was with you. Even if I have to climb another mountain, cross another sea, or brave the Barrens, I'll be by your side, annoying you the entire way." Kezra's heart swelled. A true friend was something she'd never had, nor was Lennox's friendship something Kezra deserved, but she was grateful for it. She gave Lennox a playful punch on the arm as they got ready, unsure how to cope with the vulnerable moment.

After gathering some provisions and better directions from Isa, they were on their way. Outside, in the fresh air and sunshine, Kezra felt better already. Ideas started to take root in her head, maybe the answer was in a book. They could sneak back into Tesmerin and search its extensive library. Something about a book tingled the back of Kezra's mind. She nearly tripped over her own feet when the realization hit her. Kezra already had a book. One she knew contained spells, specifically a bonding spell. She'd been trying to interpret the book on her own, but it was hopeless. However, as an acolyte of Altheia, it was possible Lennox would know the language. Kezra had meant to ask her, but in the chaos of the past few weeks, she'd forgotten all about it. That answer had been with them all along. Kezra wasn't sure how Lennox would react to seeing the reminder of the temple, but hopefully it wasn't too painful. She just had to think of the right way to approach the subject. Suddenly, everything seemed brighter. There was hope after all.

Kezra half listened, nodding along to Lennox's idle chatter on the trek to the stream, all the while thinking of the best way to approach her. All thought fled from her mind once they found the stream, though. It was easily the most beautiful place Kezra had ever seen. Blades of green grass grew with yellow and purple flowers peeking up between the blades. The stream was a perfect light blue, surrounded by glittering gray stones that sparkled in the sun. Tall green plants with thick stems and broad green leaves bordered the stream. But the most magnificent part was the one no one had told them about. A waterfall trickled into the stream as water flowed down rock from the surrounding mountain. The beads of water captured the sunlight, casting the occasional rainbow onto the rocks. It was breathtaking.

"Praise Altheia," muttered Lennox. Kezra could only nod. Surrounded by such beauty, it was easy to believe in the benevolent goddess. Lennox settled in the grass, plucking food from her bag.

"What are you doing?"

"Setting up a picnic, of course," Lennox answered.

"We're meant to be gathering ashwart," Kezra said, drying and failing to hide her exasperation.

"And we will. But Isla packed us a lovely picnic. The ashwart will still be there when we're done, and I'm starving. Have you eaten today?" Kezra's traitorous stomach growled. Begrudgingly, she joined Lennox for the picnic. She was right; what difference would a few more minutes make? They dug into the lunch Isla had packed - sandwiches filled with salty meat and creamy cheese, along with fruit and a small flask of ale to share. Eating under the sun, next to the beautiful sight, Kezra couldn't imagine a better place to bring up the book. She took a deep breath to start.

"Lennox," Kezra started. Lennox looked up, strawberry juice dripping down her chin. Kezra paused, contemplating what to say next.

"Yes?" she prompted.

"I was wondering - wait, did you hear that?"

"Hear what?" A roar sounded, echoing across the waterfall. The color drained from Lennox's face. Kezra scanned the valley, looking for places to hide, but came up empty. They were surrounded by open field. Maybe with Lennox's magic they'd stand a better chance.

"Can you summon your magic?" Kezra asked her.

"I don't know, maybe?"

"That will have to do." Grabbing her daggers, Kezra poised them to throw. A shadow loomed over the valley. Giant wings darkened the sky. Cold sweat trickled down Kezra's forehead and her throat dried. They couldn't outrun this thing, and fighting it wasn't an option. The beast roared again so loudly Kezra's bones vibrated. She quickly filtered through places to throw her daggers - should she take out the wings, go for the eyes? What gave them the best chance of getting away? A gust of air blasted her, almost knocking Kezra off her feet as the beast sailed to the ground, just feet from them. Iridescent scales glittered in the sunshine, glimmering black, blue, purple or magenta depending on the light.

The beast beat its giant, leathery wings once more as it settled to the ground. Its snout alone was larger than Kezra. What chance did they have against this thing? Its beady black eyes locked onto Kezra's as its tail flickered back and forth. Long, sharp talons struck the ground, and Kezra had a sudden flashback of those same claws emerging from red mist to impale its screaming victim. Tylan's beast had found them, and it was more terrifying than she'd imagined. Strangely, it wasn't attacking, just contemplating us. Kezra whispered to Lennox, not breaking the dragon's stare.

"Back away slowly. Then let's make a run for it. What are you doing?" Lennox had a hand out and was taking careful steps toward the dragon. "You can't just walk up and pet it, Lennox." The dragon huffed, steam erupting from its snout.

"I don't think she likes being called an it," Lennox said as she moved closer. Kezra's heart pounded as Lennox approached, convinced the priestess would be devoured at any moment.

"She?"

"This is Nithe. It's okay, Kezra. She knows me." Lennox placed her hand on the beast's snout and, to Kezra's great surprise, was not immediately eaten. A low rumbling noise came from its throat.

"Is it -" the dragon gave her what Kezra could only describe as a glare. She gulped and started again. "I mean, is *she* purring?" Lennox continued patting the dragon's snout as if it were a cat.

"She'd like you to put your daggers away." Kezra hadn't realized they were still in her hands, and she reluctantly put them back. They wouldn't help anyways.

"How do you know what she wants?" Lennox scrunched her face, contemplating the answer.

"It's hard to describe. I can feel it. It's almost like she's talking to me, but I can feel her will instead of hearing her voice." Lennox shook her head. "I sound insane." Kezra shrugged.

"No crazier than you claiming this is Nithe."

"She is Nithe."

"Sure, this is the goddess of death's dragon somehow possessed by

Tylan."

"She doesn't serve Tylan." Kezra raised her eyebrows at that; she knew for a fact this was his pet. "Of course not. What does Nithe want then?" Lennox was quiet for a moment, concentrating.

"We need to get on."

"What do you mean by get on?" The dragon lowered its body, sliding its wing at an angle, like a ramp, clearly intending for them to climb on. Lennox scrambled up. "No way. It's going to take us straight to Tylan. Lennox, get down!" The dragon - Nithe - snorted again, more steam filling the air.

"She really doesn't like being called an it. It'll be okay Kezra, trust me," Lennox said.

"How do you know?"

"I just do. I trusted you, didn't I? Just have faith in me this time." Lennox held out a hand, and reluctantly, Kezra joined her on top of the dragon. Nithe rose, spreading her wings.

"Hold on!"

"To what?" Kezra screamed. Then Nithe launched into the sky, as Kezra clung to the dragon's back for dear life. As they rose higher and higher, Kezra vowed that if they approached Tylan, she'd throw herself to the ground rather than wind up back with him.

They flew up and up until the air was thin, and her chest felt tight. The only good thing was that a fall from this height would certainly kill her. They skimmed the top of a mountain, the one protecting Kitsummit's back. And just as Kezra thought her lungs would burst from lack of air, Nithe descended onto a plateau at the mountain's peak. The landing was far more gentle than Kezra would have thought a creature of her size capable. Lennox made an uncharacteristically smooth descent, chatting with the dragon all the while. Kezra gazed around, looking for a trap. She still wasn't convinced this beast hadn't taken them straight to her master. She slid down the dragon's back, onto fresh, powdery snow.

"That's a much faster way up a mountain," Lennox said as she turned toward the dragon, patting its muzzle. "Thank you for carrying us, Nithe."

"I think I prefer using my own feet," Kezra muttered, feeling queasy. "You seem oddly familiar with i- Nithe." Lennox blushed beet red.

"We may have met before."

"What? When?"

"Tylan let me ride her once, when you were away," Lennox said, not meeting her eye.

"So you know she belongs to Tylan, and you still had us ride her? She's led us into a trap, Lennox." The dragon snarled.

"I told you, she doesn't serve Tylan, and she certainly doesn't belong to anyone. She likes you saying that even less than being called an it."

"And you know all of this, how? Just some feeling?" Lennox nodded.

"Like I said, it's hard to explain, but I can sense what she's feeling. I think my magic is allowing me to communicate with her somehow."

"Right… so, what are we doing here if not to be delivered to Tylan?"

"We need to look for something. There's something important waiting here for us," Lennox stated. Kezra rolled her eyes.

"Yeah, the trap her master set for us." The back of her neck heated as she jumped away from Nithe, who was blowing steam at her. "What was that for?"

"I told her. She really dislikes you implying that she belongs to anyone, especially Tylan." Nithe seemed to nod at that.

"Fine, I'm sorry. I won't do it again. Did she give any indication about what exactly we're looking for?"

"Erm - no. But we'll know it when we see it."

"Great. We're taking vague directions from a dragon." Kezra started inspecting the plateau, looking for anything unusual, but all she saw were standard rocks and snow. Then she saw it: a faint golden-hued shimmer in the air. It rippled, fading and brightening again, as if it wasn't fully there.

"That's it." Lennox breathed. She rushed toward it.

"Wait!" Lennox stopped. "Maybe don't go rushing off toward weird lights." Kezra pulled out her daggers. "Let me test it first." Cautiously, she approached the shimmering gold light. Up close, it looked like a long crack. One that couldn't decide it wanted to heal itself or break apart entirely. Kezra took the tip of her dagger and prodded at the light - nothing happened. The blade passed right through. She glanced back at Lennox, who shrugged. Using the tips of her fingers to touch the light, Kezra braced herself for a burning sensation, pain, a trap to be sprung, but again, nothing.

"Let me try," Lennox said, taking Kezra's place.

"What are you going to do?" Lennox closed her eyes and held up her palm. A tiny orb of silver light appeared. The orb tugged in the direction of the golden light, pulled toward it. "Are you sure that's a good idea?" Kezra's instincts were screaming at her to stop this, but she was rooted in place, curiosity overriding caution.

"This feels right. Just trust me."

Kezra gulped, not at all trusting the situation, but unwilling to stop her. The gold light sucked in Lennox's silver magic, devouring it, and the crack in the sky grew brighter.

"Lennox, I have a bad feeling about this," But Lennox didn't seem to hear. More magic poured from her, and the crack in the sky continued to grow. Until, with a burst of light, it seemed to explode. Lennox fell to the ground.

"Lennox!" Kezra ran over to her. She was breathing, but her magic had winked out. Slowly, Lennox's eyes fluttered open, and she tried to sit up.

"What happened? Did I do it?" A smoky laugh stopped Kezra from answering.

"Nithe!" Out of the golden light a figure had appeared, clad in scaled armor with dark hair braided down her back and a longsword at her hip. She looked exactly like her painting.

"Niveran?" Kezra asked, confused. The goddess paid no attention to them, focused solely on her dragon. Was her tail wagging? Did dragons wag their tails?

"Can you not pay attention to the task at hand, Niveran? Can't you see that one of them's hurt?" A second figure had appeared beside the first. She had flowing hair the color of wheat. Flowing crimson robes were tied together with a golden cord, and gold bracelets clanged on her wrists. Her piercing green eyes peered down at Kezra.

"Altheia," Lennox whispered, straining to sit up. Her face had lost all color. She looked like she might faint again.

"Oh dear, she doesn't look good at all. Didn't you help her open the gate?" Altheia asked. Kezra pinched her eyes shut, sure at this point that she had to be dreaming. When she opened them, the goddess was still standing there, an expectant look on her face.

"Niveran, get over here. Stop playing with Nithe and come help me. We've little time and both of them look as if they might faint."

"You're just jealous of our bond. I don't see why you can't handle this on your own, *goddess*," Niveran retorted. The last word was delivered with such sarcasm, it woke something in Kezra. They had said time was limited, and what was this gate? Kezra shook Lennox, who still seemed to be fluttering in and out of consciousness.

"Wake up, we need to pay attention...I need you right now," Kezra pleaded. The shake helped, and the color slowly started returning to her face.

"Help me up," Lennox said, so Kezra scooped her under the shoulder to help her stand. Altheia stood in front of them, framed by the glittering golden light. The tear appeared smaller than it had been just moments before. Altheia was glaring at Niveran, who was still preoccupied with Nithe. Altheia's eyes alighted on them.

"Oh good, you're alright. I was afraid all of this had been for nothing. Niveran, they're alright."

"Praise be," Niveran answered, not turning her attention from the dragon.

"Ignore her. Really, she's happy to meet you; as am I-"

"No, I'm not." Niveran interrupted. Altheia glared at her before starting again.

"Now, I'm sure Peter told you much already, but we'd like to help fill in any blanks. Where is Peter? Didn't he come with you?"

"Lochlan is probably too busy gallivanting across the human lands," Niveran said, finally turning her attention to them. Altheia looked ready to combust.

"He prefers to go by Peter; we will respect him, even if he didn't deign to join us. I'm sure he had a good reason."

"I refuse to call one of our most powerful Fae princes by a human name. It's an insult to our kind." The golden tear in the world was definitely shrinking; in fact, both the goddesses were looking far less solid, like they weren't really here.

"Stop it, Niveran. We don't have time for this debate right now."

"Um, excuse me - your goddesses," Kezra said, unsure of the honorifics to use in this instance, "but we don't know Peter. Also, you seem to be fading." Altheia's jaw dropped and Niveran stomped in front of them, arms crossed.

"How did you find the gate without Peter?" Lennox jumped in, quickly recounting the story of Nithe bringing them up the mountain. Niveran beamed. "That's my girl, Nithe." Altheia, on the other hand, looked less amused.

"So, you know nothing about who you are, or who we are?"

"Everyone knows who you are. Lennox has lived her whole life dedicated to you, goddess."

"Something's wrong with that one's magic," Niveran said, pointing to Kezra and wrinkling her nose. Altheia waved a hand in Kezra's direction, and she felt an invisible force burrow into her brain. It felt like it was pulling at something, a door that wouldn't budge. Altheia paled.

"Oh, child. Who tethered you? No, no, no this is not going to plan at all. You know nothing, and we're running out of time."

"What do we need to know, my goddess?" Lennox asked, kneeling. "Just tell me what you require, and we will serve you."

"Oh, get up." Altheia sounded exasperated. "First, we are not goddesses. Where the humans got the idea, I don't know."

"Why did you do that, Altheia? I quite liked the bowing. You always spoil my fun," Niveran said.

"You, sister, are not helping."

"Fine, I will help. Have either of you heard of our sister, Elowen?" Lennox and Kezra shook their heads. "She was one of the most powerful Fae in centuries, and she gave up her immortality to marry her human lover." Niveran shook her head in disgust. "She and her lover were viciously murdered by one of our kind during her weakest moment, giving birth to twin girls." Lennox and Kezra exchanged a puzzled look.

"But what does that have to do with us?" Kezra asked.

"Imbeciles. You are her twin daughters, obviously. And we need you to use your mother's magic to open the gate permanently." The world spun. Twins? Their mother's magic? It was all too much.

"That was poorly done," Altheia scolded. Niveran shrugged, walking back to her dragon.

"We are almost out of time, sister, and our nieces needed to know." Altheia glanced again at the fading golden light.

"Perhaps you are right." Altheia met their eyes. "I understand this is much to take in. I had hoped to give you more answers, but we don't have the time now. Find Peter. You will need him to un-tether your magic. And then, together, you can reopen the door between our realms. It cannot remain sealed or the consequences will be dire."

"But how will we find him?" Lennox asked, desperate.

"He will be looking for you. He is Fae in disguise and he will stand out by his extraordinary grace and height. Look in major cities and ask around. People will remember him. You must find him. Then free us. I know you can." Niveran looked at them.

"I don't. This encounter has shown me that we're all doomed. Take care of Nithe for me." She scratched the dragon under the chin one last time. With a snap, the golden tear closed completely and with it, the goddesses disappeared. Nithe let out an earsplitting roar as Niveran faded away. Kezra turned to Lennox, her sister, her twin. It was too much to take in.

"What now?" Lennox asked.

"I guess we should get down the mountain and find this Peter." Lennox nodded, not mentioning the rest. Kezra appreciated that. She needed time to process the information before she could discuss the implications. "Where do we start?" Lennox asked.

Suddenly, the memory of a man with curly brown hair rescuing her from a lemon tart surfaced. Kezra smiled, recalling his grace as he glided around the castle.

"I think I have an idea," Kezra said. Mounting Nithe, they prepared to descend the mountain, their lives forever changed.

Epilogue

Footsteps echoed across the empty palace corridor as made his way to the throne room. He had always hated the seat of Oscana's power with all the simpering nobles running around, asking for favors and expecting them for free. Even more, he despised this king, an inescapable thorn in his side. The powerless, petty fool was always making demands, and then grand threats if the commands were not carried out swiftly enough. But breaking a magical oath had consequences, and Tylan had once been desperate enough to swear one to the pathetic king. And so, instead of crushing the man, turning him to dust, Tylan answered his summons, then smiled while the king made his ludicrous commands.

The throne room was blessedly empty upon Tylan's arrival, save for a lone man with his legs slung across the side of the throne. The king paid no attention to Tylan as he entered, although there was no way he hadn't heard him arrive - a show of disrespect. Nothing irritated Tylan more than being made to wait, especially on such a mediocre individual. Realizing the king intended to continue ignoring him until he received his "proper respect", Tylan dropped to one knee in front of the throne, bowing his head.

"Your Highness, you summoned me?"

Lazily, the man swiveled his head to gaze upon Tylan's kneeled form. The king stood, circling around Tylan.

"Indeed. How nice of you to answer in person this time. I seem to remember you sending a silly girl in your place when I last summoned you." Tylan smirked at the memory, wishing he could have seen the look on the king's face when Kezra showed up in his place. The fool didn't know the girl's value. He probably dismissed her as a silly gift, when the thing he wanted most in the world had been right under his nose.

"Apologies, My King. I found myself temporarily indisposed."

"Yes, preoccupied with our new asset, I hope?" Tylan grimaced. He was not looking forward to bearing this news. He still didn't understand how Kezra had managed to subdue the bond and steal Lennox away from him. Just days ago, he'd felt like he'd had her back in his grasp. The bond had been pulling her back to him, and everything was almost right in the world. But at the last moment, a wall had slammed shut, cutting him off from Kezra and her supply of magic. No, the king would not be happy at all.

"Indeed. Although there has been an - unexpected development, I'm afraid."

"Oh?" The king stopped walking. Tylan swallowed, steeling himself to continue.

"The girl seems to have run away."

"Run away! Run away? How could you let this happen!" Furious, the king kicked Tylan in the ribs. He'd been ready for it, but it still hurt. "Stupid, stupid man. She was supposed to lead us to the twin." Tylan hid a smirk, he'd already had both twins, but the king didn't know one had been in Tylan's grasp all along. His fists clenched involuntarily as he recalled how he'd lost them both. Now was not the time to gloat. "We need them to seal the gate. If they find each other and open it before we catch them, it could destroy everything I've worked for!" The king continued to stomp and pout like a petulant child, but he wasn't wrong. The twins' escape was a problem - one Tylan needed to rectify quickly.

"My error is inexcusable, Your Majesty. But not to worry, the dragon, Nithe, has her scent. Soon we will have Elowen's child back, and she will lead us to the twin. Then, we can seal the gate permanently." Once Tylan had them back, he would break this wretched oath and seal the king behind the gate himself. It had been a mistake not bonding the priestess immediately, but he had wanted the girl to trust him, to do it of her own will. No matter, he'd have her back soon enough, and it was not a mistake Tylan would make again. Soon, he would control the only sources of the world's magic. Then, Oscana would be his.

Acknowledgments

I've spent my whole life reading other people's stories. Somewhere along the line, I told my husband I wanted to write one myself, mostly joking, but he encouraged me to go for it. Writing this novel took roughly 18-months; I almost gave up multiple times, but there was always someone in my corner, encouraging me to keep at it. Without the love and support of my family and my best friend, I wouldn't have completed this novel; I wouldn't be able to call myself an author. Thank you to my husband, Greg, for putting up with me while I half paid attention to conversations as I focused on my book instead, to my best friend for believing in me, and to my son, whose confidence in my ability to succeed never wavered. A special thank you to Paiton. Your refusal to read my book until I published it was the motivation I needed to get it done.

Printed in Dunstable, United Kingdom

81015027R00201